Mrs. W.B. McGuire
2612 Cornwallis Ave
Roanoke, Va

Return postage guaranteed

D1283499

BLACK WILLIAM

WITH admirable mastery Robert Neill swings the setting of his new novel from the brittle, unreal gaiety of the coronation celebrations of George the First in London to the vigorous countryside about Gateshead, where 'folk do their own thinking'. It was undoubtedly a sudden change for Miss Mary Lawley, niece of Lady Chandler, from dancing at her aunt's fashionable routs, to making pig's liver pudding in the great kitchen of her new home in the north, where everyone called her 'Mally' without ceremony. Yet one link remained: in London she had seen the 'loyal' toast drunk over a bowl in which a white rose floated, and adherents of the 'King over the Water' were no fewer by the Tyne than the Thames. The mysterious Captain Marriott, whose vigorous defence of her honour had made him the innocent cause of her banishment from the capital, appeared again as the Pretender's emissary to the northern Jacobites. It was inevitable that Mally's sympathies should go, as do those of every woman, to the side to which the man she loves belongs, but by this time she had met Black William's son, whose loyalty was to King George, and she was even less sure of her heart than of her politics.

Robert Neill
has also written

Mist Over Pendle
Moon in Scorpio
Rebel Heiress

BLACK WILLIAM

ROBERT NEILL

HUTCHINSON
Stratford Place
London

Hutchinson & Co. (Publishers) Ltd.

London   Melbourne   Sydney
Auckland   Bombay   Cape Town
New York   Toronto

First Published · 1955

Printed in Great Britain by
WILLIAM BRENDON AND SON LTD
THE MAYFLOWER PRESS
(late of Plymouth)
WATFORD

CONTENTS

CHAPTER I

MALLY

It was nearing midnight, 17th October 1714, and there were lights at Lady Chandler's door; otherwise Jermyn Street was dark.

Lady Chandler's door was open, and there was a guest departing. In the hall a Sedan chair was waiting, carried in that she might enter it in the light and warmth. Her two footmen stood stiffly behind it. Outside, below the steps, the linkboys waited, and the plumes of flame from the links lit the tall graceful door, the gilded canopy above it, the flags and streamers that hung from upper windows. The light quavered as the pitch flared among the tow, and gleams of gilt and colour sparkled from neighbouring houses too. Jermyn Street was beflagged for an occasion, but the occasion was not yet. It was Sunday night, and late, and the street was empty.

There was a movement in the lighted hall. A woman was coming down the stair, cloaked against the chill of night, with her hooped skirts rustling and her fan tight-clenched in her hand. Her white powdered face looked hard and strained, her lips were pressed tight, and she had nothing to say to the man who walked at her side. He was much younger; perhaps in his early twenties, tall and well shouldered, carrying easily his long full-skirted coat of wine-red velvet. His face looked as if it could smile pleasantly, but now it was gravely formal; and he, too, had nothing to say.

She looked stiffly before her, and she held her head high as she walked to her chair. He handed her in and shut the door, and then he was bowing over her hand as he murmured something inaudible. For a moment her fan was seen, and then the chairmen bent to their poles. There was a creak of leather as their shoulders met the slings; and slowly the chair was carried out. The footmen came behind; the links were lifted high; and the man in velvet went courteously beside the chair.

On the lowest step he bowed his farewell, and then he stood

watching as the chair was borne away. The linkboys walked in front; the footmen walked on either side, their cudgels ready in their hands. Six pairs of feet went tramping; and the light of the links, red and smoky, fell on house after house as the chair went by. Each house was gay and beflagged, and each gave a glint of colour in the wavering light. Then the links receded, and Jermyn Street was dark; except for Lady Chandler's door.

It was still open. The man was in the doorway now, staring after the departing chair, but perhaps he was not seeing it. His eyes had clouded, and a look of distaste was in his face, as if he had not liked what he had had to do. He was brooding, with his thoughts far away; and he did not see that another woman had come to the stair, and was watching him.

She was younger even than he, and she had a look of sturdy health that was not in the mode this year. A languishing pallor was what the mode required, and she had done her best with the powder. She had hidden the fresh young colour of her cheeks with a film of white, and in one cheek she had put the black silk patch that the mode commanded. But it was not a success, and perhaps she was not expert with the powder. The air of vigour stayed, and with it was another quality, also not to be concealed; something in that slim young face could command attention, and hold it.

She had come a few steps down the stair, very slowly and carefully, and she was standing in utter silence, watching the man below. The hall was very quiet. The doorman, gorgeous in gilt and crimson, was as stiff and wooden as the door. The man beyond had not moved. He was beneath the lintel, sunk in his thoughts, and she could see only the back of him; but perhaps that was enough. She stood intent, and her eyes were shining.

He gave no warning that his thoughts had changed. He turned suddenly on his heel, and he took her unawares. She was looking into his eyes, and a hot flush leaped to her cheeks, half hidden by the powder.

For the instant he was perhaps as startled as she. He stood rigid, staring at her; and then his face changed. He stepped inside the door, coming fully into the light, and again he was looking up. They were eye to eye, intent upon each other; and neither of them spoke.

There was a faint easing of breath. A quick smile came to his face, lighting it, making it vivid with life. Quietly and slowly, as if drawn by a force beyond him, he moved up the stair towards her. She stood waiting, and she did not move, though the flush had deepened in her cheeks.

He stopped, and still he looked up at her and was intent. Neither of them heard the door that opened beyond the stair.

"I've seen you before." He spoke softly. "I've seen you a dozen times, but always there have been others there, and no one has presented me. It's Miss Lawley, isn't it?"

"Yes." It was a fresh and easy voice that answered him, and she hoped it was steady. "I—I'm Lady Chandler's niece."

"Lady Chandler is fortunate. I'll call myself fortunate too —now."

"Oh!" She sounded breathless, and she was guiltily aware that she should not have thrust herself down the stair like this. "I was looking for my aunt, and——"

"Were you?"

It came coldly, a clear voice from the top of the stair, and it cut her short like a blown candle. She turned; and Lady Chandler herself, formidable and imposing, was standing there. She did not sound pleased with her niece.

"Why, pray, should you be looking for me down there?"

"I—I was just going to bed, ma'am, and——"

"I thought one went *up* to bed, not down."

"Why yes, ma'am. But—but I thought I heard her Lady-ship departing, and——"

"You probably did." Lady Chandler turned abruptly to the man. "Her departure, Captain, leaves Mr. Willoughby alone in the card room."

"Indeed, ma'am?"

"Yes. He—er—grows a little impatient. He says he came for play, and has not had it."

"I'm sorry for that. I was not sure that he sought the cards tonight."

"Perhaps he didn't—at first." For one quick instant her eyes were on her niece. "But he does now. And since he's of some importance, you'd perhaps better go to him."

It was plainly a command, and if there was reluctance in him he hid it with accomplished skill. She was perhaps twice his age, and she was, moreover, the hostess. There was nothing else that he could do; but a tightness had come into his face, as if he did not welcome Mr. Willoughby.

"I'll go to him at once. I doubt if it will be to his profit."

"It isn't needful that it should be. All that's needed——" She broke off sharply, and then the tone of command returned. "He's in the card room, and he's impatient."

"Then you'll give me leave, ma'am?"

His tone expressed nothing. He bowed lightly to her. For an instant he turned his head to the girl who stood silent, and his smile seemed to hint at something shared. Then he went quickly up the stair, and the wide double doors shut behind him. He was gone, passing through the gilded salon to the card room beyond, and Lady Chandler turned slowly to her niece.

"Mally, I despair of you. I don't remember such a feather-witted girl in any family."

"I—I'm sorry, ma'am. I——"

"We need not talk here." Lady Chandler was glancing sharply down. The door was shut, and the doorman in his alcove now. Only his legs could be seen from his hooded chair, and again Lady Chandler turned to her niece. "Go to my parlour. I'll speak with you there. You may ring for my milk."

"Yes, ma'am."

She went hurriedly up the stair. Lady Chandler leaned over the rail, and her voice brought the doorman jumping from his chair.

"There is Mr. Willoughby still to leave, and Captain Marriott. Then you may bolt the door."

Again she glanced sharply at him, wondering, perhaps, if he thought it odd that the cards should be out on Sunday night, and that he should be kept at his door so late. But his face stayed wooden, and slowly Lady Chandler turned away.

She pushed one of the double doors half open, and glanced into the salon. It was empty now, and dimly lighted, and in the two fireplaces there was no more than a dying glow. At the farther end the card room door was shut, and again Lady

Chandler seemed satisfied. Below her, in the hall, the clock struck midnight, and sleepily she stifled a yawn. Sir John Chandler, like a sensible man, had been in bed an hour ago, but his wife had still something to do. She had turned fifty now, and she felt the strain of these late hours; but her face was firm as she walked to her own neat parlour.

It was a trim and elegant room, warm from a flickering fire, bright from candle-light on the golden oak, the deep red rug, the lacquered cabinets of painted china. Her elbow chair was set before the fire, and by it was the silver jug of milk and the decanter of brandy. She sank into the chair, and for a moment she was thoughtful. Her niece stood waiting by the hearth, a little apprehensive now. She was ward as well as niece to Lady Chandler, and after three years in the house she could read the signs.

"It's more than time, Mary, that you were wed, and how it's to be accomplished I don't know. You seem beyond teaching."

Lady Chandler's eyes were on the milk that she was carefully pouring. Her niece stood a little more stiffly, and found this ominous. Like others of the name she was commonly addressed as Mally; and this frigid use of Mary was a sign of displeasure.

"What will Mr. Willoughby think of you tonight?"

"Mr. Willoughby, ma'am?"

"Will you not bray his name back at me like that? I distinctly said Mr. Willoughby."

A north-country burr, usually most carefully suppressed, had appeared in Lady Chandler's speech, and it was another danger sign. It was not lost on Mally.

"I should scarcely think, ma'am, that Mr. Willoughby thinks of me at all."

"He probably won't, after your display tonight. He's entitled to some courtesy, is he not?"

"Why yes. But——"

"*All* my guests are entitled to courtesy, but he had none from you." She turned aside, and carefully added brandy to the milk. "He spoke to you a half-dozen times, and you could scarcely answer him. You had dreams of a prettier face, I suppose."

It was uncomfortably near to the truth. Mr. Willoughby

was a plump young man of twenty-three, who had far too much money and thought he was entitled to deference from everybody. He had tried to divert himself with Mally during the evening, and she had not found him charming; and certainly her thoughts had been elsewhere.

"It would be Captain Marriott, no doubt. I saw him looking at you."

"Ma'am! I——"

"I never did think that girls had any sense. A man of that face gives one look at 'em, and they coo like doves. You with the rest, I suppose? You'll say your little heart went flutter, and you lost what silly wit you have?"

"If you please, ma'am——"

"What sort of a picture do you think you make—skipping after him like a performing monkey?"

Lady Chandler had no belief that girls are fragile creatures who must be handled gently. She had a good brisk way with her when roused, and she preferred the frontal attack. She stared grimly at her niece.

"You haven't yet told me what you were doing down that stair with him. Displaying yourself, I suppose?"

"No. I——" Mally was wilting visibly, and she was plainly in difficulties. "I saw the chair, and I—I thought——"

"What sort of a fool do you take me for? Apart from the propriety of it, has it yet slipped into your addled head that Captain Marriott is a man of the cards and tables? And has perhaps more to do than give heed to your vapourings? How old are you?"

"One-and-twenty, ma'am. But——"

"Then it might be supposed that—— What the Devil!"

Her Ladyship's tone changed abruptly, and perhaps with cause. There had been a perfunctory tap at the door, and now it was pushed noisily open and Sir John Chandler came in. His wife gasped aloud, and then seemed to freeze. Mally swung round, disposed by this time to thank Heaven for anything that came, and she had some ado to hold herself steady while she made her curtsey. Sir John, certainly, was not in his best appearance. He had apparently got out of bed. He had his breeches, his shirt only partly stuffed into them, and a green Indian gown tied loosely round them. He had some battered old slippers, and his nightcap pulled awry. In one hand he had a candle, which was dribbling wax over his breeches; and between that and the rest he did not look at all like the merchant-prince he was. But Sir John Chandler, when it suited him, had a way of disregarding such details. He could afford to.

He took the centre of the floor, big, portly, rubicund, and even in his present garb the centre seemed the proper place for him. He came to his point at once, and the north-country burr that was sometimes heard in his wife was plainly heard in him. Sir John was from Gateshead-on-Tyne, in the far north of England, and to his wife's annoyance he would never pretend that he was not; he almost seemed proud of it.

"Ma'am, is this become a gaming house?"

"No, sir." She answered him as sharply, and she had not moved from her chair. "It is a house of the mode and fashion, proper to what your rank requires. Why, pray, do you come at this hour?"

She was looking him coldly up and down, from the night-cap to the slippers, and he seemed to notice nothing of it.

"Does your fashion call for gaming on a Sunday night, ma'am? You have your routs and your receptions six nights a week, but I thought you at least left Sunday quiet."

"It *is* quiet. We have had merely a half-dozen guests for cards. That's permissible on Sunday."

"At this present moment it happens to be Monday. Never-theless, when I looked into your card room just now——"

"Good God!" She said it distinctly, and then she jerked up in her chair, scandalized and furious. "You went before my guests, looking like——"

She was all but choking as she saw the loosely tied gown and the shirt half out of his breeches. He nodded calmly.

"Never fear, ma'am. Your guests won't be put off. They get what they come for. What *do* they come for?"

He flung the question suddenly, and Lady Chandler sat very still. Deliberately she seemed to compose herself. He stood waiting, and Mally saw how shrewd and keen his eyes had grown; which did not surprise her. She had known for some time past that Sir John Chandler was anything but a fool.

"My guests, sir?" His wife spoke with a careful calm. "They come for the diversions of the polite world."

"Including the losing of their money, I suppose. Who *is* this Marriott?"

Again he flung it sharply, and again his wife seemed to ponder before she answered. Mally stood alert, for she, too, wished to know of this. There was something of mystery about the charming Captain Marriott. He had appeared in London scarcely a month before, and no one knew where he had come from. But almost at once he had been moving in the best society, especially Lady Chandler's society. She had, indeed, launched him in London, and he had been an immediate success. He was a man of the cards, allowed to be the most skilled and charming player in the town, and there were gentlemen in plenty who now came to Lady Chandler's house on his account. There were some ladies too, for Mally had not been alone in noting his face and bearing, but the question who he was remained unanswered. It did not lessen interest in him, particularly among the ladies, but it remained unanswered; and Mally was in hopes that it would be answered now.

"Captain Marriott?" The answer came almost languidly. "He conducts the cards, sir. I'm told he's most accomplished."

"Why must he conduct the cards?"

Her Ladyship yawned, and politely raised her fan.

"You surely know, sir, that persons of the best quality seek the house that has the best play?"

"Meaning he's a little fish to catch the bigger ones?" He eyed her grimly. "I believe you'd ask the Devil himself here, tail and hooves and all, if you thought he'd bring a Marquis with him."

"I find you tedious, sir, and a little offensive. Captain Marriott is a gentleman of the best breeding."

"You haven't yet told me where he comes from."

"I haven't asked him. The question might be—er—difficult."

"It certainly might, this year. Would he, perhaps, come from France?"

There was a moment of utter silence. Lady Chandler sat very still, and the ivory fan swept slowly to show how much at ease she was.

"I certainly don't know." She had a cool air of candour as she spoke. "It's a tale that's told of him, but I don't know if it's true. Some details of dress could start a tale like that. I don't believe all I hear."

"Nor do I, ma'am. Is he, perhaps, to have a part in this rout of yours on Wednesday?"

"He'll be among our guests, no doubt."

"Then let's hope he'll have changed his dress. It could be—unfortunate."

"So could some more. May I hope, sir, that you'll have changed your own by then?"

Again she was gazing icily at the nightcap and the Indian gown, and again he nodded calmly.

"For your rout, do you mean? I'm expected to take a part?"

"On that day, of all days—you are." She spoke with sudden emphasis. "What would be thought, pray, if you did not?"

There was a faint stir of feet as Mally relaxed. This, at least, could be understood; for Wednesday would be no ordinary day, and this was no ordinary year. It was 1714, and Queen Anne was dead.

She had died in August, and this was October. There was a King in the land again, and he was a German out of Hanover, who called himself George. He had landed at Greenwich in mid-September, and he had brought his German ministers, his German mistresses, and a whole horde of German cooks, grooms, ushers, and fly-by-nights. The only thing he had seemed not to bring was his wife, and that was because she was in prison.

He was an oddity indeed, but here he was. He was King; and within the next week he was to be crowned in the ancient style and with the ancient pomp. That was why Wednesday would be no ordinary day; it would be 20th October, the Coronation day of this new King George. That was why Jermyn Street was hung with flags and streamers; that was why there was a gilded canopy above the door; and that was why Lady Chandler had arranged for Wednesday night a rout that was to surpass all other routs. She was a social climber, and this was a chance not to be missed. She did, indeed, speak in the sourest terms of this German King. She would have preferred another, a King over the Water, who dwelt in France; and she had been heard to express the hope, for two distinct reasons, that there would be another Coronation soon. That, however, was by the way. This was an occasion not to be missed, and her Coronation rout was to be a rout of routs, as Mally well knew. There had been a bustle of preparation which she had not been allowed to escape.

"Also——" Lady Chandler shut her fan with a snap, and she waved it gently to emphasize her words. "Also, we have some other guests to think of."

"Your damned relations?"

"You may be as offensive as you please. But if Julia and her husband are to be with us this week, I expect some good impression to be given of my house. I expect help from both of you."

Again Mally understood. Cousin Julia and her husband—she was cousin to Mally and niece to Lady Chandler—were to arrive next day, as guests for this momentous week. They were from Newcastle-upon-Tyne, and were said to be of some consequence there; and Lady Chandler plainly meant them to learn that she was herself of some consequence here. Hence some sharp instructions she had already given to Mally; and hence, quite certainly, the icy gaze she was again directing at her husband's present clothes.

"Aye, aye," he said calmly, and his voice was suddenly sardonic. "But let's see Julia first."

He addressed that to Mally, as if she could share it with him, and she had a little trouble to find a safe answer. She had not met cousin Julia, and she had no great wish to. Also, she liked Sir John. But his sense of humour was dangerous; it was sometimes outrageous, and it sometimes tempted her to laugh when she should not. This seemed such a moment, and prudently she gave him a colourless answer.

"We shall see her quite soon, sir."

"We'll wait till then. If there's a whiff of the Tyne about her, I might like her."

"I think you have said enough." Lady Chandler came abruptly to her feet, as if to make sure of it. "It's time we were all abed. I hope you both understand that we must show a courtesy to Julia."

She paused. Then she was looking steadily at Mally.

"I was saying it before, and I will repeat it now for Sir John. You are to show a proper courtesy, not only to Julia, but also to Mr. Willoughby, if he should require it of you. And you are not—*not*, I say—to detain Captain Marriott, or interfere with him in any way. He has something else to do."

"Has he?"

Sir John spoke sharply, and for a moment his eyes were very keen and searching. Then he came back to Mally.

"I know nothing of Willoughby," he said slowly, "except that he's a fribble. But with one thing and another I think you might be wise to keep clear of Marriott."

"Yes sir."

She said it dutifully, but her thoughts were not happy as she went up to bed. There was something here that she did not wholly understand, something deeper than she had expected; and no doubt she would do well to heed these warnings, and to keep clear of Captain Marriott.

But if he should seek her again, and should look as he had looked tonight, she might find that difficult.

CHAPTER II

THE HIGHFLYERS

COUSIN JULIA and her husband arrived next day in time for dinner, and Sir John Chandler had therefore to wear his wig.

This annoyed him, for it was not his way to wear a wig at dinner. A full-bottomed wig, he said, was not a thing to wear at dinner. It had three great masses of curls, one tumbling down his back and the others in front of his shoulders, and they trailed into the soup and got mixed in the gravy; and if he then wiped them on the tablecloth, he was in trouble with his wife, who thought this habit undesirable. It was evident, she said, that Sir John had not yet learned how to manage his wig; and once, as a reminder of his humble origin, she had said she could well understand that in Gateshead they did not wear wigs at dinner. To which Sir John had retorted that in Gateshead they didn't wear wigs at all; they weren't such damned fools.

It was at such moments that Lady Chandler found her husband trying.

It has to be admitted that he was a self-made man. He was in these days a merchant, and a very wealthy merchant too, but he had certainly started from very little; and nothing infuriated his wife more than the gibe she sometimes heard that she had married a Chandler who was one. It hurt the more because it was true. Thirty years ago young Jack Chandler had been exactly that. He had been a tallow-chandler in Gateshead-on-Tyne, working with his brother William, riding the countryside to buy raw fat from the butchers and the farmers. It had been a humble trade, and one best not remembered in the hearing of Lady Chandler, but the brothers had known what they were about. More and more often the stench had poured from the shop at Gateshead as the cauldrons bubbled and the fat was strained; more and more wagons went rumbling to the river quays, more and more hogsheads of 'rough' and 'best refined' were slung into the ships for

London. It had been an expanding trade, and it had brought momentous changes to young John.

It had brought him first a wife, and of a family he could not have married into without money; for Lady Chandler had been Katherine, only daughter of Sir Francis Lawley, Knight. Sir Francis was of a family of wealthy merchants in Newcastle-upon-Tyne; but his services to King Charles, in the days of the Rebellion, though they had brought him honours and a Knighthood, had left him impoverished by fines; and it had been only the lack of a proper dowry for his daughter that had induced him to bestow her on the rising young merchant. It had, indeed, been a condition that she was not to live above the shop at Gateshead, but that had readily been granted; for John Chandler had been ready to go to London, there to have charge of the selling, while brother William stayed on Tyne-side to do the buying.

It had proved an admirable arrangement. John Chandler had found markets in London for more than tallow, and soon brother William was sending him salt from the pans at Shields, bottles and other glass from Sunderland, lead from the mines in Allendale, sword-blades from Shotley Bridge, grindstones from the quarries on Whickham Fell; and, above all, coal, the sea coal from the Tyne that every London hearth must have. Nor was this all; for the brothers had remembered that trade goes in two directions. Soon John Chandler was shipping to the Tyne an assortment that only he could have thought of: sugar and tea and chocolate, tobacco in small neat casks, brandy and wines and prunes from France, hops from Kent for the ales of Newcastle, cotton from Cyprus for the weavers of Darlington, dyestuffs from the wide world over for the dyers of Morpeth and Carlisle—indigo and galls and logwood, copperas and cochineal. John Chandler shipped them all; and always, at a profit, brother William sold them. It was a trade far from the tallow that began it, and it led John Chandler to wealth and position; first to a house and warehouse in Coleman Street, then to civic dignities that brought a Knighthood, and at last to his wife's ambitions and the house in Jermyn Street.

Yet he was annoyed as he sat now at the head of his table. He did not like this fashionable hour of two o'clock. In his youth he had always dined at noon, which he thought a very sensible hour for dinner; and he did not see why he should wait two hours, and then wear a wig, just to impress his wife's relations. So Sir John was annoyed, and when he was annoyed he was apt to be interesting, as Mally knew. Sir John had a north-country style at least equal to his wife's; and something in Mally was able to appreciate it. So she waited hopefully.

She did not have to wait long. Sir John, indeed, had little to say during dinner, for he had a homely belief that dinner is a time for eating, not talking; but once the fruits and wines were on the table he leaned back comfortably. Then he went at it.

"I'm to suppose, ma'am, that this rout of yours on Wednesday is to be a sink of sedition, as usual?"

"You suppose wrong, sir, also as usual." His wife stared back at him, no whit abashed. "Why should you suppose it?"

"At your rout the other night I heard you speak of the King in words that would put you in Bridewell if they were published. It's not decorous."

"Decorous?" She almost snorted her contempt. "What is there decorous about this German, pray? Have you seen his mistresses? There's another just arrived."

"Do you refer, ma'am, to the Baroness Kielmansegge?"

"If that's her name. She looks like a maypole to me. She's as thin and as brightly painted. Where's his wife, pray?"

"In prison, ma'am—for adultery."

"A German cuckold, is he? *Most* decorous! He keeps his wife in prison and his mistresses in his bedchamber."

"Where else should he keep 'em, pray? It's where he'll want 'em."

There was a gasp of fury from Lady Chandler, and from Mally a splutter which she hastily suppressed. She knew perfectly well that Sir John talked like this only when he wished to annoy his wife. He was as capable of the decencies as any man, but he seldom used the niceties of verbal fencing; he was better with the bludgeon.

"Will you recall yourself, sir?" Her voice came acidly. "Be pleased to remember that I have two nieces at this table."

Her glance moved from Mally, very still and decorous now,

to cousin Julia at Sir John's right hand. Julia was the daughter of Thomas Lawley, Lady Chandler's eldest brother. John, the second brother, was a widower, and now owned the house and estate where old Sir Francis had tried to settle as a country gentleman, a few miles up the river from Newcastle. The third brother had been Mally's father. Julia was therefore cousin to Mally, and was some few years older. She had been married five years to Henry Deane, who now sat silent at Lady Chandler's side.

"I spoke with intention." Sir John's voice came steadily, and now he seemed to be more in earnest. "Mally has still something to learn, and Julia is strange to London. It's proper she should know your routs are a rabble of Highflyers."

"Is that an insult to me, or to my guests?"

"It's a mere statement of truth."

Lady Chandler sniffed contemptuously.

"My guests, sir, are persons of quality, ladies of elegance, and gentlemen of wit and pleasure. They are always of some note in the polite world."

"That's a fine word, ma'am, for—what?"

"For the polite world, sir. I'm aware that Gateshead does not belong to it. Nor does the boiling of tallow."

Her Ladyship, also, could achieve a direct style when she chose, and Sir John was breathing heavily.

"If it were not for the tallow and some more, you'd now be tending pigs on your family's thin estate. You may despise trade, ma'am, when you're grown too nice to spend what it brings."

"So you have said, sir, some score of times before. When you insult my family, will you have in mind that it's Julia's also?"

"Mally's too, I think. I had it exactly in mind."

"And how?"

"I'm recalling that your father was a fine High Tory. Your brother John is another. You're of a Tory family, ma'am, and not far from Highflyers. And we know where that leads."

There was silence. She faced him steadily, making no quick retort; but her eyes had narrowed, and when she spoke again her tone was careful.

"What shall that signify?"

"It might be why you now fill your routs with Highflyers, and some others."

Her face tightened, and there was obstinacy in it, held back perhaps by caution. Again she seemed to watch him, and this time she was saved an answer. Cousin Julia thrust herself suddenly into the talk.

"By your leave, Sir John——" She leaned forward in her chair, a woman nearing thirty now, confident and sure of herself, with strong tight lips and unwavering grey eyes. "By your leave, what is a Highflyer?"

"A Highflyer?" Sir John turned in his chair to face her. "A Highflyer used to mean a Tory of the High Church. Now it means a Tory who spouts sedition as he swills October ale."

"I see," Julia nodded slowly, as if in understanding. "And you, Sir John, I should guess to be a Whig?"

"You guess correctly. I've wit enough for that."

"And for much more, I don't doubt."

Her smiling nod seemed to put the matter aside, but her grey eyes were keen as she glanced from Sir John to his wife. Across the table, Mally noted that Julia had given no hint of what her own thoughts were; and that might be the way of Julia. It might also be the way of Julia's husband, if anything could be judged from the silence he seemed to be keeping.

At that exact moment he broke it. He had stretched his arm along the table, and suddenly he tapped with his fingers, as if he were demanding attention. There was something imperious about it, and that seemed to fit the rest of him. He was short and plump, scarcely older than his wife, and with some air of importance. For Henry Deane, at the age of thirty-three, was already of some note; and was likely to be of more. He was a member of the Fraternity of Hostmen of Newcastle-upon-Tyne, which had a monopoly of the coal trade there, and a finger in some other trades as well. No member of the Fraternity, if he had diligence and a decent competence, could fail to rise in the world; and Henry Deane, with his dark eyes and secretive face, looked as if he had at least his share of both.

"If you'll pardon me——" He spoke with a smooth assurance. "That these Tory gentlemen hunt foxes, I can believe.

But sedition is another matter, and a graver one. May I know more exactly what you have in mind?"

"What's that?" Sir John sounded impatient. "Are you telling me you don't know on Tyneside which way the Tories look?"

"You mean they have some affection for the—er—other King?"

"We'll say the Pretender, if you please."

It came out truculently, and for a moment Mr. Deane looked almost startled. Then he nodded.

"Quite so, sir. I understand."

So did everybody else. It was a matter that nobody could not understand. For here in London was the King who was to be crowned on Wednesday, and he was King because an Act of Parliament said he was. And there over the water was the Chevalier de St. George, James Edward Stuart—*Jacobus, Dei gratia Angliae Scotiae et Hiberniae Rex,* as he now styled himself; for which reason his friends called themselves Jacobites. He was the only son of the dead King James, and was therefore King by right of birth. Only an Act of Parliament stood against him, an Act to make it sure that none but a Protestant should rule the Three Kingdoms. But could an Act of Parliament over-ride a right by birth? There were some who thought that a right by birth was a right that God had given.

"Quite so." Mr. Deane was nodding as if to show that he wholly understood. "But in these days, when there is perhaps a doubt which King——"

"There is no doubt at all." Sir John spoke forcefully, and as the uncompromising Whig he was. "It's the undoubted right of the nation to say who they'll have as King—or won't. And they won't have James Stuart."

"No." Again Mr. Deane was gently tactful. "But if the Tories think otherwise?"

"The common Tory we might forget. Give him ale and foxes, and he's happy. But round the Tories there's a fringe of lunatics, and I've called 'em Highflyers."

"Oh?" It sounded sharp. "And you think they will cause trouble?"

"I don't know what they'll do. Perhaps they don't know themselves. You heard my wife just now, with her sneers at the King and her sneers at his friends? That's your Highflyer, and as she speaks, so do they all, and she fills her routs with them. Which is why I've turned the talk this way."

"Indeed, sir? But I don't——"

"I've said you're new to London ways. You're my guests, both of you, and I make you welcome. I hope you have pleasure of it here, and see something of the Coronation. See something of my wife's routs, too. But please to remember that there's dangerous talk to be heard. You'll be prudent to guard your tongues, and that's my warning to you."

His firm tones died away. The room was hushed. Henry Deane was still and silent, and his wife had her eyes on his. Lady Chandler sat taut and grim, as if she would bide her time. Sir John leaned back in his chair; and then Julia was speaking quickly.

"But, Sir John——" She spoke lightly and almost gaily. "I hope you don't say it's all Tories and fox-hunters at Aunt Katherine's routs?"

"I certainly don't." Sir John seemed to respond to the change of tone, and now he was almost sardonic. "Top-boots and hunting horns aren't what she fishes for. They're not polite enough."

"I'm relieved to hear it." Julia's eyebrows lifted eloquently. "Henry and I had hoped to see some elegance in London."

"If that's what you seek, you'll probably find it. She had two Barons and a Viscount here the other night."

"I hope you found them—polite?"

"I didn't." The sardonic note seemed to be deepening in Sir John. "They don't talk to me. They merely drink my wine."

"I'm sorry for that, sir."

"My wife isn't. It's this polite world of hers. She'll invite anything that swims high in it, and for Wednesday she'll probably do better. Perhaps it will be three Barons and two Viscounts. What do you say, ma'am? You're oddly silent."

She answered him placidly, quite recovered now.

"Indeed, sir, you've talked so much and so loud that I didn't care to interrupt. That's all."

"I was asking you a question, ma'am. Is it to be noble lords again?"

"It is. I did not choose to mention this before. I've kept it as a surprise for Julia. But our rout on Wednesday is to be graced by one higher than a Viscount."

"Indeed?"

"Indeed. On Wednesday we are to have the honour of the Earl of Derwentwater, and his——"

"*Who?*"

Sir John's question cracked like a pistol shot, and for a moment it cut her short. Then she answered him forcefully.

"I said the Earl of Derwentwater and his lady. His Lordship is——"

"He's a papist, isn't he?"

"I haven't asked. I'm not concerned with the devotions of my guests. His Lordship derives of the royal blood."

"In a way, I think he does."

"What might that mean, sir?"

"I think he derives from our late King Charles, so we'll guess what the way of it was. He's an odd Earl for you to choose, ma'am."

"I haven't your Whig disrespect of royalty, sir. I honour his high descent."

"Thus speaks the Highflyer. He was reared at St. Germains, wasn't he—with the Pretender?"

"Again, I haven't asked."

"You might have been prudent if you had." He spoke with a snap, and suddenly he turned to Julia. "You'll hardly suppose that this noble Earl will be hot for King George?"

"No." She hesitated, and she had plainly seen the warning in his eyes. "I—I hope you don't say, sir, that even a word with his Lordship would be wrong, if it should be offered?"

"I'll not say anything so useless—to a woman. In any case, I don't doubt it's all contrived and waiting." For an instant his eyes were on his wife again. "But I suppose it's harmless. All that's needed is to guard your tongue. Don't talk of Kings, or Pretenders either."

"Will his Lordship?"

"No." Sir John pursed his lips and considered. "Probably he won't. But there may be some in his train who will. It's the quiet men who need to be watched."

"Yes." Henry Deane intervened suddenly, and his fingers

tapped again on the table. "I feel sure, sir, that you do not see much danger in these routs, or you would not permit them in your house."

"A rout's like a syllabub, all froth and nonsense, and in the main it's harmless. But there's a sly fellow here and there who's more adroit than he looks. That's all."

Sir John sat back and sent the wine splashing into his glass, as if he had done with this. Then, with the glass half lifted, he seemed to have an afterthought. He turned, and he was looking directly at Mally.

"Can you think of such a man?" he asked. "He'd be smooth, and adroit, and he might come from France."

CHAPTER III

LADY CHANDLER'S ROUT

IT was fortunate that Sir John Chandler had a talent for making money. His wife had a pretty talent for spending it.

She had certainly spared nothing for her Coronation rout, and if Sir John had disapproved he had apparently not hindered. When darkness fell her windows were gay with hanging lanterns, and her door was bright with torches, flaring and sizzling as they lit the flags and streamers that festooned the street. There were grooms to hold the horses, and lackeys to run to the chairs and coaches, and then stand stiffly as the guests alighted. Under the gilded canopy there was red matting on the steps, redder in the flaring torchlight; and above the door, huge and glinting in the light, was a *Vivat Rex*, in gold on blue. It was all very loyal and proper, and only Sir John had been so crude as to ask which King it prayed for.

But that had been in private, and in public he was supporting his wife as a husband should. He was with her at the head of the stair, a stair that had now a wall of flowers, set against ferns and palms ; and he was very dignified and assured as the guests came slowly up, two by two, with a rustle of skirts, a gleam of brilliants, and a low murmur of talk. He had his full-bottomed wig, curled and shining, tumbling over the shoulders of the long-skirted coat of cherry-red that fell almost to his knees and was richly embroidered in gold ; he had the big buttoned pockets and huge embroidered cuffs that the fashion called for ; he had a cravat of the latest mode, long and straight, falling half the length of his chest in a froth of the whitest lace ; and he matched his coat with his white silk stockings and cherry-red shoes. He made a fine and dignified figure, and not the less because his long embroidered waistcoat, of white and gold, was running into horizontal creases ; in two distinct senses, there was quite a lot now to Sir John Chandler.

He was affable, too, and his greetings to his guests were of good sense, and well chosen. He had not played his part in the civic life of London without learning how to do this sort of thing; and Lady Chandler, splendid in a gown of leaf-green satin, slit down the front to show her diamond-studded stomacher and her stiff hooped petticoat of gold brocade, had nothing to complain of now. She almost seemed to be pleased with him, and with the promise that her rout was showing; it was good already, and there was an Earl expected soon.

Mally was in the background, and her clothes were most uncomfortable. Lady Chandler had suddenly decreed that her niece must have new clothes for this occasion, and Mally was therefore in the latest mode, which she did not find comfortable. Gown and petticoat alike were of the painted Indian calicoes that were now called chints. It was a gown slit down the front, and coming to a waist some inches smaller than anybody's waist could be. It was from this that the discomfort came. Her aunt had insisted on stays of the English sort, which were more ruthless than any other, and the effect on Mally was a feeling that she had not only been pulled in, but also pushed up. Decidedly it was not comfortable, but it achieved its purpose; it gave her a waist that nobody could have, and it allowed the slit gown, of cream-and-pale-blue chint, to flare widely open to show the petticoat, and it was the petticoat that mattered. It was of cream and gold, and it was stiffened with hoops of whalebone, sewn into the chint, so that it spread and swayed like a hanging bell, taking the over-gown with it. It took a deal of room on a floor, and seemed to take more on a stair; for Mally at the ankles was nearly five feet wide, and she was not used to it. She had never worn this before.

The throng grew thicker as more and more guests came up the stair. Everybody seemed to be in the salon, and Mally could guess why. The guests of the evening, the Earl of Derwentwater and his Countess, were not yet come, and nobody would miss their arrival. There was expectancy in the air, heightened by the restless pluck of strings as the musicians made ready, and the temptation was on everybody to crowd into the doorway for a better view. Yet nobody did so. This was the polite world, and the room was full of chattering groups, intent, as it seemed, only on each other, and nobody had an interest in the tall double doors that were so eloquently open. And Sir John and Lady Chandler were still by the head of the stair.

Mally became alert as she caught sight of Mr. Willoughby pushing himself through the crowd. He seemed to be looking for someone, and she slid discreetly behind a group of talkers. It was an encounter she had no wish for, and she moved quietly along the wall, as if she, too, were in search of someone —as indeed she was, though she knew it was a dangerous search. Orders not to hold Captain Marriott might be hard to obey if he should be at her side again, as she well knew. But she moved along the wall and forgot all others. Her eyes were in the throng; but she did not see Captain Marriott.

She came to the end of the room just as Sir John and Lady Chandler walked quietly through the open doors. Sir John raised his hand in signal, and at once from their corner the musicians went gaily to a lilting tune. Sir John lost no time. He led his wife into the dance almost as the floor was clearing, and his guests were prompt to take the hint. The floor filled at once, with a whirr and rustle of skirts, the tap of heels, and the lilt of strings and drums; and Mally pressed back to the wall again. Nobody had asked her to dance, and that was her own fault; she had avoided everybody's eye.

Sir John and his wife were doing no more than give a lead. They made a single circuit of the room, and then slipped discreetly through the doors again to the head of the deserted stair. The Earl of Derwentwater and his lady must have been delayed, and the guests had been put to dance; but host and hostess must keep their vigil at the stair.

No one took heed of Mally as she stood alone by the wall. Mr. Willoughby was not in the dance. Captain Marriott was not to be seen, and she hardly looked for him now; she knew too well that he was not in the room. Cousin Julia and her Henry were deep in the dance, and Mally noted with satisfaction that Julia was not in the latest mode. She was about ten years behind it. She had a waist that was probably her own, and she had a petticoat that wanted hoops and was held out by no more than its own fullness; and it was decorated, too, with a series of satin flounces that were no longer in the fashion at all. Mally was not displeased. It was true that a fashion would take a long time to get as far as Newcastle, but Julia could surely have done better than this; and the thought almost reconciled Mally to her own tight discomfort. She was not lost in love for cousin Julia.

"Miss Lawley is pensive tonight. Could one ask why?"

She heard the voice at her side, and she moved in what should have been a languid turn and was more like a startled leap. It was not lost on Captain Marriott, and under the periwig his eyebrows twitched with amusement.

"Now don't say you're startled at *me*. I'm wholly harmless, and most of all to you."

He must have come through the doors while she stared at the throng, and his face had his own light smile as he waited for her answer. He was in a deep-blue taffeta, faintly shot with gold, and the gold brocade of his waistcoat seemed the richer for it. It was a contrast quieter than most, and it seemed to suit the man, as if he were himself too colourful to have much need of colour.

Mally wrenched desperately at her thoughts. She knew she must answer something; but he was forbidden, and her aunt was just through that open door, waiting for the Earl of Derwentwater.

She took the first thought that offered.

"I think we are all pensive, sir. Or at least, we are impatient. We await a guest."

"His Lordship, you mean? He's a little late. He's new to London, and he has affairs."

"I'm glad he's to come soon. Everybody awaits him."

"I expect they do." His cool glance round the room had amusement in it. "Half of them, I suppose, expect to be presented. There'll be some disappointments."

"Oh?" The quick thought came that she would not weep if cousin Julia were disappointed. "His Lordship is aloof, then?"

"Far from it. He's most friendly. But he doesn't like formalities, or climbers either."

"I see. It almost sounds, sir, as if you know his Lordship."

"Tolerably." The Captain nodded easily. "That's to say——"

The musicians stopped abruptly, and nobody needed to be

told the cause. The company turned with one accord, turned
to the open doors, where the footmen seemed to stand more
stiffly, and the candles to burn more brightly. Sir John and
Lady Chandler were there; and between them, standing in
smiling composure, were the guests-of-honour, the Earl and
Countess of Derwentwater.

Sir John gave an impeccable lead. He waited till everybody had seen; then he turned to the Earl, and without any
haste he bowed. He was followed at once by all of them, and
for the instant the great room was alive with the click of heels,
the swish of skirts, the glint of candles on sword-hilts and
jewels. It was almost as if they saluted royalty in this pleasing
young nobleman.

He was young, perhaps no more than five-and-twenty, and
the clear soft lines of his face suggested a modesty and friendliness. But there was something of pallor, too, and a tightness
in his forehead, to hint perhaps at cares that were unwelcome.
He was in deep-red velvet, with a white shower of lace in his
cravat, and an equal shower at either wrist, and the richness of
it enhanced his pallor. There was proof of his rank in the
ribboned Star that hung from his neck, in his jewelled sword-
hilt and the brilliants in his shoes; and there was perhaps
further proof in his demeanour. He stood for a moment in
smiling silence. Then he turned to his lady, and together, with
an easy confidence, they made their bow and curtsey in acknowledgement. It was admirably done; and the Countess of
Derwentwater, certainly no older than her husband, was as
confident as he.

The Earl turned calmly to Sir John.

"It's too much honour, sir." His voice came lightly and
easily. "But I'd be unhappy if I should disturb the dance.
Pray bid them continue."

Sir John waved his hand to the musicians, and at once they
began again. The floor filled quickly, and Mally pressed back
against the wall. Disappointment, she thought, could be seen
in a face or two, as if some had hoped for more from the Earl
and less from the musicians.

"Neatly done!" There was a smile on Captain Marriott,
and he spoke crisply. "Milord grows wary, I think."

"But wary of what?"

B

"Presentations. They'd have kept him at it for an hour if they'd had their way—each led up in turn, according to rank. Now they're set to dance instead. Very pretty!"

"It's natural, I suppose."

"To ask presentation to an Earl?"

"Shall we say—to a handsome Earl?"

"Oh, I see. But I almost feel jealous, since I'm less well favoured. However——" The quizzical smile was suddenly on Captain Marriott, and the periwig quivered on his shoulders as amusement seemed to take him. "It almost sounds as if——"

Sir John moved slowly past them, with the Countess at his side. Close behind them came the Earl, with Lady Chandler, and the Captain turned quickly to make the bow that formality required. Mally went as quickly to her curtsey. Lady Chandler turned her head in smiling acknowledgement; and then, for an instant, her face darkened as she saw her niece at the side of Captain Marriott. It was for an instant only, and then she was smiling again; but it was enough, and Mally knew that she had been warned, and that her aunt was in earnest about this.

"Ha!" At her side the Captain seemed to have noticed nothing. "I was saying, it sounded as if Miss Lawley had hopes of presentation also—to a handsome Earl."

"Did it?" Mally looked at him steadily, and knew that she would be wise to turn this talk towards an end. "But it had not been in my thoughts at all. I shall certainly *not* be in that favoured few."

"No?" The Captain's smile was broadening. "Now the ladies are so often right, and I so often wrong, that I'm delighted when it's the other way."

"How?"

"That this time *you* are wrong, and I am right."

He had a calm assurance, and he was still smiling as he glanced up the room to where a group of favoured guests were round the Earl. Mr. Willoughby was there, pleased and a little pompous, cousin Julia and her Henry, and Lady Chandler in the forefront with an air of swelling pride. The Earl seemed to smile dutifully, as though he were wearied of this.

"Come."

The Captain spoke crisply, and with no leave asked he

took Mally by the hand, as if to lead her forward. She stared at him, disbelieving for a moment, and then in consternation when she could disbelieve no longer. But he took no notice of that. He was laughing openly as he calmly turned her and led her forward; and with her hand firmly held she had to go.

Lady Chandler had just found the moment ripe, was just extending her hand to cousin Julia, when Captain Marriott came slowly past her, firmly escorting Mally. And Mally was given no choice in what to do. The Captain led her before the Earl, and then bowed with perfect confidence.

"Milord——" There was the same assurance in his voice. "Milord, give me leave to present Miss Lawley." For a moment his smile was quizzical again, and he looked the Earl directly in the eye. "Miss Lawley is a lady who has no concerns save those proper to her sex. She is of the North country, sir—your own North country—and not its least charming lady."

Mally gasped; and from the corner of her eye she had one glimpse of her aunt's face, taut and hard, and of cousin Julia, with bulging eyes. Then she had to hold herself steady to make her curtsey. She was within a yard of the Earl, and already he was beginning his bow.

"It's I that am honoured." His voice came pleasantly and easily. "I'm always pleased when I meet a lady from the North, and the more so when she's concerned with what delights us. Madam, your servant!"

He glanced quickly round him, saw perhaps the moving throng of the dancers, and relief seemed to come to his face. His smile broke out, quick and approving.

"We all dance in the North. I'm sure it's your skill for my delight. Permit me, please."

He had stepped forward, and was offering his hand; and he was leading Mally to the dance before she had even understood his meaning. Beside her, as she went, she saw her aunt's head rear in anger, and the white disappointed face of cousin Julia; and then she was on the floor, with an Earl's hand holding hers.

She was almost beyond speech. She had been given no choice, and she could have done no other, but she had no doubt at all of what her aunt would think of this; and between that and excitement she was in a mood that might at any moment set her falling over her own feet or his. The prospect appalled her, and she had to force herself to a concentration that drove all else from her mind. His Lordship, moving easily beside her, had to speak twice before she heard him at all.

"I was asking——" He paused, as if to be sure that she was heeding him. "I was asking what part of the North you come from ?"

There was nothing for it but to let her feet take care of themselves while she gave her mind to this.

"I fear I don't know the North Parts myself, milord. I was brought to London when I was only two years old."

"Alas for that ! But your father ?"

The lilting beat of the music slowed, and there was a roll of drums to hint that the dance was at an end at last. There was a final tap of the drum, and then breathless gentlemen were bowing to their ladies and speaking words of thanks and compliment. Mally sighed with relief, thinking this was over, but his Lordship was of a different mind. He stayed placidly in the centre of the room, where every eye was on him, and he pursued his question again.

"Of your father, you were saying ?"

"He—he was from county Durham, milord."

"The Bishopric is what we mostly call that county. A Bishop of Durham is no common bishop."

"No, milord. But it was from Newcastle that my grand-father came. He was Sir Francis Lawley, and——"

"Old Sir Francis ?" His Lordship was suddenly pleased. "But we have all heard of *him,* dear lady. He went to live up the river, did he not ?"

"Aye, milord. Near——"

"Near Dilston. Ten miles away, would it be ?"

"I don't know, milord. I don't remember it at all. I was only——"

"Only two. I'm sorry. Then you won't know Dilston either ?"

"I fear not."

"It's my own home, and it also looks at that river. But your father ? Does he live there ?"

"No. He—he died. It's my uncle John who is there now—my father's brother."

"I've heard of a Mr. Lawley there. But——"

It was Captain Marriott who disturbed their talk, and Mally was almost startled when she saw him standing close, plainly waiting his chance to speak. She had been giving her whole attention to the Earl, noting nothing of the room around her, but now she saw that their talk had roused the interest of everybody. She felt herself redden as she saw it; everybody was at a respectful distance, but every eye was on them.

There was a quick smile of thanks from Captain Marriott as she gave way to him, and then he spoke briskly.

"You'll pardon me, milord—but there are some who wait."

"I expect so."

It came wearily, as if his Lordship had no pleasure in this. But he glanced quickly up the room, and then he seemed to nod.

"I'm sure you're right."

His eyes were still on the waiting group as he spoke, and Captain Marriott answered him briefly.

"I am, milord."

There was firmness in the tone of it, and it could almost mean that the Captain was in some way a manager of the Earl; and to Mally's surprise the Earl seemed to accept that. He turned to her in quick apology, and then, with the Captain at his side, he went slowly up the room to those who waited.

What followed was as surprising for Mally as it was unexpected. She was no longer obscure. The ear and smile of an Earl had been hers, however briefly, and her status had therefore changed. His Lordship's attention might be hers again, and for longer, and it would be prudent to be on good terms with her. If that was not plain to Mally, it was certainly plain to some others, and they lost no time about it. There were gentlemen with requests to dance, and ladies with ripples of talk and invitations to their houses; and Mally had to give her mind to that. Only occasionally was she able to give a thought to how others were faring, and what little she saw was not exciting. His Lordship seemed to be holding what was almost a reception, and for the most part it was Captain Marriott who was doing the presenting. It was perhaps an oddity, and it was certainly another hint that the Captain had in some way a management of the Earl's affairs.

There was another oddity just before supper. Mally became aware of a slow drift of people to the salon. She and her group followed; and in the salon they found that the dancing had stopped, that the musicians had departed, and that glasses of wine were being offered. At the head of the room a small table, in smooth French walnut, had been set on the polished floor. It stood alone; and on it was a shallow bowl, of thick cut-glass, gleaming and sparkling in the light. In the bowl was water; and floating on the water was a single rose.

Behind the table the Earl of Derwentwater stood still and silent, and his young face seemed taut and pale. It was Lady Chandler who carried to him the brimming glass, and she had the air of one who performs a solemn rite. He took it from her in silence, and a moment longer he waited, while the guests made a silent circle. Then he lifted his head, and his voice came slowly and quietly.

"This is a day, and a night, that we must not take lightly, or suppose to be of no importance. What has been done this day is of consequence, and it will not lightly be undone. It is therefore fitting, and our most proper duty, that we should pledge to the King this night, in humble loving loyalty."

He stood very stiff and still. He looked round the silent circle. Then his hand lifted, carrying his glass above the table and the bowl, above the water where the white rose floated. For a moment he held it so; and then his voice came sharply in command.

"Ladies—gentlemen—the King!"

Every glass in the room rose high with his, upturned as the wine was drained. Then, in the same grave tone, he spoke again, and oddly. He seemed to suppose that he would be understood.

"We had hoped to have another here tonight, the man without a name, whom we are to know as Colonel Storm. He comes from our father's house, and could have told us what our duty is, and what is now required. But he is not yet here, and we are not to complain of that. They will be alert at the ports this week, and he must travel with proper care. But come he will. We think of him as we pledge our loyalty."

He ended; and for a moment he stood pale and silent, looking gravely upon them all. Then he relaxed, spoke a smiling word to Lady Chandler, and walked with her to the supper room. A buzz of talk broke out as the guests made haste to follow; and perhaps only Mally noted that Sir John Chandler had not been present when that toast was drunk.

The supper room was crowded and talkative, and Mally had to give her mind to it. She had hardly a chance to consider the oddities of this, and the meanings it might have; and when at last the room began to empty, she had an encounter that recalled her sharply to what she had all but forgotten. At the door she met her aunt, and Lady Chandler took the moment quickly.

"So you think my warnings are a jest, do you?"

"Madam, I——"

"Do I give routs for *you*—to go dancing with an Earl, presented before my most honoured guests?"

"If you please, I——"

"Presented by Captain Marriott, I think? Did I not say he was not for you?"

"Yes, ma'am. But——"

"I'll talk to you tomorrow."

Lady Chandler turned abruptly away, and Mally was left with a wave of alarm surging through her. The events of the night had not been of her making, but she could see how they would look to another's eye. Lady Chandler had been roused, and there was no prospect of pleasure in tomorrow's talk.

It took a half-hour and another glass of wine before she was recovered enough to give attention to the rout. She wondered where Captain Marriott was. The dancing had begun again, and this was the hour when gentlemen would think of cards. The Captain was no doubt in the card room now, and she stood against the wall and considered it. She knew well enough that she must not disturb his play; but the lure was strong, and perhaps the other glass of wine had disposed her to be reckless. She remembered that tomorrow might end all hope of seeing him again. If she could have no more she would at least have a last sight of him at play; and her chin was tilting as she went quietly down the room, and very slowly opened the card room door.

She was mistaken. There were no gentlemen at play. The green table was deserted and the cards were stacked in their box. On the side table the glasses stood clean, and the wine unpoured. Even the chairs were neatly against the wall. But the candles were lighted and the fire was bright; and in front of the hearth, leaning comfortably against it as he stood to face the door, was Captain Marriott. He was alone in the room, and he had the air of waiting for someone.

The smile was in his face at once.

"It's beyond my deserts," he told her. "You come most happily."

"I'm sure I don't." She faced him with a rueful smile, well knowing that she had intruded when she was not expected. "I'm most untimely. But——"

"Yes?"

He asked it gently as she broke off and struggled with what she knew she must say. Then, in silence, he came closer, till he was almost against her.

"Yes?" He repeated it quietly. "You are not untimely. You couldn't be. But what more was there?"

"Everything." She looked him in the eye, and tried to speak lightly. "You are beyond my deserts, it seems."

"Now what the Devil?" It came sharply, and his voice had changed. "Has someone told you that?"

"It's plain, isn't it? I——"

"Who told you?" Suddenly he took her by the elbows and turned her to face him. "*What* have they told you?"

"Surely I must not keep you from your—affairs?"

"What affairs?"

"I don't know." She had noted the quickness of his question. "There will be gentlemen who wish for play."

"Hardly tonight, I think." His glance turned to the un-wanted cards, stacked in their box. "Four Kings on cards are not worth one live Earl. For the rest, do they think I have nothing in life but affairs?"

"I don't know. I don't even know what affairs."

"It's perhaps as well that you should not. But believe me, you were not untimely here. And——"

"Captain Marriott?"

It was Lady Chandler's voice, courteous and restrained, as it always was when she addressed the Captain, but it set Mally turning hastily to the open door behind her. Lady Chandler was standing stiffly there, and at her side was Henry Deane.

"Madam?"

The Captain seemed wholly undisturbed as he moved forward, and her Ladyship matched him in courtesy.

"You'll forgive my intruding, sir——"

"There's no intrusion, ma'am."

"Perhaps there is." For an instant her eyes were on Mally. "But I fear you're asked for, Captain."

"Indeed, ma'am? Then I must surely comply." His face betrayed nothing as he turned courteously to Mally. "You'll give me leave?"

"Of course, sir. I——"

"Thank you. Now, ma'am, to whom may I be of service?"

He was in quiet talk with her as they moved away together, and suddenly the card room seemed quiet and empty. Mally moved slowly to the hearth, and she had come almost to it, and was staring into the fire, before the click of the latch set her turning quickly. Then she saw that she was not alone in the room. Henry Deane was standing with his back to the door; and he looked portentous, short and plump and sure of himself. There was the same quality in his voice when he spoke.

"That was injudicious." He regarded her gravely. "I understand that this—ah—Captain is not good company for you."

"No." Mally's answer was short. "But at a rout one has sometimes to fall in with what the moment calls for."

The door was flung noisily open, and Mr. Deane almost fell over his feet as he turned hurriedly. Mr. Willoughby was in the doorway, the wealthy Mr. Willoughby whom Lady Chandler seemed set to please; and Mr. Willoughby was the worse for wine. His face was flushed and shining; he was rocking on his feet as he stood, and one hand grasped the door as if he would hold himself steady.

"Are you—are you Mr. Deane?"

It came out suddenly, and Henry Deane stared icily at him.

"Does it concern you, sir? You'll note that we're private here."

"Private?" Mr. Willoughby seemed to consider this carefully. Then he lurched suddenly into the room as the door swung in his grasp. "I'm for the cards. What I'm here for. What Cap—Captain's here for. But he's private. Lady."

His eyes turned to Mally, who had pressed against the wall by the hearth. He blinked, as if he did not see her very well, and then a wave of his hand seemed to point her out to Mr. Deane.

"Captain's lady. But he's private. Other lady. Not right."

He shook his head with awful solemnity, and in doing so he caught sight of the wine that stood waiting. His face brightened as he carefully picked his way towards it, and the wine went splashing over the glass as he tried to pour.

"Im—immorality of present day. Awful. Can't stop it. Private."

He hiccupped noisily and seemed to stare disconsolately at the half-filled glass in his hand. On the table there was a sharp tap of fingers that were more testy now, and suddenly Henry Deane went hurrying from the room, presumably to learn what all this might be about. Mally stayed by the hearth, not at all pleased by the thought that she was now alone with Mr. Willoughby.

There was a noisy gurgle as he drained his wine, and then he was blinking as he peered at her.

"Captain's lady. I know."

He seemed pleased that he had seen who she was. Then he was blinking again, as if he were grasping for some thought that was just beyond him.

"I—I know." His face cleared suddenly as if he had just got it. "Captain's private, with a lady. Now—I came for cards. But can't have 'em. No Captain."

"Yes. But——"

"Can't have Captain. He's with a lady. Now you're Captain's lady. Captain has lady, and I have Captain's lady. It's——"

"Mr. Willoughby! Will you please——"

"Eck—eck—equity. That's it."

He got it out triumphantly, and then he was lurching towards her. She backed away in something like panic, and she forgot the table behind her. She backed into it, and suddenly he was against her, pressing her against the table while he grasped her elbows, and if his wits were clouded his strength was not. He held her tight, and her struggles seemed only to amuse him. She heard him laughing as he forced her back over the table. She twisted her head frantically, trying to see the door through which the music of the dance came loudly; and in that instant it was flung sharply open.

It was Captain Marriott who was there, and at his side was Henry Deane. Behind them, sharp-faced and suspicious, was Lady Chandler, and her first glance through the door was for her niece. But Mally had for once no eyes for her aunt. She felt the grip on her arms relax, and then she staggered from the table and pressed herself against the wall again as Mr. Willoughby went swaying towards the Captain.

"Cards!" It came out jovially, as if he had nothing to oppress his thoughts. "Now we'll have——"

He got no further. Captain Marriott had eyes only for Mally, and one sweep of his arm sent Mr. Willoughby aside as he came to her.

"What is it?" he asked her tensely. "Has there been——"

"No."

She answered him breathlessly, and tried to collect her thoughts. There were others in the doorway now, all with ears agog, and she must do what she could to lessen scandal.

"No." She said it again, and more firmly. "It's merely that Mr. Willoughby was a little——"

"Was a little drunk."

He finished it for her contemptuously, and he turned suddenly on Henry Deane.

"Have you no more thought than to leave a lady with a drunkard? Or is it sense you lack?"

"Really, sir!" Mr. Deane was open-mouthed, plainly flustered for his dignity. "I am not spoken to as——"

"You'll be spoken to as you merit. Just now you merit nothing."

"Captain Marriott!" From the centre of the room Lady

Chandler spoke frigidly. "Mr. Deane, if you please, is——"

"Is a fool with a swollen head, if I know the breed. And as for you, ma'am, you might properly show some feelings for your niece."

The Captain was plainly unrepentant, and the tone of it swept even her Ladyship into silence. He turned as fiercely on Mr. Willoughby.

"As for you—do you find me offensive?"

"Damnably." Mr. Willoughby came slowly forward, and seemed to disapprove of something. "Not gentleman. Not right. You have one lady, I have the other."

Captain Marriott moved slightly, a movement that took him nearer to Mally and no farther from Mr. Willoughby. He spoke in a tone that seemed even harder.

"I think you'd best go home."

"Go to Devil!" The answer came thickly. "Lady loves me."

He lurched, and Mally pressed back along the wall as he came groping for her. In the same moment Captain Marriott forgot the polite world and what it expected of a gentleman. He behaved, as it was later said, like a lackey. The wealthy Mr. Willoughby, hit across the jaw by a fist that had a diamond ring on it, went sprawling at Lady Chandler's feet in a stream of blood; and, overcome by that and the wine, he rolled across in a retching vomit.

CHAPTER IV

SCANDAL

THE scandal was appalling.

If Captain Marriott had behaved as a gentleman, if he had sent his friends to Mr. Willoughby to discuss a piece of level ground and a time when there would be a light for small-swords, the polite world would have forgiven him. It might even have found diversion in asking why he was so concerned for Miss Lawley. But the Captain had gone to fisticuffs like a linkboy or a lackey, and such ill breeding was not to be forgiven. The polite world was agreed, and it straightway removed Captain Marriott from its memories and knowledge. Ladies ceased to pine for him; gentlemen had no wish to play with him; no house invited him; and nobody doubted that the last had been heard of Captain Marriott.

Of this, however, Mally knew very little. She had not been allowed to know. Lady Chandler, white with fury, well knowing that her rout had come to a disaster that would hum through the Town for weeks, had taken one scorching glance around her, and had seen in the throng her most cherished guest, the Earl of Derwentwater, standing as silent witness to her humiliation. She had turned even whiter; and in the next instant Mally had been ordered to her room.

There had been nothing for it but to obey; and in utter silence, and with every eye upon her, she had made her curtsey to her aunt, and then—foolishly, but she was beyond prudence—a second and deeper curtsey to the man who had protected her. He had stood stiffly before her, and then he had bowed very deeply and had quickly taken her fingers to his lips; and he had bowed again as she turned to walk from the room. It had been a gesture by each of them, finely made and as finely returned; but there could hardly have been anything more defiant, or more likely to increase Lady Chandler's fury, and Mally had no doubt at all that she would herself be the first to feel that fury.

She waited in a mounting anxiety, and to her surprise nothing came. She was kept strictly to her room, and she saw nothing of her aunt nor of anybody else of consequence. She was merely left to wait, to think, and remember.

It was from the girl who brought her meals that she had some forbidden scraps of gossip. Captain Marriott had disappeared, and nobody had heard of him. Cousin Julia and her Henry had departed hastily, and it was believed that they thought their social position in jeopardy from this. Mr. Willoughby had called on Lady Chandler, and had been received with deference and apology. And that was all. There was no hint of any consequence for Mally; and as the time passed her anxiety grew keener. She would certainly not be forgiven, and something was being prepared.

It was a monotony that gnawed at both strength and courage, and it did not break until the third day, and then not by Lady Chandler's contriving. On that day the girl who brought in supper paused after she had put down the tray, looked mysterious, and then produced a sealed and folded sheet which she had no doubt been bribed to bring. She whispered an urgent request for secrecy, and went hurrying from the room; and Mally was left to stare at the paper, directed to herself in a writing she did not know. Then a hope flared in her of who this might be from; and with all thought of supper forgotten she ripped through the seals and scanned the bold and level script:

Madam:
　　These are to express what, indeed, I can never express, my sorrow that anything on Wednesday should have brought displeasure upon Miss Lawley. Believe me, I had no thought in the world, when I gave quietus to the unspeakable Willoughby, but to protect you from what you must have found unwelcome. Least of all did I have any thought to bring displeasure upon one whose merit surpasses mine as greatly as does her charm, and whose regard it shall ever be my purpose to deserve.
　　Of what shall come I know nothing. I, too, have incurred displeasure, and am no longer welcome at Lady Chandler's house. How I shall contrive to see you again I know not, nor

*where nor when. Yet I hold faith bright that another day shall
come; and until that day I do lay before you, and do pray you
to accept, the devotion of*

your most true servant,
Anthony Marriott.

That was Saturday, and it brought a warmth and a happiness that had no roots in logic, for the chance of more between
her and the Captain was small indeed. But at least she was
not forgotten; and the thought of it buoyed her through a
dismal Sunday and into a grey wet Monday morning. Then,
at last, she was summoned to her aunt.

She went in trepidation; and the parlour was as she had
always known it, warm and cosy from the fire and the painted
china, and somehow cosier from the grey wet window beyond.
Lady Chandler sat by the fire, as still as granite, and she
wasted no words about it.

"I told you that you were not to consort with Captain
Marriott, and were to show courtesy to Mr. Willoughby. You
have disobeyed me in each. And I thought that even *you* had
better manners than to fling yourself into the face of milord
of Derwentwater."

"Madam! I——"

"Quiet! What disgrace you have brought upon yourself
you will perhaps learn as the years go by. Or perhaps you are
too stupid to learn. Either way I care nothing. All that concerns me is that you are no longer my niece, and no longer of
my house."

Lady Chandler paused for an icy stare, and Mally stood
very still; whatever it was, they were coming to it now.

"I have cared for you, provided for you, and tried to train
you, and my reward for it is—this. I'll have no more of you. I
remove you from my care, and my memory. Did I bid you
speak?"

Her head had reared sharply, and Mally hastily took warning. It was plainly not her moment.

"It's fortunate that I'm not alone in the shame of you."
A tap of the fan gave emphasis now. "There's my brother
Lawley beyond Gateshead, and you are as much niece to him

as you ever were to me. So he shall have you. You go to him this week."

Again Lady Chandler paused, and Mally held herself as stiffly. This would be John Lawley, brother to Lady Chandler and to her own father, and therefore her uncle. He had the estate and house now, the house that had been her grandfather's; but she had never seen the house or him, and she knew no more than that of him.

She roused herself as the fan tapped sharply.

"A letter has gone to him bidding him expect you. He's now without a wife, I'm told, and there's your cousin Jane to keep his house for him. She's Julia's sister, and since she's your elder you'll be in her charge. She has a scratching tongue and the manners of a pig, so she'll perhaps be suited to you."

The note of it was menacing. There was another pause, and then a change of tone.

"You leave this week. Saturday, I think it is, but Sir John takes order for that—and why he should have such goodness I don't know. Being a man, he's perhaps a fool with girls." For a moment there was a glitter in Lady Chandler's eyes. "That is all. Go back to your room."

If it was all, it was enough; and Mally had plenty to think of as she sat alone in her chill grey room, watching the splash of rain and considering it all. It was too much for her to take in all at once. All that was clear was that she was to go from here, to go from her aunt and the ways of the polite world; and for that she had no feeling but relief. The thought of it warmed the whole grey room, until she remembered that it would also be a going from Captain Marriott. Gateshead was a vast way off, some three hundred miles she thought, and no doubt it was a barbarous place. She could hardly keep hope of Captain Marriott there.

The room went grey again as the thought came in, and she had to rouse herself by turning to what else she had been told. What reception she would have from this Uncle John she could not even guess. And what of this Jane who kept his house for him ? She gave herself to remembering the family of old Sir Francis. Thomas had been the eldest, and was the father of Julia and this Jane. Then came John, whom she was now to live with; after him came Katharine, who was Lady

Chandler, and her own father had been the youngest. So John must be uncle to both herself and Jane; and since Julia was in her thirtieth year, Jane must be a little less than that. But what had been meant by a scratching tongue and the manners of a pig? Mally's heart sank at the thought. She had not liked Julia, but Jane sounded even worse.

But there was nothing she could do about it, and nobody she could ask about it. She had to be content. There was nothing more until the next day, and then came a mercer and a milliner, who between them fitted her with a travelling cloak and some lesser things. It was proof that preparations were in hand, and it turned her thoughts to the prospect of a journey. She looked at the rain that still spattered on the window, and she thought it a bad prospect, even an alarming one. This was not weather for coaches. Henry Deane and Julia had come by coach from Newcastle, and that, in a dry October, had meant nine bruising days; and now it was wet, and all but November.

It was an alarm that proved needless. She was summoned again the next morning, and this time it was Sir John who sent for her. He was in his own austere parlour, and he was not sitting. He stood with his back to the fire, and regarded her gravely.

"So you're to leave us, lass?"

He spoke almost whimsically, and not at all as if he thought this a tragedy; and to her own surprise Mally found herself smiling. It was the first time she had smiled since the rout.

"Yes, sir," she said simply. "I'm told I must."

"Aye." He still seemed to be musing upon it. "It's perhaps as well. You'll be better with John Lawley. There's nothing for you here."

"No, sir?"

"No." He came from his musings and was brisker. "It's no house for you. You know what company my wife keeps. You'll be better with John Lawley, and I've said so. Do you know him?"

"No, sir."

"I've met him once. He's a Tory and something of a fool. Perhaps he's a Highflyer. But I think he means well, which is more than you can say of some of my wife's fine friends."

"Yes, sir. I—I mean——"

"You mean you know it, but you don't like to say it. May I give advice?"

"Surely, sir."

"When you're in the North, if you know it, say it. They like you better that way."

"Yes, sir?"

"Ye-es. Make sure you *do* know it, though." Sir John had a happy smile for a moment, and then his tone changed again. "Now of your journey. You leave this time tomorrow."

"Tomorrow, sir? But——"

"I know it's haste, but the wind serves. And ships don't wait."

"Ships!"

Mally was appalled, and Sir John looked at her with amusement.

"What comes from Newcastle?"

"Why—why, sea coal, sir."

"It's called that because it comes in ships. And ships have to go back.

"I suppose so."

"It *is* so. They like a cargo, if there is one, and sometimes they carry *my* cargo. They will therefore carry my passenger too, if I ask it. There's nothing to fear, and you'll be better by sea. These are not coaching days."

"As—as you command, sir."

"That's ordered, then. They'll put you ashore on a staith. Do you know what that is?"

"No, sir."

"You'll learn. But don't wear your newest clothes. Now once ashore, you'll be met."

"Yes, sir."

"There'll be someone—I don't know who—and he'll conduct you, or at least arrange for you. I've written to my brother on that. You know I've a brother there?"

"Yes, sir."

"Now one thing more." Sir John was suddenly graver, and he was looking very straightly at her. "I've written to my brother on a little more than having you met. I've asked him to keep an eye on you when you're in the North. So remember it."

"Surely, sir. And thank you."

"But *do* remember it. Don't suppose it's one of my wife's fine politenesses. It means something."

"Yes, sir."

"Will rides about Tyneside a good deal. He counts for something there. So if you're in trouble, or you need some help, remember that you may write to Will. Esquire Chandler, at Gateshead—that's address enough. You can remember?"

"Yes, sir."

"So will he, and I don't think he'll fail you." Sir John looked keenly at her, his eyes shrewd and steady, and then he nodded. "Tomorrow, by the afternoon tide. So you'd best be packing."

CHAPTER V

SMOKE OF THE TYNE

MALLY'S first view of the Tyne was of a cloud of smoke drifting across a sunlit sea; that, and nothing more.

It surprised her; but this passage to the Tyne had been full of surprises. Sir John had himself taken her down past the Tower to the Pool of London, and the ship had not been the cramped and dirty thing she had expected. It was a full-rigged ship of at least three hundred tons, with its deck clean and wet from the hoses, and only here and there a trace of coal dust lingering. The Master, a short and burly man with a beard and a twinkling eye, was plainly proud of his ship and zealous for its looks, and he had some cause to be proud of the shining cabin he showed her to. She looked at it with delight, for she had been in dread of the quarters she might be given in a ship; and then, to her final relief, she had learned that the Master's wife sailed with him. That had removed another anxiety, and Sir John's dry smile had hinted that he had known of it, and had deliberately chosen this ship for her passage.

Mally had perhaps not understood what an influence Sir John had in this seaborne trade to the Tyne. She had known him only in his own house. But here he was the Merchant Prince, and she was a lady he had personally brought on board; and she was very well looked after. Even the weather had helped. The south-west wind had stayed comfortably on the quarter, where the ship seemed to like it, and today she had been on deck to see a cool clear dawn, with the eastern sky a blaze of red and gold while the blue of night still hung above the land. That had been an hour ago; and now a bright sun was climbing, and they were standing in, close hauled, towards the drifting smoke. Mally stood by the poop-deck rail, muffled in her new long cloak, and asked herself what it was.

It was a problem outside herself and it seemed to fit her mood. Something had happened to Mally in these few days. Being at sea, she had discovered, was wholly different from being on land. There seemed to be a magic in it. The ship was the centre of the sea and sky; it was a world by itself, where nothing counted but the wind and sun, the heave of the deck, the changing colours of the water, and the thought of what might be for dinner. There was healing in it, and a bringing of calm; and she had hardly an interest in new neighbours and a new home, in Uncle John and cousin Jane. They existed, no doubt, but they must wait their turn; at this moment she was concerned with the smoke that was blowing from the land.

She peered at it again. Newcastle, she remembered, lay north of the Tyne, and Gateshead was to the south. So since this smoke was blowing from left to right, it should be blowing from Gateshead to Newcastle. But why?

She turned as she heard boots on the deck, and she saw the Master, bearded and jovial, watching her with amusement. She put the matter to him, and his amusement deepened.

"Gateshead?" He planted his feet squarely, and seemed to lean back against the heave of the ship. "Not in this world, it isn't. It's ten miles up river to Gateshead. That's Shields."

"Oh? But why the smoke?"

"It's the salt-pans. They boil the brine from the sea, and it leaves the salt behind. It's not all good coal that comes from pits. A lot of it's small, no bigger than eggs, and that's how they use it. They turn the sea into good hard salt, and you'd be in straits for your winter meat without it."

"It makes a lot of smoke."

"Aye. But not what we'd call a trouble, not with this wind. In a nor-wester it comes straight in your face, and we're thankful to sight the Middens. But here's where we heave to. We put our ballast over."

It made an absorbing day. They hove to, and the slings were rigged from the yardarms, and basket after basket of the loose stone ballast was put into the sea. In the river, the Master explained, it might be dumped only at specified ballast shores, where dues were heavy. So he took advantage of the calm sea, and dumped while he waited for the tide. Then they were under sail again, over Tynemouth bar, into the river and past the drifting smoke from the pans. It was a river comparable with the Thames, as busy and a deal less dirty, and the Master's wife came now to Mally's side to point out what was to be seen: the town of Shields, with the huge and land-locked pool that was its harbour; another town beyond, which she said was Jarrow, ancient and holy; and then a succession of salt-pans and quays, mounds of stone which were the ballast shores, and long wooden wharves piled high with heaps of coal. These she called staiths; and suddenly Mally remembered that Sir John had used this word, and had said she would be landed at one.

It was a slow passage, impeded by islands and mudbanks, by anchored ships and the small craft that were under the bows of every ship that moved. The quays, it seemed, were reserved for general cargo, and ships loading coal had to anchor in the stream and have it brought out to them from the staiths by squat and rounded boats called keels, slow moving, deeply laden, and by no means disposed to give way to anybody. There were other craft too, sailing hoys with passengers for Shields and Tynemouth, the jolly-boats of shipmasters, the yachts of merchants, and the smart launches of the Customs men. Between them they made fast passage impossible, and it was therefore past one o'clock when the ship nosed into the northern shore at what the Master said was St. Anthony's. Here, he said, he must part from Mally. Her further journey lay across the river, and Esquire Chandler would no doubt have arranged it.

Esquire Chandler had. In a matter only of minutes a sloop-rigged launch swept alongside with a flap of canvas and a surge and swish of water, and over the side came a young man in serviceable russets, neat and unpretentious. He looked Mally in the eye, and then named himself as Richard Chandler. He was here, he said, in place of his father, who was away on affairs; and he was therefore at Miss Lawley's service.

Miss Lawley did her best to look at ease. She had never even heard of this Richard, and for a moment she was at a loss. Then she saw the likeness to Sir John, the dark hair, the big nose and mouth, the wide shoulders and air of burly strength. Certainly this was a Chandler, and she noted, too, that he did not wear a wig. It was his own hair, trim and tidy, and the rest of him matched that. His russets were warm and good, but they were very plain; his shirt was a fine cambric, but his cravat was of the plainest; his breeches had riding-leathers, and there was no gleam of a buckle in his neat strong shoes. It was all very practical, but there was nothing here of display.

He spoke again before she had found an answer, and there was a burr in his voice to remind her again of Sir John.

"I hadn't heard of you till the other day."

"Nor I of you, I'm afraid."

"Then we can't complain. I've heard of Mr. Lawley of course. Is he your uncle?"

"He is. But I've never met him."

"I'm to take you to him. Are your bags up yet?"

He took charge with a brisk confidence, and Mally soon knew about it. Gentlemen in the polite world had either ignored her as beneath notice, or had treated her with an elaborate courtesy; but Richard Chandler did neither. He merely told her what to do, and then made sure that she did it. He sent her below to collect her last oddments, and when she was on deck again he was already standing in the boat. A length of Jacob's ladder, all rope and slats, trailed precariously down, and Mally viewed it with dismay. She balked at it, and he dealt briefly with her. He had hold of her before she knew it, and he swung her in a wide arc through the air and settled her firmly in the stern-sheets of the boat. With the same calmness he settled himself next to her, and then the launch was heeling to the wind as the bowman pushed off. Mally shook out her skirts and tried to get her breath back. She was not used to Richard Chandler.

The mainsail took the wind. The launch heeled and lurched as the helm was steadied, and a shower of spray came over, shining and gleaming in the sun. It went spattering across her knees, chilling and wetting, and she hastily pulled the cloak tight.

"Just so," he said. "Now fasten it to the neck. You can get cold on the water, and we've a little way to go. Have you seen Newcastle?"

"No."

She gave it him abruptly, and with no more attention to the courtesies than he had given her. She looked quickly away again, giving heed to the sunlit river, the busy traffic of boats, the wharves and buildings on its shores; and half her mind was on that, and half was on this man who was nothing she had ever known. He was something she had to puzzle out. He showed no courtesies, but he was perhaps not discourteous. He was merely direct. Her thoughts played on that for a moment, and she turned her head for a glance at him; and to her quick confusion she saw that he was studying her.

He was not at all disturbed. He looked steadily at her, and she saw that he was smiling.

"I don't know anything about you," he said.

"Nor I of you, sir."

"No?" His amusement seemed to be growing. "I suppose in London I should have to call you Madam?"

"It's the custom."

"It isn't here. And you don't call me Sir, either. We keep that for our elders." He spoke quickly, and she saw that he was watching her carefully. "You won't mind if I tell you something?"

"No."

She was watching him just as carefully, and some sort of confidence was returning to her. For all his blunt ways, this seemed a man she could talk to.

"Our ways are not London ways. We don't waste as many words. So if you're coming to live with us, use our ways as soon as you can. It will help you."

"I'll try."

"Do." He answered her heartily, and then turned in his seat to face her more directly. "You know who my father is?"

"Sir John's brother."

"Yes. I expect you'll meet him soon. I'm his only son, and they call me Dick. So do you, by the way."

"What!"

"Oh yes." He seemed to take it quite calmly. "I'm only Richard when I'm on duty."

"What duty?"

"Acting for my father. He often sends me to do things for him. He calls me his Lieutenant." For a moment his smile was almost a grin. "Now what about yourself? Tell me the same things."

For a moment Mally hesitated, and felt herself shy and awkward. She was used to the formalities and the escapes they offered; but this was all in the open, and London would have called it rustic. Then she remembered that this was not London, and she nerved herself to speak in his own short style.

"There isn't much. I'm Lady Chandler's niece. I'm called Mally. I'm only Mary when I'm in trouble. I'm not anybody's Lieutenant, and I'm not important at all."

"Are you sure? But look——"

He swept her attention suddenly away. The launch had turned another bend, and before her was what she knew must be Newcastle; and it was not the mean and rugged place that London would have thought. She said so, and Dick Chandler looked pleased. He was evidently willing to speak up for his town, and soon he was busily pointing things out to her. That great yard to her right was the ropery, and had she ever seen a bigger one? That clutter of little streets beyond it was the Sandgate, where the keelmen and the wharf-porters lived. And did she see the quay?

She could hardly miss seeing it. Ahead of them, perhaps a half-mile distant, a stone bridge lay across the river; and all the space along the north bank was one stone-faced quay, with the ships moored two and three abreast along its length. He was zealous in pointing out. The old wall of the town ran here, he said, and the quay was the space without the wall. Within the wall were the houses of the merchants, and those narrow lanes between the houses were the chares; and when she asked who lived there, he grinned broadly and said she had better not ask. But what did she think of the bridge?

They were almost up to it, and she thought it as fine as London bridge. He was pleased with that answer, and at once he was telling her how it led to the wealthy quarter called the Sandhill, and then he was pointing out the huge stone keep of the Norman castle above, and the rearing tower of the church that stood behind it.

They were beyond the bridge now, and he was at it again. That was the Mansion House yonder, where the stairs went up from the water; it was for the Mayor to live in, and it had cost six thousand pounds. Those were the merchants' houses left and right of it, in a street called The Close, which she must certainly look at some day. And now here they were! His father owned this staith.

The launch had turned sharply inshore, to the south bank

that she had hardly heeded, and almost at once they were
swishing alongside the wooden stairs of the staith, while the
mainsail came down as a cloud of flapping canvas. He handed
her out, and as she went up the stairs there was a crunch of
coaldust beneath her feet. It lay like a black and shining carpet,
and when she came to the top there were mounds of coal piled
left and right, and a scattering of lumps of coal for the unwary
to stumble over; and the staith, as she quickly saw, was not a
place for the unwary. It was a low timbered wharf, no more
than that, and alongside it lay three of the squat blunt boats
that had been named to her as keels. A wagon piled with coal
was being pushed to the face of the staith, and it was no
ordinary wagon. It had wheels that ran on wooden rails. The
rails, strong and neat in oak, ran across the staith to its face,
where they turned to run parallel with the water. Here the
wagon now was, and at that moment two men grasped its side
and heaved. The body of the wagon tilted. There was a crunch
and a rumble, and suddenly its load of coal went sliding and
roaring over the edge of the staith and into the waiting keel
below. Mally jumped back hastily as the black dust rose in a
storm; and before it had cleared the truck had been pushed
along the rails to where they turned to the inland again. A
horse was hitched to it, and in the same instant another loaded
wagon came rumbling down the gradient and across the staith.

"Better stand back," said Dick. "You got the dust that
time."

"I know." The gritty stuff was even on her lips, and she
had to pause to lick them. "Is it always like this?"

The second wagon tipped, and again the choking dust came
blowing. Mally moved warily to windward, and then peered
over the edge to see the loaded keel move off with two men tugging at the heavy oars. Already another keel was moving
beneath the tip, and the rumbling of an approaching wagon
grew louder. Mally watched intently, knowing that this was
far indeed from her aunt's polite world; and then he tapped on
her arm and broke her reverie.

"Your bags are up now, and it's late enough."

The sun was falling in a clear pale sky, and Mally made
no demur. She followed him from the staith to where a two-
horsed chaise was waiting, with her bags already loaded, and

two mounted servants sitting on their horses; and as she climbed into it she was noting the speed at which they did things here, and the smoothness of it all. Dick Chandler might lack the graces, but he knew what he was about. There was no detail wanting.

The chaise moved off, clattering and bouncing along a rutted road, and he had a word about that. Almost everything was carried on the river, he explained, so there was less need of a road. Then he was pointing inland to show a great iron works that reared into the sky, smoking and flickering; and with the air of one giving the Devil his due he admitted that Sir Ambrose Crowley, who had built it a dozen years ago, was really a Londoner. He made chains and anchors, and all heavy ironwork, and he had a second works to make pins and knives and saws. And this stream they were crossing was the Derwentwater.

"Is that where milord Derwentwater lives?"

Mally interrupted sharply. He had revived a memory for her, and for a moment she was back in Lady Chandler's house; there was a bowl of water where a white rose floated, and a slim young nobleman was holding his wine aloft.

"No. He lives by Corbridge, up to the north yonder. But do you know him?"

"I was presented to him, once."

She said it briefly, and her thoughts were with the Earl who took his title from this Derwentwater, and had danced with her, and spoken graciously. All the rout was passing through her mind, glittering and hard; and then she was in the card room, and alone, and Captain Marriott was standing by the hearth.

"Mally——"

She jerked out of her reverie, and Dick Chandler was at her side, watching her gravely.

"You were far away that time."

"I'm sorry. I——"

"You needn't be. You're allowed your thoughts, and they're private. That was Blaydon we've just passed through. The house yonder is Stella."

He was allowing her to escape, and showing her the way of it. He had turned from her, and was pretending an interest in what was passing; and Mally sat staring at his burly neck and the shoulders of his russet coat. She had told herself a half-hour back that Dick Chandler lacked the courtesies.

Dimly she was aware that the chaise had left the river-road and was climbing a stony hill. The clatter of the wheels had slowed, and the horses were straining; and Mally hardly heeded. She was remembering some other matters.

"Dick——"

She spoke suddenly and sharply, with her cheeks reddening that she should have called him so. The thought was with her of Captain Marriott, the careful courtesy she had had to use to him, the outrage it would have seemed if she had addressed him plainly. But Dick Chandler seemed to find nothing odd. He turned with a half-smile on his face.

"Yes?"

"Do you know why I've been sent from London?"

"Not really." He seemed to be watching her carefully, and suddenly she was aware of his eyes, and the shrewdness that was in them. "It's not my father's way to tell all he knows. All he said was that there'd been a quarrel."

"There had."

It came surging back to her, the last scene in the card room, the scandal of it, the disgrace it would reflect, the letter that would have gone to her uncle whose home was up this hill. She had no cause to expect a welcome; and it was not reassuring.

She forced a wan smile as she spoke again.

"I was nobody at my aunt's. I didn't count for anything. But there was a man who thought I did—or should."

"He was right."

She looked up sharply, thinking he had made an obvious politeness, and then she knew that he had not. He was looking at her very gravely and steadily, and he had spoken as if he meant it.

"You'd count for something anywhere. Some girls do. They're born that way. You're one of them."

"Thank you." She looked hurriedly away, pleased, yet unwilling that he should know it. "But I was thought——"

"What was thought in London won't count here." He interrupted quickly, as if he would guide her thoughts on this.

"You'll find that folk here will do their own thinking. They'll think of what they see you are, and there'll be nothing else that matters."

She stared at him, mutely grateful, and without words to express the tangle of feelings that were in her, the rising of hope that had not been there before. She saw the smile come to his face again; and suddenly, for one quick instant, his hand closed over hers as it lay on the cushioned seat. She felt the quick warm pressure of it, strong and encouraging, and then it was gone, and he was smoothing his cloak.

"Don't fret."

The two words came firmly, and for a moment longer his eyes held hers. Then he looked away, and he left her to her thoughts.

The sun was down when they came to the crest of the hill, and there was thin grey cloud in the west to dim the light. On the upland a wind was blowing, setting the long grass rippling, coming into the chaise with a chill that set her pulling at her cloak. She leaned forward, peering in the fading light; and she saw that the river was gone, and that here was undulating ground, where always an upward sweep cut off the view. The grass looked rougher, and the scattered trees were bent and torn by wind. This was not the valley of the Tyne; and it was not the world of Jermyn Street and Lady Chandler.

In the last grey of the dusk they turned from the road, passed between timbered gates, and up the curve of a stony drive. They passed through a grove of shielding trees, and so to a sweep of grass; and there, very grey and dim, was the house.

It was of no great size, and of no pretensions; a simple building, long, gable-ended, and with a grey slate roof. It had a projecting porch with thick stone pillars, a line of windows above, and some dormer windows to break the slope of the roof. In the grey light it blurred against the sky, and the details were hard to see, and only a dim light showed from a window beside the porch. There was no sign of welcome, and nothing to take the eye; yet Mally's first thought was that this was a house proper to the place. It sank into its surroundings, and it fitted.

The chaise lurched to a halt, and Dick stepped quickly out, stamping his feet on the ground as if he had felt the cold. He plied the knocker briskly, and then came to give his hand to Mally. She climbed out slowly, stiff from sitting, and knowing that she was tired. She moved at his side to the door, trying to walk steadily.

A brighter light appeared, as if another candle had been brought, and there was the slide of a bolt and the creak of dry hinges. The door swung open, and a lad in shirt-sleeves and faded breeches stood peering at them; and he was far from the gilded lackey who swung Lady Chandler's door. Mally stood numbed, trying to repress a shiver as the cold wind caught her. Then a woman appeared in the lighted hall, young and assured. She came slowly forward, and Mally stood quiet and still, unwilling to be the first to speak. This must surely be the cousin Jane she had heard about.

Dick Chandler swept his hat off, though he made no attempt at a bow. The burr in his voice seemed strong as he spoke abruptly.

"Miss Lawley, would it be?"

"It would."

She answered him as crisply, and her voice was young and clear. He nodded calmly.

"Here's another Miss Lawley. I've brought her here."

"What's that?"

She was showing no surprise at his abruptness, but she had turned quickly to Mally. There was a moment of watchful silence, and then she spoke again.

"You'll be cousin Mary, I suppose? I'm Jane Lawley."

"Yes, I——"

"We heard you were coming."

It was the same cool tone, and it gave no hint of her thoughts. Mally stood hesitating, and Dick quietly took charge. His arm came lightly round her, and she was gently pushed through the doorway. He came with her, his arm still lightly on her, and for a moment they stood so, he almost as her protector, while Mally gave eye to this new cousin. Jane was perhaps in her early twenties, sturdy and strong, with a brown and pleasant face that had an impudent nose and a mouth a shade too wide. She was standing very still and watchful, with her face composed and her brown eyes keen and steady, and she was not to be taken lightly. Mally was swiftly sure of that. As friend or as enemy, this Jane could be a force; and this might be a decisive moment.

But it passed. At the back of the hall a door creaked open, and a man came slowly into view, a man heavy and middle-aged, in an old red coat and a homely woollen waistcoat. He checked at the sight of them all, and Jane took the same pungent tone.

"Here's your other niece, sir—sent as your sister promised. It seems she travels fast."

"Does she?" He sounded vague, as if he had no good grasp of this. "Aye, we did think next week."

It was not unkindly, but he was staring at Mally as if he did not know what to say next. She looked at him carefully, noting his round plump face, his high colour and heaviness of build, and her quick thought was of too much to eat and too much October ale. There was a thickness in his face that did not suggest the sharpest mind, and there was a hint of obstinacy too; but it was a kindly face, surely well meaning, and she was suddenly sorry for him as she saw his awkwardness, and almost his shyness at being confronted with her. She took it for granted that he was John Lawley, and her mind had leapt quickly to some contemptuous sayings of Lady Chandler about her rustic brother.

"I'm sorry, sir, if I come too soon." She was speaking quickly, to break this silence. "I came by sea, and had good passage. Now I've been escorted here, and——"

"Aye, aye." There was a ring of relief in his tone. "But it's no matter. We'll make you welcome. Jane will see to you."

"Jane always does. It's what I'm here for." Jane's retort came sharply, but she had a smile that took offence out of it, and then she turned to Mally. "But it's true that you're welcome, and there'll be supper soon. But how of your—er—escort? You haven't named him to us yet."

It was a sharp reminder, and Mally turned quickly, and at once she was aware of what seemed an oddity. Dick Chandler had almost faded into the background. He had not spoken, and he had never moved since he brought her into the house. He was standing just inside the door, very still and silent. He had drawn no attention, and seemed to wish for none; and suddenly Mally was asking why.

But it was John Lawley who spoke first; and he, too, sounded as if he had neglected something.

"Aye, aye." He said it hastily. "We're indebted to you, no doubt, for bringing her. And you'll be better for ale, and supper."

"I doubt if I'm for supper, sir." Dick was answering for himself, and his voice rang a shade too loud. "She's safely brought, and perhaps that should be an end. It's not far home, and I'll take no hurt."

"Aye, aye. But in decency we must——"

"My thanks." He was speaking steadily and firmly. "I must tell you that I'm Richard Chandler, from Gateshead."

"Who?"

It was Jane who flung the word, and there was a sudden crackle in her voice. He turned to her quite calmly.

"I think you heard. I'm Richard Chandler, and it's no long way to Gateshead."

"Aye, we know that." John Lawley was taking it up again now. "But we've asked you for supper, and——"

"I doubt if I'm very welcome, sir. At least, it didn't sound like it." He turned suddenly on Jane. "Would you have asked me if you'd known my name?"

"I——" Jane sounded as if she were for once in difficulties. "We don't know much about your name, Mr. Chandler. We know your father's name, and——"

"And you don't like it. Well, I'm not here to apologize for my father. I don't think I've any cause to."

"You needn't shout it at me."

"I have to be heard somehow. There's too much said about my father, and I know what it all is. So I'd better go."

He stirred, quickly pulling on his gloves, and Mally stood aghast as she saw what hostility had flared, and how bluntly it was spoken. This was certainly not the polite world she had known.

He spoke again, and now differently. There was a quick smile on him, and his voice was softer.

"Don't think I've been unrewarded in this journey. It's a work I've enjoyed."

His quick glance at Mally made his meaning plain. For a moment he stood in silence at her side, facing John Lawley across the pool of candlelight. Then he inclined his head sharply, as if in farewell, and with no further word he turned and went through the door. Mally stood staring, feeling that something she wanted, and could lean upon, had gone. It brought a cold dismay; and in another instant, confusedly and without knowing why, she went running after him.

It was all but dark. The lanterns of the chaise had been lit, and were casting a yellow glow upon the horses. The driver was ready upon his perch, and the mounted servants behind. The wind struck cold, and by the door of the chaise he was a dark shape, muffled in his cloak.

"I haven't even thanked you."

She spoke hurriedly, knowing that she must at least say something; and he turned.

"There's no reason why you should. You gave good company, and I liked it—and you."

A dim glow from the candles showed his face as he looked to the lighted doorway, and then he was speaking quickly.

"They'll say all the world against my father in such a house as this. Don't believe all of it, will you?"

"No."

"Good night."

It was abrupt, and for an instant he was looking down at her. Then, before she knew it, or had even guessed it, he had pulled her to him and kissed her lightly. He turned away, and pulled the chaise door tight. A bell tinkled, and with a clop of hooves and a crunch of wheels the chaise moved off.

Mally stood alone, her thoughts whirling. She was dazed and confused, and there was nothing clear at all; but he was gone, and it was cold and dark, and she was lonely. Behind her was the house, and she would have to face them there.

From the lighted doorway Jane called crisply.

"You'll be getting cold out there. Hadn't you better come in?"

C

CHAPTER VI

THE NON-JUROR

If Jane had charge of this house, it seemed that she knew her business. She had no comments to make on what had just passed. She merely whisked Mally up the stair to a bedroom; and in some few minutes more the fire was crackling finely, the bags had been carried up, and Jane was looking suspiciously at the sheets and giving orders about warming-pans and hot bricks. She declared that supper would be in twenty minutes, and then she was gone; and Mally stood in the centre of the room, not knowing clearly what had happened to her.

She looked round more carefully as her thoughts began to flow. This was an old-fashioned room, low and dark, with the oak beams showing in the ceiling, and the plastered walls hung with faded tapestry. It had furniture that matched it, a canopied four-poster, an old-fashioned clothes-press, a tiring-table with a little mirror, and a pair of leather-topped stools. It was very clean and trim, as if Jane had a sharp eye, and perhaps a sharp tongue too; but it was old and faded, and nothing had been done to bring it up to date. There was nothing here of the elegance of Jermyn Street.

That was true of some more in this house. Mally made what hurried toilet she could; and when she went down the stair again, still uncertain of her welcome, she found that supper was prompt to the minute, and admirably cooked; but the staple of it was rabbits, with home-made cheese, a home-brewed ale, and a coarser bread than London knew. The cloth on the table was home-spun linen, and in the place of silver there was old and well rubbed pewter. This was simplicity, and the country ways.

It disturbed Mally not at all. She had not found much happiness in Jermyn Street, and she had no great wish to be reminded of it; and she had sense enough to know that what mattered here was not the furniture but the people. All that they would know of her would have come from Lady Chandler,

66

and it would hardly be to her credit; apart from which, they might have no wish for a stranger in their house. There was no cause for being sure of welcome, and Mally was watchful and alert.

To her relief they came to it quickly, and it was John Lawley who brought it on. He rested his knife and spoke sharply.

"So you're at odds with my sister, are you? Why?"

His bluntness was less disconcerting than it might have been some hours ago. She was getting used to this sort of thing now, and his tone had not been unfriendly. She went at it cautiously.

"I think, sir, I had too much notice from those her Lady-ship thought above me."

"Above you? She thinks most of her friends are above *me*. That's since she got money. Who were these who noticed you?"

"Why, sir——" Mally looked at him carefully, and decided to play the ace. "There was milord of Derwentwater——"

"*Who?* You mean of Dilston, here?"

"I think so, sir. I was presented, and——"

"The Devil you were! He was at my sister's house?"

"Yes. It was the Coronation night, and——"

"What a woman! I knew she was reaching high, but I'd not heard it was as high as that." He blew his breath out indignantly. "She married tallow once, and was glad to."

"Was my sister there?"

It was Jane, cutting crisply into the talk, and Mally turned quickly to note the difference between Julia and this Jane. She would hardly have guessed that they were sisters.

"Yes." She spoke slowly. "She was there."

"Was she presented? She'd be near mad if she wasn't."

If uncle John did not like his sister, this sounded as if Jane might not like hers. Mally gave a dry answer.

"She was—afterwards."

"After what?"

"Me."

"Ho-ho!" Uncle John slapped noisily on the table, and flung his head back in merriment. "No wonder they don't like you. She mostly thinks she's first."

"Always." Jane corrected him blandly. "But this is news. It's a detail Henry didn't tell us."

"Henry?" Mally was suddenly sharp on it. "Is that Mr. Deane?"

"It's that chubby little toad my sister married. He was here yesterday. He came, as usual, for what he could get."

"Oh?" Mally tried to take this in, and then put it firmly aside. Instead she turned to her uncle, determined now to bring this to a head. "I know, sir, that I've been forced upon you, and it's not good cause for welcome."

"Let alone, lass—let alone. You're welcome enough." He seemed to hurry it, as if he were embarrassed at having to say it. "There's not much here and not much to offer, but to what there is you're welcome."

"It's good of you, sir."

"No." He pushed his chair back and got heavily to his feet. "These are bad times, and hard, but I may still give some hospitality in my house—and glad to."

He went wandering to the hearth and picked a tobacco jar from the litter there, and he was turning it in his fingers as he spoke again.

"How did you come to be with young Chandler tonight?"

It was almost as if she had something to explain. She took it steadily, and then gave him the simple answer.

"He met me in the ship. I think Sir John had written to his brother here, and——"

"William? Aye, we all know of William."

He had opened the tobacco jar now, and his thick fingers were groping in it. He almost seemed intent on that.

"So William sent the lad to meet you, did he? Well, we'll not hold that against you."

"No, sir."

"You could be a thought less friendly, though, if you're wise. With any Chandler."

"Yes, sir."

It was not a matter to be argued, and to her relief he seemed to think the same. His final comment had a change of tone.

"There's not much here, but you're welcome to what there is. And if you could like Jane, it would help. It's quiet here for

Jane, and it will be quiet for you. You could help each other in that."

There was one country girl to take away the supper; which was not what Lady Chandler had had. Nor did Jane stand aloof. She gave some hand herself, and Mally was quick to take the chance. She went to help, and was glad that things were so. She could more easily establish herself in this sort of house, and more easily come to terms with Jane; which, as she now thought, might not be difficult. She was beginning to like Jane.

She learned some more of Jane before the evening was done; for in no long time a man came in who had the air of a neighbour, come for a friendly call. He was an elderly man, tall and spare, with a gaunt and scholarly face, and the bands and black of a divine. He was presented as Mr. Peaver, and he showed a grave courtesy to Mally before transferring attention to his host. Plainly he and John Lawley were old friends, and it soon appeared that he had come to play backgammon. Jane brought out the board and pieces for them, and soon they were settled by the fire, content and friendly. It was all very proper to country life, but they would be happier left to themselves; and when Mally declared that she had not yet unpacked her bags, Jane whispered that she would come up too.

She perched herself on the edge of Mally's bed, and seemed disposed for gossip.

"He comes about twice a week," she said, and she was plainly referring to Mr. Peaver. "Other nights John goes to him."

"Who is John?"

"Our uncle."

"You don't call him *that*, do you?"

"I certainly don't. Nor will you. But it will do when we're alone."

"Ye-es." Mally was still not quite sure what to make of Jane. "Mr. Peaver being the Rector, I suppose?"

"I wish he was."

The pungent tone had suddenly returned; and Mally, on her knees unstrapping a bag, sat back on her heels and looked up.

"What is he, then?"

"He isn't anything. He just happens to live here."

"You don't sound as if that's all."

"Don't I?" The pungent tone faded, and a smile came slowly to Jane. "You've some sharp senses, haven't you? But as to Peaver, he's a Non-juror, so he hasn't got a parish. He hasn't had a parish since '89."

"I see."

There was nothing to misunderstand. For in 1688 there had been the Revolution which the Whigs called Glorious and the Tories did not. It had tumbled King James from his throne and sent him in flight to France. Then the Dutchman had been called King William, and soon it had been required that every man who had office in Church or State should swear allegiance to him. The Whigs had sworn it willingly, and most of the Tories unwillingly, having no love for a Calvinistic Dutchman; and some few had refused to swear at all, saying they had sworn allegiance to one King and could not without mortal sin swear it now to another. These were the malcontents, called Non-jurors because they refused to swear; and if Mr. Peaver were one of them he would have been deprived of office like the rest. That was the trouble with the Non-jurors; they had no work to do, and brooding in idleness had not done them any good.

"I see." Mally repeated it slowly. "I remember some Non-jurors in Lady Chandler's house. This one's your neighbour, is he?"

"Yes. He had a parish across the river yonder, in Northumberland, and he had a little money, so he didn't starve when he was deprived. He was in one place and another, and then he came here. There's a house on the estate that John let him have, and now they play backgammon together."

"You still sound as if it isn't all." Mally heaved herself to her knees again and began to unpack the bag. "Is—*do* I say John?"

"If there's no one listening."

"There isn't. Is John a Non-juror, too?"

"He hasn't told me." Jane pushed herself off the bed and wandered to the fire. "Let us just say he's a High Tory. And they play backgammon together."

"Again you sound disapproving."

"It's hardly my place to disapprove, is it?"

"Perhaps not. But I don't know what your place *is* here. Or mine either."

"Poor relations, aren't we?"

"I am. I don't know about you."

"Then you may as well know. I'm exactly that, and in my father's house. Did you know I was born here?"

"No."

"I was. So was Julia." Jane had moved from the hearth now, and she was standing by the bedside, speaking soberly. "After all, my father was the eldest son."

"Of old Sir Francis?"

"Yes. It was Sir Francis who first had this house. Please don't think we're an ancient family of this County, because we're not." Jane sounded grimly amused. "If you listen to Julia, or our precious Aunt Chandler, you'd think the Sieur Something de Lawley came riding here with Norman William. Well, he didn't. We weren't heard of till Sir Francis made his money, and he made that in Newcastle. He made it out of coal. Just like Black William."

"Who's he?"

"Black William?" There was a sudden twitch of Jane's eyebrows. "Black William is Esquire Chandler of Gateshead, father of that young man who was kissing you just now."

"Jane! I——"

"You needn't turn red. If you say it was all his fault I'll believe you."

"Jane, what *has* this to do with Sir Francis?"

"I was trying to answer your question, about me and the place I have here."

"Oh, I'm sorry." Mally did her best to look interested. "What did Sir Francis do?"

"He bought this house and land. Then he called the attorneys in, and they made a settlement that takes a week to read. He didn't leave the estate outright to anybody. He settled it on all his male heirs, one after the other, to the end of time. It meant that when my father inherited the estate he didn't really own it. He only had the use of it. He couldn't sell it, and he couldn't bequeath it. It had to go to the next male heir, and then to the next and the next. That's how you make a landed family, you see. You tie the family to the estate. I think it's called an entail."

"It sounds ingenious."

"Does it?" A grim note was in Jane's voice as she went slowly on. "Sir Francis planned how his heirs should live. He thought of everything for them—except what came."

"And what was that?"

"Civil war. King Charles and his Parliament, and Sir Francis fought for the King. So the Parliament put fines on him. They left him his land, and they took all else he had. Then he died, and my father had the house and land alone— and it's poor thin land. There's no fat rent-roll here. And we can't sell one acre of it to raise some money."

"I see."

Mally spoke softly. She looked round her at the room that was old and faded. She remembered her uncle's shabby clothes, the simple supper, the pewter and the home-spun linen; and she began to understand. It would be easier for her here, for this matched her own means; but she might, perhaps, be a burden.

"What about Julia?" She spoke suddenly, as a memory came. "She doesn't look short of money."

"She isn't. That's Henry. He had a wealthy father."

"Then why did he marry Julia. Had she a dowry?"

"She had something better."

"What?"

"The estate. Her son is the heir-male, after John. So he's bound to have it."

"But you say it isn't worth much."

"It will be to Henry."

"Why?"

"The coal pit's finished. Henry has money to start a new one. John hasn't. And he can't sell any land to get it."

"I don't think I quite understand."

"I'll show you tomorrow. But that's why Henry keeps coming here. He wants a lease of the coal. But meantime, you know why I'm the poor relation, and what I'm doing here. I keep the house for John. That's all there was, after my father died."

She turned away, and for a moment she stood staring at the

fire. Mally stood by her forgotten bags, and in the silence she heard the hiss and flicker of the flaming coal. Perhaps even that had come from the estate, as the rabbits had ; and certainly this was bleak for Jane.

"Mally——" Jane turned suddenly by the hearth. "I think it's time we went down."

"To the parlour ?"

"I think we ought to. Those two will be talking now."

"Shouldn't they ?"

"No." There was a change of tone, and Jane's voice had hardened. "Backgammon's one thing, and talk's another. Peaver's a Non-juror."

"What of it ?"

"Don't you know what Non-jurors talk about ?" There was anxiety suddenly in Jane. "These are not times for such talk. It could be dangerous."

CHAPTER VII

THE COAL PIT

JANE kept to her promise that she would the next day show Mally something of the estate.

She had, indeed, no choice, for she and Mally found themselves engaged to drink tea with Mr. Peaver; and if this did not please Jane, she had only herself to thank for it. For when she had gone down the stair with Mally, the night before, she had found what she feared; that the game of backgammon was ended, and that Mr. Peaver was leaning his tall spare figure against the hearth while he talked politics. He was eloquent about it, with a fervent voice and glittering eye, and Jane had promptly swept him out of it. She had unblushingly declared that Mally was greatly interested in the coal pit, and Mr. Peaver had at once put aside his politics. There was an old-fashioned courtesy in him, and a kindliness, and he had at once said that the pit was near to his own small house, and he would be delighted to show it to her if she and Jane would drink tea with him on the morrow. He had been charming about it, and there had been only one possible answer, little though Mally cared about coal pits; and when, later, she had said as much to Jane, she had been bluntly told that little things like that were sometimes needed to keep Mr. Peaver from his politics.

It thus came about that Mally had to adventure upon a horse; which gave her no pleasure at all. She had not used horses in London, and she had all but forgotten the few short lessons of childhood. She looked very doubtfully at the two shaggy beasts that were led from the stable, and she rode out with Jane at a cautious walk; and now, for the first time, she saw the house by day. It was grey and simple, of thick old stone, with moss clinging to the slated roof, as if to hint of rain enough in winter. The windows were dull and faded, the shutters were as grey as the stone, and in the drive there were ruts and hollows. Mally read the signs, and noted, too, what rustic horses they were riding. It fitted with what Jane had said of there being no money here.

They passed through the belt of shielding sycamores, and beyond them were the gates and the dusty road she had used last night, no wider than a slender chaise would need. Jane led across it to a bridle track in the fields beyond, and Mally began to give heed to her surroundings. She was on the rolling upland that she had noted last night, where always there was an upward sweep and no long view of anything, and over it a wind was blowing, westerly and cool. They were skirting a stubble field, not yet ploughed, and Jane had a word about it.

"That's a harder stubble than you'd have down south. It's thinner, too. Look at that grass."

They had passed the stubble and were riding across rough pasture, and Mally could see what was meant. This was no soft meadow, rich and lush; it was a strong rough grass, wind-blown and tufted, and even in the afternoon light it was hard and weather-beaten.

"It's the same with the wheat." Jane's voice came gustily on the wind. "Our winters aren't worse than others, but the north-easters blow in the spring, and they keep us cold and hold the sowings back. The wheat hasn't time to grow. That's why it's thin. I told you it was poor living here, and no fat rent-rolls. Now look——"

They had come to the last of the rolling crests, and Jane had pulled her horse to a halt. Before them the land sloped steeply, down and down, and at the foot of it, perhaps five hundred feet below, the Tyne was a broad and shining ribbon in the bottom of the valley. Beyond it was a level strip, and then the rising ground again, rolling and climbing to the north until it was against the sky and blocked all further view.

"That's Northumberland, across the river." Jane spoke slowly, and seemed to be looking to the far distance. "There's God's plenty of Non-jurors there."

"Oh ? That puts me in mind of Mr. Peaver. Where does he live ?"

"Yonder."

Jane was pointing down the slope; and there, tucked into sheltering trees, was a house, small and neat. It seemed to stand almost on the edge of the slope, and yet in a tiny dip that

gave it privacy. It would command every view there was; and
yet, with the dip and its grove of trees, it was so screened and
hidden that Mally had not even seen it before Jane pointed.
She said so, and Jane nodded.

"It suits Peaver," she said calmly. "Folk look past him,
and that's perhaps as well—with a Non-juror."

Jane put her horse to a steady walk down the slope and
Mally followed.

"How does he come to live here?" she asked suddenly.

"Peaver? John felt sorry for him, I suppose, and let him
have this place. It was empty."

"Is it John's house, then?"

"Yes. It's on the estate. Our land ends down there."

They came to the house and found Mr. Peaver on the stone-
paved path to the garden gate. He was without his gown now,
but he was still in his clerical black, with the white bands
fluttering at his neck; and it was plain that, parish or no parish,
he was abating nothing of his cloth. But he seemed glad to see
them, and he had a smile that was almost benevolent. He held
their stirrups for them while a lad came quickly from the back
of the house to lead the horses round.

Mr. Peaver did not live in discomfort, as was soon apparent.
His house had a parlour of good size, a low square room with
a plastered ceiling, a panelled wall, and a good stone hearth.
It was furnished perhaps more as a study than as a parlour;
there were bookshelves on two walls, a fine large writing-table
in the window, and another by a side-wall that was a litter of
books and pamphlets; there was a big brass inkstand, a brass
sand-shaker, a jar of pens, and a trimming knife set ready. But
there was comfort too. There was a bright fire of coal in the
hearth, with a soft rug spread before it. There were two good
elbow-chairs, and a low stool set handily between. Poker and
tongs were of brass, and on the mantelshelf there were candle-
sticks, a blue-and-white tobacco jar, and a clutter of long white
pipes; and above the hearth, oddly, a large clear map of Tyneside hung from the wall.

There was a housekeeper too, a woman of something past
middle age, who had some fond looks for him, as if she were
devoted to his service. She brought in the silver teapot, the
blue-and-white cups, the cakes and biscuits, and it was Mr.

Peaver himself who insisted on pouring for his guests. He had them in the elbow-chairs, and for himself he brought his writing-chair from the table. He stretched out his long legs till they touched the low stool where the teapot was, and then he turned benevolent eyes on Mally.

"Ah, Miss—*may* I say Miss Mally?"

"But of course."

"It might otherwise be perplexing, with *two* Miss Lawleys here. But indeed, you are most welcome among us, if you can bear with our simple ways. It was a surprise when we learned of your coming. We had not expected so much."

"Nor had I, sir—to deal quite truly. I must hope I can deserve such welcome."

"We may be sure of it, quite sure of it. But you were with Mr. Lawley's sister, were you not? I'm told that her Ladyship is of excellent disposition."

"No doubt, sir."

It was not quite Mally's opinion of her aunt, but that could be passed over. Then it occurred to her that Mr. Peaver might be talking politics here.

"Sir John," she said quietly, "is also of excellent disposition."

"Sir John Chandler?" Mr. Peaver pursed his lips and looked almost ruffled. "But I'd supposed he was a Whig?"

"He is," she answered smoothly, and made due note that her guess had been correct. "But he showed me some kindnesses, and it was those that I remembered."

"To be sure, to be sure." He still seemed a little put out. "It's very proper that you should remember. I have not met Sir John, and perhaps we ought not to judge him by his brother."

"Brother? Do you know Esquire Chandler, sir?"

"I do not. I only know *of* him. A pestilential fellow, and a spy of the government, too. You may put him quite from your mind."

"Then so I will," said Mally, and knew very well that she would not. "Is he perhaps another Whig?"

"He's a Whig, and a traitor, and a damned scoundrel too."

"Oh!"

She had not expected so hot an answer from this elderly divine; and he seemed himself to sense that it was startling. He made haste to get away from it.

"Put him from your mind, Miss Mally. Perhaps—perhaps I should not have said that of him. But put him from your mind. Now what was it that you came here to ask me. There was some question, was there not?"

He was all benevolence now, and Mally stared blankly at him, unable to remember what she had come here to ask. Jane came quickly to her rescue.

"Coal," she said promptly. "Mally wants to know why there's no profit from our coal pit here."

"Coal it is." Mr. Peaver sounded pleased to be reminded. "Strange, is it not, how talk of Chandler leads us to talk of coal? But it always does. Each word seems to mean the other. Now let me see——"

He had walked to the window and was peering out at the cool clear afternoon, the pale sky and the flecks of gold in the thin cloud. He nodded as if he were satisfied.

"The light holds well. Shall we walk across? It's but a few minutes, Miss Mally."

"Gladly, sir, if we may trouble you."

There was no other answer possible. She would have preferred to stay with the fire and the tea. But if this eccentric divine was convinced that she wished to know about coal pits, and was valiantly going from his fireside to show her one, then the least she could do was to look pleased about it. She came resignedly to her feet, and she contrived a quick grimace at Jane while Mr. Peaver was hunting for his gown; and Jane calmly winked at her.

They walked together along the rim of the slope, treading on the tufted grass, till they came to a gentle rise. They passed over it, and there at their feet, not a quarter-mile from Mr. Peaver's house, was the pit.

It was just that. It was a great hole dug in the ground, and it was nothing more. It was some forty yards or more in width; and Mally guessed its depth at sixty feet. Gently sloping tracks went curving down the side of it; and at the bottom there was water, black and stagnant, streaked and shining with iridescent dust. It was desolate and lonely, utterly deserted of man, and only the crunching dust of coal, thick over all the ground, gave hint of what it was.

Jane stood on the rim and planted her feet firmly.

"This," she said calmly, "is our uncle's coal pit—or was. Perhaps, sir, you would explain it to Mally. She's burning to know."

"Ah, yes—yes. Well now——"

He swung round, slender and eager, with the air of one about to give a lecture, and Mally turned her back resolutely on Jane. There was an edge in the wind up here, and Mr. Peaver was clutching his gown as he began to speak.

"You will understand," he said, "that one cannot open a coal pit anywhere. There is not coal everywhere. Or at least, it is not at the surface everywhere. There are thin sheets of coal, and they do not follow the ground. They dip, and they rise again. I do not understand this fully."

That was perhaps fortunate. It checked his flow, and it left him staring thoughtfully at the dark black water in the pit. That seemed to provide him with a fresh topic.

"There is also water, and not only rainwater. There are underground springs. They flow, it seems, in places where there is some inequality in rock. Persons skilled in Natural Philosophy say——"

A gust of wind came noisily, blustering up the slope, making nothing of what those persons said. He grasped tightly at his fluttering gown, and when he could be heard again he was better worth hearing.

"We may therefore dig a coal pit only where the coal-streak is at the surface, and where no spring flows. Such places are not many. This is one of them. There is another up yonder, a half-mile distant."

He was pointing up the slope again, to the higher ground they had come from, and Mally thought she should make some comment.

"And is that one like this?"

"No, no." He was quite brusque about it. "It is not even opened, not dug at all. It would not pay to do so."

"But why not? I——"

"Come down the track a little."

Mr. Peaver did not wait for assent. He led down the curving track that descended the side of the pit, and Mally had to follow. She looked round with distaste, and saw the twitch of of amusement in Jane; and, at once, she hooked her arm in Jane's. There was then no choice but for Jane to come also.

They followed Mr. Peaver down the grimy slope, with the wet dust crunching beneath their feet. Below the rim the wind was lost, and the air was dank and chill. There was a silence, too. Every sound of wind and birds was lost, and there was nothing but their own crunching feet and the soft splash of water as tiny rills from the rock went dripping to the stagnant pool. It was a place lost to the world; and perhaps no human foot would ever come here again.

At the bottom, by the edge of the water, they halted, and Mr. Peaver looked up to the pale circle of sky that filled the mouth of it.

"Above us," he said, "there once was coal, but that has been dug away. We can go no deeper, for beneath us there is rock. See——"

He went clambering a few feet up the slope, and then he stopped to point.

"It was a thin streak of coal, slanting to the surface, and where it met the surface there could be no rock above it. So we could dig. Here it is slanting down into the earth, and perhaps there is miles of it. But now it has rock above."

The light was dim in the depths of the pit, and Mally had to peer with care before she made it out. The pit had been dug through earth and soil, but here at the bottom it touched the rock. Its wall here was of rock; but for a space perhaps a yard in height, and stretching horizontally across the pit, the rock was interrupted. This streak was of coal, black and solid, with rock below and thinner rock above; and the face of it had been scooped out, to leave what was almost an indented gallery, dug into the coal, and running half round the pit.

"There it is," said Mr. Peaver calmly. "A streak of coal, slanting deep into the earth, and only God may know how deep. But do you see the workings?"

Again he was pointing, and Mally saw that tunnels had been dug into the coal shafts a yard across, following the slope of the coal into the earth. She looked at their black forbidding mouths and shuddered.

"Did men work down *there*?" she asked.

"But of course." He seemed to take it for granted. "That's how coal is won. We cannot take *all* the coal, lest the rock above should fall, so it has to be small shafts only. And these, unhappily, are at an end."

"But why?"

"Water. There must be a spring that runs, and a short way down there's water. They go some thirty feet, and that's an end."

He seemed to be at an end also. He lapsed into silence as if there were no more to say, and Mally looked round her at the dank dark wetness of it all; and her thoughts were of the men who must once have worked in here, and of the life and bustle that must once have been.

"It's dead," she said slowly. "Forgotten. There'll be none to come here again."

"Why should there be?" He looked carefully around him. "What man should ever wish——"

He broke off, as if some thought had come to him, and then his gaze seemed to be intent on the streak of coal and the forgotten shafts that opened in it. A silence came, and seemed to pin them down. It lengthened, and Jane's foot scraped impatiently.

"I think we should go," she said abruptly. "It's damp down here, sir, and cold. It will do you no good. There'll be a rheum on you if you stay."

"Aye, aye." He seemed to rouse himself into attention. "Perhaps we'd best——"

Above them, at the rim of the pit, there was sound of a foot, and a little clod of earth came falling. They looked hastily up and saw a tousled head against the sky as a man peered down with interest.

"Hey, hey!" Mr. Peaver was suddenly calling up to him. "It's Geordie Wade. How are ye, Geordie lad?"

CHAPTER VIII

THE FIFTH OF NOVEMBER

Mr. Peaver went scrambling up the steep track to the top, his interest in the fellow having seemingly caused him to forget the ladies. They followed at leisure, and when they came to the sky and the wind they found him already deep in talk; and Mally, something out of breath, conscious of filthy boots and a coal-daubed skirt, was glad enough to stand back and let him. But, as usual, she was taking note of things. This Geordie Wade was plainly some sort of labourer. He had a rough leather jerkin, some serge breeches faded beyond any colour that could have a name, and heavy boots that seemed to be tipped with bars of wood. He had a battered hat clutched firmly in grimy fingers, and he was showing a mop of tousled hair above a cheerful freckled face. He was an odd fellow to be in talk with this meticulously dressed divine.

But Mr. Peaver seemed unaware of that. With his gown still tight about him, and his bands still fluttering in the wind, he was beaming with goodwill, and as soon as he saw Jane he turned animatedly to her.

"I've been asking Geordie where he's been these late weeks," he said. "I haven't seen him since—how long is it?"

"Months, I should say." Jane, also, seemed pleased to see the fellow, and she had a friendly smile for him. "Where have you been, Geordie?"

"I've been to London. Twice, we've been."

"We?"

"Aye. Master Nixon, and me, and the beasts."

"Are you set up as a carrier, Geordie?"

"Aye. Master Nixon it was. But it's done now, and I'm turned off."

"Oh, Geordie!"

"Ye-es." Mr. Peaver nodded his assent. "Geordie was just telling me of it. He says that when Nixon was turned off from here he tried to set up as a London carrier, and he kept Geordie for the beasts."

"Yes?"

"Well——" Mr. Peaver pursed his lips and looked regretful. "There are carriers enough at that work, and they have all the trade in their hands. There was none of it for Nixon, or not enough."

"So it failed?"

"I fear so, and Geordie's out of work again."

"I am that." Geordie was suddenly answering for himself, and the burr in his voice made it hard for Mally to understand him. "It's why I came up here—to see if there might be a hand working again."

"I'm afraid there isn't, Geordie, and there won't be." Jane answered him gravely, and she seemed to think she must go further. "There's not much for you at the house, but if you wish to give some hand in the stable again——"

"I'd be right glad to."

"Come in a day or two, then. I'll speak to Mr. Lawley of it, and——"

"Geordie——"

Mr. Peaver had intervened suddenly, and he seemed to have forgotten Jane. He spoke slowly, as if he were thinking it out.

"Geordie, you could find Mr. Nixon, couldn't you?"

"Oh aye. He's at——"

"Then you tell him to come to me. Just that."

"Aye, if you say it. But——"

"Just that, Geordie. Just that. Tell him to come to me." He was emphatic on it, and then he turned quickly to Jane. "After all, we must do something for Nixon, if we can. He deserves well, you know—a most worthy man."

"I expect he is. But what can you——"

"Now just that, Geordie. Remember to tell him. Goodbye, goodbye, God bless you."

He came out in a whirl of words, and suddenly he was shivering in the wind. Jane linked her arm through his and marched him firmly towards his house; and when they arrived she took the initiative just as firmly in calling to the housekeeper for more hot tea. Mally, feeling cold enough herself, was more than glad to see it; she was not used to the wind that blustered on this moor.

She learnt a little more about affairs when the tea came in. She found herself left to pour it; and Jane, kneeling before the hearth as she mended the fire, thankfully took her cup and then turned to Mally.

"Geordie used to be our stable boy. Then he took work with Nixon. Joe Nixon was carrier for the pit."

"What does that mean?"

"It means that coal is no use till you've carried it somewhere. You must carry it to where you can sell it. We haven't a wagonway, so it had to be a carrier. That was Nixon. He'd a score or so of packhorses for the work. Galloways, we call them." Jane, cup in hand, was watching the fire critically. "It's slow, and it's expensive, and it's half the reason why the pit didn't pay, but it was the best we had. We couldn't afford a wagonway, or a wayleave either."

"I'm not quite sure," said Mr. Peaver suddenly, "that Miss Mally knows what those are."

"I think I know a wagonway. I saw one when I came. On the staith."

"Yes." Jane nodded. "That would be a wagonway."

"But do you mean that those rails have to go all the way from here to the river?"

"It's no good going anywhere else. If you'd sell coal you must take it to the water. As for a wayleave, it's just leave to carry coal over someone's land."

"But how——"

"It's quite simple. If you carry coal by horses they can go by the road. But a wagonway can't. It must always go downhill, and that nearly always means over someone else's land. You need leave for that, and the owner makes you pay for it. That's a wayleave, and we can't afford one, or a wagonway either. And that's an end."

She spoke with resignation, as if she could see no hope against this pressure that was always on a house that could not pay its way; and Mr. Peaver nodded.

"It's been an end to the pit, indeed. And now Nixon is out of work, and Geordie too. Can you find Geordie something?"

"He may help in our stable if he will, but there won't be much money."

"No. It's another pit that's needed, and that needs a wagon-way. We must hope that affairs will mend."

"There's no harm in hoping it." Jane seemed to put it aside, and then she glanced carefully through the window. "I think, sir, we should go. We've had the best of the light, and it's a rough road home."

There was no dispute about it, and in the waning afternoon Mr. Peaver went courteously down the garden with them as the horses were brought to the gate. He helped them to mount, and then he had a word for Jane.

"I see you on Friday?"

"Of course, sir. It will be all prepared."

"Thank you. Tell Mr. Lawley, pray, that there will be one guest more, if he will give leave. A Mr. Patten, the Reverend Robert Patten. Tell him of it, if you will."

"I'll remember it."

They rode away in a fading light, and it seemed that Jane had something to brood upon. She rode a mile in silence, and when she spoke her voice was sharp.

"That's what Henry wants."

"Henry?" Mally was completely at a loss. "Please——"

"Julia's Henry. I told you he'd been here. He wants that coal."

"But—but I thought it was finished?"

"There's another pit up there—or could be. Peaver told you."

"Yes, but——"

"It isn't dug yet, and it will take a deal of money to dig it. It's too far from the river for horses, so it'll need a wagonway, and a wayleave too. We can't afford any of those things. Henry can. So he wants a lease."

"What's that?"

"Leave to work the coal. John can grant that, you know. He can't sell, and he can't mortgage, but a lease doesn't change ownership, so he can do it."

"Then why not?"

"Because Henry's too mean to pay for it—properly." Jane almost snorted. "He wants a twenty-year lease, and he knows

John won't live that out. I've told you the land must go to
Henry's son, which means Henry, really. It would fall right
into his hand before that lease was done, and he won't pay
decently even for that. There's no give-it-away in our fat
Henry."

The sky was dim and grey when they turned through the
faded gates and rode through the trees to a house that was
blending with the dusk. Jane led round to the stable yard; and
it was not till they were returning on foot that she had more to
say. Even then she seemed to speak half to herself.

"Who the Devil is Patten?" she mused.

"Who?"

"Patten. The other guest our Peaver spoke of, for Friday.
Reverend, wasn't he?"

"The Reverend Robert, he said. What *is* this of guests
for Friday?"

"Dinner. For a dozen odd. There's some work in it for
you and me."

"But is it an occasion?"

"It's the fifth of November."

"I suppose it is. But dinner on the fifth? Is there to be a
bonfire?"

"Not unless you make it yourself. It's not that sort of
occasion. It's the other sort."

"What sort?"

"Remember your prayer book. What does it say for the
fifth of November?"

"Oh! Service of Thanksgiving?"

"To be read in every parish church. Do you think they'll
attend?"

"Why not?"

"Where are your wits, Mally?" Jane halted in the shadow
of the pillared porch. "What's the thanksgiving for?"

"Deliverance from the Gunpowder treason."

"What else?"

"Oh!" A gleam of understanding was coming to Mally.
"The coming of King William?"

"To Torbay. On November the fifth, 1688. He came to
chase away King James, who was father to this Pretender we
hear of. Do you think men like Peaver will attend the parish

church for *that*?" Jane paused, with her hand on the door, and the sardonic tone was with her again. "They'll have their own Service—here. Peaver will conduct it. And it won't be thanks for King William."

CHAPTER IX

DINNER FOR TWELVE

JOHN LAWLEY was not unfriendly, as Mally soon learned. He did not, indeed, show much interest himself, but as a companion for Jane he plainly welcomed her; and that was for the moment enough. Mally's interest was with Jane, and Jane was glad to have her. She had been starved of company for too long, and now she made no secret that she was glad of someone to talk to.

She began by discussing the arrangements for this dinner next Friday. As house-keeper, she was responsible for it, and she would have to do more than merely arrange it. This was not a house with a vast staff of servants. A waiting-maid, a cook, and a lad to fetch and carry made all the indoor staff; and, said Jane, the waiting-maid was new and raw, and the cook was a fool. So it was clear that Jane would have to take charge herself, and that Mally would have to help; and the first thing to do was to decide on the details.

It was at this point that something emerged. Jane began by considering the guests. There would be Mr. Peaver and this Mr. Patten, whoever he might be. There would be a half-dozen gentlemen of the neighbourhood, all certainly Highflyers and possibly Non-jurors; and there would be Mr. William Harvey and his son. Mr. Harvey, said Jane, lived across the river in Northumberland, and he was uncle John's brother-in-law. John Lawley had married Will Harvey's sister, and now, as widowers, they remained firm friends. Will Harvey was therefore an important guest, and there would certainly have to be a hog's-liver pudding, which he loved. Jane was practical about it.

It was when she spoke of his son that she was perhaps less practical. Jack Harvey, it seemed, was twenty-six, and ought to have been married three years ago; but his bride-to-be had died of the smallpox, and he had not shown any disposition to marry anybody else. Jane said this in a carefully flat tone, and

88

Mally came to attention. The tone, she thought, had been a shade too flat. So she asked whether this Jack, like his father, had some favourite dish, and she was answered that he liked a roast of pork, served with a sauce of lemons, butter, strong ale, and the brains of the pig; and Mally remembered that she had already heard Jane asking if there were lemons in the house. She nodded with no show of interest; but she was alert now, and not disposed to miss anything. She had an interest in Jane.

But that had to wait, for she had more to do just now. This dinner was to be an occasion. The guests would expect a festive meal, and Jane was taking no chances. The cook, she repeated, was a fool, and whatever had to be done well would therefore have to be done by herself and Mally. She added, as an after-thought, that John no doubt supposed that a dinner for twelve would fall from Heaven like manna; which it would not.

November, as she further pointed out, was not a good season for dinners. Except for the milking cows and pigs, the farm stock had been killed a month before, and it would there-fore have to be salted beef. There could be pigeons, of course, and a duck, and the stew-pond would yield some fish. There could be a pig, for the liver pudding and the roast of pork; but beyond that, if John wanted anything fresh he would have to go out and shoot it.

She told him so; and then, in the great stone-floored kitchen, she and Mally fell to work; and it was well for Mally that she had not spent all her days with Lady Chandler. She would not have learned such work there, and Jane was taking it for granted that she knew what to do. She had to draw now on the earlier years, when life had been simple and her own mother alive; and fortunately her memories were keen.

This was Thursday, and they began with the pig. It was killed by the lad in the stable-yard, and then Mally found her-self entrusted with the liver pudding for Mr. Harvey senior. The roast and the special sauce for Mr. Harvey junior were apparently Jane's concern, and Mally made no comment on that. She had enough to do without making comments. The pig's liver had to be cut into cubes and lightly boiled, and then beaten to a pulp in a mortar; then the eggs and bread-crumbs and suet had to be mixed to it, with the proper season-ing of blood whipped with birch twigs; then the flavourings had to be stirred in, currants and spices and salt and sugar, before the whole mixture could be gently boiled and Mally could find her breath again. Tomorrow it would be wrapped in its suet crust and boiled again, but this was enough for one day.

Round her in the kitchen the others were as busy. There were the pigeons and the duck to be plucked and drawn, and leaves of sorrell set to soak in the bottled gooseberries to make the sauce for the duck. There were the jellies and tarts and a great apple pie to make; there was a syllabub to make of beaten cream, with almonds and rosewater and sweet white wine; there was a confection of marchpane, to be painted with white-of-egg and decorated with nuts and cherries before the cream could be added tomorrow; and when Jane had chopped the pig's head open to get the brains for the special sauce she had to leave them gently simmering while she prepared a big pudding of suet and flour and oatmeal, which had to boil in milk before the dates and currants went in. There was work and to spare for them all, and it was not made easier by the huge hot fire and the wisps of steam that filled the kitchen. And in the middle of it John Lawley came walking in from the outer door, leaving a trail of mud from his boots on the scrubbed stone floor. He had a gun under one arm and a brace of hares in his other hand, and he dumped them on the table with the air of a man who has done his duty. He went strolling out by the inner door, leaving another trail of mud behind him; and Jane looked from the mud to the hares, now oozing blood on the white scrubbed table, and said in her softest tone that she supposed somebody would now have to jug the brutes.

The morrow found Mally alert and watchful, but she was by no means free to move as she pleased. Jane was in the same mood of mistrusting the cook, and that meant that she and Mally were in the kitchen themselves, getting the roasts of pork and beef ready on the spits, stuffing the duck and pigeons and putting them on lesser spits, setting the liver pudding and the date-and-currant pudding to boil in the thick iron pots on chains above the fire. There was work for all of them, and it began at eight o'clock. Dinner was to be at the old-fashioned hour of twelve that Sir John Chandler still approved of, and the guests were expected at nine o'clock. Whatever rites they intended would fill the forenoon, and then they would dine at ease and leisure. It was Jane who explained all that, and then she drove the work at a speed that Mally thought unreasonable—until she remembered that Jane, too, might wish to welcome the arriving guests, or some of them.

So it proved. Jane so drove it on that by nine o'clock the dinner could be left for an hour to the others; and Jane and Mally, a little disturbed by thoughts of what their hair might smell of, had tidied themselves to some sort of looks and were hovering watchfully. Mr. Peaver was the first to come, now in a cassock, and with a bag in his hand that looked much as if it might contain a surplice; and with him was his fellow divine, the Reverend Mr. Patten. Then, at a quarter past nine, Mr. Will Harvey and his son came riding to the door, and John Lawley was out to greet them. Mally had an interested glance for Will Harvey, noting quickly the round and boisterous face, the genial air, the thickness of lips and nose to hint at perceptions not too acute, and the thought came quickly that here was a man in whom the heart might lead the head; she could imagine him as a Highflyer, confident and hearty, drinking his Tory toasts in strong October ale, and not seeing very clearly what their true import might be.

But it was for his son, standing quietly behind him, that she had the greater interest. Jack Harvey was not a copy of his father. He was taller, more spare of build, and something of this was in his face as well, as if he had a perception that his father lacked. It was a good face, firm and clear, but it was a face that seemed to stay in repose, as if he would show no eagerness, nor betray what thoughts he had. For a long moment he stood so, waiting while his elders moved slowly into the house; and then his eye lit on Jane, very still and silent by the porch. At once his face was transformed. He was interested and friendly, and there was a light in his eye, and the next moment he had gone quickly to Jane. Whatever he said was quietly spoken, and Mally heard nothing of it; but at once Jane brought him across to her, and he was formally presented.

There was no time for more than a formal word. He and his father had to go to join the others in the parlour, and Mally took the chance of a look in also. It surprised her. They all had solemn faces and grave looks; and the dinner had so filled the hours for her and Jane that it was hard for her to remember that it was not what these people had come for. They were here because they would not attend the parish church this day, and would have instead their own service here; and she must suppose that their dinner was an afterthought to that.

It could not be an afterthought to herself and Jane. The roasts of pork and beef were sizzling before the fire as the spits turned slowly, driven by a cord-and-pulley to a tread-wheel high on the kitchen wall, where a caged dog was trotting steadily. Above the fire the steam was curling from the black iron pots as the two big puddings boiled; and at the side, in the lesser heat, the hares seemed to be jugging themselves. The lad was carefully putting more coal on the fire, and the mistrusted cook, red-faced and sweating, was as carefully basting the roasts with the fat that dripped beneath the spits. Jane took it in with one sharp glance, and then gave orders. There must be more water for the puddings, and water for the dog to drink; the duck must be set to roast; the sauces must be thought of soon, and it was time somebody began the fish. She had them all busy, and another half-hour passed before she took a critical glance round the kitchen and declared that they might now take it in turns to slip away; and Mally might go first.

Mally went willingly, and after the sweating kitchen the house seemed cold and wintry. But a voice could be heard, quiet and steady, and it drew her to the hall where the parlour door had sprung ajar, as it was wont to do; and with curiosity rising in her, she went on tip-toe, and looked and listened.

They were all on their feet in that well-warmed parlour, and Mr. Peaver, with his back to the fire, was the warmest of them all. He was in canonicals now, in surplice and scarf, and with a prayer book in his hand he was reading steadily: "O most mighty God, terrible in Thy judgements, who in Thy heavy displeasure didst suffer our gracious Sovereign King James II to be taken from us by the hands of cruel and bloody men: We Thy sinful creatures here assembled do, in the behalf of all the people of this land, humbly confess that they were the crying sins of this nation which brought this heavy judgement upon us. O gracious God, lay it not to the charge of the people of this land, nor let it ever be required of us or our posterity . . ."

The kitchen door creaked softly as Jane came quietly out. It was Mally's turn now to watch the spits, and she had heard enough. There could be no more doubt of Mr. Peaver's sentiments, and what he had just read was certainly not in the Service for Gunpowder Day. It was of his own, and it spoke the sentiments of a Non-juror.

The knocker on the outer door clattered suddenly, and Mally, busy with the sorrell leaves and the gooseberries for the sauce the duck would swim in, turned in sharp surprise and ceased to think about Non-jurors. She pulled the kitchen door a little open as the big iron knocker went clattering again, and then it was pushed further open as Jane flung her apron in; and Mally remembered that there was no one but Jane to go to the outer door.

She held the kitchen door ajar, and stood listening. She heard the slide of the bolt, and then voices, first Jane's and then a man's. There was a tread of booted feet, and they seemed to go towards a dim cold second parlour that was seldom put to use. There was a jingle of spurs, as if this were a traveller; and from the greater parlour the voices rose again as Mr. Peaver began the Litany.

Steps came sharply, and the kitchen door quivered as Jane flung it wide open; and Jane was all but quivering too. She stood for a moment, and then she spoke abruptly.

"It's for you," she said. "He asks for you."

"But who is it?"

"Black William."

"*Who?*"

"Black William, I said. Listen!"

The antiphon of the Litany was swelling through the house, clear and fervent from the parlour, and Mally had to wrench at her thoughts.

"You mean Esquire——"

"I mean William Chandler of Gateshead, father of your Dick of the other day. He's a damned Whig, and a spy of the Government. And he comes here now, asking for you."

"But why——"

"Mally!" Jane spoke slowly, and as if to a child. "He's come here now, and he's asking for *you*. I can't tell you why."

"I'm sorry. I——"

"Have you chopped that sorrell yet?"

Jane moved helplessly to the table, as if the work must go on above all. She turned by the table and spoke softly.

"I go to the door, smelling of pork, and my face shines like a beetroot. I gape at him when he says who he is. I take him to a second parlour that hasn't a fire and smells as if it never had one. I have to say he can't see John. So I said he wasn't well. And at that exact moment we hear 'em at the Litany— which shows that I'm a liar. He wants *you*."

There seemed no answer, and Mally moved slowly to the door. She had her hand on it when Jane spoke a final word.

"You'd perhaps look better if you took that apron off."

CHAPTER X

BLACK WILLIAM

HE was undoubtedly Mr. Chandler.

One glance at him was enough, and that helped to clear Mally's wits. Here was Sir John Chandler's brother, and she was in no doubt of that. It was the same face, the same big nose, the bushy eyebrows, the direct and level gaze. He was standing by the cold hearth, standing with his hands behind his back and his feet firmly planted, as if he were sure of himself in anybody's house. He had even the build of Sir John, thick and burly, the sober way of dress, the air of being always a merchant. He was in coat and breeches of brown, a waitscoat of deeper brown, and a slim and plain cravat. Below the knee he was in riding boots, spurred and muddy, and they seemed to add to the vigour of him while taking nothing from his air of being a merchant; they merely signified that the merchant had affairs today.

But it was to his face that Mally looked again, once she had swiftly taken in the whole of him. It was Sir John's face indeed, but younger. This man would hardly be fifty yet, and there was a tan in his face to hint that the riding boots meant a healthier life than London. He had his own hair, trim and tidy as if he scorned a wig, and it had not yet greyed as Sir John's had done. There were no more than some flecks of grey in the black of it; and it was this, with his burly air of vigour, that put her in mind of his son. She looked again, noting the big shoulders, the neatness and the air of confidence, and she could almost see Dick Chandler here. She could see Sir John as well, but it was of Dick that she was thinking now. With the passing years he could become exactly this, and the thought came that he would not need to regret it if he did. There was nothing of elegance here; but there was something that impressed, and took the eye.

He stood for a moment, still and impassive, and considered her gravely. He made no attempt to bow, and she guessed that he saw little use in what was purely formal. Then his face eased, and a slight smile came; and he was more than ever like Sir John.

"So you'll be my brother's niece, hey? Miss Lawley?"

"Yes, sir." She gave him the answer quietly. "I'm Mary Lawley."

"Miss Mary, is it?" His eyebrows went up in a style that had certainly been Sir John's. "It was Miss Mally when my brother wrote."

"If I know Sir John, sir, I doubt if it was 'Miss' at all."

"It wasn't. Would you wish it?"

"No."

She gave it him in his own blunt tone, and suddenly he was nodding approval, and as suddenly Mally was at ease. She could talk with this man. He had Sir John's bluff ways, and she was growing used to them now; she had seen them in Dick as well.

"I must give you some thanks," she told him quickly. "You gave me much help in my journey here."

"It was Jack who did that."

"Who?" For the moment she was puzzled, and then she knew that Jack must be Sir John Chandler. "No doubt, sir, with the ship. But in the river I was met, and——"

"Aye, aye. Jack bade me give an eye to you. That lad of mine saw to you well, I hope?"

"He was most kind."

"I told him he'd better be. How is it now, in this house?"

That was coming to it quickly, and she was glad she had a truthful answer.

"They are most kind also."

"So they should be." He was looking at her very straightly now. "Jack wrote to me to give an eye to you, and I wrote back that I would. That was a promise, and I'm telling you of it."

"Yes, sir?"

"Yes." He paused, and then seemed to think he must explain himself. "It means that if you want any help you can tell me of it. That means *tell* me—not wait till I chance to come. Is it plain?"

"Why, yes, sir. It's very——"

"Good!" He cut her short quickly. "But all's well just now? No help needed?"

"None, sir—I do assure you."

"How are you for money?"

It came so quickly that for a moment she was at a nonplus. Then she gave the proper answer.

"I—I think sufficiently, sir."

"You don't sound so sure. You'll be right in that, no doubt."

"How?"

"No lass has enough when she goes to buy ribbons. Or I've never known her have. Here's to help along."

There was a clink, and a gleam of yellow gold in the chill grey room as he poured a dozen guineas on the bleak bare table; and Mally stared with widening eyes, wondering what she could say.

"Sir!" She did her best at it, knowing that she must. "It's most kind of you. But I'm sure I should not accept so——"

"Every lass says she shouldn't. She always does."

He sounded quite sure about it, and the sudden smile that came upon him seemed to put an ease on everything. It convinced Mally that she need dispute about this no longer; and some thoughts about the costs of clothes were already in her mind. She tried to speak another word of thanks, and he promptly cut her short.

"No," he told her calmly, and then he looked her in the eye again. "I came here at Jack's wish, because he asked me to. But that's my own. I like the look of you."

"Sir! I——"

"Aye, aye." Once more he cut her short. "But that's the shape of it, and I think Jack was right. Perhaps Dick was, too."

"But in what, sir?"

"Now which of 'em?" The smile had changed, and now it was almost a grin. "As for Jack, he said he knew a dozen of your folk, and they hadn't the wits of a louse between 'em, excepting you."

"Oh!"

"As for Dick, perhaps I'd better not tell you. It might be bad for you. What do they say of me here?"

It was another sudden shift of topic, and it put her at a loss

D

again. He watched her with his amused smile, and then he put his question more lightly.

"What do they say of me here? Do they call me Black William?"

"I—I did hear that said."

"You probably said it too." His amusement stayed, as if he would not at all mind that. "What more do they say? That I'm some sort of scoundrel?"

"I——" She was thinking of what Jane had said of him. "They said you were a Whig, sir."

"That's to say a scoundrel—here." He nodded, quite unperturbed. "John Lawley is a Highflyer, isn't he?"

"I scarcely know, sir."

He made no answer, but he cocked his ear towards the door, and through it came the sound of Mr. Peaver's voice, high and loud and fervent. Black William listened, and then he looked Mally in the eye again.

"He goes to that trouble to show he's disloyal. Are *you* a Highflyer?"

"No, sir."

"I didn't think you could be. A Highflyer has to be a fool, and you don't look one."

"I'm glad."

"So am I. That lass who received me just now—is she his daughter?"

"My cousin Jane. His niece also."

She explained it simply, and he nodded.

"Is she a Highflyer?"

"I don't know. I'm new here."

"It was the way she looked at me. She thinks I'm a Whig, and a rogue, and perhaps the Devil too. She does not attend these—devotions?"

Again he cocked his ear, and it seemed that Mr. Peaver's voice was gaining strength. Mally spoke hastily in Jane's defence.

"She certainly does not attend, nor myself either. Our part is to make their dinner for them."

"It smells good."

He sniffed, and Mally was suddenly and acutely aware that neither she nor Jane had offered him any sort of hospitality.

She was thinking guiltily of it when he spoke more briskly.

"Since I may not see the master of this house, I think I should have a word with this cousin of yours. Will you call her?"

A note of command had come into his voice, crisp and sharp, and Mally knew it for what it was. She went quickly from the room, and in the kitchen she found Jane seasoning the brains of the pig with the lemons and the ale. It was the sauce for Jack Harvey, and Jane seemed intent on it.

"He asks for you," said Mally briefly. "William."

"In Heaven's name, why?"

"Because he can't see John."

"Of course he can't see John. He can hear Peaver, can't he?"

"I'm afraid so."

"What does he want with me?"

"I don't know. But he's some sort of guest here, and——"

"Don't I know it?" Jane wiped her fingers on her spattered apron. "I'm sorry. Mally. But he *would* come at this time! What do I look like?"

They went back together to the bleak and inhospitable parlour, and William was leaning placidly by the empty hearth. Jane saw it, and seemed to think that even to him an apology was needed.

"I'm ashamed that there should be no fire for you, sir. That's not our way, and it was not of intent."

"I'm sure it wasn't." He sounded as unperturbed as ever. "I should no doubt have remembered the date."

Mr. Peaver's voice could still be heard, almost passionate now, and for a moment William seemed to listen. Then he turned to Jane.

"Since I am in Mr. Lawley's house it would have been proper for me to speak a word to him. It's to be regretted that I can't."

"I'm sorry for it, sir." Jane spoke stiffly, and she was plainly embarrassed. "It's not by discourtesy that he can-not——"

"To be sure it isn't. It's not a discourtesy at all. It's just a foolishness. But tell him, if you please, that next time I pass this way I'll make myself known to him. I think he could expect that of me, since I've had talk with his nieces in his house."

"I doubt, sir, if there's need——"

"Perhaps you don't. But I do."

He said it as if he were not to be argued with. Then he stepped to the side-table to take up his gloves, and on it were the guineas, sleek and shining in the light. There was an audible gasp as Jane saw them, and William turned quickly. He spoke to Mally.

"You'll remember that if you need help you should tell me of it. Don't wait for someone else to tell me."

"Thank you."

Jane turned sharply, keen-eyed and perplexed, and William missed nothing. He spoke directly to her.

"I came to bring goodwill to my brother's niece. Assure Mr. Lawley of it, pray. I'll extend the goodwill to him—and to you also, if you'll permit me. Now I'll take my leave."

"Oh!" Jane seemed to be wrestling with something, as if she were between two minds. "You'll take a cup of ale, sir, before you go?"

"Thank you, no." He was courteous, but as firm as ever. "The next time I'm here, willingly. But now I should go."

He led out of the room without waiting for more, and they both went with him. Jane handed him his hat, and for a moment he stood in silence, with his head a little aside as he listened. Mr. Peaver seemed to be at his peroration, and here in the hall the words could be heard.

". . . it is truth, it is loyalty, it is the good man's path. Yet loyalty now commands that a man shall *do*. To pray for the King is but the half, for he needs our service too. Wherefore do I end as I began, for here, in our text, is courage, and guidance too. Be assured, my friends, the night is far spent, the day is at hand : let us therefore cast off the works of darkness, and let us put on the armour of light."

His voice ended, and there was a stir and a scrape of chairs in the room as unseen men came hastily to their feet. Black William turned, with his face impassive. He settled his hat comfortably on his head, and then he walked slowly through the door as if he had heard nothing. Jane spared one anguished glance for Mally, and then, side by side, they followed him.

No one could doubt what sort of sermon had been preached on such a text as that.

Outside the house there was a servant waiting, holding his own horse and his master's. William climbed slowly into his saddle. He settled himself and adjusted his gloves. Then, just as he seemed to be going, he turned and looked down at them. He leaned from his saddle to speak quietly.

"What we heard there——" The stab of his whip towards the house displayed his meaning. "What we heard there is foolishness. Perhaps you know it is. If it stays at talk there'll be no harm done. But if it goes beyond talk——"

He paused, and his eyes moved from the one of them to the other, and Mally felt a strange quiver within herself. There was a force in this William, and he was in earnest.

"In these days, with the tales that run, and the government awake, that talk could lead to a hempen tippet, and quickly." Again he paused, and Mally felt the quiver turn cold as she took his awful meaning. "I've heard nothing of John Lawley save that he's an honest man, and I've no wish to see him hanged. Keep him from it if you can. It's God's work and your own. Fare you well."

He waited for no more. He swept his hat in a courtesy they had not expected, and then there was a clop of hooves and a jingle of harness as he went trotting down the drive with his servant after him. He did not look back, and as he disappeared behind the trees Mally turned helplessly to Jane.

"Jane! He—he didn't mean *that*?"

"Didn't he?" Jane was standing taut and tense, and her eyes were still on the trees that hid him. "It happens to be true."

"What!"

"Oh, it is. It's true, Mally. I've known it these twelve months gone."

"Jane! You mean that John could——"

"Yes." Jane turned abruptly on her heel. "Damn Peaver."

She went walking slowly to the house, as if she could bear no more of it, and Mally trailed after her. Then, in the beginning of the porch, Jane turned fiercely.

"It won't come to anything. It was Black William trying to frighten women. That's all."

"Yes."

"Couldn't you say it better than that?"

"Oh Jane! I——"

"I'm sorry!" Jane seemed to shake herself, as if she would grasp realities. "Mally, what were those guineas on the table?"

"He gave them to me."

"Lucky you! I don't think, Mally, that Black William is quite what I've been told."

"You don't think I did wrong, to take those guineas?"

"Don't be a fool." Jane sounded herself again now. "Mally, we're so pinched and starved for the half of a guinea that I'd almost take them from the Devil. At least I'd take them in any decent way that offered. Count yourself lucky."

"I do. Oughtn't we to go in?"

"Why?"

"There's the sauce to make."

"Oh Hell!" Jane stared wildly at her. "It's guineas and Non-jurors, Black William and a talk of hanging, and we've to make sauce!"

"But we *have*."

"Lemons and brains! Oh, my God!"

CHAPTER XI

THE MESSAGE FROM COLONEL STORM

JANE and Mally had been invited to dine with the gentlemen, but they had decided against it, and that was what was really expected of them. Their duty, said Jane in her best sardonic tone, was to feed the men till they grunted, and then get out of the way while they drank themselves silly. As a fine afterthought she corrected that to sillier, and then she turned to hauling the hog's-liver pudding from its steaming pan.

It thus came about that Mally had yet another experience that had not been hers at Lady Chandler's, and it let her see and hear without being snared in talk. She did not, indeed, hear all the talk, for she was in and out of the room as they dined, but she heard enough to show that Black William was not a fool. He had known what manner of men these were.

It began as might be expected between neighbours who did not meet often, but soon, as the ale sank home, it began to change; and the ale was sinking fast. Soon the neighbourly inquiries turned to complaints and condolences. It was the same tale with all of them, the low price of corn and coal, the troubles with pits and wayleaves, the pressure of taxes and mortgages. Mally listened attentively, and noted that at least they found nothing to complain of in the dinner. The roasts of pork and beef, the jugged hares and the hog's-liver pudding, the duck and pigeons and carp, all went the same way home, each man mixing as he chose; and little by little the talk became franker. Their troubles were all due to someone else, and it had not been so in an older day. It was the government, putting taxes on this, duties on that; or if it was not the government, it was the Hostmen of Newcastle, with their monopoly of exporting coal; or if it was not the Hostmen it was Black William; and Mally's attention grew keen when she heard that name.

The apple pudding came, and the tarts and jellies, the syllabub, and the masterpiece in marchpane. They went the way of the roasts, and as quickly; and even more quickly went the talk. Black William would buy wayleaves, and then refuse the use of them so that a pit had to stop; then he would buy at a starving price and work it himself at a fine fat profit. If a pit were to be sold he would be there first, offering a price that no gentleman could give; and then he would undersell the neighbours, until their pits too were ripe for his plucking. Black William would do this and do that, all for his own profit and the ruin of honest men. His spies and agents swarmed, to bring him word of every chance of gain; and this vast knowledge he put to further use as a spy of the government, giving them word of every tale that ran. It was a government of Whigs, and William was a Whig; and William, as it almost seemed, was the very Devil too.

Thus it ran; and Mally was beginning to think she had the measure of it when another memory was roused, and sharply.

There were three bottles of claret for drinking the King's health, and she went to see if Jane needed help with these. To her surprise she met Jane coming from the kitchen with a wide bowl of water. It looked as if in summer it might be a rose bowl, and Mally spoke in surprise.

"What's that for?"

"To drink the King's health." Jane's voice was carefully without expression. "Over the water. Will you bring the claret?"

Mally stood staring, and for a moment the Coronation rout came before her sight again; the glittering company, the walnut table and the cut-glass bowl, and the Earl of Derwentwater, with his glass high above the water where the white rose floated. That too had been the King's health, drunk over the water.

It was John Lawley who gave the toast today, and again it was a rite. The glasses rose above the water as each man leaned with outstretched arm, then back again as they drank to the King who was over the Water—James Edward Stuart, who was a pensioner of France, and dwelt at St. Germains. It was solemnly done, but it ended the claret, and then it was time for the ale mugs to be filled again. Tobacco was brought and a box of pipes, and soon they all were at ease in friendly talk. They could be left to themselves now, and Jane led Mally

from the room. It was their own turn now, she said, to have
something to eat.

It was perhaps a half-hour later when they went to the room
again, each with a great jug of ale, and what they saw was
disturbing. It was not a scene now of chatter and idle talk.
The men were hushed and intent, too intent even to stir when
the door was opened, and the centre of their interest was the
stranger, Mr. Peaver's friend, the Reverend Mr. Patten. He
was on his feet, and he was addressing a hushed and seated
company. His voice came sonorously.

"In more ways than one, in even the smallest way, those
words are true that were in our text today. For the day is at
hand. Gentlemen—" He paused impressively. "I have it in
command to tell you that our father has not forgotten us. He
does not forget. He is sending his own officer and envoy.
Colonel Storm is coming, and indeed he will raise a storm."

There was a quick stir in the room. Men sat up in excitement; and in the doorway Mally stood very stiff and still as
another memory came. Lady Chandler's rout was before her
eyes again; the toast had been drunk above the water, and the
Earl was speaking of a Colonel Storm, who should have come
from France but had been delayed. It must surely be the same.

Mr. Patten coughed, and his gaze ran the length of the
silent table. All were intent, and nobody noticed Jane as she
quietly put her ale-jug on the floor. Mally did the same. If
Jane was bent on hearing this, so was she.

"I spoke of Colonel Storm as our father's envoy. He is an
envoy in that he comes from France and can speak our father's
words. But he is *Colonel* Storm, sent to command, and it is
for us to obey."

Mr. Patten was portentous about it. They hung upon his
words, and in his own time he began again.

"Colonel Storm has crossed from France. From London he
wrote to his Lordship, and some part of that letter I have leave
to read to you."

He brought out a folded paper. His listeners sat tense and
eager; and Mally and Jane stayed silent and forgotten as he
spoke again.

"The Colonel writes, you understand, as his Lordship's
man of business. A needful caution." Mr. Patten coughed with

sagacity. "He first declares that he is himself making the journey hither, and he promises to—er—'to present myself before your Lordship before the month shall be out, and sooner if God so grant'. That is plain enough. Now——"

Mr. Patten coughed importantly. He produced some horn-framed glasses and settled them on his nose. Then he came to it again.

"Colonel Storm thus continues: 'I trust I shall then offer such advice as may best ensure that your Lordship's kinsman shall soon recover his whole estate again, an event, I am assured, to give satisfaction to many of his tenants. Certain goods will, however, be needed for this transaction, and I look to your Lordship to have proper quantity of skins ready for the market.' Hmm! Hmm!"

Mr. Patten peered through his glasses and looked very wise indeed.

"The skins will no doubt have men in them. We look to you, gentlemen, to furnish each his quantity of—er—skins. However——" He turned to his paper again. "Colonel Storm goes on: 'Other merchandise I have gathered here, at my father's charges, and I must beg that your Lordship's friends will be at the trouble of removing it. At call are twelve kegs of tea, three of prunes, and three of long-cut tobacco. The short-cut I have not as yet been able to obtain. There is also a box of galls and two of cochineal; and these your friends may have if they will ask of your Lordship's aunt, at her house in Jermyn Street.'"

Mr. Patten swung round in alarm. In the doorway Mally had moved, startled into it by a leaping thought, and he had suspicious eyes as he saw her. She stood helplessly under his gaze, and it was Jane who carried it off. She spoke as if she were in no way frightened of any of them.

"We bring you more ale," she said calmly, "but we did not care to disturb you."

She picked up her ale-jug from the floor and marched to the table, with Mally at her heels. At once the tension broke, and there was a scraping of feet and chairs, and a sudden outburst of chatter, as men held their mugs to be filled. Mally worked steadily down one side of the table, filling each mug in turn, and with her hearing alert to every scrap of talk. It came

to her disjointedly, one voice after another, and she could not
wholly piece it together.

"Aye to be sure we must meet . . ." "End of this month
. . ." "I've heard of prunes being pistols . . ." "Fresh from
France, and Colonel Storm's a good name . . ." "No, *my*
house. We're off the roads, d'ye see, and yet near Dilston. . . ."
She swung round at that, for she remembered talk of Dilston,
and it was bluff Will Harvey speaking; and at once her
thoughts were of Jane, and of young Jack Harvey who was
embroiled in this. Then the voices took her ear again. "No, I
don't know galls, nor cochineal either . . ." "Ask Patten . . ."
"Who *is* he? . . ." "This day fortnight, if Storm's here by
then. It's young Jack's birthday, d'ye see, and that's excuse
to meet. . . ."

She came to the top of the table, and filled John Lawley's
mug; and as she poured, she was looking keenly at him, noting
his greying hair, his honest eyes, his face red with ale. Something stabbed through her as she looked, for he was her host,
and kind to her; and she heard Black William's voice again,
who had no wish to see John Lawley hanged. And, oddly, she
had liked Black William too.

The voices broke out again in thanks, and she saw that Jane
had finished pouring too, and that the men had been glad of
the ale. But she and Jane had been taken for granted. They
had been thanked for the ale, and would perhaps be thanked
as cooks; but that was all. There was no hint of awareness that
they might, perhaps, have understood what they had heard;
and again she was looking down the line of men, the honest
faces, the heavy lips, the eyes dulled now with food and ale. At
root, she thought, they were all alike, honest and decent, a
little muddled and a little fuddled; loyal to the older ways, and
not the breed from which conspirators should come.

But the ale had been poured, and there could be no pretence
of staying longer. They had to go, and to shut the door behind
them; and then Jane had Mally firmly by the arm and was
guiding her to the other parlour, where Black William had
been that day. It was neither warm nor comfortable, but it was
private; and Jane looked urgent.

"Are these people mad?" was her beginning. "Who *is*
this Patten? That letter's plain treason."

"It isn't exactly Patten's letter."

"He brought it here, didn't he? He was preening himself like a peacock when he read it, and he didn't seem to care who heard him. He never even noticed us."

"We're the women of the house."

"Not worth noticing. Who's this Colonel Storm?"

"I think I've heard of him."

She explained it quickly, and Jane's eyes widened.

"From France? With a pocketful of treason?" She sounded shaken to the roots of her. "He's to start a rebellion?"

"Jane!" Mally had not faced it as clearly as this. "It's surely not as bad——"

"Isn't it?" Jane was snapping angrily. "You heard that letter? Milord—that'll be Derwentwater—is to have skins ready, and skins mean men. What was that other gibberish? Tea and prunes and cochineal——"

"I heard one say that prunes are pistols."

"They would be! Tea, I suppose, being powder for the pistols. *Isn't* it rebellion?"

"I—I suppose it is."

"It certainly is. Do they think nobody has any wits? Tea and prunes and cochineal! Would anyone believe it?"

"I don't think William would."

"William!" Jane seemed to explode. "They have this crazy meeting, with their Peaver and their Patten and the rest, and they hatch a wild mad treason—and it's on this exact day that Black William must walk in! He talked about hangings. What *are* we to do?"

"You mean it's for *us* to do something?"

"It won't be for anybody else. You've seen what their wits are like. And our John happens to be mixed in this."

"Ye-es." Mally was answering thoughtfully. "Isn't there another mixed in this?"

"Now what——"

Jane stopped short, and a touch of colour had come to her cheek. It was one of her rare moments of confusion, and Mally understood it quickly.

"I'm sorry." She looked Jane in the eye. "But I did not mean Jack Harvey."

"I don't know what you mean. Who is this other?"

"It said in that letter that those prunes and things could be had of his Lordship's aunt in Jermyn Street. He hasn't got an aunt in Jermyn Street. I used to live there."

"With your aunt?"

"She's your aunt, too, isn't she?"

"Mally, do you mean——"

"I don't know. But she's just the sort of woman who'd be mixed in this. And if this Colonel Storm came from France, hers would be the house he'd go to."

"It's Sir John Chandler's house, isn't it? He's a Whig. He's Black William's brother."

"I know, but he lets his wife do all she pleases. I don't know why, but he does."

"Well, we can't see to that. We've enough to do here."

"You mean it's our work to protect——"

"John." Jane cut in firmly, as if no other should be mentioned; and she was looking grave and worried. "How do we do it? How *can* we?"

"If we warned him?"

"Do you think he'd take advice from women? And on politics? He'd order us from the room. I suppose we've time to think."

"We haven't. They were talking of another meeting. This day fortnight, they said."

"Where? Who said it?"

"It——" Mally glanced nervously at Jane. "It was Mr. Harvey. At his own house, he said."

There was an intake of breath that could be heard in the quiet room, and then Jane was standing very still. She spoke softly.

"I see. That will put *him* in the centre of it."

"And his son, too."

"Need you tell me?"

"I'm sorry."

"It's nothing. We, I suppose, won't even know what's done there, or what they talk about."

Across the hall a door opened. There were footsteps and a murmur of voices, as if to show that the meeting was breaking up. Jane turned, and went quickly to the door.

The men seemed pleased, and the scraps of talk, as they sat

in the hall pulling on their boots, made it plain that they would indeed meet again in two weeks' time. The Reverend Mr. Patten had three of them round him, and seemed to be conveying some last instruction. Mr. Peaver, ascetic and benevolent, was by the open door, ready with a word for each who went. John Lawley, between farewells, was trying to talk to his brother-in-law; and Jack Harvey, a little apart from them, was soon in talk with Jane. Mally went to join them.

"I think I'm discourteous," he told her quietly. "I spoke two words to you when I came, and I haven't noticed you since. Now apart from your being Jane's cousin, you are yourself so——"

"Keep your compliments for Jane, sir. She better deserves them, at all times."

"You pin me to the wall. How can I answer, that shall not seem offence to one of you?"

"Then perhaps you should not answer. Let us agree that you have been occupied this day."

"I have indeed. I've been dutifully sitting beside my father."

He stressed it a little, as if he would have them know that he had not been there from choice. Jane pounced quickly on it.

"You might be more wise if you were less dutiful."

"Should I?" He answered her gravely, and without evading her eyes. "Now what shall that mean?"

"You know what it means, Jack. We've ears, haven't we, and eyes?"

"You always had, Jane."

"Say I always had a tongue as well."

"But you've had no chance to use it today. That's what I deplore."

"Jack, I mean this. Will you——"

"Now what's to do here? What ails you, lass?"

It was Will Harvey, the father, who had intervened. He had been standing with his back to them, in talk with John Lawley, and it might have been Jane's rising tone that set him turning. He stood there now, bluff and genial, beaming upon them all, and somebody had to answer him. Mally took it on herself, and she tried to do it lightly.

"It's being said, sir, that Jane has had no chance to talk today."

"She was starting to make up for it, from what I heard." He turned heartily to Mally. "You're new here, aren't you, lass? Welcome to the North, then. We're glad of a new face, and the more when it's a pretty one. When shall we see more of you?"

"Why, sir, whenever——"

Mally stopped short as a thought came darting, and at Lady Chandler's she would have put it instantly aside. But here, in the North, boldness seemed to be tolerated, and suddenly Mally was risking it. She spoke sweetly to him.

"I heard a gentleman say, sir, that it's your son's birthday in two weeks' time, and that you are entertaining."

"Why, so I am! Well said, lass! Come ye, then—both of ye. You too, John. Come the day before, and stay the day after."

"Aye, but Will, it's affairs."

John Lawley's protest did not sound very vigorous, and Will swept it aside at once. He had perhaps dined too well for careful humours.

"And what of that? The affairs take half a day, and you'll come for the three." He was boisterous about it now. "It's a poor life that's all affairs, and it'll do Jack good to see a lass i' the house. He's a dull dog these days, hey?"

He dug his son gaily in the ribs, and then went rolling to the door, with his rich laugh booming across the hall. Jack took the moment for a quick word.

"I'm so glad." He was speaking first to Mally. "I wanted to ask it myself, but I feared that Jane——"

"You feared *me*?"

"Of course, dear Jane." The quick smile showed that he certainly did not. "I asked myself what you'd say if——"

"Jack!" His father's voice came ringing from out of the door. "Where the Devil are ye?"

"Aye, sir. Just coming. Jane, I'll count the hours. And Miss Mally, my——"

"Jack! Jack! Are ye dead? Ye've had time enough to kiss 'em both."

"Aye, sir. I'll have to fly. You heard him. He's right too —thus."

In an instant he had an arm round Jane, had drawn her close and had kissed her firmly before she could speak. She gasped, and at once he did it again. He released her, and then his laughing eyes were on Mally.

"I don't know you well enough yet, but——"

He went from the door at a run, and swung gaily into his saddle at the side of his impatient father. John Lawley was bare-headed between the horses, and Mally and a speechless Jane were in the doorway to see them go. At the curve of the drive, where they came to the trees, Jack turned with a gay flourish of his hat; and in silence, Jane waved back.

There was a crunch of feet as John Lawley came slowly back. They stood aside to give him passage through the door.

"Well said, lass!" He had checked in his walk and was speaking to Mally. "It's more than time we were at Will's again, all of us. You'll be at ease at Will's. Send me some ale to the parlour, Jane. It's a dry day."

"Aye, sir."

He was humming cheerfully as if no care lay on his mind. The parlour door shut noisily; and in the deserted hall Jane and Mally looked at each other. It was Jane who spoke first.

"Mally, you're as brazen now as a doorknocker. Thank you. I wondered when somebody would think to ask me there again."

"There'll be some other folk there, too—for half a day."

"Why did you say it?" For a moment Jane's face had hardened, and her lips were pressed tight. "This day two weeks, and weaving a rope to——"

"Jane!"

"As you will." Jane let it pass, but her angry eyes roamed over the grass and trees, and then came back to Mally. "Blast this Colonel Storm!"

CHAPTER XII

THE BROODING GENTLEMAN

JANE'S prediction that John Lawley would not take warning from his nieces was soon fulfilled. He had no belief that they could speak on politics, and he thought it an insolence. Jane had known of this; yet it was she who forgot it, and made the trouble.

He was quiet through the next day, which was perhaps as well after his hospitalities, but in the evening he revived and seemed to want talk and company. He began the talk himself, and he had grace enough to thank his nieces for the dinner. Jane looked as if she had not expected this.

"It's in our work, sir. You could complain if we did less." It sounded formal, but there was a warmth in it, as if she had been pleased. "But it's to be someone else's work in a fortnight, we're told?"

"Oh aye, at Will's house." He seemed unaware of anything that might have drawn Jane's thoughts towards that house. "The same company again, and you added, and Mally. They'll make you welcome at Will's."

"I'll have a word for someone, if they don't," said Jane. "Will you be talking again all day?"

"You know well enough that we've affairs." He turned suddenly to Mally. "You can keep your mouth shut, can't you?"

"Yes, sir."

"Good!" He was eyeing her straightly. "You'll have met these affairs before, at my sister's? That's a house for honest men, isn't it?"

"I've seen men of all sorts there, sir."

"I expect you have. But you know plainly what I mean. Men of decent loyalty, who know where——"

He checked abruptly, and for a moment he eyed her suspiciously. His face was hardening as he turned to Jane.

"How much did you girls contrive to hear of yesterday?"

It was sharp. He looked from the one to the other, and then back to Jane; and Jane's face was hardening as his had done. Her answer, when it came, was not well chosen.

"We heard of skins and prunes, and of a Colonel Storm."

"Oh?" He sat erect and looked disturbed. "Are you keeping your tongues still?"

"Perfectly. We've no wish for the hangman in the family."

"Good God!" He came almost out of his chair. "What's that you say? Are you from your senses?"

"No."

"No?" He stared at her in unbelief, and seemed stung to deeper anger by the shortness of her answer. "Do you know what you're saying?"

"Only too well." Jane was taut and white, but she was facing him unflinchingly. "We know what's at risk."

"God help you!" His breath was coming noisily now. "What's this rant of a hangman?"

"It's not rant. Treason doesn't respect persons."

He was suddenly on his feet, blustering and speechless, and Mally was on her feet in the same alarm, desperate to make the peace, and not knowing what to say. She had not seen a man so stirred before.

"My God! We're to be schooled by women, are we?"

"It's hardly that, sir. It——"

"I should damned well hope it isn't. Your place is in the kitchen, not schooling your elders."

"I'm sure it is." Jane spoke bitterly; and then her tone changed, as if she knew she must seek an end to this. "It's only that we have some love for you, Mally and I. And because we think so of you, we shall not love Colonel Storm, nor any other who disturbs your peace. That's all."

"All? If you were half as mannered as a horse you'd know it was a damned sight too much. There'll be no more of it." His anger flared suddenly, as if the enormity of it were sweeping through him. "Get out of my sight."

"Sir! I'm sure I——"

"Get out, I say." His voice rose wildly. "Go to your room —now. Don't let me see you till you've found your senses. Get out."

It ended in a shout of fury, and Mally stood aghast,

frightened for what might come next. Jane was stiffly erect, her face white and her lips pressed tight. For a long moment she looked steadily at him. Then she inclined her head in assent.

"As you say, sir."

She spoke it without expression, then turned, and walked quietly to the door. It latched behind her; and Mally, as stiff and silent as her uncle, noted that he was shaking.

She forced her mind to it, torn between a loyal urge that this must be shared with Jane, and a steadier thought that her part was to make the peace. There was no one but herself to make it, and she must go about it by whatever path should open.

He retreated to the hearth, standing with his back to it, and she heard his angry mutter.

"The whole damned family! One takes from the other."

He said it to himself, and she scanned him intently for any weakness she could work on. He was still red in the face, still puffing and blowing, and the thought came darting that here was a troubled man, a man drawn farther than he wished to go. Yesterday he had talked too much, hot with the wine and ale, and he could not in pride draw back nor in sense go on. He had made a fine bold picture of himself, and Jane had butchered it. In one ghastly sentence she had shown him the cold truth ; and now he must face it. No wonder he had flared into fury at that.

She lifted her head. The need now was to divert him, and reassure him.

"Pray, sir," she asked him, "what did you speak of ? Which takes what from the other ?"

"That ?" He blinked at her, and then had to wrench his thoughts back to it. "They're alike, aren't they ? They think I'm a country clod, because I struggle to keep this house. I'm a poor relation, and rustic. I'm shabby, and I can't have any wits."

It rang bitterly, as if it had eaten at his pride for years, and the whole sweep of it was suddenly in Mally's eyes again ; his shifts and savings, his slow fall in a world that did not need him, his resentments against the rising men, against the government—and the German King. He was looking to the past, when he and his kind had mattered.

"Alike, aren't they?" He said it suddenly again. "They rise in the world, and then they push you under. That sister of mine—didn't she treat you so?"

"Aye, sir. She did."

"And Jane's sister and her damned husband? A pretty high-riding pair they make! They're waiting for this to fall ripe too—waiting for me to die."

His glance round the room showed what he meant. Mally looked at it too, noting the faded shabbiness, the wear and tear, the lack of means to put things right; and in that moment a further understanding came. It was the resentments in him that had led him to this madness, had tied him to the Peavers and the Pattens, and the resentments sprang from his lack of consequence; which meant, in the end, his lack of money. He could not make the figure that his fathers had done; he could not live and dress as they had done, nor even keep his house as they had done, and always there were little things to tell him so. A little more money might heal him and sweeten him, give him sense and balance; and even save him from treason and a traitor's death.

Her eyes turned back to him, his brooding face and the bitter thoughts that held him. He was a man sick in mind, and she must not scruple here. Any way that would serve must do, and the glimmer of it was in her mind as she judged his mood. She would have to go deviously; and he must be calmed and not excited.

She spoke calmly, and there was nothing in her young face to hint what her real thoughts were.

"It's a pity, sir, that some of Mr. Deane's money can't be had. I'm told he has plenty."

"He could feed his cows with it. You think it's to be had, do you?"

"I scarcely know, sir. But it was Mr. Peaver who was saying——"

She left that in the air while she looked about for ale. She had noted that it sweetened most men, and when she poured it he took it without comment and settled himself in his chair.

"Ah!" He emptied half the mug and then stretched his legs comfortably. "What was Peaver saying?"

"Oh, he—er——" She was finding him his tobacco as she

spoke. "It was the other day, when he showed me the coal pit, and he said something of Henry wishing a lease of it."

"The Devil he did!" There was a grumble in his tone, but the note of anger had left him. "What else did Peaver say?"

"I scarcely know, sir." She was lighting a splint of wood, and she held it to his pipe as he puffed and drew. "The fact is, sir, I didn't understand him."

"I don't suppose you did. What did he say?"

He was almost affable now, and by the time she had filled his mug again he was willing enough to talk. It was an easy topic for him, and one on which he could be knowledgeable. It was well enough, he said, for Henry to ask a lease of the coal, but Henry was demanding a twenty-year lease, and that would permit no fines. It was all but making a gift of it to Henry.

Mally looked politely baffled, and asked what fines might be. Between more puffs of smoke he was pleased to explain.

Leases of land, he said, were made in this County for very small rents, by which no owner could profit. But it was the custom that when a lease ran out the tenant should make a payment called a fine. It was the price of renewal, and it was usually twenty years' rent. It was therefore from the fines, and not from the rents, that the owner made his profit, and that was why the duration of leases was important. Long leases meant few fines, and were therefore desired by tenants; short leases suited landlords.

He was growling with indignation now. Henry Deane, by demanding a twenty-year lease, was all but refusing to pay a fine at all. John would hardly live twenty years; his death would end the lease, and Henry would pay the fine to his own son. It was no wonder he was urgent for a lease, on those terms.

Mally gave him more ale while she thought this out. She had no difficulty in believing it was the sort of bargain that Henry Deane would ask for. But if there was no bargain there would be no money; which meant that discontents would stay. She picked her words carefully.

"What, sir, would be proper for such a lease?"

"I've offered him three years. I'll live so long, I hope, and then he'll have to pay."

Mally nodded, and was too wary to offer contradiction. But the pit, she remembered, had stopped altogether. A new one must be dug, and Henry would need to lay out a deal of money before there was any coal at all. A three-year lease was perhaps a shade ungenerous; but surely there could be something between?

"That put the damned rat off. It sent him packing, and he won't come back."

It burst out suddenly, and the growl was in his voice again. Mally sought quickly for a soothing answer.

"I'm sorry of that. It seems a pity to leave him with all that money. He'd be better after parting with some."

"Part he won't. It's not in his nature." Again the resentment was swelling in his voice. "Money isn't all, and we'll be the sweeter without him—coming here as if he owns it already."

"So much?"

"Much!" He banged his ale-mug passionately to the table beside him. "If you so much as give him ale you can see him note what the mug will fetch when he sells it. It's so with all things. You can see it in his eye, and I wish no more of him."

He was growing excited again, and Mally decided that for the moment she had said enough. More might antagonize him, and she had put a thought into his mind that he could be left to brood on. Also, she wanted a word with Jane.

She marched briskly into Jane's bedchamber, and found her comfortably in bed. But the curtains were undrawn and the candle still burning, and she was plainly wide awake. She spoke sharply.

"Is there more trouble?"

"Not yet." Mally was remembering that she had perhaps been negligent of Jane this last hour. "How's it with you?"

"As you see."

"I don't see much."

"You heard me ordered here. Did you think I should walk about all night?"

"I didn't know what you'd do. Is it John's way?"

"He has a temper. Most men have."

"I'm afraid you roused it. I've been trying to turn his mind from things."

"You'd have done better if you'd turned his stomach. A purge is what *he* needs."

"Jane!"

"Oh yes, it is." Jane heaved herself higher on her pillows and spoke incisively. "His stomach's sour from yesterday, and why it hasn't rotted through I can't guess. He had stewed carp, and hog's-liver pudding, and roast pork, and about half a duck. Between-times he had jugged hare——"

"That too?"

"He shot the damned things, didn't he? Then he had apple pie, cream syllabub, currant pudding and some marchpane. He'd what-you-like of ale, and a glass of claret to help it swill. Now his stomach's sour."

"I suppose it is. But——"

"That's all there is to it. He ate too much and he drank too much. Now he has to turn on someone, and I'm packed off here like a twelve-year-old."

"I'm sorry for that, Jane." Mally dismissed it briefly, and turned to what she thought mattered. "When do you think we shall have Henry here again?"

"Never, I hope. If he comes here again, *I'll* need a purge."

"I'll give it to you myself. How can we get him?"

"Who?"

"Henry." Mally spoke crisply, and then settled herself on the edge of the bed. "If a letter were sent to Henry, saying there was now good chance of a lease, what effect would it have?"

"Like fish to a cat. He'd be here next day."

"That's just what we need. You'll write that letter." She waved a protesting Jane into silence. "Now, listen——"

CHAPTER XIII

THE HOSTMAN

JANE wrote the letter. She grumbled, but she wrote it.

She wrote it on Sunday afternoon, while uncle John was comfortably asleep by the fire, and then she cast about for a way of sending it. Geordie Wade could do that, she said; and Mally had to be reminded that Geordie Wade was the carrier's boy who had spoken to them at the coal pit the other day. He had been offered some odd work in the stable here, and he would have time enough to ride to Newcastle with a letter.

Jane came back looking puzzled. Geordie, she said, had been to the stable only once. He had cleaned some harness and then had disappeared. He had not been seen since, and she had had to arrange for the other lad to take the letter. But there was no difficulty.

Then Jane contributed another notion. Uncle John, she said, would more readily swallow Henry if he thought he was doing it for the Cause; and she blandly asked him if he had noted how Mr. Peaver looked at church yesterday. She had seen clergymen look like that before, she said, and it usually meant that parishioners were to subscribe for something. Mr. Peaver would no doubt expect his friends to subscribe for the skins and prunes.

Uncle John looked startled, and Jane let the matter drop. When you planted an idea in his head, she told Mally afterwards, you could be fairly sure that in twenty-four hours he would think it his own idea, and therefore a good one; which, she tartly added, was usually the best way to deal with the old fool. She had apparently not wholly recovered her temper yet.

The lad rode with the letter on Monday morning, and it had exactly the effect that Jane had foretold. It brought Henry to the house next day, a half-hour before noon, when John was hungrily awaiting dinner, and Jane was in the kitchen seeing to it. It was Mally who saw him first, and she saw him with some dismay. This was sooner than they had expected, and it was hardly to be supposed that John was in the right mood yet. He was more likely to quarrel than to grant a lease; and Mally went running. She thought she had better get a word in first.

It was the same Henry, plump and prosperous, shrewd and assured. He had a dark-blue coat and yellow breeches now, with silver buttons and a touch of silver lace, and over his neat small wig he had a wide black hat that removed all gaudiness and served to proclaim that he was a merchant out of Newcastle, busy and dignified. He had a liveried servant with him, stiff and wooden on a sleek black gelding; and every detail of the picture fitted.

He brought his toe carefully to ground with a gleam from his polished boots, and he turned as Mally came hurrying out. Plainly he recognized her, and he sensed at once that there was an urgency here. He listened alertly as she spoke.

"If you please———" She was hurrying it, and with a quick glance back to the house. "That letter Jane sent to you— Mr. Lawley does not know of it, and it would be better that he should not. He'd be angered, we think, and———"

"Ah!"

His soft exclamation seemed to show understanding of this, and then he nodded almost testily, as if to say he knew much more than Mally. He turned and walked slowly to the house, and at once she saw that she had been no more than in time. John Lawley was in the porch now, and there was no look of welcome on his face. He was stiff and wary, and the best that could be said was that he was frigidly correct. He acknowledged Henry's bow with a very slight one, and then he had nothing to say. Henry was not at all disconcerted.

"I've taken it upon me to visit you again, sir." It was the same smooth voice that Mally remembered. "I'm always sorry when I can't be in agreement, and I'm willing to try again."

"At what?"

The tone of it would have put most men off, but Henry let it go past him.

"At some agreement that may work to the profit of us both. It's to our common interest."

"That's why the profit won't be all yours."

"Which is what I hope to convince you of. Ah, dear sister!"

He had just seen Jane behind her uncle, and Jane had her self in hand. She slipped past uncle John to greet dear Henry, and she had a bright smile and some proper inquiries about Julia and the children. Then she walked with him to the door, and when John followed them he found Henry already in the parlour, and a hospitable Jane promising dinner within half an hour. Mally stayed carefully in the background.

Uncle John went slowly into the parlour, and Jane promptly came out of it. Then she drew Mally into a whirl of activity. Dinner must be hurried, she said, but the immediate need was ale, and not a small ale either. It would have to be the best October, and Jane went plunging into the cellar to get it, leaving Mally to give a final polish to the pewter mugs. That took perhaps five minutes, and when they made their way to the parlour they found that the men were already in talk. They were standing together by the hearth, propping their shoulders against it, and in the stance of each there was wariness. They were arguing about the length of lease and Henry was still demanding twenty years, and John refusing more than three.

"There's no profit in rents," he was saying. "Twenty makes it a gift to you."

"An expensive gift." The rejoinder came promptly. "Consider what I'm to lay out on wagonways."

"That comes back to you. It becomes your own."

"My son's, if you please."

"That's all one, and I'm concerned with what comes to *me*. Do you think I can wait twenty years?"

"Well——" Henry reached absently for the ale mug that Mally was holding to him. "Well, perhaps a shade less."

"A deal less, if we're to do anything at all." John took a mug and then glared truculently at Henry. "Even three makes longer than I care to wait. I thought I'd been generous."

"Generous?" The tone was still smooth, and Henry had not lifted his voice. "If you'll give me leave to say it, I am of the Hostmen's Company, and I have much experience of these matters."

"I don't doubt it."

"The opening of a new pit is not a small venture. The man who seeks a new pit may ride home on a lean horse." His voice was a little harder now. "I must tell you plainly it's a great risk, and a fine after three years is almost payment in advance."

"And why not? You can afford it."

"Give me leave to know what I can afford."

"Give me leave to know what you won't get."

It was John's voice that had hardened now, and Mally had seen the urgency come to his face as Henry made mention of a payment in advance. It had perhaps started a thought in John. A payment in advance was what he needed.

"I shall *not* pay in advance." Henry was answering with a calm certainty. "It is not to be expected."

"Then the coal's not to be expected either. We waste our time."

It was an angry answer, hot and uncompromising, and he was not far from an outburst that would wreck the whole of this. Mally stirred slightly to glance at Jane, and a flicker of the eye showed that Jane knew all about it.

"I think," she said calmly, "that dinner is all but ready. I'll ask you to finish the ale, and perhaps let coal pits wait."

"It's the dinner that will wait." John spoke gruffly, and still kept his eyes on Henry. "I think we'll have an end to this, and I'll have it before I dine. Is there more to be said?"

"I hope so." It was still expressionless, but Henry's fingers were tapping on the mantelshelf as once they had tapped on Lady Chandler's table. "But perhaps Jane is right. There might be wisdom in letting it wait while we dine."

"You haven't yet been asked to dine."

"Oh!"

It was a gasp from Jane, as if even she were shocked by the rudeness of this. Without haste Henry put his ale mug down on the table. It was still untasted, as it had been handed to him.

"I think perhaps I'd better go," he said. "But it's to be regretted. We could have come to an agreement that would be to your profit and my son's." He spoke with finality, and without any haste he turned to Jane. "Julia asked me to say that she has not seen you for many a day, and wishes to. She desires that both you and cousin Mally shall make a visit to us soon. I do not think you will find us inhospitable."

If that last was meant for John it went unheeded; and Jane had herself wholly in command as she made the best of this.

"Thank you," she said. "Pray thank Julia too. We shall

be your grateful guests when you've appointed a day. Have we your leave for it, sir?"

She had turned calmly to John, and he almost shook himself as he came out of his thoughts.

"Oh, aye," he said hurriedly. "I'll not stand between you."

He turned away as if it had no interest for him, and Mally knew this to be pretence; under it he must be seething with anger, and perhaps with disappointment too.

Henry turned quietly to Jane, and in spite of his calmness there was a tightness in his face that Mally had not seen before.

"I'll tell Julia she may expect you," he said quietly. "And now I'll take my leave. You'll understand why I don't linger. Acquit me of discourtesy."

He walked firmly to the door, and John went as firmly after him, as if to be sure of seeing him safe away. Jane followed, and Mally came in the rear, sure that there were tempers strained to the limit, and that a very little could make an outburst now. Yet in one small corner of her mind a question rose, and would not be put away. Had Julia really sent that invitation? Or had it been Henry's smooth device to keep a channel open for another day? That might be like Henry.

They were out of the house, and Henry was taking his bridle from the servant when the trouble began; and it was what she had foreseen. The tempers broke.

Henry climbed carefully into his saddle. The servant held his stirrup and hastily mounted his own horse. Henry turned for a last word.

"I'm sorry you will not agree. We might both have come to profit here."

"If you think I'm for haggling you waste your breath. I'm not a merchant."

"I wish you were. You'd know then how to develop an estate."

It was the first hot answer that Henry had given, and for once it did not come smoothly. Plainly his own temper had risen now, and Mally saw it all too well. Vaguely and from behind her she heard hoofbeats among the trees, but she was too intent to give any heed to that. She heard John's heated answer.

"I don't ask guidance from you. The estate isn't yours yet, even if you think it is."

"It would be paying better if it were. And you'll not develop it without me."

"I'll sell my coal as I please, and not ask *you*. You're not the only buyer."

"Am I not?" Henry's face was flushed now, and he turned further in his saddle, stabbing the air with his whip as if he would drive his words home. "Now that's exactly what I am. I'm your only buyer. There's no man will touch your coal but me."

"What the Devil do you mean?"

"What I say. You've forgotten I'm a Hostman, haven't you? We alone may market coal."

"There are other Hostmen."

"They won't touch *you*. I'll see to that."

"Or anything that fills your pocket. Do you note that this is still my land?"

"I do."

"Then get out of it—now."

"As you will." Henry gathered up his bridle. "You'll find no other buyer, and I'll leave you——"

His voice died as if a gust of wind had swept it. Mally turned sharply, and for a moment she was bereft of speech. The other horse she had vaguely heard had come close and had stopped; and its rider, as still and silent as the horse, was Black William. He was wholly at his ease, and so like his brother that for a fleeting instant Mally was not sure which it was; she could almost have supposed that here was Sir John.

"What are you doing here?"

It was Henry, with a crackle of furious anger in his voice; and William received it placidly. He sat comfortably in his saddle, and looked Henry up and down.

"I make a visit," he said cheerfully. "I hope it will end more happily than yours."

There was silence, and Mally heard Henry's hard intake of breath. It had been thrust and parry; and suddenly she knew that it had not been the first, and that these two men were enemies of old.

"Are you pushing your damned nose into this? I'll make you sorry that you've ever——"

"I'm sure you'll try to."

"What!"

It was furious question and cheerful answer. Fleetingly Mally turned her head, and saw Jane tense and watchful and John staring and puzzled; and she remembered that he did not yet know Black William. Then a raging Henry snapped again.

"The coal here is mine and none other's. D'ye hear?"

"You seemed to be complaining just now that it wasn't."

"You know damned well what I mean. If you thrust in here I'll take you to the King's Bench for it."

"Are you sure they have a writ?"

"Now what the——"

"Better say Chancery. There's more to be had from Equity."

What that might have meant was never known. John thrust himself suddenly into the talk.

"What the Devil!" he exploded. "Will you tell me, sir, who you are?"

"Willingly." There was a calm nod of assent from William, and Mally had seen Sir John look exactly so. "I'm the plague of all the Hostmen, and my name is William Chandler."

Even the voice was Sir John's, the bluff and hearty tone he would use to tease his wife, and Mally had never a doubt that it was just as intentional in William. It was cool provocation, meant for Henry though addressed to John, and Henry spluttered into the fury she had expected. There was nothing smooth about him as he rounded now on William.

"That's the first truth you've spoken in your thieving life. You're a damned grasping scoundrel, grubbing into every trade that isn't yours, and why God kept you from boiling in your own tallow I'll never know."

"It wasn't God."

"What's that?"

"It was the Devil. He always watches his——"

"Shut your damned mouth, will you?"

"No."

There was a splutter of laughter from John, who seemed more than ready to enjoy this discomfiture of Henry. Mally saw it in one wondering glance, and the quick thought came that she had not yet the measure of this bluff and simple William. There was perhaps a purpose in this.

"I didn't come here to shut my mouth," said William placidly. "I came for a word with Mr. Lawley, but that may wait. Pray end your business, sir."

"There's no business for me."

"I thought you were buying coal."

"Then you thought wrong." Henry swung suddenly to John, and some semblance of calm was his again. "I'll wait for you to consider further. But do not suppose it's to be sold to any other. It's a Hostmen's monopoly, and among the Hostmen it's mine. Short of being a fool I'll stretch to the limit. I'll come to twelve years with you, but I will *not* be beaten into paying for what isn't yet got. Consider it, please."

He had almost regained his dignity as he shook out his bridle, and William lifted his hat courteously. Henry almost recoiled from it, and then he was clear, trotting down the drive, with his servant after him; and suddenly Mally was asking herself why William was here at all.

He was not slow to tell them, and she noted how completely his manner changed. He swung from his horse, thick-set and vigorous, and he was all dignity and courtesy as he moved to John. He spoke easily.

"You'll have heard my name, Mr. Lawley, and certainly I've heard yours. I think it's time we met."

"Indeed?" It came a little stiffly, as if John were not sure of his answer. "I was not expecting it."

"Yet you might have done."

It was not easy to be hostile to William at this moment. He had created a sympathy by his rout of Henry, and his bearing now was impeccable. He offered courtesy, and he had the dignity that demands it in return.

"Miss Mally here——" William turned to her with a smile that put Sir John alive before her. "Miss Mally is your ward, but she was once my brother's, and he has asked me to do her what service I can."

"Oh?" John seemed to be struggling between suspicion

and courtesy. "I don't know that there's a service needed."

"Perhaps there isn't." William was wholly disarming about it. "I learned so the other day. You yourself, sir, were engaged, and I didn't linger."

He had lingered long enough to hear Mr. Peaver preach, and long enough to give a warning. But that seemed forgotten, and he went easily on.

"Having been in your house, I felt I must make your acquaintance."

"To be sure." John seemed to have remembered what a gentleman must do. "Come into the house, sir. It's cold here."

"Thank you." William made slowly towards the door. "I'm sorry if my coming marred your business."

"Ugh!"

"Ye-es." He seemed to interpret that without much trouble. "I doubt if my coming hindered anything to your profit."

"It damned well didn't."

"That's the way of Hostmen. They're a little harsh with their monopoly. Do you know my trade?"

"Coal, isn't it?"

"Mostly. I buy it in spite of them and ship it in spite of them, and they do not love me."

"The law being against you?"

"There are ways past the law, if you have good money and a good attorney. I continue to buy the coal." In the arch of the door Black William halted his walk. "I will buy yours, Mr. Lawley, if you will let me. I *do* pay in advance."

CHAPTER XIV

THE MAN OF BUSINESS

For a moment there was silence.

John stood speechless, plainly between temptation and a thought of what his neighbours would say. Mally stood as silent, suddenly aware of a serpent's skill in William. It was Jane who spoke, and she sounded merely practical.

"Will you now be pleased to dine?" she said. "It must be half past twelve."

"What's that?" John seemed to come hastily from dreams. "Are we late?"

"A half hour late, and everybody famished."

"Aye, so we are." He seemed suddenly to realize that he had a duty and no alternative. "You'll dine with us, sir."

"Thank you." William was affable about it. "Miss Jane says we're famished, and I never quarrel with the ladies— unless, of course, the dinner's scorched."

"I'll believe any man would quarrel at that." Jane's eyebrows lifted suddenly. "But I'll go and see. Mally, will you——"

She was leading to the kitchen without more words, and Mally went hastily with her. A word with Jane would be welcome now, and she lost no time about it.

"Jane, is it all right—about selling to William?"

"I haven't sold to William."

"I know you haven't. But from the way you invited him to dinner——"

"Oh!" Jane, busily superintending the removal of a roast of mutton from the spit, abruptly left the work to the cook. "It's a chance from Heaven, isn't it, to sell that coal?"

"If William comes from Heaven. I'm not quite sure he does."

"Mally, it's not a matter of where William comes from. It's a matter of finding John some money."

"I know. But——"

E

"Then don't stand talking. William's money is as good as Henry's, and he's probably got more of it. Do you remember some guineas he gave you the other day?"

"I did ask you if I should take them."

"And I told you not to be silly. That's true of John as well. I'd take guineas just now from William or anybody else. Now go and see if those men have got some ale. They'll expect it."

"Yes. It's only that I——"

"For Heaven's sake stop talking. Go and see to that ale."

Mally went, and what she saw surprised her. The two men were leaning comfortably against the hearth, John with his ale-mug in his hand, and William with what was surely the mug that Henry had held and then put down untouched. She opened the bottle of October that was warming by the fire, and they absently held out their mugs, not taking their attention from each other; and to her surprise they were not discussing coal. They were talking about horses; or William was. He was saying he had been breeding from the Barbary strain; and John, the country gentleman, looked deeply interested. Mally went on tiptoe from the room, noting again that William was not as simple as he looked. He was genially coming to terms with the man before he so much as mentioned coal; and once more she began to think that she had the measure of William.

Before very long she doubted it again. William kept on about his horses while they sat at dinner. It was fifty years and more, he said, since King Charles had brought the Barbary to England to improve his sport at Newmarket, and it was surely time for them on Tyneside. He had some help from his brother in this. John had a liking for horses too, and occasionally took a day at Newmarket to see them run; and sometimes, if he saw a horse he liked, he would buy it.

William went calmly on. John, he said, had from time to time sent him a stallion and a mare or two, so he now had what he chose to call a very decent stable. The Barbary seemed to cross well with the local horses, and the strain he had come to had a Barbary fire and yet was docile. He went into some details, and he answered his host's questions with a knowledgeable ease. Then he turned to Mally and asked if she had ridden Sir John's horses when she had been in his house.

She had to answer that in London they had always used

the coach. William looked sad, and remarked that she would certainly have to use a horse here. It was almost as an after-thought that he asked her what horse she did use.

Again he knew how to steer the talk. In five minutes he had it out of them that the only good horse in the stable was John's, and that she and Jane had to make do with a pair of cobs. William looked benignly down his nose, and said he would send her a cross-bred Barbary.

Mally gasped. John let his knife clatter against his plate, and even Jane looked startled. William sat placidly, and Mally could not even turn her mind to an answer. It was filled by the leaping thought that William had been gently leading up to this since his first mention of horses over the ale, when she had not even been in the room. She knew that to be a guess, and she was blindly sure that it was true.

But William was speaking again.

"In these parts you'll need a horse, and one with some legs and some wind as well. I'll send him to you."

"It's too good, sir. I——"

"I'll send him tomorrow."

She knew that she must somehow thank him. She had no notion of the worth of a Barbary, but it was surely a greater gift than had come in her life before; yet when she tried to speak some thanks he swept them aside.

"Don't make too much of it," he told her. "I don't *buy* these Barbs. They—er—just come."

"No doubt, sir. But——"

"I can't ride them all myself, and I've no wish to sell. That would mean my neighbour on a horse as good as mine. Oh no!"

His chuckle left her wondering whether he meant it or not, and she was quite able to believe that he did. Then he was grave again, and was speaking quietly to John.

"That's all to your mind, I hope? You'll not forbid the lass——"

"Oh no—no." Again John was answering hastily. "It's proper enough, to be sure, since she came from your brother's."

"Oh aye. But there's the other lass." He turned suddenly to Jane. "You're not to ride a shag by the side of your cousin on a Barb. I'll not allow it."

"No?" It was Jane's turn to look surprised. "I don't see how I'm to——"

"The younger cared for, and not the elder? What do you take me for. There'll be a pair of Barbs—one for each of you."

"What!"

He seemed to enjoy it. He sat with a smile on his face, while a floundering Jane tried to know what to answer—exactly as Mally had done.

"It's more than I should take, sir," she said at last. "Truly, you can't send——"

"You try stopping me."

"Oh!"

It sounded as if for once she did not know what to say next, and William promptly took that as settled. He addressed himself to John.

"I'll send the Barbs tomorrow, the pair of them. You've stable room, no doubt?"

"Oh aye. It's generous of you."

"Wait till you see what they eat." His smile was whimsical now. "You'll need to sell your coal when you've had 'em for a month."

It was beautifully done, and Mally was far enough back in her wits to see it. He had made time for soothing dinner and the forgetting of Henry, he had established himself as part-guardian to Mally, he had won everybody's goodwill and put everybody under obligation; and now, at the exact moment, he had flicked easily to business with the lightest of touches. It was perfect, and Mally sat marvelling at it until the thought came quickly that this was how Sir John might have done it. She lifted her head, seeing Sir John in every line of him, and knowing that diplomacy must be a very part of him, as it was of Sir John. These brothers would never have risen as they had done if they had not had some skills in the managing of men.

Her head dropped again, and suddenly she was disappointed. She had been pleased that he should think so well of her and Jane, and it chilled to believe that it had been no more than the prelude to a bargain. But so, no doubt, it was; he would drive his bargain, and have back a dozen times the worth of his horses.

Once again she was wrong. Instead of the haggling she had expected there was no trouble at all.

William spoke very simply, and from his manner they could have been two old friends having a last look at what was agreed.

"I've told you I'll pay in advance," he said calmly, "and I supposed the trouble was about the length of lease. What was Deane asking?"

"Twenty years."

"And you?"

"Three."

William nodded, and spoke with crisp certainty.

"I think three is a little short, since it's yet to be dug, but I'll give you five—and the advance. What's the rent?"

"I——" John seemed a little out of breath. "I think it should be fifty—fifty pounds a year."

"And a fine in five years?" William hung on it for a moment. "Agreed, and I'll pay you the five years in advance. I'll need an option to renew, of course. Is there any more?"

John was gaping at him.

"You haven't *seen* the land yet!"

"I don't need to. I know every seam of coal that's mapped. That's my trade. Is there any more?"

"There's the digging of it. And a wagonway."

"There's a wagonway now on your neighbour's land, and I have rights in that. We have only to join it. Give me credit for sense." William was smiling now. "I should not buy your coal if I were not sure I could get it away. Are we agreed?"

"I think we—yes."

John was suddenly decisive, and there was relief in his face that he had emerged with what he asked for. There was satisfaction plain upon him, and Mally felt a throb of relief that it had come to him at last. He would be easier to deal with now, and safer. Across the table she caught Jane's eye, and read the relief there too. John scrambled to his feet as if he could sit still no longer, and William rose lazily. He too seemed pleased, and the air of business had dropped from him. He spoke lightly to Jane.

"We've sat two hours over dinner, and broken the work of

the house to pieces. So I'll plague you no longer. I'll take my leave and be gone."

"It's no plague, sir."

"At least it's half past two, and dark before I'm home. Could my horse be brought?"

"If you say it." John was answering him now, and again he seemed to remember what a gentleman must do. "I'll ride to my boundary with you."

"Do. We might then agree on the line of the wagonway."

"That will be easy."

It might have been; but getting him away to do it was not so easy. First he could not find his boots. He had left them at the side of the hearth, and they were not there now. Jane told him they certainly were not; they were drying in the kitchen, as he might have guessed. He spluttered indignantly, and Mally went to warn the stable boy about the horses.

When she returned she found William placidly in the hall, ready in a long deep-skirted riding-coat of the modern sort. He was waiting amiably, while John stamped about in his stockinged feet looking for his spurs, and when Jane found them behind the clock he asked who the Devil had put them there. Jane told him that he had probably put them there himself, and she went to find him his cloak and hat and gloves. She laid them in a row in the hall, and when he came hurrying out in his boots, apologizing gustily for keeping William waiting, Jane had to help him into his thick old-fashioned cloak while he stood there breathing heavily. William waited placidly. He looked at the hat and gloves; and from those he looked to Mally.

"That puts me in mind," he said calmly.

It had the air of an afterthought, and Mally was alert at once. She did not believe any longer that William had afterthoughts.

"Ye-es." He had another look at the hat and gloves. "Did my brother furnish you with riding-clothes?"

"Why no, sir. He——"

"Then he should have done. I'll do it for him."

He plunged his hand into the deep pocket of his coat, and came out with a monstrous fistful of guineas, and once again he had Mally gaping at him. She thought he had thirty or forty guineas in his hand, and she saw the bulge in his pocket as if there were more there still, and she was too taken aback to have a word to say.

He turned to the oak bench beneath the window, and calmly counted a dozen of them into a neat pile.

"There you are," he said. "That will make your riding-habit, and perhaps your gloves as well."

"Truly, sir——" She had to gulp for breath. "You've done that before. I'm sure I should not——"

"You may leave John to say that. I'll put it into account with him, and he may charge it to his wife's routs. What do they cost, do you think?"

"I *couldn't* think, sir."

"Nor could I, from what he tells me. So what's to a dozen more?" He was chuckling happily now. "He should have paid this before he sent you north. As it is, he'll have to pay twice."

"Twice?"

"Aye, aye. We'll not part the younger and the elder." Again he fished in his pocket, and again there was a clink of gold as he counted the guineas out. "That's for you, lass."

"Me!" Jane sounded startled out of her manners. "*Me?*"

"You." He was beaming at her. "And don't start telling me you can't, because you can. Have you met my brother?"

"No."

"It's time he heard of you. I'll tell him who they're for."

"But really, sir——" She sounded at her wits' end now. "I—I have a riding-habit."

"I've not heard of a lass yet who didn't need another. Don't be so soft."

A genial slap reduced Jane to a gaping silence, and William flung his hat on and moved to the door. His chuckle came again, and he had no more to say. He was in his saddle with surprising agility, and then he went trotting down the drive with John at his side. They passed out of sight behind the trees, and Jane and Mally were alone outside the porch. In silence they looked at each other.

"Is—is he mad?" asked Jane.

"No." The images of a dozen Williams were drifting

before Mally, images all subtly different, and none less real than the others. "He's not mad."

"Why did he give all that money for the coal?"

"I expect he knows. He seems to know everything."

"He seems to know too much." Jane's eyes were troubled as she looked at Mally. "I hope John's all right."

"Why shouldn't he be?"

"He's a child—to William. I don't understand all this. I don't know where he's leading us."

"I don't either. But——" Mally had looked away uneasily, and then quickly she turned back. "I like William."

"What did you say that for?"

"Oh? That sounds as if you do too."

"Don't be silly."

"I'm not being. Why did you take his money, and his horse?"

"Why did you?"

"I suppose I could answer, because I liked him."

"I suppose you could, if you were fool enough." The old pungent tone was suddenly back with Jane. "You took his guineas, Mally, for the same reason that I did. I couldn't help it. He made me feel about six years old, and he wasn't to be argued with. I've not met a man like that before."

"You probably won't meet another."

"I'm not sure that I want to. Or do I?" Jane was suddenly thoughtful as she turned to the door. "Perhaps *you* do."

"Now what does that mean?"

"Nothing." Jane was still watching, but there was a twitch of amusement in her now. "I thought you might be wondering if his son's like that, too."

CHAPTER XV

FRUITS OF AGREEMENT

THAT had been Tuesday; and Wednesday gave a glimpse of what might follow.

At mid-morning a liveried servant came riding to the door, and produced a letter, which he had carried from Newcastle, he said, by command of Mr. Henry Deane. It was from sister Julia, to dear Jane. Julia was eager to see her sister again, and cousin Mally too; and she hoped they would accept the invitation, and with no delay be her guests in Newcastle. The forbearance of uncle John in sparing them for some few days would be gratefully appreciated.

There was a sniff from Jane, and she tossed the letter to the table. Evidently, she said, Henry meant to have that coal, and he would worm himself back to favour this way. There was silence; and it was left to Mally to say that they could hardly accept the invitation.

"Why not?" said Jane.

"Because the coal is already sold. And if she's asking us because she hopes——"

"She doesn't say so."

"Of course she doesn't. But——"

"She's my sister, isn't she? Why shouldn't I go to visit her?"

"Yes. But——"

"What about that riding-habit? Where do you think you'll buy it, if you don't go to Newcastle? I need a few things myself."

It was at this point that the next disturbance came. They heard the sound of horses, and it was a small cavalcade. Two riders had the look of grooms, and each led a spare horse, but it was the leader who took Mally's eye and brought her leaping to her feet. She could not mistake those broad shoulders and that air of youthful vigour. This was Dick Chandler, and she hastily followed Jane to the door.

Dick seemed glad to see them. He pulled his hat off, almost with a flourish, as he swung quickly from his horse.

"I'm here again, you see. I'm bringing horses, for both of you. They're from my father."

He directed that last at Jane, and she had to answer him.

"Thank you." She spoke a little stiffly. "He's generous."

"Ye-es. I did say I don't apologize for him."

"Oh!" There was a sudden gasp. "That's a barbed answer."

"Shouldn't it be?"

There was another little gasp from Jane. Her mouth had tightened, and Mally intervened hastily.

"It would be easier for *me*," she said, "if you two would stop quarrelling. I don't see the need for it."

"Nor do I."

He said it cheerfuly, but he turned back to Jane as if he were ready for anything. Jane was still bristling, and again Mally spoke hurriedly.

"Then please don't invite it."

"I'm not inviting."

"Good! Then Jane——"

Jane stood sullen, as if she would neither advance nor retreat, and for a moment the silence held. Then uncle John came wandering out of the door, looking as if it were time somebody told him about this; and he was a changed man. He had made his peace with the father, and that seemed to include the son. Also, he had an interest in horses, and the Barbs took his eye at once. He was quickly in talk about them, and then he was bawling for the stable boy, and Mally felt more at ease. She suggested ale, and John was loud in approval as he led to the parlour fire.

It gave her another view of Dick Chandler. He took two minutes over talk and ale, and then he gave attention to uncle John, and came quietly to business. He had been entrusted with more than horses. He produced a roll of papers and a canvas bag. The papers were a plan of the land, with some boundaries neatly marked, and an agreement already signed by William. The canvas bag held two hundred and fifty pounds in gold, five years' rent, exact to William's word. Mally looked, and had to suppress a gasp of surprise. She had not thought William slow, but she had hardly expected such speed as this.

Dick explained it crisply. The map, he thought, was correct; it showed precisely what Mr. Lawley had agreed with his father. The agreement set out what had been discussed, and Mr. Lawley would no doubt satisfy himself of that. The money was the amount that had been promised; and, by way of showing that, he began to count it into piles, with expert flicks of his fingers and a steady clink of gold.

It was something new to Mally. She had never pictured Dick Chandler as the competent main of affairs. Yet here he was, dealing with the lease and gold in a way an older man might have envied. He knew exactly what was needed, and he was very sure of himself. He ended his counting of the gold, and he made no attempt to hurry John's slow reading of the lease. Instead, he came across to Jane and spoke in a quiet undertone.

"I'm sorry to burden you with two servants. Some escort seemed wise, with——"

He glanced at the gold, and Jane seemed to be cooler now.

"Of course." She nodded absently. "Your father seems to move quickly."

"It's how he builds his business. He has a way of being there first."

It came quickly, as if he were glad again of a chance to justify his father. He watched Jane steadily, and then he pressed it home.

"A half of what's said against him is said by those who come too late."

"When he's made his bargain, you mean?" She answered him almost grimly. "I can all but hear them say it."

She looked quickly to the table, where the letter lay, the letter from Julia, which in fact meant Henry. He, too, would soon be saying it.

There was a muttering from John, still poring unhappily over the lease. He looked up, with his brow still furrowed, and Dick went at once to his side.

"Is there anything I can explain, sir?"

"Why can't a lease make sense?"

"It's the way the attorneys write them. That one's in the usual form."

"It reads like it. One long jabber."

"Yes." Dick sounded bland and soothing, and he made no attempt to argue. "You'll let your own attorney read it before you sign?"

"I—I suppose I should."

"It's as well, sir."

The quiet rejoinder seemed to suit the way of this, and it was not lost on Mally. If this was the way of the Chandlers, it seemed an honest way. There was no pressure, and no taking of advantage. There might be more in William than appeared, but there was surely no malpractice here.

"Aye, my attorney——" John's voice broke into her thought. "But he's down by the river there, at Ryton."

"Then perhaps we could ride——"

It was at this point that the next interruption came. Mr. Peaver had not been seen since Friday, and he chose this moment. He came on foot, and when they were all too occupied to hear his gentle tapping, he took the privilege of an old friend and walked in. He opened the parlour door, and there he was.

He was surprised, and he did not hide it. He saw the papers and the gold, and he stood there blinking. Then he began an apology, and John cut him short.

"No, no. There's nothing here at all." He was hasty about it. "It's just a little business."

"Indeed?" Mr. Peaver's eyes seemed drawn to the gold. "It means, I hope, that you sell, and not that you buy?"

"Oh yes, yes. It's the coal, do you see? I—er—arranged to sell——"

"Splendid!" Doubt seemed to drop from Mr. Peaver. "That's news to me. I'm pleased indeed."

"You are? Why then—er—this is Mr. Chandler."

"Who?"

Mr. Peaver's eyebrows had gone up, and his quick glance at Dick was piercing. It was received stolidly. Dick stood quietly waiting, and uncle John did the best he could.

"Mr. Chandler, I said. He—he's the son of Mr. William Chandler."

"Oh?"

"Yes. We—er—do business. Mr. Chandler—Mr. Peaver."

The slightest of bows acknowledged that, and Dick stayed silent, apparently seeing no reason why he should be involved in this. Again it was not lost on Mally. He was certainly showing some good sense; but a touch of the graces might have made this moment easier.

Again uncle John had to do his best.

"Yes. We're just thinking of Ryton—my attorney there."

"Then I must not detain you."

It was frigid. John looked unhappy. Dick stayed in the same silence, and Mr. Peaver had no more to say. Jane had to take charge.

"Do you dine in Ryton, sir?"

"Of course we do."

"Then you'd better hurry, or you'll be too late for it. I'll find your boots. Mally, will you find his horse?"

"I will."

She moved quickly on that, thinking anything better than this threatened quarrel which involved Dick Chandler too, and to her surprise he came with her. He said there were his own men to be roused, as well as the stable boy, and he would do that himself.

It ended with their standing together in front of the house, while the horses were made ready, and then he had a word for her.

"Who is he?"

She knew he meant Mr. Peaver, and she answered in the same brief style.

"A friend of my uncle's. He's a neighbour."

"A Tory?"

"A Non-juror."

"Oh!" It was short and dry, and it made plain what he thought of Non-jurors. "Does he come often?"

"Once or twice a week."

"He doesn't seem to like my father. How about Jane?"

"She—she's easier than you'd think."

"I hope so. I'm coming here again."

"Oh?" She was watching him carefully. "Affairs with my uncle, would it be?"

"No. You." He said it tersely, and then he turned to face her. "I told you before that you would count for something anywhere. You might count for a lot."

She found her breath coming quickly, and she was still without an answer when Jane came walking to join them. For once, perhaps, she was unwelcome.

"I've found him his boots," she said. "And his hat and his spurs, and pretty nearly dressed him. He'll be out in a moment."

"Thanks." Mally had found her voice again. "Where's Peaver?"

"By the fire. Sulky, by the look of him."

"That's me," said Dick calmly. "I've been telling Mally I'll be coming here again. Will you mind?"

"There's nothing to stop you from coming, if you wish to."

"I do. As a matter of fact I'll probably have to."

"Why?"

"This coal from your land. There's a wagonway to make, and I'll have to oversee it. That means some visits here, about the details. Are those the horses?"

He turned quickly at the sound of them, and that ended the talk. John came bustling from the door, booted and spurred at last, and wrapped in his thick old cloak; and then he and Dick were away together, seemingly in busy talk, and with the two servants trotting behind. They went noisily, and at the bend by the trees Dick turned in his saddle to wave. Mally found herself waving back, and her head was still a whirl of thoughts when Jane spoke sharply.

"Careful! Here's Peaver."

He was standing in the open door, as if he had come there to see the riders go, and his lean face was troubled. Jane put a warning hand on Mally's arm, and they walked back slowly to the house. Mr. Peaver eyed them sombrely.

"I don't like it," he said abruptly.

"No?" It was Jane who answered him, and there was a patient note in her voice. "What don't you like, sir?"

"These dealings with Mr. Chandler. It's imprudent."

"To deal with Black William? He seems to have paid for the coal."

"Oh, yes—yes. And a little money will be useful. We need it. But it's still imprudent. The man's a spy."

"Is he, sir? But how?"

"I don't know. I wish I did." He was speaking jerkily now. "Let us just say that he knows a great deal, and that what he knows is soon known to the government. That makes him a spy."

"But uncle John has only sold him coal. He can't go spying in a coal pit, surely?"

"No, no——" Mr. Peaver seemed even more disturbed, and he spoke almost tartly. "To be sure, he can't. There's nothing in coal pits for him. Nevertheless he now has free access to this land. He may ride it as he pleases. And at this juncture——"

He ended in a clucking noise, and Jane looked as if she were finding patience difficult.

"Why at this juncture? Is it special?"

"Ah!" His glance grew suddenly keener, and he looked warily round him. Then he nodded sagely. "Now that's what I wished to tell you of. I've been away since Sunday."

"We thought we hadn't seen you."

"No. I—I've been at Dilston."

"With milord Derwentwater?"

"Yes. It's what I came to tell John about. Pray tell him when he returns."

"Yes?"

"It is tidings indeed. You know we are to meet next week, at Mr. Harvey's, which is near to Dilston?"

"Yes."

"I have it from his Lordship that Colonel Storm will be at Dilston then, and will bear his Majesty's commands."

His voice was hushed, and there was a glitter in his eye to tell of the fanatic that was in him. Mally stood very still, and Jane spoke without expression.

"I'll tell uncle John, sir."

"Thank you. But his Majesty's commands will not be idle. And to have this man here, riding freely upon this land——"

Mr. Peaver shook his head in agitation. Then he spoke a sharp farewell, and went hurrying off. He was almost stumbling with haste as he passed out of sight, and Mally stood staring after him.

"The Devil!" said Jane, slowly. "What's upsetting Peaver?"

"He doesn't like William."

"I'm not sure that I do."

"Then you'd better not say so."

"Why not?"

"Because you've taken his guineas and you've taken his horse. So have I. Let's look at those horses again."

They moved slowly towards the stables, and Jane seemed thoughtful.

"Why did William buy that coal?" she asked suddenly.

"I suppose he knows what he's doing."

"I'm quite sure he does. But what *is* he doing?"

"Now what——" Mally stopped in her walk. "Jane, do you mean it was what Peaver said? He wants to spy on John?"

"Well——" Jane almost drawled it, and suddenly there was a gleam of amusement in her eyes. "I should have thought it might be simpler. You seem to be throwing some charms at Dick."

"I'm sure I'm not. I——"

"Just as you like. Let's put it this way, then." Her amusement was open now. "Dick brings you here in a chaise, and what he said on the way I don't know. But he—er—gives the appearance of kissing you. Then he goes home to tell father——"

"He didn't! He——"

"Father comes here and buys the coal. Which gives Dick a reason for coming here again—often. I'd have called it obvious."

Mally stood staring. Then, slowly, and as her thoughts began to clear, she knew that she was not convinced. It might have been obvious with someone else; but not with William. Nothing was obvious with William.

CHAPTER XVI

THE WARNING

THEY went to Newcastle on Friday, and in spite of some protests from Mally. She still had doubts about this invitation, and Jane made short work of those. The acceptance, she said, matched the invitation, and if the one was doubtful, so was the other. For her own part she meant to do some shopping, and if Julia didn't want them she shouldn't have asked them. As a crushing afterthought she added that the invitation was already accepted; she had sent a letter back with Henry's groom the other day.

That seemed to settle it; and Mally, with some thoughts that flickered between Dick Chandler and this coming visit to the Harveys, could see some excellent reasons for turning William's guineas into a riding-habit. So she gave way gracefully, and off they went. Jane gave minute orders to the cook for the care of John, and then they departed—though not with the Barbary horses. Even Jane shied at explaining those to Henry, and they took the shaggy cobs from the stable. They took the stable boy as well, partly as escort, and partly to lead the spare horse that had their baggage. There would be the more need for it, as Jane pointed out, on their way home.

They rode in a drizzling rain, and they came into Newcastle in the middle of the afternoon, entering by the great mass of stone that was the Westgate, and had a gallows outside it to take the last cheer from the afternoon. They passed through the arch, and Mally roused herself for some sight of Newcastle, and what she saw surprised her. Fine timbered houses were set apart in deep wide gardens, girt about with trees and lawns, and even through the dripping rain they looked well kept. The paint was clean, the lawns were trim, the paths well rolled. A pride was evident, as if neighbour vied with neighbour, and had the means to show it. They were the houses of substantial men, with elegance joined to solid comfort, and one of them was Henry's.

He must have been watching for his guests, for as they came to the gate he appeared in his doorway, cheerfully waving them in; and a change had come upon Henry. Here, in his own home, he was different. His smooth and calculating air had gone. There was a warmth in him; which, as Jane afterwards remarked, made him almost human. He gave them a welcome, and he seemed to take a pride in it, as if they were now his guests and must learn what Newcastle hospitality could be. He was out in the rain to help them dismount, and then he led them to the door where Julia was waiting; and she looked as pleased as he. She almost pulled them into the house, and then she had wit enough to commiserate upon the weather, and to ask if a dish of tea would be pleasing now.

It was admirably done, and it was more than Mally had expected. She was disposed to be grateful for it, whatever its cause, and soon a sense of amusement added to her well-being. Something seemed to touch a memory; and soon, as they sat with Julia over the tea, she realized what it was. There was something here of the polite world of Lady Chandler. She looked round her, noting the blue-and-white cups, the chased silver of the teapot, the lacquered china cupboard in black-and-red. There was even a thick red rug on the polished floor, and Mally carefully suppressed a smile. Julia had evidently not missed much when she visited Lady Chandler.

She played the hostess well, and she showed a thoughtfulness. She herself suggested that they might wish to do some shopping in Newcastle, and she offered to conduct them; and Henry promptly hinted that he was of some note in the town and could obtain some discounts for them. Also, he would himself show them something of the beauties of Newcastle. He was affable about it, and friendly; and nobody even mentioned coal.

Julia took them out on the morrow; and it made a tiring day. They went on foot, walking down the Westgate street, then threading through a churchyard, and so, by the narrowest of lanes, to a place of markets. Julia led them on past a greater church, hard by the grey stone castle, and then down a steeply sloping street which seemed to fall to the river. At the bottom she told them that they were now in the merchant quarter of the town, and that it was called the Sandhill, though it did not look like that to Mally. Then Julia turned into another narrow climbing street which seemed to be given to the shops of butchers, and which led them at last, with Jane looking wearied and Mally out of breath, to a street as fine as the Westgate they had started from. This, said Julia, was Pilgrim Street, and here they might do all the shopping they could wish.

They did not do quite all they wished, and it was Mally's riding-habit that gave the trouble. There was not here the gay range of colours that London would have shown. Newcastle seemed to think that a riding-habit was something to go riding in, not merely to be seen in; and what was offered was practical. It took account of weather. These were habits of fuller cut than those of London, high in the collar, and furnished with the cloak that London now disliked. Mally supposed they suited the weather. But for the most part they were of useful russets; and Mally, remembering that Jane's habit was exactly that, wanted something slightly different. Julia knew which shops to take her to, and in the end she had a fine mulberry serge, soft and warm, with a cloak a full tone darker. It was not quite what she had hoped for, but it would do. At least it was not the same as Jane's, and she could perhaps get further contrast from hat and boots.

That, however, had to wait, for at this point Henry appeared. First he took them to dinner, and then he insisted on showing them more of Newcastle. He led them down again to the river, down through a lane he called a chare, which was as narrow, and perhaps as unsafe at night, as anything Mally had known in London; but from this they came to the great quay that Mally had seen from the river, and the quay made amends for the chare. It was, said Henry, the finest quay in England, and Mally believed him. Along all its length were ships, moored three abreast, and it seemed to Mally that every merchandise of the world was being loaded or unloaded here; and beyond the quay the river was dotted with busy keels, taking coal to the colliers, or hurrying to the staiths for more. Across the river was the town that must be Gateshead, and at once she was wondering where Black William lived, and Dick, and what they did this day. And which house had been Sir John's, when he had made his humble start with William and

seethed the tallow there? She turned, looking again to the
bustling quay, and the thought occurred that one of these ships
might be unloading what Sir John had sent.

It was at this point that Henry made his first mention of
William and the coal, and he led to it very neatly.

He took them along the quay toward the great stone bridge,
and from there he turned into the triangular cobbled space
that Julia had called the Sandhill; and here, by the waterfront,
was the oddest building that Mally had yet seen. There was a
square tower with a squat spire; half-way up the tower a Gothic
arch disclosed an entrance door, with two balustraded stair-
ways climbing the face of the tower to reach it; and above the
arch was a statue of King Charles II, dressed as Julius Caesar,
which did not suit him at all. Jane took one withering glance,
and asked if the masons had been drunk; and Henry ignored
that as he pointed out a graceful hall that sprang from one side
of the fantastic tower. It was, he said, the Guildhall, where the
Mayor and Corporation met; but it was also the meeting place
of the Hostmen's Company.

He went firmly on to say a little more; and there was a note
of purpose in him now.

The Fraternity of Hostmen, he said, had been in Newcastle
since beyond the memory of man; and for this last century and
more they had by royal charter been a corporate body, able to
sue and be sued, to own and demise property, and to have their
own seal. They had the exclusive right to load and unload coal
and grindstones in any part of the Tyne between the Sparrow
Hawk and Hedwin streams. He recited it carefully; and then
he looked steadily at Jane.

"Such men as William Chandler," he said, "are therefore
flouters of the law, and may be called to account. It would not
be wise to sell coal to such a man. That could bring great loss."

He had no more to say of it. He turned to speak of some
furnishings in the hall, but Mally knew that he had not spoken
idly. He had spoken with intention, and he could return to it
when he chose.

He returned to it the next evening. He presided at supper,
very easily and hospitably, and when supper was done, and
wine was on the table, he came again to coal. It was Sunday
evening, and Jane had been insistent that they must return

next day. They could take an hour or two to complete their shopping; but they must return next day. She could not leave John for longer in the care of a cook and housemaid.

Henry pursed his lips and looked regretful.

"That can be understood," he said, "and we'll not detain you. We shall both hope to see you again soon."

"Of course."

"I shall myself hope to see you even sooner, and at your house. My visit the other day was surely unfortunate. Mr. Lawley has some oddly wrong beliefs."

Suddenly his finger was tapping on the table, as it had once tapped on Sir John Chandler's table, and Mally became alert. She remembered that tapping finger.

"Ye-es." He was speaking slowly now. "He thinks his coal is worth more than it is. He does not understand the cost of winning it. It is impossible that he should receive such sums as he speaks of—not, at all events, from an honest man."

He seemed to be arranging his thoughts as he poured the wine again—and it was Tory claret, as Mally noted, and not the Lisbon wine that a Whig would have poured. He spoke slowly and thoughtfully.

"We do not take lightly our privilege to deal in coal at Newcastle. There are strict rules for our trade. We have heavy dues to pay on the coal we ship, and they amount to a great charge. Also, every Hostman must keep to his bond, and he dare make no bond he cannot keep. A Hostman must be more careful of his promises than less responsible persons, and I—er —regard it as most unfortunate that such a person as William Chandler should have intruded as I was taking leave."

"It was a little—difficult."

"It was more than difficult." He spoke incisively now. "I don't understand what brought him there at all."

"I think he came to see *me*." Mally spoke quickly to help Jane. "I was ward to his brother, and I think Sir John had asked him——"

"You're sure he didn't think of coal? Did he speak of coal when I was gone?"

For a moment she held her breath, and she knew that there was only one answer. This must be answered truthfully.

"Yes."

She said it carefully, and she saw Jane tense and watchful. Henry's face darkened, and for a moment he was silent. Then his voice came with a snap.

"Did he talk of making offer for it?"

"He did."

"He'll promise anything. What did he offer?"

"I could not properly say. I don't well understand such matters."

"What did your uncle answer?"

"I——" She tried desperately to evade this one. "I think he seemed surprised."

"I'm glad he had wit enough for that. But certainly I must go to him at once. This——" He turned abruptly to Jane, as if a dreadful thought had struck him. "He did not make any promise?"

"I'm afraid he did."

"He——" Henry was open-mouthed now. "*What* promise?"

"What you might perhaps have expected." Jane spoke firmly, as if she knew that it must now come out. "Mr. Chandler made some offer, which my uncle accepted."

"What!" His chair scraped, and there was a splash of claret as a jerking finger shook his glass. "You tell me he——"

"Henry!" Julia was leaning forward, with her fingers on his arm. "I do not think it is the fault of Jane, or of Mally either."

"No." It came grudgingly, and he seemed to collect himself and put a face on it. "I did not mean that. I beg your pardon, Jane."

"There's not the need to. I'm afraid it must be——"

"God pity him!" It burst out as if he could keep it in no longer. "Chandler, of all men! Does he know what company he keeps?"

He sat stiffly at the head of his table, his breath coming noisily as he waited for the answer. The smoothness had gone, and he was speaking now what he thought. This was not the careful Hostman, and even the lines of his face had changed; there was a shrewdness now that was almost a shock to Mally.

"Company?" Jane was speaking calmly. "It's a matter, surely, of buy and sell, not of——"

"There'll be Chandler and his men on the land, won't there? Chandler riding to the house to ask of this or that?"

"Does that matter?"

"Matter! You know what a high fool your uncle is, with his Non-jurors, and his King over the water."

"I know he's a Tory, but——"

"A Tory sober is a Jacobite when drunk. They're all of the same mould, ripe for the same end."

An icy chill came suddenly on Mally. This was the true Henry, speaking of what he knew. Black William had given the same grim warning; and even Mr. Peaver had spoken of indiscretion. The room was hushed and still. Julia had shrunk to nothing, and Jane was taut and silent. Mally spoke slowly.

"Would you tell me," she said, "the truth about Mr. Chandler?"

"Do I need to tell you? You were in his brother's house. What company does your aunt there keep? You know, I suppose, that her house is the meeting place for every Jacobite in London?"

"I fear it is."

"Fear is the proper word. If there's any rogue come from France, he makes straight for Lady Chandler. He'll have wine and comfort there, and all his friends to talk with. And talk he does! The wine sees to that."

Her thoughts were moving swiftly as she listened. A Colonel Storm had lately come from France, and he had surely gone to Lady Chandler. Now he was riding north, and next week, at Will Harvey's——

"A pretty nest of traitors." Henry's voice broke in again, and jerked her back to the present. "Sir John Chandler is a Whig, isn't he?"

"Yes."

"Then why does he buy their wine?"

"Oh!"

The chill was icy now. She had asked herself this a hundred times, and had never understood it. Now, with the question put like that, she knew the answer.

"Exactly." He had his eyes intent on her, and he saw that she had guessed. "He lets every plot in London be hatched in his house, and loosened with his wine. There's no Jacobite can keep his tongue still. They drink too much and they talk too much. Have you noted that?"

She had. Her uncle seemed disposed to talk to anybody; and Black William had listened at the parlour door while Mr. Peaver preached.

"Exactly." He said it again, as if he would drive this home. "Sir John Chandler has noted it too. He sees all and hears all, and it's no wonder he's in favour with the government. That's why we get no satisfaction when he and his William break every law there is. What's a Hostmen's charter against news of plots?"

It rang bitterly, and Mally cared nothing for it. Her thoughts were with her uncle, and Black William, and a Colonel Storm; and again she brought Henry back to it.

"How does this touch William Chandler?" she asked. "Is he a spy too?"

"Of course he is. He's told by his brother of all that hatches, and then he knows where to look for the proof of it. There's a rope at the end of that."

She sat speechless, and his words came savagely.

"This—*this*—is the man your uncle must have on his land! Your uncle! And could there be a more marked man, with a sister like that in Sir John's own house? My God!"

His chair creaked back, and he came to his feet, dominating them as he stood above them.

"Do not ask again why William Chandler dare buy this coal, against every rule and law. He's protected. But if you can speak one saving word, keep your uncle from these follies. You might save his life that way."

He moved slowly to the door; and as he reached it he turned for an afterthought.

"You might save the estate as well. It's our family inheritance, and you'd not wish it bestowed on William Chandler—for services rendered."

CHAPTER XVII

DERE STREET

THE first news that greeted them when they were home was that the arrangements for this visit to Will Harvey had been changed. They were to go a day sooner than had been planned, on Wednesday instead of Thursday; and Mr. Peaver was to travel with them.

They thought that ominous. They had a word together, and then they set themselves to learn the meaning of it. Jane said that a drink or two would soon loosen John. So she gave him October ale, mulled with sugar and ginger and yolk of egg, and she had the tale from him in half an hour. This meeting was to be on the Friday, and it might perhaps be addressed by Colonel Storm. But on the Thursday there was to be a meeting with some gentlemen from Scotland; and that was why they must now travel on Wednesday, Mr. Peaver with them.

It was not reassuring, but Jane seemed to think it must wait till they got there. Then she fell to work with a smoothing iron, and suddenly Mally understood. Friday was also Jack Harvey's birthday, which had been the excuse for their being invited; and Jane had more in her thoughts than a meeting of Jacobites. Mr. Peaver was not in the front of her mind.

They were, somehow, ready for Wednesday morning, and Mr. Peaver appeared on a horse so good that Mally wondered what his need of it was. She mounted the Barbary that was William's gift, and it gave her a medley of thoughts as she and Jane went trotting after the men. It was somehow of a piece with the rest that William should supply their horses for a Jacobite journey that smelt of treason.

They rode down the Stanley burn towards the Tyne, and then westwards up a track that touched its winding bank from time to time. They would do ten miles of this, said Jane, until they came to Corbridge, where they would cross the river; and, she added, she would then point out the demesne of Dilston, where milord of Derwentwater was awaiting Colonel Storm.

The name roused thoughts, and Mally gave herself to recalling what she knew of him. The Earl of Derwentwater, when he had proposed that toast at the rout, had distinctly said that the man without a name, whom they were to know as Colonel Storm, was coming from France. He was to have been at the rout, but he had been delayed by alertness at the ports; so he was evidently of importance. Whoever he was, he would have arrived by now, and he would have been to Lady Chandler's. Now he was on his way north, with orders from the King over the Water, and no doubt he was well named. He would indeed bring storm, and probably ruin too; but perhaps not to himself. He would not be a beginner. He would be a sly and seasoned plotter, who would know how to stay in secret, and he would not come on the stage while his puppets worked the play. He would perhaps be back in France when his storm broke out in England.

Mally's thoughts grew harder as they cleared. What of these others, these muddled country gentlemen who were to do his work? She lifted her head, and saw John and Mr. Peaver jogging their untroubled way; she thought of Jack Harvey and his jovial noisy father; and she remembered their talk and indiscretions. They were not the stuff that conspirators should be; and they had even let Black William hear words through a parlour door. That reminded her of Henry, and the cold warning he had given. There was Sir John Chandler in London; he was buying wine, and listening.

She roused from her broodings and spoke to Jane.

"This Colonel Storm," she said. "He's a puppet-master, isn't he?"

"With Peaver as the Merry Andrew. He's fool enough."

"I'm serious. Do you think Colonel Storm knows what sort of men these are?"

"Does anybody, except us?"

"Perhaps he'd go elsewhere if he found out."

"He's bound to find out."

"But perhaps too late. I'm wondering if he could be told."

"You don't think he'll ask us, do you?"

"No. It—it was your Jack I was thinking of."

"Now what——"

"I'm thinking that we need some help. A man might say what we can't."

"I expect he could." There was a cold bitterness in Jane's tone, as if her thoughts were hard. "But he seems to be pulled into this himself. He was at that meeting last week, and I suppose he'll be at this one tomorrow."

"That's what we must see to."

"How?"

"Ye-es." Mally let that wait for a moment, and then her tone changed. "Jane, I haven't seen this house of the Harveys'."

"I know you haven't."

"Then just remember it. I expect to be entertained, and shown the country. So do you."

"Do I?"

"What have we got new horses for? Certainly we expect to be shown the country, with proper escort. I shall be slighted if we're not, and I shall say so."

"Oh!" A brightening of the eye showed that Jane had understood. "You mean Jack as escort? You seem to have some wits in you."

"One of us needs to have. What's this place?"

They were dropping down a hill, and below them was a sweep of level ground, green and lush, with the river running through it. The sun was behind them now, so they must be riding north, and the river was flowing to the east, broad across their path. Across it, nestling on the northern bank, was a grey little town, low, and old, and mellow. By contrast, a fine stone bridge soared across the river, and was surely new and modern.

"Corbridge," said Jane. "Our only hope of dinner."

"What's beyond it?"

"Something you haven't seen. But look—up on the hill."

They were coming down to the bridge, and Jane was pointing to her left; and there, high above the river, the grey keep of an ancient castle could be seen. A modern house rose beside it, set about with trees.

"Dilston."

Jane spoke briefly, and Mally's attention was keen. The

house had size and dignity, as befitted the seat of a nobleman who had wealth and place, and perhaps some royal blood. But it was Stuart blood; and because of it he might soon be seen at the head of rebellion. That would be expected of him, and suddenly Mally shivered as she thought of what his end might be. He had talked and danced with her, and he had shown a charm that lingered warm and bright; and perhaps that, too, derived from his Stuart blood.

She turned her eyes hurriedly away, and she gave attention to the bridge as they walked the horses carefully across. Then there was an inn that would give them the dinner they hoped for, and would bait the horses too; but they had to wait for dinner while the men made sure of the horses. In this country, said Jane, the horses came first.

They walked through the little town while they waited, and in the churchyard was an old stone tower, squat and massive, set apart from the church. It seemed to lack windows, and Mally asked what it was.

"It's a pele," said Jane.

"A what?"

"A pele. This wasn't a safe place in the older days, when the raiders came out of Redesdale, and the Scots from beyond the border. Men liked a refuge then. You'll see another before the day's out, and bigger. Wait and see."

After dinner the horses had some work to do. They were hardly a mile from the town before they were climbing steeply. Up and to the north went the road, straight as a tightened bow string, hard and narrow; but the ruts were few, and never deep, and under the dust the hooves were finding something solid. It was a road of a new sort, and Mally was moved to ask about it.

"No," said Jane. "It's old. It's about sixteen hundred years old."

"What!"

"Yes, it is. The Romans made this road, and they put down the stones we're riding on. This is the Dere Street. Ask Peaver. He can talk for hours on it."

Mally did, and Mr. Peaver's face lit with delight that she should have an interest in this. It seemed as if he were indeed going to talk for an hour about it.

The Romans, he said, had indeed built the road. It was
their road from York. It was called the Dere Street, and it ran
past Corbridge to the north. Did she know there had been a
Roman town at Corbridge?

He went on and on, and Mally listened carefully. She was
interested in this queer old road which seemed to be built on
stone instead of on mud and clay. It was so much better than
any road she knew that she was still marvelling at it when they
came to the top of the rise; and then she saw that they had
climbed to a great high ridge that seemed to run east and west,
mile after mile, blocking the way to the north. Behind her was
the valley of the Tyne, also east and west. Before her, a short
fringe of trees seemed to run with the ridge; and by a gap in
the trees, where the road ran through them, a horseman waited.
He gave a flourish of his hat, and came trotting down the slope
to meet them; and another half-minute showed that he was
Jack Harvey.

He was wholly unchanged, still with the quiet air, the face
that seemed to stay in repose, and he greeted them in the same
quiet voice.

"I thought I'd guide you in," he said. "It's a poor track to
the house."

He ranged himself with Jane, and Mr. Peaver turned in
his saddle and beckoned to Mally as they approached the line
of trees that ran across the road; and now she saw that there
was more to it than trees. There was masonry here, grey and
heavy, cluttered with moss and fern, running straight and true
in line from west to east. It was out of all reason on this wind-
swept moor, and Mr. Peaver halted.

"That," he said, "is the Wall."

She saw now that it had indeed the look of a wall, or of
what had once been a wall. But it had been of a size exceed-
ing any wall she had ever known, and she turned to him for
explanation.

"No." He was smiling into her puzzled face. "It is no
common wall. It is the wall the Romans built and it's nearly
as old as the road."

It was of very varying height. It had parts that were full six
feet high, and parts that were not six inches, but all, as she
could now see, had once been a continuing whole, and perhaps

some ten feet thick; and exactly where the road ran through it, it opened out to a hollow square.

"You see?" Mr. Peaver was smiling at her again. "This is where the Dere Street ran through the Wall, and there was a little fort here. Do you see the gateways?"

"But what was it for?" she asked.

"Defence." Mr. Peaver's answer came promptly. "This was the northern frontier of Rome, and beyond it were the barbarians. So the Wall ran all the way across England. Do you note the ditch?"

Again he was pointing. The ditch was some twenty feet beyond the wall, skirting its northern face, and even now, choked with weed and earth, it had her staring in surprise at the size of it. It was some ten yards wide and ten feet deep, and all of it hewn from the living rock. It ran round the little fort, and was interrupted only where the road went through.

"A useful ditch," said Mr. Peaver.

"Yes." Again she was looking round her, marvelling. "I suppose all this was useful once."

"It's useful still," said Jack Harvey.

"But how?"

She had not known that he was so close to her, but there he was, with an amused Jane at his side. He answered her clearly.

"For the one thing, it makes us a road. You may ride all the way from Newcastle along the Wall, and it's the best way there is. In parts you ride on the Wall, and in parts beside it, but you get along. It wouldn't take a coach, of course, but for a horse it's fair going."

"I see. But why is the Wall so broken?"

"That's from its other use. It builds our houses. It's the quarry we dig in when stones are needed. And there's plenty of it. There are still some stones to take."

"And when they're gone?"

"We'll need to quarry our own."

"Is there more about this dam'-fool Wall?" John had come edging forward impatiently. "You can show this Wall another day. It will still be here tomorrow, won't it?"

"I expect it will, sir. Let's move then."

They moved briskly, trotting through the ancient gateway,

northward by the same hard-metalled road. Jack had the lead now, and Mally was watching him thoughtfully. Perhaps there was a chance here for what she wanted.

She spoke with a careful lightness.

"You'll remember what he said, won't you?"

"What was that?"

"You can show us the Wall another day. It will still be here tomorrow."

"You wish to see it?"

"I do. So does Jane."'

Her quick glance at Jane was imperative, and Jane made no mistake.

"Yes," she said quickly. "You may show us more of the Wall—tomorrow."

"There's a meeting tomorrow."

"Then you won't be at it."

"I've no wish to be. But——"

"You can't be." Mally cut in sharply, to give support. "I'm a stranger and a guest, and I need looking after. I'll tell them all so, if I have to."

"You're growing like Jane. I'll do what I can, though. Now here's where we turn off."

The road was dropping now. In the distance they could see it rise again, soaring over the distant hills; but here, to the left, a narrow track ran off, and Jack led along it. It went curving along the side of the hill, and soon it brought them to an oddity of a house, a shape that Mally had never seen before. The nearer part of it was a great square tower, solid in mortared stone, and of size enough to be a house itself. It had turrets at its corners, and a door half-way up the wall. It was grim and forbidding, its tiny windows high in the wall, with a sheer sweep of stone below. At its side was a newer house, seeming to be built against it, and having some looks of comfort. But it would always be an afterthought; the grim square tower rose above it, and dominated.

"That's the bigger pele," said Jane. "It's what all the houses here used to be."

"But why?"

"They had to be." Jack was answering her now. "That's stables now, and storerooms, but my great-grandfather lived

in it. He had to. He was a deal too close to Redesdale to be safe
without it."

"Jane spoke of Redesdale. Where is it?"

"Up to the north-west there, and it isn't safe yet. There's
every kind of thief and cattle-snatcher there. To this day they
won't have a Redesdale lad as apprentice in Newcastle. They
say he comes of a thieving brood, and he'll hark back when he
can. And they're probably right." The amusement seemed to
have left him as he looked to the grey high tower. "In great-
grandfather's day they didn't stay in Redesdale. They came
out raiding and murdering. Hence the peles. You'll find them
all through this country."

There was a garden now, set around the house and pele,
with a decent gate and a curving path to the door. They went
jingling through, and he led them to the pele, where the stables
were. It was Mr. Peaver who helped Mally to dismount, and
there was a light in his eye as he pointed to the fine trimmed
stones that made the pele. Mally looked, and could not mistake
his meaning. These were stones from the Wall. Their size
and shape left no doubt of that; and at the corner of the pele
there was one he pointed to in triumph. It was big and flat,
and it had lettering cut upon it. It was built sideways into the
pele, and she had to lean her head to read it : D— M— ALAE
SABINIANAE MILITES CVI PRAEST——

It ended abruptly, where the later mason had trimmed it,
and Mr. Peaver chuckled as he watched her puzzled face.

"But what does it mean?" she asked.

"To the Gods and the Departed Dead! The soldiers——"

Whatever it told them of soldiers had to wait. Will Harvey,
boisterous as ever, came round the corner of the pele in noisy
greeting. He was seemingly pleased with life just now.

"Aye," he was saying. "We meet the Scots tomorrow.
Milord's to be there in person, and he hopes for Colonel
Storm. Then on Friday our friends come here."

"Aye, aye."

John was acquiescing, and Mr. Peaver was looking pleased.
Mally steadied her breath and spoke out boldly.

"What of Jane and me, sir? We're not to be left forgotten?"

"Now who the Devil should forget you, lass?" He sounded

in high good humour. "I'm not so old as that, and Jack isn't."

"Now that's just it, sir. We're hoping he'll show us something of these parts. I've not seen them, and I wish to. You'll not command him to your meeting?"

"Oh, that's it, is it? And the dog put you up to say it, hey?" He was shaking with laughter now. "He likes your company better than his father's. I'd ha' done too, at his age."

"Aye, sir. But——"

"Don't spoil it, lass. But you may have him for the day."

"Thank you." She was smiling in quick relief. "We'll remember it, Jane and I."

"You'll remember the old fool's soft, you mean. Aye, aye —but you must be at the inn by afternoon. You're wanted there."

"Inn, sir? I——"

"Aye. It's where we meet." Quite suddenly he had sobered, and now he was looking at her gravely. "Milord's been asking of you."

"*Who*, sir?"

"Milord of Derwentwater. He remembers you, it seems, and he commands a word with you." He paused, and his eyes were steadily on hers. "I've a notion that Colonel Storm has some message for you."

CHAPTER XVIII

THE INN BY THE RIVER

THERE was nothing to do but accept it; and if Mally had some doubts Jane dealt shortly with them. They found themselves sharing a bedroom, which gave them the chance to talk in private, and Jane was forthright. His Lordship, she said, was of almost royal eminence here, and his commands were almost royal commands. If he sent for Mally, then Mally would have to go; and that was that.

Apparently it was; but Mally's thoughts kept circling round it, doubt blending with excitement. This word of a message could surely mean only one man. Colonel Storm would certainly have been to Lady Chandler's when he arrived from France. He was a Jacobite agent, direct from St. Germains; and Captain Marriott, as she had now very little doubt, was another. They would surely have met in London. They would probably have a duty to meet; and she could therefore hardly doubt whose message this was. It would be an obvious opportunity; and the Captain had no doubt relied on the Earl of Derwentwater to find where Mally was, and to bring her in touch with Colonel Storm. His Lordship seemed to be doing exactly that.

It was certainly exciting; and it revived some vivid memories of the Coronation rout, of her days in her own grey bedroom after it, and of the letter that had been smuggled in. But it also brought some doubts. His Lordship and Colonel Storm were between them the leaders of this plot, and she had no wish to help it. She had set herself to hinder it, not to help it; and to hinder it might be difficult if she were indebted to them both. It could be awkward, and possibly embarrassing. She said so, rather incautiously.

"And who," said Jane, "is Captain Marriott?"

That was disconcerting. She had spoken only in general terms of her departure from Lady Chandler's, and now she had to be a little more precise. Jane's eyebrows seemed to quiver.

"He pursues you, does he? Now I thought it was Dick Chandler who——"

"Jane!"

"All right, all right! But what worries you?"

"I've told you. If they——"

"They won't talk politics to you. If they do, it's easy."

"How?"

"Just look lovesick. Too stupid to be anything else. They'll probably believe you."

"Thanks. It happens that I'm not lovesick."

"Then don't be silly. You ought to be feeling flattered. Most women here would be if his Lordship sent for them. You probably are."

"Well, I suppose in a way——"

"Exactly. Now are you ready yet? We might learn more of this at supper."

They did learn a little, though it was hardly about Colonel Storm. Will Harvey held forth gustily throughout the meal. The meeting tomorrow, he said, would be at a quiet inn some three or four miles away. From the north of the county there would be a Mr. Forster, with the Reverend Mr. Patten; from Scotland there would be some emissaries of the Earl of Mar; and from Dilston there would be his Lordship and Colonel Storm. It had been thought wise to meet at a lonely inn, since there were some men of rank involved; but his Lordship and the Colonel would have to leave by four o'clock. Mally should therefore be at the inn a little after three; but if that were kept to, Jack might escort the ladies wherever they pleased. Will chuckled noisily, slapped his son on the back, and said that from the look of the sky tonight it would be a windy day.

He proved a good prophet. The morrow was exactly that, a day of blue sky and blowing cloud, with a kicking wind from the north to set the dry leaves whirling and the dark cloud-shadows sweeping. It was a day alive with movement, when every green thing quivered, and nothing could be still. Jack said it would be windier before it was done, and a scarf tied over hats would help to keep them on; and Jane snorted, and asked if he thought she was as green as a salad.

But she heeded him, for all that. They let the elders ride out first, and then they followed at leisure. Jane's russet riding-habit was enriched by the new hat and the yellow boots she had bought in Newcastle; and she had contrived some yellow plumes for the hat, to match the boots. She looked sturdy and gay enough at Jack Harvey's side, and Mally had to remind herself that this was not her day. The others would wish to talk apart, and it would be her own turn when they came to the inn. For her appearance she was modestly satisfied, and she thought she had spent Black William's guineas well. The mulberry serge looked rich in the sunlight, and brighter for the darker cloak. She had soft black boots, and a wide black beaver hat, with two white plumes to flutter in it; and she was admiring these in the mirror when Jane arrived behind her and firmly tied a scarf over the hat and under her chin. It might spoil the looks of it, said Jane, but it was better than losing the hat; and Jack was not such a fool as she might think.

He led them out by the way they had come yesterday, and soon they were on the hard stones of the Dere Street, trotting up the sunlit road towards the fringe of trees that lined the ancient Wall. Mally lingered behind to let the others talk, and the mood of excitement came to her again, born perhaps of the sun and the sailing clouds. Her thoughts were running quickly now, guessing at this message that was to come to her; and her memory was keen of Captain Marriott, who had kept his word and had not forgotten her. If she had hoped for it she had not truly expected it. Her thoughts had played with it in quiet moments; but in the waking day she had placed him in the past, in Lady Chandler's world, which she would never see again. Now, it seemed, something was coming from that world, coming to this northern world of wind and sun, and coal, and Black William.

The thought struck oddly. It recalled her to things; and above her a white cloud turned to grey as it passed beneath the sun. Its shadow went sweeping up the road, killing the whiteness, taking the gleam from the dazzling dust, and suddenly she was in gloom to match the shadow. Black William was real; and he did not fit with Jacobites at a lonely inn, with the charming Earl, and Colonel Storm. A cold light was playing on her thoughts; and suddenly, in one cold flash, she saw what a deadly game these men were playing, with their plots and their meetings and their intent of treason. But it was real, not a game, and William understood reality.

She pushed that hurriedly aside, seeking anything that would clear her mind of it; and from nowhere the picture came of Dick, quiet and friendly, here with the others this day to make the four. She told herself it was silly, but the image stayed and teased, and it was pleasing. She looked up the road to Jane, riding with Jack at her side; and suddenly she was lonely.

She shook out her bridle, and on the horse that had come from William she went jogging after the others. They were waiting where the road ran through the Wall, and here the wind was a solid thing. The Wall, as she now saw, ran along a ridge. It clung to the highest ground there was, and the wind from the north was sweeping up to it with exultant force, buffeting and roaring in a style that made her glad of the scarf round her hat. Not a leaf was left on the trees, and even the dust had been blown from the half-made track. But it was clean and sweet on this forgotten frontier. There was a cheerfulness here; and then the grey cloud streamed from the sun, and all was a dazzling light, a chequer of blue sky and green grass, dotted with moving patches where the dark cloud-shadows ran. Mally felt better.

They rode slowly along the line of the Wall; and Mally, in a mood of conscience now, did what she could to keep apart and leave the others free. She revived the pretence of an interest in the Wall, and she lagged behind to look at it; and little by little the pretence became reality. The thing took her mind, and she let it. At least it kept out other thoughts. She loitered along, seldom keeping to the track, and moving as the whim took her. It was a manner that suited the Wall, for the Wall, too, had its whims and moods. Here it stood a dozen courses high, and here it had been pillaged to its bare foundations. The great ditch was deep and sharp, and a litter of stones by its rim might have been of yesterday. There was another ditch, too, behind the Wall, and what it had been for she could not guess; but there it was, and running near it was a track that had smooth tight stones under a sweep of grass. Again she knew nothing of it, but it made good riding; and looking for it kept her occupied, and her thoughts from other things.

Somewhere on the heights they stopped to eat what they had in their saddle-bags. They sat in the lee of the Wall, facing south and with the full sun on them, and now the ground was falling. The Wall was dipping steeply here, dipping to a wide flat valley where a river flowed, and Jack explained it crisply. This was a branch of the Tyne, flowing down from the north, and the Romans had once had a bridge to take their Wall across. But that was long forgotten, and now there was another bridge, a little way up-stream. This too was old. It was three centuries old, decayed and none too safe, but it was the only bridge there was; and hard against it, just across the river, was the inn where they were to meet milord.

They lingered till the sun gave warning of the time, and then they picked a careful way down, grateful for the age-old track that seemed to march with the Wall. They came to the flat green valley, and the Wall struck straight across it, and beyond the river they could see it soaring on. But here at the foot of the slope, running down the valley, and passing easily through the flattened ruin of the Wall, was a broad trodden way that could hardly be called a road. It was a way trodden in grass and mud by countless hooves, and again Jack told them why. This was a noted river-crossing. Three miles away, near Hexham, there was a crossing by boat, but this was the only bridge, and the pack-horses and cattle droves must come this way. This trodden track took them to Hexham, where they found the Newcastle road.

It was soft and sticky going, and they kept to the grass outside it, helping to make it wider; and soon another track joined it from the north, from Redesdale of evil name. But the main track curved to the river, where a weather-beaten bridge rose steeply on four high arches. They crossed it warily, noting the crumbling stone and the pieces flaking off, and the track turned away at once, following the river bank; but that was not their concern. For here, nestling under the bridge, and facing the bend of the track, was the inn.

It hardly looked an inn. It was of no pretensions, low and

simple, with thick stone walls and a slated roof. It had tiny windows and a blackened door, with no sign hanging to tell its name. It looked what it surely was, an ale-house for the drovers and carriers who must use this way. It was remote and lonely, an ale-house by a river, set beyond the Wall, and it was surely nothing more. No man of rank would ever think of using it; which was perhaps why an Earl was using it this day. The thought of him was keen as Mally came slowly down the bridge; this was far indeed from the gilded salon, and Lady Chandler's rout.

They turned their horses to the patch of river gravel that made an approach, and they knew that the meeting must have ended. There were horses on the gravel, with a fellow holding them, and by the door a group of men were taking leave. Will Harvey was among them, with John at his side, and the tall figure of Mr. Peaver could be seen behind him. Will came bustling forward as he saw them, and he was as boisterous as ever.

"You're no more than in time," he said. "His Lordship's been asking, but I promised you'd be here. Now——"

He had seized Mally's stirrup, and she slipped carefully to the ground, but she was given no chance to think. Jack was already helping Jane, and then they were both at her side.

"Now for it," said Will heartily. "His Lordship waits, and that's not proper. Do ye come with us, Jack?"

"It depends on Jane, sir. I don't know what she wishes."

"She's coming." Jane was answering trenchantly for herself. "I've not been presented to an Earl yet, even if Mally has, and——"

A roar of laughter from Will made an end of that, and his one hand slapped her shoulder while his other pushed at Mally, and in high good humour he propelled them both to the door. Jack came quietly behind, and from the group of departing men uncle John came with them.

They passed under the weathered lintel, where the green moss clung to the stone, and there was a gloom that was all but dark after the brightness of the afternoon. Before them was a low stair, and at the foot of it a candle burned. There was a door to the left and a door to the right, and that was all. Mally halted, confused and uncertain, and it was Jane who had wit enough to step behind her and untie the scarf from her hat; and at that moment there was a creak of hinges to their left. She turned, to see the door open and lights within; and slim and straight in the doorway was the Earl of Derwentwater, as lithe and graceful as he had been in the glitter of the rout.

He did not glitter now. He was discreetly in homespuns, brown and simple, and nothing about him hinted at his rank. But he was the same man still, as suave and charming, and he did not wait for Mally to make her curtsey. He was bowing to her at once, and suddenly he had taken her hand and had carried it lightly to his lips. She steadied her breath, and from behind her she heard Jane's gasp of surprise.

"Madam——" He was speaking in his crisp clear tone. "I must hope I have not put you to trouble today."

"You could not do that, milord. The honour is wholly——"

"Mine—and another's also." He was smiling as he saw her forehead pucker. "There's one whom you'll have heard of, a Colonel Storm. It was at the Colonel's asking that I begged that you should come. He was urgent for it."

"Milord, I——"

"He may speak of it himself, and say what he seeks. Here he is."

There was the scrape of a shoe on the boards behind him, and a man came quickly to the door. His Lordship stood aside; and Mally was speechless, while her breath fluttered. The man came a step forward, into the full light of the candle, and not a doubt was left. He was Captain Marriott.

CHAPTER XIX

WIND ON THE BRIDGE

In the moment that followed it seemed to Mally that time stood still; or even that time had blurred, and was running back on itself. There was a past that was as close and vivid as the present, and there was this present too, unreal and fantastic, with the quality of a dream. It was remote, having nothing to do with her. She stood at the centre of it, and had no part in it. Dimly she was aware of the others, of Jane's jerk of the head and Jack's unnatural stillness; yet all was remote, and she could find no word to say.

It was milord who broke the spell, and he tried to take it easily.

"I need not, I think, present Colonel Storm to Miss Lawley. You'll have met before. But, Mr. Harvey——" He was addressing himself to Jack, whom he seemed to know. "Permit me: Colonel Storm——"

It was an affable lead, and Jack was quick to follow it by presenting Jane. Mally moved back against the stair, away from the centre of this, and she was in some manner collected when Captain Marriott turned to her again.

"Madam——" He was speaking very quietly. "I did never doubt that we should meet again, but I did not think of so small an inn as this, and set in such a desert."

The smile that had made him known through the routs and card rooms was with him now, and Mally felt herself unsteady and her forehead wet. The inn was reeking hot, as if there had been fire and tobacco for hours while the men had talked, and she had to press for support against the stair behind.

"Steady!" He was suddenly at her side. "Are you not well?"

"It's hot in here. That's all. I——"

"It certainly is." He seized on it sharply. "A turn in the air will help. Permit me——"

He had taken her in charge before she understood. He tied her cloak for her, he snatched his own from somewhere, and he was shepherding her to the door before she could speak. The others stood quietly, and there was proof that they had noticed something in the care with which they made no comments.

The wind from the north was cold. It set her cloak fluttering and her ears tingling, and it was good medicine. It cleared her mind and blew the last trace of mistiness from her; and suddenly on the wings of it a spatter of rain came down, chilling and wetting. She turned to it, holding her face to the splashing drops, and she almost laughed in relief. She knew now where she was. She was in the far far north, by a river beyond the Wall; and it was not Lady Chandler's rout.

"You get wet."

He was solicitous at her side, and she almost laughed in his face.

"Does it matter—here?"

"No." His answer came back promptly. "Hence this."

He was tying his cloak, and he was smiling grimly at it. It was an old-fashioned horse cloak, full and long, and suddenly she was smiling too at the sight of him wrapped like this. In London it would have been a long tight-waisted coat, the lightest of swords, a beribboned cane and a gold-laced hat. A change had come to Captain Marriott; and abruptly a change came to Mally's thoughts as amusement left her. Was he Captain Marriott? Or Colonel Storm?

The rain-spatter passed, whirled away by the wind, and for a moment she was intent on the sky again. There was wet sunlight now, and grey cloud driving, and she saw that the wind had veered. It was almost from the north-east, colder than before, and becoming gusty. There would be rain in plenty before the night was done.

His arm touched hers, turning her, and she went without protest. They walked to the river-bridge, and it was he that spoke first.

"Did you have my letter? I sent it to your aunt's after that—that rout."

"Yes."

The mention of it softened her thoughts, and she turned

to the sky again as she went slowly up the arch of the bridge. At the top she leaned against the parapet, with her face still to the wind.

"I don't understand," she said sharply. "Who are you?"

"Tony Marriott. It's very simple, really." He had to speak more loudly now, with the wind roaring over the bridge, and for a moment he was looking down at the white froth in the black and tumbling river. "What was that fellow's name?"

"Willoughby. You hit him."

"I had to. But then I was out of fashion. I was very much out of fashion. I was thought unfit for gentlemen to play with. I wasn't welcome at the tables."

"Because of—me, do you mean?"

A clatter of horses broke through the wind before he could answer, and she saw a string of riders coming at the bridge, his Lordship, Mr. Peaver, John, Will Harvey and some others. She pressed back to give them way, and on the high crest of the arch his Lordship stopped.

"You'll forgive us if we do not stay for you, Colonel?"

"Aye, milord. You'll permit me to come later?"

"I'm sure you're well engaged. Madam, your servant always!"

His hat swept as he rode away, and then it was John who stopped.

"Jack says he'll see you safe home. He's down yonder with Jane. Remember the light's going."

He went hurrying after the others, and Mally watched him go. She turned again to Captain Marriott.

"You were telling me something?"

"Yes." For a moment he looked down again at the dark tumbling water, and his eyes came back to hers. "What work did you think I did in London?"

"You lived by gaming, didn't you? Or so it was said."

"Yes." He looked steadily at her. "Do you know what a Non-juror parson is?"

"I do. But why?"

"My father was one."

"What!"

She spoke in blank surprise. That the polished Captain Marriott, skilled with the dice and cards, should be a parson's son, was a new thought to her.

"But he was." His voice came again, firm and convincing. "He was chaplain to—let us just say to a nobleman—who followed King James when he went away in '88."

"Yes?"

"My father went with his patron. There was nothing else he could do, for he would not swear allegiance to King William. So he went to France. I was born there, the next year."

"Oh! But what then?"

His shoulders lifted, almost helplessly, and for a moment he looked down again to the black water, blacker now in the fading light. Mally saw the darkness of it, and then she looked to the inn, and saw Jane and Jack Harvey standing by the door, as if they were waiting. She looked to the sky, and saw that the gold had gone, and it was all a deepening grey. Certainly it was time to go.

"It was a mad life." He was speaking again, and it set her turning hurriedly. "Nobody had any money. The nobleman hadn't much, and his chaplain hardly any. But we played the forms of royalty. A puppet King with a puppet Court, and we were the Court, or the fringe of it. Very much the fringe, I fear."

"Why?"

"Because my father was a chaplain, and he was not of their Church. That put us out of what chances there were. I was a soldier with them for a time, but there was no hope of advancement."

"Did you wish to be a soldier?"

"I wished advancement. They were kind to us, you understand. We had admission everywhere, but no employment." His shoulders shrugged again. "A mad life, as I've said. No money and the best society."

"Then what did you do?"

"I took to what I found. I learned more about gaming than anything else. There was no lack of that."

"Exiles?"

"Yes. They'd nothing else to do. I came to support myself by it. And then my father died, and truly he died for the King. That life had killed him."

"Ye-es. But what then?"

"Nothing—for a time. I learned some more of gaming. I wanted some proper work, and in the end it was offered."

"What?"

"What you know of. I was to call myself Captain, and come to London. Introductions would be arranged."

"Oh!" A memory stirred her suddenly. "We did ask, all of us, how you came from nowhere, and were at once in the best houses."

"That's how it was. I was there for King James. Was nothing more whispered of me than the play?"

"I never asked."

"Did you not hear that I was of some repute? That men would visit the house where I was known to play?"

"There were some who came to my aunt's because you were there."

"And some of them were desired there for—other purposes. Mr. Willoughby was one."

"What purposes?"

"The King's. Sometimes a man could be persuaded to the cause if he were brought to the house. Also——" For a moment he hesitated. "Sometimes a man could be better persuaded if he had lost more than he could pay."

"Oh!" She stared at him unbelieving. "You lent yourself to *that*?"

"I lent myself to the King." He corrected her firmly, and his voice took a sharper note. "I came to serve the King, and it was not for me to choose the work. I did what I had the skill to do."

"But——"

"It was needful. A King in the dark cannot be served in the light of day. I served as I could, and truly, I was of service to the King."

The wind blurred the tone of it, but she saw the lift of his head, and she knew he had a pride in this. For a moment she turned away, and she saw Jack Harvey in the road outside the inn, with Jane at his side. They were hatted and cloaked, as if ready to go; and Jack waved his hand and pointed to the western sky. It was hint enough. The sun was down. It was dusk, and would be dark within the hour; and decidedly it was time to go.

She turned to tell him so, and he had already seen.

"I know," he said. "It's getting late. But there's just this. That trouble with Willoughby in the card room—you see how it ended my use? There was scandal. Men would not play with me, and I could no longer be of use that way."

"Yes. I understand. Now I think we ought to——"

"Not yet." He had her quickly by the elbows, and his voice was urgent. "Haven't you understood? I waited there in hopes, trying to see you, and I couldn't. Then they offered me another work." He almost shook her, as if he would make her listen. "It was only in London that the scandal worked. Out of London I still could serve. There was a man new come from France, and I had known him there. He had the King's orders, and was to be known as Colonel Storm."

"I heard some talk of him, at a rout, and——"

"Never mind that now." There was an urgency in his tone as he cut her short. "I could no longer do my work, but he was as skilled with the cards as I. It was thought we could do each other's work, and it was arranged so. He took my place, and I his. I was to call myself Colonel Storm, and carry orders——"

"You carry more than orders. It's treason too."

"Listen!" There was no doubt about the shake he gave her now. "When they first spoke of this change, I almost begged for it. Do you see why?"

"No."

"Because I knew you had been sent to your uncle's. I bribed Lady Chandler's maid for that. And I knew that if I were in the North I could find you somehow, find you and talk with you. Now do you see it?"

"Oh!"

"And I *have* found you. When I learned that your uncle was among those I was to meet today, I thought it a working of God. I asked his Lordship——"

"To send for me?"

"To contrive that we should meet. I could not instruct him how he should do it. If that seemed a deceit, forgive it."

"Yes."

She was too dazed to take in the whole of this, or to know what her true thoughts were. She needed a respite now, and a chance to think, and the excuse for it was more than ready. She looked at the inn again, and the horses had been led out and were waiting.

"We'll talk another day," she said. "It's much too late——"

"It's not too late for you to say one word. It couldn't be."

"Now—now what does that mean?"

His tone had changed, and so had hers. He had a softer urgency now, that could hardly be mistaken, and she had responded with bland ignorance. Her shoulders had gone back and she watched him carefully.

"I've told you of how I came to the North, and why. Is there no word in answer?"

"Answer?" She looked him over coolly. "I suppose I should felicitate you."

"On what?"

"Safe journey. Happy ending."

"Will it be happy?"

"Is it for me to say?"

"It's for none other. Will it be?"

"Now that's difficult. I must think of it."

Something had happened to Mally. She was holding him off with a lightness that had never been hers in London, and she was detached enough to know it. She was pleased at it, and she leaned farther back against the bridge as she spoke again.

"It would be difficult if there were only one gentleman to deal with. But when there are two——"

"Two?"

She heard the crackle of it, and hastily she pushed away a thought of Dick Chandler. That was not what she had meant, and she kept her voice steady.

"There's Captain Marriott, and there's Colonel Storm. I hardly know them apart, and the other might overhear."

"You little minx! Do you take to teasing?"

"But I have to think of this. The Colonel's important, I'm told."

Then the Fates intervened. She was pleased with her answer, and she tossed her head defiantly. She tossed it backward, and with her mind on other things she did not remember that Jane had removed the scarf from her hat. The wind remembered for her. It came in a roaring gust, as if it had seen in that tilting brim an offered sacrifice. There was a sharp cry of dismay as she felt the snatch, and then the hat was gone. She whipped round, and the wind roared gleefully through her hair, pulling it to ragged streamers. The hat went soaring, black against the darkening sky, and then down in a steepening arc till it hit the water and went floating and tossing down the stream, its white plumes fluttering still. It was hard to see, against the black and white of the water, but Tony Marriott kept his eyes firmly on it. Then he spoke sharply.

"It's moving to the bank. Come on——"

It was first things first, and Mally did not argue. He went at a run from the bridge, and she was at his heels as he went scrambling down a grassy slope to the bank of the river. It was darker here, and she knew that dusk had come, but he gave her no time to think. This was soft ground, with the wet grass squelching under their boots, and his heels flung a spatter of mud in her face as he broke into a run again. She heard him laugh as he leapt across a muddy pool, and then he was ahead of her, running fast, and she heard him shout, though the wind blew his words away. This was a new Captain Marriott, years younger than the assured gentleman of the gaming rooms, and he seemed to delight in the wind and water.

She hurried after him, and in front of her she saw the stream divide, as though there were an island here. There were trees by the bank, and one was a great gnarled willow, with its boughs low across the water. He was scrambling out on it, and he pointed exultantly. She had to look hard in the dim grey light, and then she saw that the thick low bough put branches down to the water, and that tangled in these was her hat, crumpled and sodden, with the water lapping at it. He went out for it gaily, and Lady Chandler would not have known him now. He had to lie flat on the branch to get it, clinging with hand and knees while he lowered himself to grasp with the other hand. But he achieved it, and he came scrambling back in triumph, with the bedraggled hat in his hand. Mally reached for it eagerly, but he came leaping to the grass and held it teasingly from her.

"Now——" He lifted it higher as she tried to take it. "You may give me that word of welcome."

"Let me see it."

"Let me hear it."

"Oh!" She tried to grasp it, and he swung it away. "You're very welcome, then."

"When I bring your hat?"

"It's all muddy."

"So are you. Here——"

Suddenly his arm swung round her, taking the hat behind her back. She had both hands on it instantly, and he let it go. Then, while she had still both hands behind her, he had her by the shoulders, and before she knew what he was about he had drawn her against him and had kissed her confidently.

She was never quite sure about the moments that followed. She knew that he did it again. She knew that the wind tore at her hair again and blew it against his cheek. She knew that she even dropped the hat. But no clear thought came until he eased his hold of her, and let her balance on her own feet. Then she saw that he was laughing.

"Do you see?"

He was looking up-stream as he spoke, and Mally turned hastily. She saw the bridge as a high black arch against the sky, and on it were two black figures, standing by the parapet in attentive watch. Mally needed only one guess.

"Lord!" she said. "It's Jane."

"Is it really?" She saw him shaking with amusement. "Then perhaps we'd better go."

They scrambled up the slope to the foot of the bridge, and Jane was in a fine good humour.

"We came to look," she said.

"My hat blew off."

"So we noted."

Jack Harvey came lightly down the bridge and spoke more briskly.

"You look a little wet," he said. "There's mulled ale at

the inn for both of you, and then there are horses. You'll be riding our way, Colonel—past Stagshaw?"

"I think so. I'm for Dilston."

The two men went strolling up the bridge together, seemingly in easy talk, and Jane looked Mally up and down, at the mud and the disordered hair.

"Well, well!" she said at length. "You do make the most of time."

"Jane! I——"

"If he'll kiss you when you look like that, he should do anything when you've been tidied up. I'll take you in hand myself."

"You needn't. And it's true. My hat did blow off."

"Providential," said Jane.

CHAPTER XX

DIS MANIBUS

It was not to be expected that Jane would let that pass without some questions.

There were some trying moments during the evening; for John and the others had naturally noticed that Mally had seemed to know Colonel Storm. But her quick explanation that she had met him at Lady Chandler's house was plausible as well as true, and to her relief they accepted it easily. It was, of course, in the Colonel as the Jacobite agent that they were interested, and she was able to add that she had not even known that he was that. So all was well, and she passed through the evening without embarrassment—until bedtime.

That, of course, was Jane's moment, for she was sharing a room with Mally. She came to the point as soon as the door was shut on the outer world.

"I'll suppose from the way you fell on him that this Colonel is your Captain Marriott?"

"I didn't fall on him. I——"

"We'll say he fell on you, then. He seemed willing enough. Who is he?"

"He's Captain Marriott."

"Also Colonel Storm. A most accomplished fellow. What brought him to the North? No—I'm serious." There was a change of tone which Mally recognized. "It's all very well with you and your hat and a willow tree, but he's also Colonel Storm. Or is he?"

"Now what——"

"I mean, is he just pretending to be Colonel Storm, while he comes here to pull your hair about, or——"

"He didn't. I wouldn't——"

"You looked as if you wouldn't. But I'm still serious. Is he making a plot? Is he in earnest about that?"

"I—I don't know."

"And you probably don't care. Perhaps I shouldn't,

either. But I'm afraid we must. Was nothing said to give you his mood on that?"

"He——" Mally twisted uneasily on the stool by the tiring-table. "He spoke something of serving the King."

"I see." Jane spoke quietly, and then she seemed to steady her breath. "I'm afraid we know what that means—and where it's likely to end. Black William told us."

There was utter silence. Jane seemed to wait for Mally, and Mally could find no word. The memory of William was with her again, and she could almost hear his voice as he turned from the parlour door and spoke of the end a man might have who was led by Mr. Peaver's sermons. But there was more to it now than Mr. Peaver.

"You don't like me for saying that?"

Jane had spoken again, gently and steadily, and again she had no answer. Mally sat mute, and Jane waited. Then she spoke again.

"Perhaps I shouldn't care so much if it wasn't men we know. But it is. It's John here, and——"

"And your Jack. I know." Mally almost snapped it at her. "Isn't it also him?"

"Oh!" Jane turned by the hearth, and was suddenly contrite. "I should have remembered that, shouldn't I? You mean this Captain Marriott?"

"It doesn't matter."

"I wonder. You did speak of him, I know, but rather as if it was—past."

It was not past now, and Mally knew it. She had thought it was, but in one short hour she had learned that it was not. She sat silent, looking mutely at Jane; and Jane spoke quietly.

"So he's in earnest about you? And he's in earnest as Colonel Storm also?"

"He must be." Mally roused herself to answer plainly. "His father was a Non-juror."

"Like Peaver?"

"Yes. He was born at St. Germains, and——"

"Then that settles it. His plot's a duty to him. Probably he'd call it his honour. Men do. That's how they talk."

"I know."

"So you can't ask him not to."

"I—I couldn't."

"I know you couldn't. He probably wouldn't do it, any-way, and you wouldn't think better of him if he did. We could warn him, I suppose."

"Of what?"

"Of the sort of men he has here. How they talk all the time, and don't care who hears. It might surprise him to learn how much we know."

There was silence again. Jane moved restlessly about the room, her face tight with thought, and Mally sat hushed and still. Then Jane turned, and spoke decisively.

"It's all we can do, and we'll have to try it."

"Try what?"

"Tell him how much we know, and hope he has wits to profit. When do you see him again?"

"I don't know."

"Then let's hope it isn't long. We can't go running to Dilston after him. We'll have to wait."

They did not have to wait long. They had scarcely ended breakfast next morning when a fellow rode to the house and produced a letter for Mally. It was brief. He had affairs at that same inn this morning, where he must say a later word to some who had stayed since yesterday. It would be ended before noon, and he would dine at the inn and then ride back by the Wall; and he was her very devoted Anthony Marriott.

There was some bustle in the house just then as prepara-tions began for feeding the twelve who were to dine here today. Jane was audibly thanking God that it was not her affair today when Mally pushed the letter under her nose. Jane spoke shortly.

"We'll dine at that inn."

"He doesn't say so."

"You don't think he's going to dine at an inn while we munch cold mutton on a wall, do you?"

She sounded herself again this morning, and Mally took that easily.

"We can't go there alone."

"Of course we can't. We'll have to disentangle Jack from this meeting here."

"Can we?"

"You go and press your hat. They'll be boiling it as a pudding if you don't. It looks like one."

They rode out a little after ten, Mally none too pleased at her efforts with the hat. Jack was quiet and attentive, but he was thoughtful, and from time to time he glanced at them as if he had some questions in his mind. Before they were off the Dere Street Jane went at it bluntly.

"Jack, you're not put out at missing this meeting, are you?"

"I'm not. I'm glad to be out of it. Mr. Peaver will be telling them of Colonel Storm."

He seemed to be offering a hint of what was in his mind, and Jane did not shirk it.

"It sounds as if you do not approve of Colonel Storm."

"I don't. I fear for what he may bring."

"So do I. Mally also."

"Yet it seems we dine with him this day."

"Not exactly with Colonel Storm. We dine with a Captain Marriott."

"Indeed?" He turned slowly to Mally. "It was not hard to guess that you knew him yesterday. I haven't asked questions, but——"

It would be more easily told by Jane, and she told it crisply. He listened attentively, and his face cleared.

"It's very well," he said. "I did not dislike the man. It was the Colonel, as the agent, that I wished elsewhere."

"Yes." Jane was watching him carefully. "Will you remember, Jack, that Mally has some liking for this Captain Marriott—apart from his being the Colonel?"

"Apart from his being the Colonel, I liked him myself." He turned suddenly to Mally, and the smile was on his face for the first time that morning. "I think he went to a little trouble to make his meeting with you yesterday. I like him for that, too."

They lingered a little on the Wall, and it was close on noon when they went at last over the bridge to where the grey inn seemed to sleep by the river. There was little sign of life in it now. The door was shut, the sweep of gravel deserted, and only a wisp of smoke from a chimney gave hint of life within. But it was hint enough; and as the horses went crunching over the gravel the door was pulled quietly open, and Captain Marriott stepped out.

"Welcome!" His smile made it include them all. "You're my guests at dinner, if you please. I hoped you'd come."

"Then we don't take you by surprise?"

"It's not easy to take by surprise at this inn. Perhaps that's why we use it."

"I see." Jack spoke quietly as he swung out of his saddle. "That sounded like the Colonel speaking. It makes me doubtful how to address you."

"I'm not sure myself."

His glance turned to Mally as if he were asking for a lead in this, and she gave it him at once.

"These are my good friends," she said. "Both of them."

"I take that as enough. Tony Marriott, then. But not, if you please, when others are here. That's needful."

They dined together in peace and fine accord. They sat, all four of them, in the grey low room that had yesterday had an Earl as guest, and it was no country meal that was set before them now. The inn knew more than it showed, more perhaps than a lonely inn had proper cause to know, and there was salmon from the river, capons of the freshest, a beefsteak pudding that was surely graced with larks, and tarts and syllabubs of a sort that set Jane asking how. There was even coffee, and a fine French brandy to lend it the proper tang. Nor were they hurried after that. The fire was mended, the coffee-pot placed before it, the brandy set upon the table. Then they were alone to talk, and a quick glance from Jane told Mally what was expected of her. She went at it briskly, and with some prepared phrases.

"May I address myself to Colonel Storm?"

"Certainly." He stared at her for a moment, and then his face was grave, as if he had seen that she was in earnest. "What is it, please?"

"The work the Colonel comes to do is—delicate? It requires some caution?"

"Yes."

"Do you think those others show a caution?"

"I'm assured they do."

"Then you are assured wrong."

"Oh?" His voice was even quieter. "May I know——"

"It's not the concern of women, is it? We should know little of these affairs?"

"You should know nothing of them."

"We have not wished to. But in some short weeks, not seeking it at all, we have learned—what?"

She had turned to Jane, as if asking help in this, and Jane promptly gave it. She took a fine sardonic tone.

"First, there's a plot, by which it is hoped your father will soon recover his estate. That's how King James is spoken of, I think. Skins will be needed for this, and it's a question of where to find enough. The most will be from Scotland."

"What is this?"

He spoke softly, and he was a little more erect in his chair. Jane sat very still; and Mally's thoughts had gone leaping to that dinner for twelve, when the Rev. Mr. Patten had read the letter from Colonel Storm. Jane was quoting from it now.

"Those of importance," she went on, "are the Earl of Derwentwater, Mr. Patten, Mr. Peaver, and a Mr. Forster of Bamburgh. To these are joined some lesser men and certain Scots, notably the Earl of Mar. Colonel Storm is to join these efforts into one."

"Is he?"

"Yes." Mally joined suddenly in the attack, and she had remembered that letter. "Certain other merchandise is needed. Tea, prunes, long-cut tobacco, galls, cochineal——"

"How did you know——"

"Prunes, of course, are pistols, and we know what the others are." In point of fact she did not, but she let that pass. "To those named as important, we should add my dear aunt Chandler."

"But why?"

"She has the keys of the warehouse—the prunes and the rest."

"Good God!"

He was staring at them now, startled to the roots of him, and remorselessly Jane took the attack again.

"To those named as important should be added Mr. William Chandler."

"Who?" It crackled suddenly. "You mean——"

"I mean Black William."

"Sir John Chandler's brother?"

"Yes." It was Mally again now. "Two loving brothers, and they exchange good letters. Did you never think, in London, that Sir John has eyes and ears?"

"What's that? Do you mean—— ?"

"I mean that he's no fool."

"Brother William," said Jane, "is even less of one. You'll do well to believe he knows at least as much of your plot as Mally and I do. Which is perhaps more than you supposed."

"It is indeed." He spoke grimly, and his face was taut. "Would you tell me how you learned all this?"

"We did not need to learn it. It was laid before us, to be picked up. There's not one of your crew can hold his tongue about anything. They all talk, all the time, and you can't stop them."

Mally leaned forward to make an end. She surprised herself with the firmness of her tone.

"Which is why we asked you if you were sure the others showed a caution. You said they did."

"I said wrong." He was smiling ruefully. "I said very wrong. I'm in your debt that you should have told me."

"But what follows?"

"I don't know, yet."

"You can't make a plot with men like these."

"I must do my best."

It was quiet, but it was uncompromising. There was obstinacy in both face and tone, and suddenly Jane spoke again. An edge was coming into her voice now.

"You can't make a plot with such as these. They're the wrong sort."

"Perhaps most men are." He spoke very calmly. "But I must do what I can. I have orders from the King."

"You won't serve your King with a detected plot, and a hangman."

"God forbid!"

"He hasn't forbidden it before, when plots have failed."

The edge in her tone might have ruffled any man now, but his years in the card room served him well. He kept his temper perfectly.

"What, please, is suggested?"

"That if you must have a plot you have it elsewhere, and with other men—better men."

"I don't doubt that that's shrewd. But it is not within my powers."

"I don't——"

"I have my orders, and they are precise. It is for me to serve, not to disobey."

"Yet if the risks——"

"I must accept risks." He came quietly to his feet, and he spoke with uncompromising pride. "Many have died for the King. Many more will, and it is not for me to complain. Only so can a just cause be upheld and a true King served. I must do the best I can, and with the instruments I am given. The end must lie with God."

In the quiet room he looked from one to another, as if he awaited answer. Then his mood changed, and he was almost smiling.

"Deus nobiscum, quis contra nos?" He spoke with a quiet certainty. "We may surely have some faith."

He was plainly making an end. He was dismissing this topic, and courteously telling them so. Mally looked at his firm set face, and then glanced fleetingly at Jane; and tightened lips showed that Jane was of the same opinion. For the moment they must accept this, and further argument would make it worse; which did not, perhaps, mean that there could be no more later.

There was certainly some more later, though it was a little different. They rode home early, in the clear pale light of the afternoon, and it was not long before Jane and Jack Harvey had moved a little ahead. Tony Marriott showed no sign of regretting that. He seemed well content to linger, and Mally pulled her wits together. She thought she might need them.

They were walking the horses slowly up the long hill from the river, and he moved closer to her side. He watched her for a moment, and then he spoke carefully.

"You found me unaccommodating, I fear. You will not be —offended?"

"Disappointed, shall we say?"

"I'm sorry." Again he seemed to seek carefully for words.

"If it were any matter of my own I can think of very little I would not do to serve you. You will not think of me as Colonel Storm?"

"You *are* the Colonel, are you not?"

"Colonel Storm is the part of me that is sworn to the King. All else of me is sworn to you."

It was a declaration plainer than he had yet made, and instinct warned her not to respond too eagerly; it would be better to be quiet, and not very helpful.

"You will not confuse the two? The Colonel and myself?"

His voice came urgently, and calmness stayed with her.

"I don't think I can deal with two gentlemen at the same time, who are the same gentleman, and yet not the same. It's too much for me."

"But surely it's plain?"

"It may be, to a man, but it isn't to me."

"But, Mally——"

"No." She turned to face him squarely. "There's nothing mended by having two names, and each saying he doesn't know the other."

"I never said that. I have said only that in some matters I may choose for myself, and that in others the King chooses for me."

"Yet you choose to accept his choices."

"It is a thing in honour."

For a moment she was in silence, remembering that this was a prickly topic, where men held some odd views and put things in odd proportions. She must be careful here.

"How does it touch you so nearly that I serve King James?" His voice came again, and as quietly as before. "Do you tell me that you are hot for King George?"

"I care no more for King George than I do for King James."

"But——" He was looking almost baffled now. "But what, then, do you seek?"

"I think it's life at home which matters, not which King has guards and trumpets."

"What a thing to say!"

"Well, I say it."

They were at the top of the hill now, ambling gently along

the broken line of the Wall as it traversed the open moorland, and she let her eyes turn to that while she waited for him to answer. She had no inclination to explain herself, and she thought it could be left to him.

He came at it gently.

"If you care so little for either King, why should it touch you that I serve King James?"

"My uncle has been good to me, and you'll drag in Jack Harvey too, I suppose. It happens that I care for those two. Had you thought of that?"

"They are grown men, and free to choose. You do not think that I persuaded them to this? That it was anything but their own will?"

"It's not Jack Harvey's will. I know that."

"Then why does he not withdraw?"

"How—in what you call honour—can he?"

"By merely announcing his wish. There shall be no dispute from me. Ours is not a service for pressed men."

Something in his tone, perhaps in the very quietness of it, set her looking sharply at him. She saw the tightening of his face, and when she would have met his eye he looked away, and was for a moment intent on the distant hills. Then he turned to her again.

"Persuade Mr. Harvey, if you please, to take his own road. I wish him very well, and Miss Jane also."

It was lightly spoken, but that did not deceive. There had been that glance away, and the tightening of his face; and Mally caught at her breath as understanding came flooding through her. It was a work he thought too high to press men to. It was a work of pride and danger, for dedicated men; and he would lead those who would follow. He had been born to this and reared from boyhood with it. He saw it as honour and duty, and he would neither press those who feared nor desert those who followed. He had a soldier's purpose, and eyes wide to the danger. It was all too plain; and a cold and sickening fear came to Mally for this Tony Marriott, whose face was now puckering into a smile beside her.

"Thank you." She heard her own voice speaking, and it seemed far away. "I'll remember it."

"Do." His rejoinder came pleasantly, and he seemed not

only at his ease but anxious to put her at hers. "As for these others, the elders——"

"What of yourself?" It would stay within her no longer, and it cut desperately through his words. "What shall your end be?"

"It *could* be a King's gratitude."

"It could also be something else. Do you think I've a wish for you to be taken as a traitor?"

"That's not the word——"

"Oh, my God! Is it words all the time? You know what the end will be."

"Oh yes, if I'm taken. But——"

"If?" She flung it at him wildly. "What do you suppose will come with men like these? I've told you how they talk."

"That's unfortunate, and I'm grateful that you've warned me. But it can be mended. There's no more done yet than talk."

"What of your men and pistols? Your skins and prunes, and long-cut——"

"Oh, not yet." He was airy about it. "That's for the days to come. It will be weeks, more likely months, before——"

He seemed to brush it aside. Again he looked away, intent on the sky and the play of sunlight on the clouds. The clop and jingle of the horses filled the silence, and she watched him carefully. Then he turned purposefully, and looked her in the eye.

"I had hoped that you had perhaps some concern for me also."

It was not to be evaded, and she felt her face harden as she tried to keep expression from it.

"How could I not have concern? I know what risk you run."

"Let that pass."

"I can't."

"I meant for the moment. You know why I sought you out —what my true thought was when I journeyed here."

He had urged his horse a little forward so that it passed in front of hers and brought her to a stop. He was very close to her, and she could feel his knee touching hers as he spoke again.

"You know how it was in London. It was very formal there, and always there were the cards and dice. I had to think of those first, and do as I was expected. There were those who must be entertained, and kept in play and talk. There was much duty for me."

"And you liked it?"

"Not all of it. And less after I had first seen you. Do you remember that night?"

"How—how should I not?"

He seemed more in the past than the present. Mally sat very still, and even the sigh of the wind across the Wall could be heard above his voice.

"There were some few gentlemen for the cards that night, and one or two ladies. There were always some of those."

"I know."

"They played deep. Why, I don't know, but they always did. This night there was a lady who had lost enough—which means too much. She looked unhappy. There would be some reckoning with her husband perhaps."

"Why did you let her lose?"

"She was to be—encouraged. My duties were so." His shoulders shrugged as if he would dismiss all that. "The least I could do was to escort her to the door. Her chair had been called."

"Yes."

It came very quietly, and Mally hoped that her face was still. She knew what his memory was.

"I stood in the door while she was borne away. Then I turned. You know what I saw."

"Me?"

"Yes." He seemed to be intent on the memory, as if the scene were alive for him again. "You were on the stair——"

"I should not have been."

"Do not say it. I——"

"My aunt said it."

"I never knew." He was looking gravely into her eyes. "But I feared it might have been, and I'm sorry if I brought trouble on you."

"It's no matter."

"But I think it is." Again he went quietly on, and again

the sigh of the wind could be heard above his words. "I could not help it. It was a force beyond me, and I had to seek you out. That was the other night, of the Coronation, and we know how it ended."

"It ended in trouble for you. But you were good to me."

"There was trouble for you also."

"No." Her head lifted, and for a moment she looked about her, at the sky, the windswept grass, and the grey stone of the Wall. "It seemed so, but it was not. I'm happier here, in the North."

"Are you?" For the first time there was eagerness in his voice. "Perhaps I could be happy, too—here."

"Perhaps you could, if you stopped making plots."

"Mally!"

He sounded almost shocked. She had spoken quickly, by instinct more than by thought, and for a moment she regretted what she had said. Then she steadied herself and knew that instinct had been true. There could be no happiness, for him or her or any other, while he led to what must end in ruin. That was at the root of all, and she knew that she must hold to it. For his sake and her own, there was nothing else.

"I'm sorry." She spoke quietly now, and without pretence. "But that's the trouble. I can't split you in half. There's Colonel Storm as well as Captain Marriott."

"For Colonel Storm you should blame King James. It's Tony Marriott who seeks you now. Could you not show some liking?"

"Not for the Colonel."

"The Colonel is——"

"Please!" She cut him short almost savagely. "Let's not have that again. I can't bear it, this juggling with words. It's you and the Colonel and I don't care which."

"Mally! I——"

"How will it end?" She rounded on him fiercely, careless of what might come. "Uncle John and Will Harvey, and Jack yonder, and even Peaver——"

"Peaver?"

"A soft old parson with a bee in his head, and he'll end in rope like the rest. And what of yourself, when you're the head of it all? What hope have *you*?"

"You take this too far. It will not end so."

"It won't be missed by juggling names."

"Perhaps not. But it will not end so. For myself, I've some prudence. For these others they are free to go."

"And for me?"

"That's what I hope to learn. It's what I came to the North parts for."

"In part."

"I'll admit, in part. But it's true, for all that. I'm your devoted servant."

She faced him in silence, suddenly at a loss for words, and his sincerity was plain. A shaft of sunlight was pouring through the broken cloud, drawing colours from the grass and moss and grey stone of the Wall, and the restless horses stirred and were impatient to be gone. They pawed at the ground, moving in a quick half-circle, taking him away from her, and she saw the sunlight on his calm determined face. He was looking her in the eye, steadily and of purpose, and she was left in no doubt at all. He meant what he had said, and he would not soon change.

There was a clatter of hooves on rock as he turned his horse, and she saw the half-smile on his face.

"Perhaps we had best move," he said. "Our horses give us the hint, and the others may be asking what we do."

The Barbary turned without guidance, and together they went ambling along the grassy wind-blown track, jogging knee to knee in a silence that was now friendly. They went up a gentle rise, and a half-mile away she could see the others against the sky. They, too, were on a crest and they seemed to have halted and be waiting.

He spoke suddenly, and it seemed as if his thoughts were clear.

"I've said I'm your very devoted, and I mean it so. I've meant it so since the night you were looking down the stair. In the next week I shall have affairs. But when they are done I shall seek you again, and you shall learn the truth of this."

She took leave of him where the Dere Street ran through the Wall, and the sun had a tinge of gold when Jack Harvey brought her and Jane to the door of his father's house. It was very still and quiet, and the falling sun was shining on the windows and giving a glow to the stone. At the foot of the old pele tower Mr. Peaver was standing, and Mally walked across to him. He was at the corner of the pele, and his attention was on a stone in its ancient wall. Mally looked, and saw it was the stone he had shown her before, the Roman stone with the inscription deeply cut.

"Ah!" He looked up as she approached, and there was something far-away in his eyes. "Dis Manibus, you see. Is it not a fine beginning?"

It meant nothing to Mally. She looked helplessly at the stone : D— M— ALAE SABINIANAE MILITES—— It was what she had seen before, and she turned again to Mr. Peaver.

"I don't understand. What is it?"

"What I told you. Dis Manibus—to the Gods and the Departed Dead."

"Yes?"

Mr. Peaver was pursuing his own thoughts as he spoke again.

"They revered the Gods, and the dead. They lived and died upon the Wall, thousand upon thousand of them. Does it now matter how they died?"

"Not now."

"But it did." Again his thoughts were not with Mally. "To the Gods and the Dead. Some died in the path of duty, revering the Gods. If they had not done that, they would still have died, but they would have been worthy of no memorial."

"Yes?"

"Matters of death do not change with time. There is still a path of duty, and it may still lead to death. But we must follow it, or we shall die without memorial."

A chill touched Mally. It was this man's true belief, and he would preach others into it. He would let nobody withdraw.

G

CHAPTER XXI

SIMPLE WILLIAM

They had Mr. Peaver's company for the journey home on Monday, and his mere presence was enough to keep Mally's thoughts on him and his beliefs. That linked with Tony Marriott, who shared those beliefs. On the face of things they were a world apart, the elderly country parson and the adroit and polished gamester; yet more truly, and as Mally was beginning to see, they were of the same world, a world of shining loyalty, of sacrifice and courage, and perhaps of illusion. It was a world colourful and brave, lit by a fine high confidence, demanding the best from men; and Mally had been very near it, these last few days.

She therefore felt some shock when she was reminded, before they were even home again, that she lived in a world that had also Black William in it.

They parted from Mr. Peaver by his house; and when they were passing the coal pit, on the last mile home, they became aware of activities. The pit, indeed, was as still and deserted as before, but far up to their right, where the new pit was to be dug, a mound of earth had appeared, and at intervals men with barrows came to its crest and dumped more earth. Down the slope, in the other direction, men were at work on what must be the new wagonway; and a line of slender poles, painted in black and yellow, ran up the slope to the mound of the new pit. There was a brisk efficiency here; and that, with the speed at which it had started, was hint enough of William. It would be the way of the man, and Mally found herself looking round, half expecting to see him.

For a moment she thought she did. Up the slope, by the mound, a horseman appeared on the skyline. He flourished his hat, and came cantering down the line of posts; and a second glance showed that he was Dick Chandler.

He seemed glad to see them. He was waving his hat again, more particularly at Mally, and she had to rouse herself. In hese last few days she had all but forgotten Dick Chandler; nd she was abruptly aware that now she was home she would not be allowed to forget Dick Chandler. He did not look as f he would let himself be forgotten. Nor did any of the Chandlers.

He came ranging up, cheerful and confident, and he had sense enough to give his first attention to John.

"You seem in a hurry here." John was speaking gruffly. 'You don't lose time, do you?"

"If you lose time, sir, it doesn't come back."

"That's what your father says, I suppose?"

"It's also what he does."

"I'll believe you. What's all this?"

"What was agreed, sir. There's the new pit yonder, and he wagonway down there. It's coming from the existing way, on the next land, and here's the line of it." He showed the line of painted posts, running within a few yards of the worked-out pit. "I'm in charge of the work. Shall I ride round it with you tomorrow, sir, and show you?"

"I'll find my own way." John was as gruff as before, but he did not sound displeased. "If you want to ride someone round, take Mally. She's got a new horse."

"And a new habit, too, I think. I like it."

His eyes were suddenly on Mally, confident and cheerful, and a pleased surprise ran through her. She had not expected he would have wit enough to note the mulberry serge, and make that comment.

"Thank you," she said. "I hope——"

"Will you come? Come riding, I mean. Soon?"

He said it quickly, and Mally was as quickly in a difficulty. This was a complication. She did not know what her wishes were; but dimly she knew that she had some duties here. Dick had been honest with her, and kindly.

"Thank you." She heard her own voice answering. "I should——"

"Good! I'll bring my other hat."

"What's that? I——"

"It's got some lace on it. Sundays, mostly." He was grinning broadly as he turned suddenly to Jane. "How's the horse? Not fallen off yet?"

"I haven't." Jane's head had lifted quickly. "I'm not in the way of falling off."

"I wish you were. It might ruffle you a little. Then I could pick you up, and you'd be grateful ever——"

There was a splutter from Jane which sounded oddly like amusement, and then he was laughing openly at her.

"I'm glad to see you back," he added. "I knew you'd been away. I've been to the house, with a packet for you."

He had turned again to Mally, and once more he had her surprised. He nodded calmly.

"From my uncle John in London," he said. "It came by sea, and I took it to the house. I don't know what it is."

He took leave at that, trotting purposefully down to the wagonway, and Mally had thoughts enough as they rode the last mile home. Certainly she would have no chance to forget these Chandlers. William and his son seemed to be more or less on the doorstep; and now there was this packet from Sir John, surprising and unexpected.

It was even more surprising when she came to it. She had supposed it would be a letter, but it proved to be a parcel of some size, carefully tied in canvas. She opened it in the lesser parlour that she and Jane now used, and out came a roll of silk and two rolls of Indian chint, gay and coloured. Mally gasped with surprise, and Jane seized on the rolls of chint. She took them to the window to see the colours better.

"What a man!" she said at length. "These *are* chints, aren't they?"

"They are. They're the latest, too."

"I thought chints were forbidden?"

"Yes. Silk, too, if it's Indian."

Again she was in no doubt. She remembered well enough the dismay in London when these imports had been forbidden because they were harming home trade; and she remembered Sir John's bland smile when she had asked him how he continued to have them. He had let an eyelid droop; and he had answered that to know one's way round a silly law like that was among the arts of life.

It came back clearly as Mally recounted it; and Jane took it with a sniff.

"I'll believe him," she said. "As for William, he probably knows about six ways round. Have you noticed there's a letter?"

There was, tucked into the roll of silk, and Mally opened it hastily. It was in Sir John's own hand, and it set out in short words that some chint and silk would perhaps be acceptable to Mally, and no doubt to her cousin Jane as well; with whom these were therefore to be shared.

"Bless the man!" said Jane. "I almost like him."

Mally went on reading:

You will remember a Captain Marriott who ended in fisticuffs on your behalf. He has not been seen here since, and is much mourned, I'm told, by the ladies of the town. It is now the talk that he has been packed off North to recuperate. What this means, I don't know. There are, however, some whispers. (My wife's friends, you'll remember, could never hold their tongues about anything.) One is that he may better serve the Jacobite foolery in the North, and has been given special work to do there. The other is that his real intent lies under Venus, and that he means to seek out you. My guess, for what it may be worth, is that both tales may be true.

"For what his guess is worth?" said Jane. "He seems to be exactly right."

"He usually is. So is William."

"Never mind William! What else does John say?"

Jane was imperious about it, and Mally gave heed to the letter again:

It is therefore possible that he may seek you at your uncle's house, which is why I give you warning. His coming without your expectation might have embarrassments. Where he will lodge in the North I do not know, but the tattle here has quartered him at Dilston, on milord of Derwentwater; which is likely enough. They hunt in the same pack, those two.

"God help us! The man knows it all. He *is* at Dilston."

"I know." Mally looked across with troubled eyes. "Talk about secrets!"

"Is there any more?"
"Yes."

Young Willoughby, by the way, whom Marriott was at fisticuffs with, has taken his beating very sourly, and is set to do Marriott a mischief if he can. He is stayed, I fancy, only because he can't, so far, think of a mischief to do. A hint to Marriott of this would no doubt be a friendliness. Willoughby, indeed, is no more than a powdered fribble, but he has a deal of money, which lengthens a man's arm.

Commend me, pray, to your uncle Lawley and your cousin Jane. Whatever in this is foolish you may blame upon the dotage of:

John Chandler.

"Dotage!" Jane said it softly as the letter fell fluttering to the table. "He hasn't missed a point, has he? Can you warn your Tony? When does he come here?"

"I don't know. He only said he had affairs, and that he'd seek me after those."

"He'll come." Jane began to sound sardonic. "He'll probably come the same day as Dick Chandler. What happens then?"

Again Mally did not know. She said so, and Jane looked helplessly back.

"We'll have to wait till it happens," she said at length. "It's about all we can do, these days. In the meantime, you can write to Sir John."

"Write?"

"You can't take his chint if you don't thank him."

"Nor can you."

"But you know him. I don't."

"It can wait till tomorrow."

She had, however, rather more to think about on the morrow. It began with the arrival of Mr. Peaver, who looked concerned about something. He shut himself up with uncle John, and nobody minded that. Jane said it would keep them both out of the way, and that for herself she was busy. She evidently thought that the affairs of the house needed some minding after her absence, and she seemed to want no help.

Mally, politely asking what she could do, was told that she could write that letter to Sir John.

She thought she might as well. It would not be an easy letter, and this might be as good a chance as she would get. So she cast about for ink and pens, and tried to settle in the lesser parlour; and she was still sitting there, rubbing her nose and wondering how to start, when William came.

He came jingling up to the house, as calm and purposeful as ever, and Mally had to think quickly. Uncle John was talking with Mr. Peaver, and that would hardly be suitable for William. So she pushed her head round the kitchen door and called to Jane, and then she ran to let William in. She took him to the lesser parlour, thankful that it had a fire today and a look of use. She shut the door firmly; and she knew that she must somehow hold him in talk till Jane had done something with Mr. Peaver.

William was quite unchanged. He put his back to the fire and began to warm himself comfortably, and he looked Mally over with amusement in his eyes.

"How are the Jacobites?" he asked suddenly, and Mally almost stammered in surprise.

"Jacobites, sir?"

"Aye. That parson of yours—the fellow who preached."

"Mr. Peaver, would it be?"

"It might." William was carefully warming the seat of his breeches, and it was an ample seat. "I saw him walking here as I came. So I held back to let him get here first. I hear you've been away."

Again the new topic took her by surprise, and she almost blurted out too much. She checked hurriedly, thinking that the less she said the better of where she had been, and with whom.

"Yes," she said. "Just for the few days."

"Aye, aye." He nodded affably, and made no attempt to press it. "Dick said you'd gone. He was up here last week, with some packet or other."

"It was from your brother, sir. From Sir——"

"Aye. I know it was." He suddenly had a broad smile. "What did Jack send you? Can I ask?"

"Of course."

She was thankful for a topic that seemed safe, and she decided to spin it out. She found the rolls of silk and chint and held them out for his inspection. He thumbed the silk gingerly, and then his eyes turned to the chint.

"It's a Hell of a colour, isn't it?"

"Indeed it is not, sir. It's the latest——"

"Aye, aye, we'll suppose it is." He handed the rolls back to her. "I suppose Jack knew what he was sending. Jack knows a good deal."

"He seems to know how to get chint, sir, when it's forbidden."

"Oh, that?" William lifted an eyebrow, and then shook his breeches as if they were now warm enough. "Now Jack trades in a big way. He imports a lot of things. Prunes, say, from France."

He came out with it blandly; and Mally, with her thoughts on the prunes that Colonel Storm had written of, twitched guiltily. Then she remembered that Sir John did indeed bring prunes from France; and those, no doubt, were what William was speaking of. Or was he? It was hard to be sure; and she had a dark suspicion of William.

"Yes, prunes." He sounded almost jovial, and he could surely have noticed nothing. "He brings prunes from France. He sends them to me, and I sell them for him."

"So I've heard, sir."

"Yes. But they come from France. They come in a ship, and Jack owns the ship."

"Owns it?"

"Oh yes. So if he asks it to carry a little more than prunes, it will. That's very convenient." He straightened himself, and suddenly looked Mally in the eye. "You'd be surprised what things can be carried in tubs marked prunes."

Mally twitched again, and as hastily recovered. William smoothed his breeches, and had only talked of prunes. She tried hurriedly to lead the talk along.

"At least, sir, I'm glad that Sir John gets chints. I'm most grateful. I was just about to write to him when you came."

She showed the paper on the table, and she thought she was safe with that; and again William moved ahead of her.

"How will you send it?"

She was once more taken by surprise. She had not given a thought to this; and the first thought she gave it showed some difficulties. It would have to be conveyed to Newcastle for dispatch with the weekly post boy, and she did not know how to do this. She hesitated, and William took charge at once.

"When it's ready," he said, "give it me. It can go with mine."

"If it isn't too much——"

"Of course it isn't. I write to Jack each week, and it goes by sea. Yours will go with it. It's quicker."

"Then thank you. I'll certainly——"

"Give it to me when it's ready. Or give it to Dick. I'll tell him he's to come here for it. The ship sails tomorrow night."

He spoke cheerfully, with the air of one who has it settled. He was watching her with amusement again; and suddenly he went off on another slant.

"I hope you don't write to Perkin too?"

"Perkin?"

She was completely baffled. His eyebrows lifted for a moment, and then he answered pleasantly.

"Perkin. Otherwise the Pretender—James Stuart."

"Why——" She had still no notion what he meant. "Indeed I don't write to him. I——"

"Good!" The amusement had dropped from him, and his eyes were unwavering now. "I'm told he does correspond with some he calls his subjects here, and from a few of them he has answers. It's not wise."

That came near home, and she stood in silence, with no answer that she dared to make. He waited, as if to let it sink in, and then his expression eased. He spoke more lightly.

"Dick said he had a thought to ride with you. Showing you these new workings was the young rogue's talk. It's as good as another, I suppose."

"Yes, sir. I——"

"I hope you enjoy it. It's one reason why I mentioned Perkin."

For a moment she made nothing of that. Then her

thoughts went leaping wildly as she asked herself what he was supposing, what he almost seemed to be approving. And characteristically William gave her no chance to think about it. He changed the talk at once.

"Hadn't you heard of Perkin before?"

"No." He had changed the mood as well, and Mally seized on it gratefully. "Of the Pretender, of course. But why Perkin?"

"Now that——" William was eyeing the ceiling sardonically. "Now that's a long tale. It has to do with a warming-pan."

A door creaked open suddenly. There were footsteps and a murmur of voices, and it was plain that Mr. Peaver was departing. William cocked an ear.

"Is that Peaver?"

"Yes. He's——"

"I haven't met him. It's time I did."

He was not diffident. He went striding firmly to the door, purposeful and determined; and before she could even get in his way he had jerked it open and was standing there at gaze. At the door of the other parlour Mr. Peaver turned awkwardly.

CHAPTER XXII

THE WINE CELLAR

THERE was a moment of silence. John had appeared in the
parlour door behind Mr. Peaver, and Jane was hovering in
the hall. Nobody knew what to say. They all looked at
William; and William gave the lead promptly.

"Good day to you, Mr. Lawley. I wished for a word with
you."

"Oh, aye—by all means. Much at your service."

There was nothing else that John could say. William
nodded, and then turned his gaze.

"Mr. Peaver, isn't it? I've heard of you from my son.
I'm William Chandler."

"Delighted, sir."

Mr. Peaver did not sound delighted. He was standing
stiffly in the doorway, very lean and tall, and his tone was
frigid. So, too, was his face, and even John began to look
embarrassed. He was clearing his throat when William spoke
first. William was taking this in his stride.

"You don't sound as if you approve of me."

"I don't approve of some of your ways, sir. Forgive me if
I speak my mind."

"Willingly." He was bluff and simple now. "I don't
always approve of other people's ways myself. You'd be surprised at the tales I hear of some folk."

"I don't doubt it, sir." The shaft seemed to have glanced
off Mr. Peaver. "We'll agree to differ, then. And perhaps I
should take my leave."

"Oh, don't go yet. I'm going myself." He turned suddenly to John, and his manner was impeccable now. "That's
really why I'm here, Mr. Lawley. I'll be moving more men
in next week, to get that pit opened quickly. That means some
sort of camp for them to live in, and I'd be glad to agree on a
site. Would you ride out with me?"

"Why, certainly I will. Very pleased. Now where the Hell——"

It was apparent that John had lost his boots again, and Jane took swift charge of that. Mr. Peaver bowed frigidly, and as frigidly departed, and Mally took the duty of seeing him politely away. William stayed calm and impassive, and ten minutes later he and John rode out together, apparently on the best of terms. Jane saw them go, and then she came slowly back to Mally.

"These men," she said, "would drive anybody mad. What did William say?"

"A lot in a short time. Most of it with two meanings."

She gave some account of it, and Jane heard it gravely.

"So he knows about the Jacobites," was her comment, "and he may know about the prunes. That seems the gist of it."

"I'm also warned not to write to Perkin. Does he think I would?"

"He might think you'd know a man who would."

"What! You don't mean he knows of——"

"Sir John knew about him, in that letter, so you'd better suppose that William knows too. I suppose he was taking the chance now to have a look at Peaver?"

"I expect so."

"He doesn't miss much. Now here's something else to cheer you. John wants the wine cellar cleared."

"The what?" Mally stared in surprise, and then tried to bring her thoughts to this. "I didn't know we had one."

"Most houses have one. You don't think old Sir Francis went without his wine, do you?"

"No. But——"

"It's not been used for years. There's not been any wine for years, and it's full of dirt and rubbish. But he wants it cleared. I suppose he thinks he can afford some claret, now he has William's money."

"All right, then."

"Yes. But he's in a hurry. He wants it cleared today."

"Oh, does he?"

"Yes. And I'm busy, so that means you."

"I was trying to write to Sir John."

"Then write to Sir John. The cellar can wait till the afternoon. There'll be some beetles, too."

Jane disappeared into the kitchen again, and Mally made another attempt at letter-writing, a task for which she was now in no sort of humour. But she did her best. She thanked him for the chints and silk, and she included Jane in that. She thanked him for the news of Captain Marriott, and she added that she had already seen the Captain once and expected to see him again; and she would take the opportunity to pass a warning about Mr. Willoughby. She read that over critically, to be sure she had made no mention of dates or places. Then she repeated her thanks for the chint, and remained Sir John's most grateful servant. It was not a good letter, but it would have to do. The writing of letters, she decided, required the mood, and she was not in the mood this morning. Also, she had the wine cellar to think about.

She had to do a little more than think about it. There was nobody free to help her but the stable boy, who was not interested, and in the end she had to do most of the work herself; and it was dirty work. Jane had not exaggerated the state of the cellar. It had been for years disused, and a convenient place to throw whatever nobody wanted. It was therefore a clutter of bottles, furniture, battered pans, old boots and what-you-will, the whole festooned with grime and cobwebs. Even the door creaked rustily and sent a shower of grit and dirt upon them as they opened it; and the boy's attempts to oil the hinges did not make things cleaner. By mid-afternoon they had got the rubbish out; and Mally, in the oldest clothes she could find, and with a scarf tied round her head, was almost as black as the coal pit. She was brushing the dust of ages from the flat old-fashioned wine-tables when Jane pushed her head into the cellar. The candle went flickering as the door swung open, and Mally turned sharply.

"Thank God these are flat," she said viciously.

"Why shouldn't they be flat?"

"The new way is partitioned bins. Sir John Chandler has——"

"Never mind Sir John Chandler. Here's Dick Chandler."

"What!"

"I said Dick Chandler. He's come for that letter."

"He would! What do I look like?"

"Something between a devil and a pit boy. I've told him you're resting."

"Resting!"

"Well, you can't see him like that, can you? Where's the letter?"

"I'll give it him myself."

"Are you mad?"

"Very nearly."

She flung the brush across the cellar, and slipped quickly past Jane to avoid more argument. It did not surprise her that Dick should have come at this moment. It was of a piece, she thought, with the way all else was falling out just now; and to see him like this would no doubt make an end of Dick Chandler. He would hardly come again; and that, she told herself, would spare an embarrassment. At this moment she was feeling like that.

She went scrambling up the cellar stair, to blink in the daylight, and then she marched into the lesser parlour exactly as she was, and without even a glance at a mirror. Dick was by the hearth, where his father had been that morning, and Mally came to a halt in front of him and stood truculently.

He looked at her quite calmly, which was not what she had expected.

"I came for your letter," he said easily. "I'm sorry if I've called you off your work."

"It doesn't matter, does it?"

"It might." He seemed to be taking this quite seriously. "Generally, I should say that work *does* matter. Mine does."

"Does it get you as dirty as this?"

"Try loading coal into a keel. Do you remember a keel at the staith? And the dust that blew?"

"Of course." She was staring at him in disbelief now. "You don't mean that you've done *that*?"

"I'm learning my father's trade, and I have to do some of everything. He says you can't control what you haven't done. I get a lot dirtier than you, at times."

"Oh!"

It was something she had never suspected. That Sir John

had used his hands in the tallow days was plain, and William must have done it too; but that in the days of his wealth, he should expect it of his son was some shock to her. There had been nothing like that in the polite world of London.

"It doesn't do me any harm, and it won't do you any."

His voice came again, calmly and seriously, and Mally stared as seriously back. Her ill temper had somehow dropped away, and she was more in a mood of wonder. She was thinking of some gilded gentlemen she had met at routs; and by contrast there was something very sane in Dick Chandler. There was something soothing, too.

"It's the way to learn," he said slowly. "Knowing how is worth a dirty neck. That could be true for you, when you've your own house to command."

"When!"

He did not laugh. He watched her gravely, but he made no comment that was direct. He seemed to go back to his earlier thought.

"I'm glad to know you do some work."

She thought for a moment he was rallying her, and then she knew that he was not. Whatever this was, he meant it.

"Why?" she asked.

"Because——" For once he seemed to hesitate and to seek for words. "I thought you might have London ways, and notions. I don't suppose the men you knew in London were ever dirty?"

"Not this way." She was suddenly smiling at his earnestness. "I wouldn't answer for everybody's fingernails."

"No?" His eyebrows lifted, as if he had not known this. "But if a man was dirty from work? What then?"

"He'd not be received by—gentlemen."

"Nor by ladies?"

"No."

"That's what I was afraid of. I'll be down this new pit soon, seeing what sort of coal it is, and that it's worked the right way. And if you were to meet me coming out, and if you thought like a fine lady——"

"Dick!" She was indignant, and then half amused that he could have had such thoughts of her. "Do I look like a fine lady?"

"No. That's what I'm glad of, and you don't know how glad."

It was at this point that something happened to Mally, and she should no doubt have known better. He had spoken with a solemn earnestness, and suddenly a rush of thought came to her. She began to see what he might be leading to, and why he might be glad; and her head went back, as if she would have him in better focus. In one ear the voice of sense and prudence whispered, telling her to be careful here; she had enough on hand at the moment with Tony Marriott. But in the other ear an excited little imp was whispering, and in quite a different tone. This imp was not a perfect stranger; he occasionally kept company with Mally.

"Now why——" Her head was a little farther back, and the imp was certainly in charge. "Now why should you be so glad? It's an unimportant matter, isn't it?"

"Not to me."

"Why not?"

"Can't you use your wits?"

"I am using them. Whatever I thought if I met you coming from a coal pit, it wouldn't really matter. You'd forget it as soon as you were home."

"I shouldn't."

He said it obstinately, and she noted that he had none of the airs and graces, none of the quick riposte that the polite world thought an accomplishment. But she noted, too, that his jaw had stiffened; which reminded her that the charming riposte was not always sincere.

"Oh!" She contrived to sound a little shocked, and her head tilted to the side. "You don't tell me that you go home at night and have thoughts of *me*?"

"Yes, I do."

There was no more grace than before. He seemed to think that when he had stated the fact he had done all that could be expected of him; and suddenly she was asking herself if William had been like this, and Sir John.

Then Dick did a little better.

"I thought you'd have guessed it, after that first night I brought you here. What do you suppose I thought of when I was driving home in that chaise?"

"I've no idea."

"Then do some guessing. You won't find it difficult."

Since that night had ended with his kissing her in the dark, it was indeed not difficult. But the imp would have none of that.

"I should think," she said calmly, "that you were glad to be ended with it. It was a task laid upon you, wasn't it?"

"I'll admit I wasn't pleased when I was told to do it. I thought you'd have the London ways, and be very fine and high. But you didn't seem to have, and I liked you. I've gone on liking you."

That was certainly better; and she was just deciding that he was perhaps not irretrievably clumsy when she saw that his face had lightened and that a smile had come to him.

"That's why I'm glad to see you look like that," he said. "You must be a little bit like me."

"Suppose I didn't want to look like this? Suppose it was just work I had to do?"

"That often happens. What were you doing?"

"Clearing the wine cellar."

"Then somebody ought to be grateful. Will you be clean tomorrow?"

The imp hissed excitedly, and began to dance on her shoulder.

"I don't know," she said. "I suppose it depends on the wine cellar."

"And on how long I keep you from it." He nodded cheerfully. "Then I'll go. I'll come back tomorrow. I'll have my other hat, too. I promised you that."

"Now what is this?"

"I told you yesterday. I said we'd go riding to the wagon-way, and I said I'd wear——"

"Have I said I'd go riding with you?"

"No. So I'll have to hope. Is your letter ready?"

"It's here."

"Thank you. Tomorrow afternoon, then."

"I don't know that I'll be ready."

"I don't either, if you go on talking. Get back to the cellar."

He was grinning broadly as he went marching to the door.

Mally trailed after him, with a feeling that she had somehow lost her grip on this. It could at least be said for Dick Chandler that he knew his mind and was not shy to speak it; and he had been exactly that, she remembered, when he first came aboard the ship to meet her.

He took his leave at once, and Mally went out to see him go. He waved cheerfully as he passed behind the trees, and she found herself waving back. She stood for a long moment before she moved slowly back to the house; and she had something to think about.

In the hall she found Jane waiting, and Jane spoke tersely.

"Is that the end of him?"

"End?" Mally was carefully on the defensive. "Now why should it be?"

"Have you seen what you look like? What did he say?"

"He talked of coal pits. He does."

"Very suitable for you, at the moment." Jane took a withering glance at the dirt and disarray. "And what comes next?"

"Oh——" A medley of confusing thoughts was in Mally now, and one of them seemed to dominate. "I think I'll go back to the cellar."

CHAPTER XXIII

THE THOUGHTFUL GIFT

SHE knew very well that she should not have done it. She had complications enough without adding Dick Chandler, and she knew she would not have cared to tell Tony Marriott about this. Nor, for that matter, would she have cared to tell Dick about Tony Marriott, let alone about Colonel Storm. The whole thing was a foolishness, and she did not clearly understand why she had done it. She was inclined to blame the imp, of whose presence she had been fully aware.

It thus came about that by morning she was very undecided. She remembered thankfully that she had not committed herself to anything, and had certainly made no promise to ride with him. It would no doubt be better not to, and she went so far as to consider some tactful phrases in which she could refuse; which did not keep her from a quiet word with the stable boy about the Barbary horse. Then she remembered that Tony Marriott had said he would shortly seek her out, and that gave a different look to things. She would certainly be unwise to begin something else just now. That decided her, and she went at once to ask Jane's advice. Jane gave it, and Mally expressed agreement. Then, by way of keeping her mind off things, she began to clean her riding-boots.

She disappeared after dinner, and by some cause which she could never well explain, she found herself changing into the mulberry riding-habit which had been carefully put away since Stagshaw. She added the black hat and the newly polished boots, and was pleased. Then she brought out a pair of silver-laced gloves which she had bought in Newcastle and thought too sparkling to take to Stagshaw. They were excellent with her polished spurs and the white plumes in her hat.

She could not avoid a tread and jingle as she went down the stair, and Jane came abruptly from the parlour.

"I thought you'd decided not to?"

"I have really. But I thought I'd better——"

"Better what?"

"I can't be sure what will happen."

"I can."

"You needn't say it like that. You go riding yourself, don't you?"

"I do keep to one."

"Then thank Heaven fasting. Do you like the gloves?"

"Yes. I suppose you think there's a spice in variety?"

"There is."

It had perhaps never occurred to Dick Chandler that there had been a doubt about her going. He arrived very calmly, and without even the laced hat he had promised to wear. He greeted Jane as an old friend and the Barbary as another, and he held Mally's stirrup very safe and firm while she mounted. He led her over the stubble fields and pasture to where the deserted coal pit lay, and then he seemed more interested in his wagonway than in her. He had brought her out to see the wagonway, and he conscientiously showed it to her. He showed it to her in some detail. It was certainly variety, after Captain Marriott; but it was not so certainly spice.

He led her to where they were working. The ground was being smoothed to an even gradient, ballasted with stones where needed, and planks of heavy oak were being laid on edge to form the rails. Mally's interest began to revive as a horse-team came up the completed way, drawing a wagon of the sort she had seen on the staith. It was loaded now with stones for the way, but it served to remind her, and suddenly she turned to Dick.

"You've really helped to tip coal out of those?"

"I've even tried running them."

"What does that mean?"

"Look——"

The stones had been tipped from the wagon now, and a man had mounted the little platform at one end. He released the brake lever, and the wagon rumbled down the slope to where the unhitched horses waited. It creaked to a stop as the brake was pulled on.

"You see?" He glanced across to make sure that she had seen. "You should try it when it's full of coal. It just runs wild. You hang on with one hand, and you pull the brake with the other, and those brakes aren't very good. You must get them on in time when you get near the water. I didn't."

"And what happened?"

"We went right across the staith into the Tyne—wagon, coal and all." He was grinning suddenly at the memory. "They fished me out with a boat-hook and told me I was lucky. But don't you ask if I've ever been dirty. You should have seen me then."

"I wish I had. What did your father say?"

"He said it would teach me not to be so damned silly. I gave him your letter, by the way."

"Thank you."

"He asked me if I'd seen you, so I told him *how* I'd seen you."

"You didn't? What did he say?"

"He said he thought you had it in you. Do you know he likes you?"

"No. I—I never thought of that. Were you asking him?"

"Not exactly. Anything more about this wagonway?"

"I don't think so." She looked round her, content to accept this change of topic. "How long will it take to finish?"

"Not long. This is easy ground." He glanced shrewdly up and down the slope. "Say a week to the old pit there, and another ten days to the new one. Shall we ride up?"

They let the horses jog comfortably up the slope, and the talk languished. The new pit did not take her interest. It was nothing as yet but a half-dug hole, with some streaks of coal coming into sight at the bottom. They sat their horses for a moment on the rim of it, and then Dick shot a question that surprised her.

"What has Henry Deane to do with this?"

"Henry?" She rounded on him, almost startled. "Do with what?"

"The coal here. He seems to be talking as if he half owns it."

"In a way, he does. At least, his son inherits it."

She explained it briefly, and he listened with obvious care. He seemed to think it explained something.

"He wants it badly," was his comment. "Did you know he tried to buy it from my father last week?"

"No?"

The sharp thought came to her that if Henry got the coal there would be no more of William on this land, and no more of Dick either; and suddenly she knew that she would not like that. The thought surprised her, but it was unmistakable; and there was anxiety in her voice as she answered.

"What did your father say?"

"He refused it. Don't ask me why. I don't know."

They went jogging down the slope again, riding in an amiable silence, and suddenly Mally was pondering another oddity. This silence was not embarrassing. She had no feeling that she must say something to break it. Dick Chandler did not seem to lose by silence, as some men did; and whatever attraction he had did not derive from any charm of speech. It must, she supposed, derive from something that he was.

The November afternoon was fading as they turned for home. They were crossing the pasture, and the crescent of an early moon was hanging in the sky, when he suddenly roused himself and gave some hint of what his thoughts had been.

"If this son of Deane's," he said, "takes the house and land, what is there for you and Jane?"

"Nothing," she told him promptly. "Did you suppose——"

"Of course I did. I supposed you'd inherit, you and Jane."

"Well, we shall not. There won't be——"

"Not that it matters." He cut in hurriedly, and his voice had suddenly sharpened, as if he would correct something here. "I—of course, I'd always supposed that Jane would have most of it."

That came hurriedly too, as if he wished to get off this topic. He followed it up with what hardly made it better.

"Anyway," he said cheerfully, "it's still your uncle's house, and that should last your time."

"Do you think I'm in a consumption, or something, and I shall go before him?"

"No, no." He almost laughed at that. "I meant it will last till you're out of his house and in your own."

"My own, indeed!" Her thoughts had gone leaping to what this might mean, and to what might be confusedly in his head. "And where's that?"

"You haven't vowed not to be married, have you?"

"I suppose I haven't." She was trying to head him off this now. "But that's a different thing from intending."

"I think I could foresee it, though."

"Do you have a crystal, and look into it at nights?"

"I don't believe in crystals."

"Then stop foreseeing."

"Very well." He seemed quite willing to humour her. "Tell me one thing, though. Where would you wish to live?"

"Dick! You really——"

"It's all right. I only meant——" He seemed to see for himself that he must choose words better here. "I meant, do you wish to go back to London, or is Tyneside as good?"

"Oh, that?" She thought she could answer this one, and again a feeling of surprise was in her. She had never given a thought to it before, but she knew at once what the answer was. "I've no wish to go back. There's something here I like."

"Good!" He sounded suddenly relieved. "It may wait for another day. Meantime, you're still in your uncle's house —and here it is."

He held her stirrup as firmly and safely as before, and there was nothing in his stolid air that could disturb anybody. He rode away at once, having no more than time to get home by dark, and Mally walked slowly to the door. He was more disturbing than he looked, she reflected. He had no finesse with things. He came out with them too suddenly; and anybody who rode with Dick Chandler had better keep her wits awake. She was likely to need them.

She went straight to her bedroom, and she was taking her hat off when Jane walked in.

"Did you enjoy it?"

"Yes. I wondered if I should, but I did."

"Just as well. You're probably safer with him."

"What does that mean?"

"What you might guess." Jane hesitated, and then spoke in earnest. "In these days, Mally, it might be dangerous to ride too much with—Colonel Storm. You'll be safer with William's brood."

"I see." There was a silence that neither of them cared to break; and then Mally addressed herself to the tiring-table. "That isn't all one thinks about, is it?"

"No." Jane shook herself, and then changed the talk abruptly. "Our John, by the way, is pleased with you."

"Why?"

"The wine cellar. I never thought he'd remember it again, but he did. He's been down himself to look at it. So he's pleased. He even spoke some thanks."

Jane went cheerfully away, and Mally was left to consider what she had pointed out. Undoubtedly there was a problem, but Mally was not much disturbed. She thought she had had an excellent afternoon, and Dick Chandler was more pleasing than he seemed to be. Certainly, as Jane pointed out, there was Tony Marriott too; but it might be some days yet before he came, and she would have time to think this out. There was no hurry, and she could expect a day or two of peace and quiet.

That was a comforting thought, and it lasted just half an hour. She changed her clothes and went downstairs; and in the grey of the dusk, when the candles were lighted and she and Jane were pulling curtains and fastening shutters, a horseman came quickly from the bend by the trees. He came purposefully, as if he knew his way, and he was hard to see. Mally leaned out, with a wild thought of who he was, and as she leaned he saw her and called her name; and his remembered voice woke surprise. He was Jack Harvey.

Jane got to the door first. Mally went slowly, and her immediate thought was of something wrong. There was no clear reason for Jack Harvey, so unexpectedly.

He seemed happy enough as he came through the door. He greeted Jane with obvious warmth, and Mally with a pleasing friendliness. Then he gave attention to John.

"I bring letters, sir," was his greeting. "And I've a hope you can bear with me for a day or two."

"To be sure, we can. Glad to have you, lad. But letters, do you say?"

"Yes, sir. It's—it's a little odd."

He explained it more clearly when they had him in the parlour. He stood by the fire, still in his cloak and boots, and he spoke quietly and clearly.

"It's all been as usual at home, sir, since you left us. No word from anybody, and all very quiet—too quiet." He looked suddenly at Jane with his own quick smile. "That was until this morning, and then there were letters, four of them. They'd been pushed under the door in the night."

"Who by?"

"There was nothing to tell us. But one letter was to my father, and I think he brooded on it through the morning. He didn't tell me what it was. But at noon he bade me ride here with the others."

His hand was in his pocket, and then he carefully laid three letters on the table.

"There's one to yourself, sir, one to Mally, and one to Mr. Peaver."

Mally stirred slightly. She leaned forward to see the letter that bore her name, and one glance was enough. It was in Tony Marriott's hand, and she took it quickly from the table, with some thought that it should not lie there for them all to see. The others were in the same clear hand, and John was at the table to take his own.

Mally missed no detail. She saw him move to the hearth and quickly break the seal. He unfolded the sheet, and she saw that it had only a line or two of writing; but it enclosed a second sheet, and this seemed fully written. He glanced at both, and then hurriedly folded them again; and he had not had time to read that second sheet.

"Oh aye," he said quickly. "I know of this, and it's no great matter. Jack, where's your horse?"

"Still by the door, sir."

"Then where the Devil's that boy? Jane, is there a room for Jack? He'll need a fire, won't he? And his bags?"

He was clearly breaking up this talk, and already he was bawling for the stable boy. He flung them all into confusion, and Mally seized the chance to disappear. Jane could do all this, and would no doubt enjoy it; and for her own part she had a letter to read.

She took it to her bedroom. It said briefly that he had all

but ended pressing affairs, and hoped, under God, to see her before many days were gone. In those days, as in all days, she would be ever in his thoughts; and he remained her most loving and devoted.

That was all, and it had no date and no address. She read it three times through, and then she roused herself as boots and voices sounded on the stair. It was Jane, bringing her Jack upstairs, and there would be a good deal to do. Mally thought she had better help.

He had his cloak over his arm, as he came up the stair, and his valise in his other hand. Jane was carrying the candles, and Mally hastily took one from her to light the fire that was ready laid in the cold dark bedroom. Jane lit the other candles, pulled the shutters tight, and drew the curtains across them. Then she gave critical attention to the bed, and said that a warming-pan would be up in a minute or two.

The dry wood flared and crackled in the hearth, and Mally, on her knees in front of it, looked up and saw that Jack had his eyes on her.

"I would not seem inquisitive," he said. "But could I ask if your letter was from Marriott?"

"It was."

"Thank you. So we may suppose those others were from —Colonel Storm."

There was something in his tone that set Jane turning quickly.

"Jack, what does it mean? What is it all about?"

"I've no idea at all. My father told me nothing—about that."

"Does that mean he told you of something else?"

"Yes." He turned quickly from Jane, and was looking at the crackling fire. "He told me I was henceforth to have no part in that affair, and no knowledge of it."

"Oh, Jack!" Jane moved forward excitedly, and then suddenly her face clouded as if she had guessed that there was something more. "Why did he say it?"

There was silence. Jane waited; and Mally, who had been about to put coal on the flaming wood, knelt motionless, with the tongs in her hand. Jack turned slowly, putting his back to the fire, and he looked Jane in the eye.

"He said it was no work for a man who—who might be near to marrying."

"Oh!"

There was an embarrassed gasp from Jane, and Mally hastily fell to work with the tongs to create a diversion. Jack spared her an understanding glance, and then he turned to Jane again. He seemed to speak with careful lightness.

"Could you bear with me for some few days, Jane? He told me not to return till Monday."

"But of course. We'll be——"

Jane broke off hurriedly, and again Mally thought it was left to her. She contrived a smile, and she tried to take an even lighter tone.

"Is Jane what you're to stay for, Jack?"

"No." He answered her quickly, and his voice was grave. "He did not give any reason. But I had the thought that he wished me out of the way. I think there's to be something at home I'm not to know about."

"Another meeting, do you mean?"

Jane had spoken urgently, and he turned quietly to her. "I don't know, Jane."

"It must be. Letters to your father, and to John and Peaver? Calling them to it, I suppose."

"I don't know. But it would be odd to send me here if they're being called away."

"Jack! You mean it's something worse?"

"Again, I don't know."

There was silence, tense and brooding; and Mally broke it sharply as her own thoughts moved.

"And Tony will be in it?"

"Storm?" He turned quietly to her. "Yes, I think we could guess that."

She gave no answer. The silence pressed upon them again, and the hiss and splutter of the fire was loud in the room. Then, as if some deep insight had come to her, Jane spoke fiercely.

"Jack, there's some more yet. You haven't told me all of this."

"No." He made no denial, and now he was looking her in the eye again. "There's just a little more."

"What is it?"

"My father has called an attorney in. He's having the most of his land transferred to me, by deed of gift. The house as well."

"But what——"

"Oh, it won't make any difference. He's made that clear. He'll continue in the house, and he'll continue with his rents. It will all be as before. But it will be mine in law, do you see?"

"Then why——"

"Don't you understand? The land is safe with me, if I'm out of the plot. It stays in the family, and that's what he's thinking of." He paused, and his eyes turned to Mally, and then again to Jane. "It's a thoughtful gift. It means, I suppose, that he can see a danger coming."

CHAPTER XXIV

COMMISSION OF TREASON

It seemed to Mally that she had got to a point at which she could do nothing from a single motive, nor consider anybody from a single point of view. It was all too confused. Jack Harvey's revelations were no doubt disturbing, and they ought to be heeded. But he had also let it appear that something might take shape between himself and Jane; and Mally thought that this should be helped.

It was partly with this in mind that she volunteered to visit Mr. Peaver the next afternoon. Jane had let it be known that she intended to ride out with Jack, and uncle John had promptly declared that they could call on Mr. Peaver and give him the letter that was directed to him. Mally thought this tactless. She was quite sure that Jack could find something better to do with Jane than take her to Mr. Peaver, and she therefore offered to carry the letter herself. But she had some other thoughts in mind as well. For one thing, she liked Mr. Peaver; and for another, she hoped to learn something. Mr. Peaver was apt to be indiscreet.

She decided to arrive in the middle of the afternoon. Mr. Peaver might then give her some tea; which, besides being pleasant in itself, would help to set him talking. So she had time to clean her boots again, and she even polished her spurs. There would be no harm in making the best of impressions on Mr. Peaver. Also, as one corner of her mind had noted, to get to Mr. Peaver's she would have to cross the wagonway, and there might be someone riding down it.

She met nobody, and she was slightly disappointed. She halted by the coal pit and looked left and right of her, up and down the line of black-and-yellow posts, but there was nobody of interest in sight. So she went steadily on until the ground began to dip to the river; and there, discreet in its sheltering trees, was Mr. Peaver's house, trim and neat, and, as she now thought, uncommonly private. It was exactly as it had been before, but this time it impressed her differently. It was its seclusion, its air of hiding in the trees, that pressed upon her notice now. It might almost have been contrived for a man whose ways should not be marked, whose visitors should not be known.

Mr. Peaver was unchanged. He had seen her coming, and he was out on the garden path to meet her, just as he had done before, still in his proper black, with his white bands fluttering. He came up to expectations at once, and when she was by the fire in his cheerful parlour he would hear nothing of her business until he had called for a dish of tea. He commonly had it at this hour, he said; and he was delighted that she should take it with him.

Mally disposed herself elegantly. She laid her gloves where the lace caught a twinkle from the fire. She put aside her cloak, and she made sure that she was sitting well, and with the mulberry serge uncreased. She balanced her teacup delicately, and she leaned back, smiling. Then she gave Mr. Peaver his letter.

She saw the gleam of excitement in his eyes; and then, as he broke the seals, she carefully looked away. She would not seem to have an interest in this, and there was a mirror on the wall that served her just as well. She watched his image, and she saw him glance quickly at the sheet and then unfold a second sheet enclosed. It was exactly as uncle John's had been. Then he went quickly to a writing-bureau, and pushed the two sheets hurriedly inside. Mally made no comment.

He came back almost jauntily, so pleased and excited that curiosity came to boiling point in Mally; but quite plainly she could not ask him. The only thing to do was to get him talking, and then to guide the talk.

She took what seemed the obvious opening.

"I, too," she told him, "had a letter from Captain Marriott."

"Ah, yes—yes." He spoke quickly, and still excitedly. "I was told that you had known him, and before we did. You are fortunate, Miss Mally. In London, was it?"

"Yes. At my aunt Chandler's."

"Just so, just so. But he was not then Colonel Storm?"

"No. I think that came later."

"Of course. For *us*." Mr. Peaver sounded pleased about it. "He has a special commission, and he guides our destinies."

"I hope he'll guide them well."

That slipped out before she could restrain it. It was born of fear and anxiety, and it had a tone that set Mr. Peaver staring.

"But Miss Mally!" He sounded quite shocked. "You don't suggest——"

"I don't suggest anything. I only fear for it. How many will there be to join you, if it should come to the push of things?"

"Enough, we hope. It is, of course, a question of principle, and we must hope for nothing from the Whigs. The Whigs are without principle. If it did not come near blasphemy, I should say that they are without God also."

"Black William?"

"Since you name him—yes. The man exemplifies the type. There is no principle but expediency, and the worship of Mammon. There remain, therefore, the Tories, and I fear that most of them were swearers."

He spoke with a crisp precision, and he did not refer to the language the Tories used. He meant simply that they had sworn allegiance, and were not Non-jurors like himself. It was not what Mally wished to hear about, but Mr. Peaver was not easily stopped. He seemed to be set for a lecture on this.

"They have had time to reflect, however, and they fear for the day of Wrath. They knew well enough that to resist the power is to resist the ordinance of God. The—er—the Epistle to the Romans, Miss Mally, the thirteenth chapter. They knew it well enough, whatever they pretended. I would not depart from charity, but can it be doubted that they swore to save what they had?"

"I—I don't quite——"

"Of course they did." He was speaking hotly now. "I well know what it meant to be deprived. It meant losing all, and not the Office only. The parsonage, the glebe, the stipend, all were taken, and I do *not* say it was easy. But that is why they swore, and we all know it."

"Yes. But——"

"But they have had time to reflect. It was twenty-five years ago, that day of deprivation, and certainly it was hard. But the day of Judgement will be harder still, for a man who swore for his goods. And as we grow older——"

Mr. Peaver stopped abruptly, as if his attention had shifted. He seemed to be gazing out of the window, and then he suddenly came to his feet.

"Why it's—I do believe it's Geordie Wade," he said.

Mally got to her feet also, thankful for the interruption. She looked through the window, down the stone-flagged path to the gate, and at once she remembered Geordie Wade, who had come to the coal pit on the day Mr. Peaver had shown it to her. He had been the carrier's boy, she remembered, and had lost his work when the pit stopped; and now he was standing by the garden gate, awkwardly, as if he did not know what to do, and she remembered his cheerful freckled face.

"But I must see what Geordie wants," said Mr. Peaver. "We all do what we can for Geordie. I must give him a shilling."

He went hurrying to his bureau against the wall. He jerked it open, and then his fingers were jingling coins in a drawer till he found a shilling. He went bustling from the room, and Mally remembered that he had shown a liking for Geordie that other day. So had Jane. She had even found him work in the stable, until he had abruptly left it.

Through the window she saw Mr. Peaver go down the path, and fall into talk with Geordie. They made an odd pair, the tall elderly parson and the out-at-elbows lad with the grin and the tousled hair, but they seemed to be finding enough to talk of; and Mr. Peaver's quick nods seemed to hint at interest too.

It was at this point that Mally behaved badly, and she did it deliberately. She knew precisely what she was doing. Mr. Peaver had gone so hurriedly from the room, after finding the shilling for Geordie, that he had forgotten to shut his bureau. It lay open; and in it, lying just where he had so hastily put it, was his letter from Colonel Storm. It was plain in Mally's view as soon as she turned to look that way, and temptation was immediate. That she had no shadow of right to look at it she well knew, and for a moment she stood hesitating. She took one more glance down the garden, to be sure that Mr. Peaver was still in talk with Geordie, and then she went on tip-toe to the bureau. The larger sheet came first to her hand, and after a quick glance at the door she hastily unfolded it.

It was written in a hand she thought a clerk's, and it began, as she now saw, with a seal of wax, carefully impressed. Then came the text of it:

James the Third by the grace of God King of England Scotland France and Ireland Defender of the Faith, etc.

To our trusty and well beloved James Peaver, Artium Magistro: Greeting. This is to authorize you to be, and do the office of, a Chaplain of the English Rite in the regiment of Horse commanded by our trusty and well beloved Colonel William Harvey. And to obey the orders from time to time given according to the Discipline of War.

Given at our Court at St. Germains, the 22nd day of November, 1714. And in the fourteenth year of our reign.

By His Majesty's Command.

Storm.

Mally stood aghast; and then another detail took her eye, and she felt her breath coming faster. It was all in that clerkly hand, except for the names and the date. Spaces had been left for these, and they had been done in a hand which she knew to be Tony Marriott's. But down at the bottom, in the left-hand corner, another hand appeared, one that was strange to her; and it had written a single word: *James.*

She stood open-mouthed and staring as she took in what it meant. It was a Commission in a rebel army, signed by King James, and it was a formal order to commit treason. It could hang any man who accepted it. It could hang Mr. Peaver, and Will Harvey too; and at once the memory came that Will was making formal gift of his lands to his son.

A voice sounded, as though lifted in farewell, and she thought she heard footsteps on the path. Hurriedly she flicked the paper into its folds again and dropped it where it had been. Mr. Peaver's steps were in the house already, and she knew

H

there was not time to be sitting again, as she should have been.

He found her standing by the table, calmly pouring herself more tea, and that was well thought of. It let her keep her eyes on the teapot, and avoid his; which was perhaps as well, as some further thoughts came in. This paper had been prepared with spaces blank for names, and there would be others like it. One had come to her uncle John, and it would hang him if it were found. There would be one, no doubt, for milord of Derwentwater. And what of Tony Marriott, who had signed them all?

"Well, well!" Mr. Peaver's voice was almost startling, and he seemed pleased about something. "I'm glad to see Geordie from time to time. We all do what we can for Geordie."

He was rubbing his lean hands with satisfaction, and Mally hastily turned to pour tea for him, whether he wanted it or not. She needed another moment before she could face him calmly, and she poured the tea slowly.

He took it happily, with a courteous word of thanks, and then he was insistent that she took her chair again. He sat upright in his own, with his teacup in his hands.

"Yes," he said cheerfully. "They swore to save what they had, and then they would have blamed it on the Apostle. Anything to justify themselves!"

Mally gaped at him. He seemed to be going on where he had left off, but she could not bring herself to grasp it.

"Think of Dutch William watching for our souls!" said Mr. Peaver.

"Who? What?"

"Little Hooknose. They cited Hebrews to us, if you please. The seventeenth of the thirteenth."

"Yes, but——"

Mally gave it up. He seemed the most impractical man she had ever heard of, and the frightening thought was that he believed all this. He believed it to the point of staking his life on it, and the lives of his friends as well. He had preached them into it, and now they believed it too.

She turned, and quickly put her teacup down. She could bear no more of this just now. She smoothed the mulberry serge, and she did her best at a smile as she came to her feet and announced that she must go.

He demurred, and then accepted it charmingly. He had one small request, he added. Would she stay one short minute while he wrote three lines to her uncle? There was a matter of some small importance——

He called to the boy for her horse before he wrote it, and then he sat at his opened bureau, with the Commission of King James plain in view, pushed lightly aside as he scribbled. Mally stood by the fire, tying her cloak and untying it again, while his quill scratched noisily and her eyes kept straying to that folded sheet in the bureau. The words of it were clear in her mind, and her fingers pulled at the cloakties as if she must pull at something or scream at him. But he kept his word and was brief, and he had ended his writing before her horse was ready. He could be brisk when he chose to be; and that, she thought, might make him the more dangerous.

She rode away in a daze, with Mr. Peaver bare-headed at the gate, his bands a startling white against his black. He waved to her as she went, and she scarcely heeded. She would have to tell Jane of this, which meant Jack Harvey, too. And how was she to tell him that his father was a rebel Colonel, with a Commission signed to prove it? Vaguely, as she rode, she saw the young moon rise above the hills; and her thoughts turned to his home, where the pele tower would be grey and quiet, and the Wall at peace under the moon. But it had not always been at peace, and there was a stone from it lodged in the pele, inscribed to the Departed Dead. *Dis Manibus:* and her thoughts came round the circle as she remembered Mr. Peaver's brooding.

She was so sunk in thought that she passed the coal pit without a glance, and she was between the black-and-yellow posts when she was roused by a cheerful shout from somewhere up the slope. She turned hastily, in something like consternation. Dick Chandler was coming down at a lively canter, and to adjust herself to Dick at this present moment seemed beyond her.

"I thought you hadn't seen me," he said.

"I was thinking."

"Then don't think quite so hard. I'll ride home with you."

"You needn't."

"I know I needn't, but I will. Have you had a bad afternoon?"

"I've had an entirely blameless afternoon. I've been drinking tea with a parson."

"Peaver, down yonder? He's the Non-juror, isn't he?"

"You know very well he is."

"True."

He accepted her short answers quite easily, and seemed in no way put out. Then he ranged alongside her and they rode in the friendly silence she had found with him yesterday. She felt it again at once. She was more at ease now, more able to view things calmly; and some quick flash of understanding told her that this cooling wind was coming from Dick Chandler. The thought set her turning to see him, and at once she was sure of it. There was a robust good sense in him that would seldom get excited and never tilt at windmills. It was something he spread about him, and Mally knew it. He was very soothing.

He saw her sharp glance; and again, in that odd way of his, he had caught her mood.

"Don't take Non-jurors too seriously," he said. "They've bees in their heads."

"This one has."

"They all have. They cite texts at you, about obedience and loving your rulers. Then they talk about the rights of Kings by inheritance, and King William being a usurper."

"I know. But what do you answer?"

"It's easy." A look of amusement was coming to him now. "William the Norman was a usurper. So were some other Kings. So I suppose they couldn't have had any rights?"

"Perhaps not. But——"

"So if King James inherits from those, he can't have any either. Simple!"

"Dick!" She was almost laughing at him. "Where did you get that from?"

"My father told me."

"He would! What about the texts they cite?"

"Give them the one back about rendering unto Caesar the things that are Caesar's. That always worries 'em."

"Did your father tell you that too?"

"Yes. He said it was all dam' nonsense anyway."

Which was so exactly what she could hear Black William saying that Mally dissolved into laughter. It heartened her, and made her feel better. Coming to Dick Chandler after Mr. Peaver was like coming to sunlight after dark and cloud. There was a down-to-earth good sense about him that made Non-jurors seem fantastic. Which led to the further thought that Tony Marriott was nearer to a Non-juror, and was the son of one.

They were nearing the house when Dick spoke again, and she noted that he had been watching her.

"Will you be riding tomorrow?" he said briefly. "May I come to the house?"

"I—I don't know." She suddenly saw that there was a difficulty. "We have a guest in the house just now, and——"

It was certainly awkward. She was not sure how much he ought to know about Jack Harvey, and there was not time to think it out. She hesitated, and then he gave her the answer himself.

"Then perhaps I'd better not come to the house."

"It's no matter," she told him quickly. "It's only that I don't yet know what's arranged."

"I see." He was watching her carefully.

"If I should be free, I expect I shall ride out. I should come this way again, and——"

"Then I'll watch for you. I shall be hoping for you."

She noted that he did not ride quite to the house with her. He had asked no questions, but he seemed to have taken the hint. She turned her horse and sat watching as he rode away. She had a wave for him as he passed out of sight, and for some long moments she sat motionless before she made slowly for the house. She passed through the gates, and quietly through the trees; and the light had ridden away with Dick Chandler, and only the dark was left. She was lonely, and a little frightened, and Non-jurors were not a fantasy. They existed, and there were Commissions signed by King James, and her uncle John had one.

It was nearing dusk when she had seen her horse put away. There were candles showing in the house, and in the darkening sky the moon was low above the trees. Dick would have to ride hard to be home before full dark, and she paused before the door, thinking of the buoyant confidence that was his. It was not with her now. It had gone with Dick, and it would be with him as he rode under the moon. For herself, she must enter the house; and she must tell Jane about those Commissions, and the name of Colonel Harvey.

They were in the parlour, all of them, when she entered, and the candles were bright. Jane was by the hearth, with Jack at her side, and there was something in the looks of both of them that took Mally's eye at once. Uncle John was by the table, and she saw that there was claret on it, and that he had been pouring as she entered.

"Ho ho!" he said, and she saw that he was excited. "Home at last?"

"Yes, sir. I——"

"It's these two. They go riding together, and what do you think they've done? What news for us?"

"I can't guess," said Mally; and could.

"They get themselves betrothed." His voice was loud, as if he found it a joke and a happiness in one. "They're to be wed, they say, and they want our blessing on it. Jane as Mrs. John Harvey, hey?"

"Yes."

Mally took a grip of herself; and she tried to look as happy as Jane.

CHAPTER XXV

THE GALLOWAYS

IT made one of the longest evenings that Mally could remember, although in fact it was a short one. A single thought showed her that this was Jane's evening, and that it must not be spoiled by treason and the shadows that were massing. Jane must have her evening, and King James must wait for the morrow. It must be happiness tonight.

So Mally had to sit the evening through on those terms, and it was a strain. There was too much pretence in it. Dick Chandler was far away; and Mr. Peaver was back with her now, and his fantastic purpose and the force that drove him on. He was dangerous; and her thoughts of what he might do were always interrupted, had always to be put aside for the excited talk of Jane and the jovialities of uncle John. Mally was far from sorry when he began to insist that they were tired and should be early abed. She said aloud that he was right, and then she gave a lead to it.

She slipped into Jane's room at the very last for a goodnight word, and Jane was almost in bed.

"Will you be able to manage John?" she asked. "John and the house, when I leave you to it?"

"Oh!" Mally had been too distracted through the evening to think that she would have this thrust upon her. "I expect I shall. Perhaps he won't ask me to."

"He certainly will. He's already told me how fortunate it is."

"Has he? Well, there's time to think of it. It won't be next week, I suppose?"

"Perhaps in the spring. We haven't talked of that much."

"And where to?"

"Stagshaw, I suppose. Or nearby."

Jane was smiling into vacancy; and Mally felt one quick touch of envy as she thought of the clean wide space of it, the long views to the river, and the wind that rustled on the

Wall. But the Wall led down to the river, to an inn where men had met; which reminded her of more, and she had to take her thoughts back to Jane.

"Yes," she said quietly. "I shall enjoy making a visit to you there—if you ask me."

"If I ask you?" Jane seemed amused, and then, suddenly, she sobered. "I could not have had this if you had not come here."

"What *do* you mean?"

"I couldn't have been wed without some small dowry, and John hadn't one to give. But now, you see, he has something, and that's because William bought the coal. And William came because of you."

"I suppose you're right."

"I know I am. I know too well how it was before you came —and William. It's odd, isn't it, to be grateful to Black William? I didn't expect that."

"There's a good deal, Jane, that I hadn't expected. But meanwhile perhaps——"

"I think you're right." Jane was smiling happily again, and seemingly without thought of care. "Bed and sleep, Mally. That's the need. Go and get it."

"I will. Good night, Jane—bless you."

Mally took leave and went. But bed, as she soon learned, was more easily achieved than sleep. She was soon in bed, safe and alone in the shielding dark, and she was warm and tired and comfortable; but sleep did not come. Her mind was too active, and her thoughts would not be still. There had been so much in the day to grasp and put tidy, and now she lived it through again, and went round and round the maze of it. Far away, at the foot of the stair, she heard the whirr and tinkle of the tall old clock as it struck eleven; and there were Commissions signed by King James, and milord of Derwentwater met others at an inn, and Black William had letters from Sir John, and there was none but herself to stop it. Even Jane might be less help now, for her mind would be on sweeter things; and Jane reminded her of the Wall, and the track that twisted along it, and ran to the river. She had ridden with Tony Marriott along that track, and he had told her of his boyhood at the Pretender's Court. Soon he would be riding here to see her, and then he would meet Dick Chandler. She was sure he would. It was the way things had, in these crazy days. Then her thoughts went back, as if a magnet pulled, and she was on Lady Chandler's stair, and his tall figure was by the open door as he looked into the night, and then he turned to look up; and she was breathless. Then she was in the salon, and he was taking her to the Earl of Derwentwater, and there was a bowl of water where a white rose floated. She saw the glint of the candles, and heard the swish of silk and satin; and below her, at the foot of the stair, the whirring came again as the clock struck midnight.

It was a little time after that, perhaps some minutes only, when a sound came in. It was a sound, she thought, from outside the house. It came softly, muffled by the shutters and the curtains, and she did not believe it. She put it down to fancy, or some creak in the house. But her head had lifted from the pillow, and she was very wide awake, all her attention put to listening. It came again, softly in the dark, and this time she sat erect in bed. It was surely the sound of a horse, a horse that waits, and stamps fretfully.

Mally slipped out of bed. She parted the bed-curtains and wrapped herself hurriedly in the serge night-gown that was ready to her hand; and her thoughts were leaping excitedly as she groped her way to the window. For who was it who might come in secret, and perhaps seek a word with someone? She drew the window-curtains back, and felt in the dark for the shutters; and her thought was of Tony Marriott, who might do such a thing as this. She would believe anything now, and she had to steady her breath as she gently pushed the shutters.

The house looked to the south-west, and the moon was fair upon it, hanging in a cloudless sky. Below her was the lawn with the curving drive, and beyond were the trees, hard and black against the light, and a dark pool of shadow below them. She could see nothing in that, and there was no horse to be seen; but on the lawn, full in the moonlight, a man was standing, tall and slim and black. He turned on his heel, coming half-face to the house, and she saw the linen bands at at his throat, silver in the moon. His wide hat left his face in shadow, but he was surely Mr. Peaver.

Below her a latch clicked softly. There was the creak of a door, and a man stepped quickly from the house, full into the moonlight on the grass. He was bareheaded, with his face in the light, and he was uncle John. He went to Mr. Peaver, and for a moment they were in whispered talk.

In the pool of shadow by the trees a boot crunched softly, and then a man came slowly into the light, a burly thick-set man whom she did not know. He seemed to be looking at John, and John raised a hand and nodded. The man turned, and disappeared into the shadow. There was a gentle clop of hooves, and then another man came from the dark, leading a loaded horse. He led it across the grass to the door, a wiry short-legged packhorse, with the bales made fast to its sides, and Mally was almost craning out of her window to see. The thick-set man came from the shadow again, but it was the man who led the horse who had her interest now. She thought she knew him, and she leaned farther out to see. Then she was sure. He was Geordie Wade; and she remembered the hurried letter she had brought to John this day from Mr. Peaver. It had been written after talk with Geordie; and Geordie had been a carrier's boy.

The horse stopped by the door, almost below her window, and the thick-set man began to unstrap the bales, Geordie helping. They did it slowly, plainly with a care for silence, and Mally had a chance to slip away. She woke Jane ruthlessly, whispering fiercely at her, and then almost hauling her from bed and bundling her into her night-gown. A moment later Jane was hurried into Mally's room, still only half awake, and set to look from that window; and then she was wholly awake.

"My God!" she whispered. "It's their prunes."

"Their what?"

"Their prunes and cochineal—their pistols, and the rest. They're bringing them *here*." Jane sounded appalled. "That's Geordie Wade."

"I know. Who's the other?"

"Who?" She leaned again through the window. "It's Joe Nixon. I told you. He was carrier for the pit, till it finished. Geordie worked for him."

"It looks as if Geordie still does."

"Yes. I thought he'd sold his galloways."

"His what?"

"Packhorses. It's what we call them here. He said Geordie was turned off."

"He was. You found him work here, in the stable."

"And he stayed one day." Jane sounded vicious about it. "We can see it now. I suppose Nixon *did* fail, as an honest carrier. Then Peaver found him this. It's very pretty."

A slithering noise hinted that the bales were free and were being slid from the horse. Mally looked cautiously from the window again, and now only Geordie was to be seen. He was leading the unloaded horse back to the trees; and sounds of quiet movement came from below the stair, to tell of the others in the house with the bales. Jane listened, and then spoke sharply.

"They'll wake the house if they're not quieter than that. Do they want the cook to hear?"

"Why haven't the dogs barked?"

"Because John's there, of course. He's quieted them."

"He must be mad."

"He's been mad for years. I wish Jack would wake. We could do with him now."

"Oh!" Mally had been so lost in her thoughts that she had forgotten Jack Harvey. "But couldn't we——"

"No, we couldn't. We can't go to his room at this hour. What's that?"

It was another sound from outside, and they saw another loaded horse being led to the door by Geordie Wade. The men came from the house again, and with the same slow care the bales were unstrapped and carried in. The muffled sounds came again from below, and Jane pulled her night-gown tighter.

"Where are they putting it?" she asked angrily. "I'm going to look."

"Jane, you——"

"I'm not frightened of anybody in this house. You stay here."

A faint glow of candlelight was coming up the stair, and Mally stayed rigid at the bedroom door while Jane went slowly to the stairhead. She crept half-way down the stair, and leaned over the rail. The pause lengthened, and then she came softly back. She was at the window, looking out again, before she spoke.

"They're taking it below," she said. "I think you must have been a help to them."

"Me?"

"Why else do you suppose they must have the wine cellar cleared? I don't think this is claret."

"You mean——"

"Here's another galloway."

The moon was as bright as ever on the grass as Geordie led a third horse over, and this time the bales were of a different shape. Again the men came from the house to unload, and Jane drew her breath in noisily.

"It's Peaver's doing," she snapped. "Why can't he keep the stuff himself?"

"Because he has a small house."

"John must be out of his wits. You'll note that Nixon knows about it now. He even knows where it's been put."

"So does Geordie."

"I'll have a word for Geordie that he won't like, next time I see him. But Geordie means well. It's Nixon I'm worried about. He's half a rogue, at least."

"Jane! Do you mean he might——"

"He certainly might, if someone paid him to. How much longer will they be?"

There were still two galloways to come to the door, which made five in all, and the light was aslant on the house before all was done. Then there was another surprise. Geordie had gone into the shadows, and there was the stamp of a hoof and a jingle of harness to tell what he was about. Nixon stood on the grass, short and burly, and seemed to be in last talk with John and Mr. Peaver. Then Geordie came into the light, riding one of the unloaded horses. Another followed, tethered behind it, and another, and another; and Mally found herself clutching at Jane as amazement grew. She had supposed there would be five of these horses, and she counted four-and-twenty. They went in a wide circle, making round for the path again, and the gates to the open road, and Nixon swung himself astride an unloaded one as they went. He waved an

arm in farewell, and with a clink and a jingle, and a soft
rumble of hooves, the galloways were gone.

The grass was silver-grey in the moonlight, quiet and
empty now. Mr. Peaver turned, and there was a flash of white
from his bands, and a black sheen on his gown. He spoke a
word to John, and then strode vigorously away, to go home,
no doubt, on foot. There was a lithe energy in Mr. Peaver that
matched his force of mind. His power for danger lay in that,
his power to impose himself on others; and Mally was remembering his charm and courtesy in the afternoon. But she had
not yet told Jane that he had a Commission as Chaplain, in
the regiment of Colonel Harvey.

His long stride took him to the trees, and he was lost in
the shadow. John was alone in the moonlight. He walked
slowly to the door, and below them they heard the latch, and
the soft slide of the bolt. Mally drew away from the window,
and it was Jane who spoke.

"He'll be coming up to bed. I'll have to wait here."

"Yes. But those horses—four-and-twenty of them?"

"It's the usual. Twenty-four galloways make a train."

"But five here means nineteen for somewhere else."

"There'll be other houses in this." A gleam of moonlight
lit Jane's face, and showed it taut and strained. "I'm afraid
all this is a little bigger than we thought it was."

"It's getting bigger still. Where are these other
houses?"

"I don't know. There's none close round here."

"Could it be—Will Harvey's?"

"Oh, Mally!"

"But the pele tower there?" A glimpse seemed to come
of a stone that was set in its wall, and had Roman letters cut.
"You could store anything in that."

"The whole nineteen." Jane sounded almost savage now.
"I suppose that's why Jack is told to stay here. It wasn't for
me, was it? It was to have him out the way when that lot
came."

Below them a shoe creaked softly on the stair. It was John
coming up to bed, and they stood in careful silence while his
steps moved to his own door. Faintly they heard it shut, and
then Mally relaxed. Jane, perhaps, did not.

"He must be mad," she said fiercely. "That stuff could hang him if it were found here."

"I know."

There was a Commission of King James that could hang him too, and Mally had to restrain herself. It was not the moment to tell of that.

"How's that wagonway getting on? And the new pit?"

The question came suddenly, and Mally was taken aback.

"Now why ask——"

"I want some cause for sending John to see it. We'll have him safe away from the house tomorrow. Then we'll see what's in that cellar."

CHAPTER XXVI

MR. PEAVER'S GUEST

IT was apparent at breakfast that the management of uncle John had become an art with Jane. She did not even address him directly. She addressed herself to Mally, inquiring about her ride with Dick Chandler the other day, and her inspection of the new coal pit. Mally gave the pre-arranged answer that streaks of coal had been showing at the bottom. Uncle John looked interested; and Mally, with a little free invention of her own, added that there was something odd about this coal. It was in the wrong place, or at the wrong slope, or something; she was not quite sure what, and she might even be mistaken. She put that in as a belated prudence, but uncle John hardly heard it. He was already declaring that he would go out this morning to see for himself.

He was a little later in doing it than they expected. He went strolling aimlessly out of doors after breakfast, and he was next seen under the trees, busy with a garden rake. In itself that was no oddity, for he liked pottering; but Jane watched him through the window, and declared that the galloways had evidently left hoof-marks which he was now covering with dead leaves.

It was past ten o'clock when he rode away, and Jane summoned what was almost a conference. She produced some ale to help it; and then Jack Harvey had to be told of the broken night, of the galloways under the moon, of the parcels carried to the cellar. He listened very quietly, but he was grave about it, and perhaps perturbed under his calm. Nor was that all he had to hear; for Mally knew that she must tell them now what she had spared them last night. They must hear of Mr. Peaver's Commission in the regiment of Colonel Harvey.

He took it in complete silence. It was Jane whose face lost colour.

"They're all mad," she burst out. "A Colonel! What does he know of war?"

"I think he once served in the militia."

"Militia!" She almost snorted at it. "A crew of plough-boys, to be looked at once a year by the Lord Lieutenant! John served in the militia, too."

"I expect he did. Do you think he has one of these Commissions too?"

"Of course he has. Your father as Colonel and Peaver as Chaplain. I expect John is the Major. What a regiment! Has it any men?"

"We don't know." Jack was answering her quietly and gravely. "I expect they'll enlist their tenants, and some pit-men."

"To fight King George, I suppose? Does anyone ask if they're mad?"

"Steady, Jane! We haven't come to that yet."

"We're getting nearer to it. I don't like your Colonel Storm. I don't like this Pretender either. He sits in France, and sends good men to this." She was snapping angrily, and suddenly she turned on Mally. "If we don't see this cellar soon, we shall have John coming home."

"Very well. Has it occurred to you that the cellar will be locked?"

"The housekeeper has a key, hasn't she? You need a key to everything here, even if John doesn't know it. Remember that, when you have the house."

She took her keys; she carefully lit two candles at the fire; and with a last glance through the window she led the way.

There were three great cellars under the house, opening one from another, and the first of them, clean and dry, held her stores for the winter, butter and cheese and salt, dried peas and beans, apples and salted meats, sugar and spice and raisins, soap and candles and beeswax. Jane unlocked it, and as carefully locked it behind her before she led through it to the second cellar, where the ale-store was. It was damper here, and colder, and the scent of ale was heavy as she pushed the thick door open. One side had the small-ale, ranged in its barrels on the low wooden racks, and the other the October, some ripening in barrel and some ready in bottle. The candles flickered and fantastic shadows danced as she went quickly to the farther door. This was the wine cellar; and properly it was John's concern.

Mally took the candles while Jane made sure of the key. The lock turned with an ease to hint that someone beside the stable boy had done some greasing here, and the hinges swung in silence as Jack put his shoulder to the door. Mally lifted the candles, and was the first to go in.

It was swept and tidy as she had left it, cold and dank from the disuse of years. The walls were black for want of lime, the stone floor cracked and stained. There was nothing to fling back the light, and it was darker here, colder and more secret. Only the flat old wine shelves took the light; and on them, neatly ranged, were packages in canvas tied about with cord. There were six of one shape and four of another, and two smaller ones at the side, and one glance was enough for Jane.

"Five galloways," she said. "Ten bales. Just right."

"Those two odd ones?"

"They were piled on top, on the last beast. What are they?"

She stooped to pick one up; and as she handled it a hollow rumbling sound came from it, muffled and indistinct. Jane stared in surprise, and held it gingerly.

"Now what the——" She turned, to hold it more clearly to the candles. "Jack, can we untie these cords?"

Between them they achieved it, and Mally held the candles while the canvas wrappings were parted; and what emerged set them all staring. It was a gaily painted side-drum.

"Drums!" Jane looked in bewilderment from the thing to its fellow, still wrapped in canvas on the wine table. "Will someone tell me——"

"Yes." Jack answered her sharply, and his voice was grave. "Isn't it how you start a rebellion? You ride into a town, and you strike up the drums in the market place. You pull off your hats, and you proclaim King James. You drink his health, and you make the Mayor do it too. The drums bring everyone to watch."

"Very pretty."

Jane had her lips pressed tight as she put the drum into its canvas again. In silence Jack helped her to tie it, and then she turned to the other bales. She fingered one from the set of six, and it was heavier than the drum.

"What's this?" she said.

It was a pile of clothing this time, neatly folded, and Jane shook out a horseman's cloak, long and full. It was vivid in scarlet, and on either side, below the shoulder, it was embroidered with a white rose.

"Good God! The soldiers of King James." Jack was staring at the thing as Jane held it up, and then his glance turned to Mally. "You know what the white rose means?"

"I do."

She had seen it before, and she spoke as grimly as he. It had been a real rose she had seen before, floating in the water, but that mattered nothing. This was the Jacobite emblem, and she knew it.

"How many of them?" she asked.

"Eight."

"In that bale. And six bales——"

"Makes forty-eight." Jack ended it for her tersely. "Half a Troop of Horse. About what he might enlist round here."

They looked at each other in silence. Jane grimly folded the scarlet cloak, and Jack helped her to wrap it in the bale again. Without comment they unwrapped another bale, one from the set of four, and disclosed a pile of wide-brimmed hats, packed crown in crown. They were roughly made, of a cheap black felt, and each had the white cockade. Jane held one out, and then counted the pile.

"A dozen."

"Four bales makes forty-eight. The half-Troop, you see."

That was Mally's comment, and she held the candles steady while Jack looked round the cellar, as if in search of something.

"I'd expected arms," he said. "Swords, perhaps."

"And muskets?"

"Carbines, more likely, since it's Horse."

"They're not here." Jane turned, and in the candlelight her face was hard and strained. "Jack, you don't think they've gone to *your* house?"

"Ours? Now why——"

"They went somewhere. Nineteen galloways, still loaded. Some house expected them. You were sent here and told to stay here. And that pele tower of yours——"

"Jane!"

The tallow spilled on Mally's hand as the candles shook, and irritably she turned on them both.

"For Heaven's sake, let's get out of this cellar. I've had enough of it. And we'll have John home soon."

It was, however, another hour before he came, a bleak and comfortless hour, in which they talked it over and round and through, and arrived at nothing. The fact confronted them. It was hardly to be believed, but here it was. Between the war cloaks and the Commission, a search of this house would hang John Lawley; and they all knew it.

It was John himself who was wholly unconcerned. He came home jovially, in high good humour, surely with no true thought of the risk he ran. He called gustily for ale, insisting that they all should join him; and Mally's thoughts were of London, and how little he knew of it. All his days he had lived in this lonely place, where he was the squire, secure and safe; and he knew nothing of London, and the long arm of a Secretary of State.

He rallied her on the blunder she had made about the coal. It was just where it ought to be, and at the expected slope, and he did not know what she had been talking about. She had best go back and have another look.

She gave him a soft answer. She said she would certainly look again; and later, on a second thought, she decided that she might as well do it. Jack and Jane would want each other, and it would be tactful to leave them; and it had not quite slipped her memory that Dick Chandler had spoken of being watchful for her this afternoon. She considered it thoughtfully, and then went to see about her boots.

She rode out alone in the best of the afternoon, and she was glad of a clear bright sun. It was, indeed, as fine an afternoon as November could give, and the mulberry serge seemed exactly right. There was a gleam from her silver-laced gloves, and something very near it from her boots. Her hat, too, with repeated pressing, was beginning to look less like river water, and with one thing and another Mally was feeling better. Dick had certainly said that he would watch for her; and now she was savouring the mild clear afternoon, and noting the zest the Barbary seemed to have for this. Without haste she skirted the fields and came to the line of the wagonway, where the old pit lay forlorn. By its rim she halted, and she took her time at looking round.

Up the slope the new pit was less busy than it had been. The mound of earth had been smoothed and tidied, and a gap ran through where the wagonway would go. A man in the gap was holding a saddle-horse, which might have been Dick Chandler's, but there was no rider in sight. She watched carefully, and a man pushed a barrow into the gap; but he was not known to her, and she turned to look the other way.

There was no lack of activity here. The wagonway had made strides since she had last been here, and it was hardly a hundred yards away. There were men with picks and shovels, a wagon tipping gravel, men laying long oak rails, men hovering with strings and spirit-levels; but nowhere was there a man she knew. Dick was no doubt in the new pit, and that would be his horse in the gap.

She kept her back firmly to it. She was very well placed where she was, and easily in view of anyone who chose to look, and she gave her attention to the wagonway. It was certainly making progress, and another day or two would bring it to where she now was. Another week or two would take it to the new pit, and perhaps coal would be rumbling down it soon. Black William did not waste time, and he no doubt meant to have his money back.

Behind her there was the gentle sound of a horse, a little distance away, and surely coming nearer. Mally cocked an ear, and went on watching the wagonway. She sat quite still on the Barbary; and from some far clear corner of her mind the thought came that what she showed of herself to Dick was not quite what she showed to anybody else. It was not what she showed to Jane, or to Tony Marriott. It was a blend of her qualities which he knew as her; and she was quietly getting it ready for him.

Her eyes were on the wagonway, and her attention on the hoofbeats that were coming closer. They were behind her and to her left, and now they were slowing. They stopped, and she knew he must be almost at her side. She stayed intent on the wagonway, making sure her head was up and her shoulders back; and she waited for his voice.

"Dear lady, will you spare me no glance?"

There was only one man who would speak to her like that, and he was not Dick Chandler. She turned wildly, and she all but slipped from her saddle. She gripped it fiercely, while the Barbary went capering in a half-circle, with his nostrils fluttering. At once a big calm grey came pushing close, and a restraining hand was at the Barbary's head.

"I'm sorry," said Tony Marriott. "I startled you."

"Yes."

She said it blankly. She was not quite back in her wits yet, and he was very close. His hand had dropped from the Barbary's head, but she could feel his knee against hers before he moved back. He was watching her keenly, and she saw him relax as if reassured.

"You were so intent," he said. "You never even heard me come. What was it that had all your thought?"

"It—I was watching the wagonway."

"And what, please, is a wagonway?"

"Why——"

The far clear corner of her mind told her that the fault was hers if he looked puzzled. She had been expecting Dick Chandler, and she had not changed the blend in time.

"Why, that is." She waved cheerfully at it. "That flurry of men and shovels. I think it's to carry coal along."

She would not have said that to Dick, but she was adjusting herself quickly now. She leaned back in her saddle, got her head up, and contrived a smile.

He was looking at the wagonway with interest, and she moved back a little to see him better. Where he had come from she had no notion, but he was certainly showing an elegance. He was in a fine golden brown, with a tracery of gold lace round the great cuffs of his coat. His waistcoat was of deep cream taffeta. His cravat, of the whitest Mechlin, was gathered with black silk ribbon, and he had a black three-cornered hat with white plumes flat along the brim. His short neat periwig was gathered with another black silk ribbon, and it was this that took Mally's eye. In the polite world a tie-wig was a traveller's convenience, but it was also a hint that an occasion was informal, and so, perhaps, he meant it now.

Mally let her horse move back another pace as she considered him. He thought he was dressed informally, not to attract attention. He had no bright colours, no sharp contrasts, and he supposed that to be enough. Memories of the town were with Mally as she noted the fine smooth cloth, the excellence of fit, the details that conformed to fashion. For all the quietness of it he was in the mode. He had come from a London tailor, and he looked it; and here, in the country, he would take the notice of everybody. Alarm was in her as she saw it. He was on too dangerous a work to be dressed like this; and the memory was back of the candle-lit cellar, the cloaks with the white cockade, and the Commissions he had signed.

"Where did you come from?"

"I beg your pardon." He turned instantly as she spoke, and his manners matched his elegance. "I'm most neglectful. I was watching this affair of wagons yonder. Peaver told me of it."

"You've been to him?"

"I've made myself his guest."

"What?"

She was too startled to care for manners as she thought of them together, fanatics both, and what might hatch between them. She showed it in her looks, and his face lit with amusement.

"Why not?" he said gently. "I must have quarters somewhere, and here's as good a place as another. He has a house that hides itself, and he's a man I must work with. So I arrived this morning. I've been asleep through the forenoon."

"Oh?"

"It's very convenient. I may very properly lodge there. And I did say I should seek you out. It fits very happily."

She knew he meant it. By day he would be at her side; and by night he would be in talk with Mr. Peaver, plotting, planning, plunging deeper into what was deep enough.

"I woke at noon." He spoke again, and now he was in gentle earnest. "We dined, and my one thought was of you. I asked directions for the way, and I was making for your house. Then I saw you."

He could hardly have missed seeing her, and she had to hold herself composed as he went quietly on.

"You were sitting here, and you graced the land. You were all intent on something, and you never heard me come."

"No."

"I thanked God for it. I had not known if I should find you, and here you were, and alone. You might almost have been waiting for me."

"I suppose I might."

A wind set the white plumes rippling in his hat as he nodded, smiling. Then his head lifted, as if he had seen something. He was looking up the slope, and in one sharp stab an understanding came to Mally. She turned hastily.

She had been right about the horse that waited in that gap. Dick had kept his promise to watch for her; and now he was trotting down the slope to join her.

CHAPTER XXVII

THE ESCORT

THERE was no time for thought, and Mally braced herself to meet it. She had no notion what to do. She must take this as it came, and hope for the best.

He came to a halt within a yard of her, and for a moment there was silence. The men eyed each other warily, and without, as she thought, much pleasure. Then both of them looked to her, and her duty was obvious. She steadied herself, and tried to speak lightly.

"Permit me, please. Here is Mr. Chandler. And—er—" The awkward thought intruded that she did not know what name he was using at the moment. "And—er—Captain Marriott."

If that was wrong, she could not help it. He ought to have told her, and she looked from one to the other with what she hoped was a winning smile.

"Oh?" said Dick.

"Sir——" The tricorne hat went sweeping gracefully. "Sir, I'm honoured. Your most dutiful servant."

"I'm not quite sure what that means."

"Nor am I, just now. I wait to learn more."

Mally intervened hastily.

"Captain Marriott," she said, "is—er—on his travels. He was known to me in London." She turned hurriedly to the Captain. "Mr. Chandler was so kind as to meet me on my journey, and escort me here."

"I'm glad he did. I think, Mr. Chandler, that I have heard your name."

"My father's, more likely."

"Possibly. But you'll have some concern with this—er—undertaking?"

"The wagonway? I'm in charge of it. That's my business here. I'm not quite sure of yours."

"No?" The Captain kept countenance perfectly. "A different business, sir. I fear I can't pretend to the mechanic arts."

"It's not wise to pretend to anything, round here."

"But I've no wish to. I'll proclaim my business to the world. It's to pay homage to Miss Lawley, and to make my devotion to her."

"The Devil it is! Well, you're not the only one."

"I'm sure I'm not." It came back smoothly. "It would be no compliment to Miss Lawley to suppose that. The good taste of many gentlemen must——"

"Please!" Again Mally intervened hastily. "You'll make me vain, if you say so much. I'm sure there are no gentlemen here who——"

"Mr. Chandler seems to be saying that he is one of them. I had not known of that."

He was gently reproachful, and before she could think of an answer Dick gave it for her.

"If it comes to that, I hadn't known of *you*." He said it very straightly to the Captain, and then at once he turned to Mally. "I don't think you told me of him?"

There was nothing for it now but boldness.

"Why should I?" She hoped that sounded teasing. "I haven't asked about the ladies of Gateshead. Do they languish without hope?"

"I'm sure they don't."

"I'm sure of it, too." She thought that quick and neat, and at once she turned in her saddle. "As for the ladies of the town, I know how they pine for Captain Marriott."

"Mally! They don't."

"Oh yes, they do. I've seem 'em in rows at routs."

Dick turned on her promptly.

"Were you one of them?"

"Now——" She faced him with her chin tilting. "Now, if I had been, do you think I should tell you—either of you?"

She looked triumphantly from the one man to the other, and then, with the air of one who has disposed of all this, she looked away from both of them. She looked down the slope, to the busy workings on the wagonway; and at once her idle gaze was held, and grew intent. There was a horseman at the side of the men with shovels, and he was watching her. She knew him instantly. She would have known anywhere that burly shape in the wide brown coat that was indefinably a merchant's.

He came jingling up the slope to join them, and she was sure he had a purpose and knew exactly what he meant to do. She noted, too, that they were all waiting for him. At fifty yards' distance William had imposed himself, and had silently taken command.

He came without haste, and she had time to watch his sun-browned face, and to note again that his riding-boots seemed only to heighten his air of being a merchant. He swept his hat to her, but his first word was for his son.

"How's it up yonder?" His whip pointed to the new pit.

"Well enough," said Dick promptly. "The ground's a bit wet, and we're having to timber the way up. There'll be a drop of water to pump out. Otherwise we're ready."

"Good. I'll go up there in a minute." He turned his eyes to Mally, and for an instant he was amused. "I like to see things for myself. I take some trouble to."

"Aye, sir. I——" She suddenly understood what he really meant. "May I present Captain Marriott, whom I knew in London? Captain—Esquire Chandler."

"Sir——" The tricorne hat swept impeccably. "Sir, your most humble servant."

"Yours, sir."

"I have the honour, sir, to know Sir John Chandler."

"So have I. I'm his brother."

"Yes, sir. I——"

Even the accomplished Captain Marriott was looking a little puzzled, as if he had not quite met William before. His voice died away, and William nodded affably.

"He told me of you."

"I'm much honoured, sir."

It was what he would have been expected to say in Jermyn Street. But his eyes had steadied, and his face was a shade more impassive than before. Mally read the signs, and knew he had seen danger here.

"You needn't be," said William cheerfully. "John often tells me of his guests, and who they are."

"Indeed, sir?"

"Aye, and what they do."

Mally sat tense and still. That could mean almost anything; and she knew the simple look that had come to William now.

"I'm glad to meet you," he said heartily.

"The honour's mine, sir."

"Oh, no." He sounded even heartier. "I said just now, I like to see for myself."

Mally caught at her breath. William looked big and placid. Dick, across the circle, was utterly still. Tony Marriott seemed for once without an answer; and William spoke again.

"It's easier when you've seen a man. You know how he looks then."

"No doubt, sir. I——"

"So I'm glad you've come here. I thought perhaps you would."

The words seemed to fall into silence. He sat motionless, his eyes unwaveringly on the man before him. Mally saw it all; and then, in one wild flash of understanding, she knew what her part had been in this. Sir John had known about Colonel Storm, and William had been warned that he was in the North; and had been warned, too, that he would perhaps seek Mally. Another flash of insight came, sickening and frightening, as she saw what they had done. Sir John had written to her, bluff and honest, with his gift of silk and taffeta, and she had walked right into the trap. He had written of Captain Marriott in his letter, and she had answered that the Captain would shortly seek her out. At once William had appeared, and had kindly offered to send her letter with his own. No doubt he had read it, and learned that he had only to watch the wagonway, and sooner or later his man would come. Mally sat quivering as the truth of it came upon her, and she saw what these Chandlers had done. She was the bait they had used for Colonel Storm, and perhaps even Dick had helped. He had watched the wagonway.

She turned her head, staring angrily at William, almost hating him as she thought how he had used her, and how simple he had found her; and suddenly another thought came rushing. All this depended on the Chandlers having access to the land, in short, the wagonway; and was that why William had bought this coal? Colonel Storm was important; and this might be William's way. He was moving into position before the others had even seen where the board was. It was certainly William's way.

Then, while she was still aghast at it, William spoke directly to her.

"He's now your guest, I suppose?"

"He is not. He——"

"I am *not* Miss Lawley's guest." The Captain cut in sharply, and it sounded as if he were trying to get a grip on this again. "It is the Reverend Mr. Peaver who invites me."

"That parson yonder? I've heard him preach. He's a Non-juror, isn't he?"

"I don't see what——"

"It might set folk asking what you talk of."

That was plain enough, yet to Mally's ear it had no threatening ring. He made it sound like the older man giving homely advice to the younger, and to her surprise it even sounded friendly. Yet Captain Marriott seemed to take it differently. He flushed as he heard it, and then he was very stiff and erect. He was the gentleman of the town as he answered.

"Give me leave to tell you, sir, and setting aside some double meanings I seem to have heard from you, that I am not here because Mr. Peaver is a Non-juror, nor to take his thoughts, nor to hear him preach. I did not even know of his preaching."

"I did."

"Indeed?" The flush deepened, as if he found the interruption annoying. "To deal plainly, sir, I care nothing for that. I do not probe into your affairs. But I tell you that I am here on behalf of Miss Lawley. I am here to offer homage, to lay my devotion at her feet, to declare her to excel in all——"

"You mean you're sweet on the lass?"

There was a gasp from Mally, and then, for a moment, silence. William looked helpful. Dick was as stiff and silent as before. Tony Marriott sat speechless, cut short like a quenched candle. He had been famed through the town for his fine riposte, his skill with the charming phrase; but the gentlemen of the town had not been quite like William.

"I—I do mean that," he said suddenly.

"Good," said William, and turned again to Mally. "I

don't blame the lad. I'd have been sweet on you myself at his age."

There was another gasp; and Captain Marriott, who had perhaps not been referred to as a lad before, was seen to twitch in his saddle. William sat beaming, and Mally tried fiercely to know what her thoughts were. She was so bemused that she knew neither what she thought nor what she ought to do; and William turned calmly to his son.

"Dick," he said. "They don't want us here. I think we'd better go."

"I won't," said Dick.

"Hey, hey! Haven't you any tact?"

"Plenty. But I'm not going."

He sounded dogged and determined, and he left no doubt that he meant it. He looked Tony Marriott in the eye.

"I came here this afternoon to meet Mally, and I'm not riding off because someone else has come. Also——"

"Yes?" said the Captain frigidly.

"I heard your fine words, and I won't match those. But I think as much of Mally as you do, if not a bit more, and I don't care who hears it. I'll say it to anybody."

"Hey!" said William. "Spare the lass. She's blushing."

And to Mally's deepening annoyance that was true. She was, and William nodded cheerfully.

"What are we going to do?" he asked.

It was Tony Marriott who gave him the answer first. He had recovered something of his poise now, and he spoke firmly.

"As far as it touches me, I maintain what I have said. I told Miss Lawley that I should seek her here, and I did not think she was displeased at that. At least——" He turned suddenly to her. "You allowed me to think that I should be welcome here."

"And so you are." She felt the flush in her cheeks again as she tried to speak lightly. "It's only that I did not know when. I hardly expected you so soon."

"That I can believe."

For the first time there was an edge in his voice, and his icy glance at Dick made his meaning clear. Dick remained unruffled.

"She certainly expected *me*," he said. "And she will go on expecting me."

"That, sir, remains to be determined."

It was sharper than before, and he was watching Dick unwaveringly. Mally stirred suddenly, roused to alarm by the tone of it. They were dangerously near to quarrelling, and neither man looked at all disposed to give way. Her alarm mounted, not lessened by the knowledge that either could blame her for this, and perhaps both would. Something seemed to be fluttering inside her as she looked hurriedly round the circle of them, seeking for some way to make the peace; and it was William who responded first. She might almost have foreseen that he would.

His way of it was all his own. He swung his horse a little so that he faced Mally directly, and then he edged it back a pace as if he wished to see her the better. He was still carefully jovial, and perhaps only Mally noted that he had backed his horse between the younger men. Then he looked at her whimsically.

"It's time you went home," he said.

There was a mock solemnity about it which she recognized at once. She tried to respond in kind.

"So soon, sir?"

"You've been out quite long enough. Look at 'em." He glanced solemnly round him. "There'll be trouble soon. You should keep to one at a time."

"By all means, sir. But——"

"Now you make your mind up. Which is to ride home with you?"

"Which?"

Her voice failed her as she suddenly saw that the jest had passed, and that this was earnest. Without warning he had thrust the hard choice upon her, and she sat mute and desperate, unable to say it to either of them. Dimly, to left and right of her, she saw the two men move, each coming forward a little, and she saw William edge his own horse forward to stay between them. But she found no answer. Not a word would come, and she knew that the choice was not yet ripe, and could not yet be made. Yet William had forced——

There was a slight lift of William's eyebrows, whimsical

again, and Mally's thought changed. She recognized the way of it on the instant, and she knew that once again she had been wrong about William. There was no choice for her here. It was another of William's pretences, and it would lead to something that he already intended.

"I'll ride home with you myself," said William.

"What!"

Again it was the unexpected, and for a moment she was not sure that he meant it. But he watched her placidly, and then nodded. He turned unhurriedly to Dick.

"You can go to the pit again, and see to the pumping. Captain, you'll wish to help Mr. Peaver with a sermon, no doubt."

"Really, sir, I——" For a moment he was taut and silent, and then his face eased and he was the gentleman of the town again. "I'll at all times give way to an elder, sir. That is—er —different."

His sudden glance to Dick gave point to that, and Dick responded promptly.

"If you go, I will," he said. "But I think Mally will have to make her mind up."

He stayed for no more. He gave a nod that seemed to take in all of them, and then he turned his horse and went quietly up the slope. Mally watched him go, and when she turned she met Tony's most charming smile.

"I must ask your leave to go. Believe me, your servant always. Mr. Chandler, yours. You will find me, I hope, a peaceable visitor."

He rode quickly away, returning over the rise of the ground to the hidden slope where Mr. Peaver's house was in the trees; and Mally watched him in silence, as she had just watched Dick.

"I hope we do," said William.

She turned hastily, not knowing what he meant, and suddenly aware that she was now alone with him.

"Hope we do what?" she said.

"Find him peaceable."

She let that slip past her, plain though the meaning was. It had occurred to her that she wanted a word with William about the use he had made of her; and this seemed the moment for it.

He turned his horse, and a moment later she was riding at his side as he escorted her home. Then, with indignation reviving as she thought of it, she went at it as bluntly as he might have done himself.

"You were waiting for Captain Marriott, weren't you? You knew he'd come?"

There was a hot anger in her voice, and it heated William not at all. He looked at her benevolently.

"I thought perhaps he might."

"You knew he would. You knew it from my letter. I wrote to Sir John that——"

"Oh, aye, aye." He sounded quite soothing now. "I know of your letter."

"You read it, didn't you? That's why you took it from me, and offered to send it."

"I was trying to be helpful. I always am."

His plaintive tone roused Mally to a gasp of fury. He looked hurt but forgiving, and Mally glared at him angrily, perfectly sure what this performance was. Then she steadied her breath, and tried to get a grip of herself, well knowing that she would come to no profit by this. Displays of indignation were wasted on William.

"You should tell John about it," he said.

"Tell him of what?"

"The letter. He asked me to make sure if you needed anything."

"Oh!"

"Yes. He did ask me to keep an eye on you."

It was another of his transformations. He had gone in an instant to a quiet and sober tone, and Mally roused her wits. William in this mood needed full attention.

"I don't understand," she said.

"No?" For a moment he looked at her steadily. "John said young Marriott showed you some attentions in London. It seems you weren't displeased."

"Oh! But——"

"I'm not asking questions about that. I've got a little sense.

But don't grow heated if I take a look at him. It's only good sense."

"Were you asked——"

"Yes. John asked me to keep an eye on you. I've told you he did." He cut her short brusquely, and then again he was looking steadily at her. "In one way, you might need help with this. In another, you might need help out of it. I don't expect to be thanked."

He turned away, as if he would let her think this out, and she was left without an answer. It was completely plausible, and it could very well be true. She could at least not deny that he had gone out of his way to help her, and she was at this moment riding the horse he had given her. If he said he was concerned for her well-being, she could hardly contradict him. But it was also true that an eye on this meant an eye on Colonel Storm, and it would be like William to play two hands at once. It might be Sir John's way too.

"Beyond which, Marriott's a Jacobite. Some sort of an agent, I'm told."

William had spoken suddenly, almost as if he had guessed her thoughts, and Mally's head reared at once. This was alarming, and she tried to counter it firmly.

"Is that the reason why you wished——"

"Partly." He nodded understanding at once. "It's not so small as to be overlooked, is it?"

"How?"

"Such a man could bring trouble. He could bring trouble to *you*." Again his sharp keen glance was disconcerting. "John knew that. It's perhaps why he asked me to keep an eye."

Again he lapsed into silence, and Mally's thoughts went racing as they asked how much he knew, and what he intended for Tony Marriott. His manner was quiet, but he had given no hint of intentions; and she knew that she had not yet the measure of William.

"Besides——"

"Yes?"

"Dick seems to ride after you these days, and I've an interest in that. You wouldn't expect me not to have."

Again he left her without an answer. It was sensible and

J

proper, but she had no wish to talk of Dick just now. She hardly knew her own mind about Dick, and she was glad enough to leave it alone. They jingled on with no word added, and it was a relief to come to the house. She had had enough for one afternoon.

At her uncle's gates he took leave of her, and he had one last comment.

"I've said a Jacobite could bring you trouble. He might bring it to others too."

A jerk of his head to the house made his meaning plain, and Mally sat very still and quiet. There were cloaks and drums in the wine cellar, and the cloaks had the white cockade. William had an ominous stillness as he spoke again.

"There's talk in London, I'm told, of an information laid against this Marriott, and a warrant issued."

"What!"

"It isn't here, yet, of course, and I don't know that it will be."

"But—please, what sort of warrant?"

"I don't know. The Secretary of State doesn't tell me everything."

She felt her forehead cold as she looked at him, and she would not trust herself to speak. She watched him helplessly, and suddenly his face eased.

"Nor," he said, "do I tell *him* everything—if that's any comfort to you."

CHAPTER XXVIII

CONFLICT

THAT Jane should be told of this was inevitable. She and Jack were told that evening in the lesser parlour; and to Mally's annoyance Jane's first response was amusement. She heard of Tony Marriott's coming, and her eyebrows began to quiver.

"Difficult," was her comment. "Perhaps you're used to such incidents."

"I certainly am not."

"What lie did you tell?"

"I didn't tell——"

"Did you say you waited for Dick?"

"Of course I didn't. He——"

"Suppose he'd come?"

"But he *did*. That's just——"

"Oh dear!" Jane began to shake perceptibly. "No doubt you had a tale ready?"

"Will you be serious, Jane? It was bad enough like that, but then William came."

"Don't say you've made another conquest?"

"You try conquering William. Now listen——"

She told the whole tale of it, and Jane's amusement faded. There was nothing of it left when Mally ended; and Jack Harvey, who had been silent through it all, looked grave indeed when he heard of the warrant issued.

"Does Marriott know?" he asked quietly.

"I don't know." Mally was feeling desperate by now. "I don't understand about warrants. How bad is it?"

"I'm told a general warrant allows search of any place. It will be a warrant for Marriott, of course, and the charge will be that he's Colonel Storm, however they've worded it."

"But what of our cellar?"

"If it were not for Marriott I should call that safe. There are a lot of cellars in this County, and without him there'd be nothing to lead to this one. But if they find Colonel Storm as the guest of Peaver, and plainly linked with this house——"

He stopped; and Mally was suddenly aware that both of them were watching her. But no answer would come, and it was Jack who had to say it.

"I've no word against Marriott. I like the man. But for his own sake he would be wise to be off before he's noted. That would bring safety to some others, too. I think, Mally, that you are the only one who could persuade him to it."

"Jack——"

It was Jane, speaking quickly and with her hand on his arm. She had understood what this might mean, and her eyes were on Mally.

"That's what Dick wants, isn't it—to send him away? But what do *you* want? I wasn't going to ask you."

"But I don't know. I don't know anything." Mally's voice was near to cracking now. "What *am* I to do?"

"There's only you can decide that, Mally. You'd be showing some sense if you chose Dick. But that isn't all of it, is it?"

"No. Why should I be showing sense?"

"Tony's a romantic. If he escapes from this he'll have to run for it, and be in hiding. He has his head in the air, and he'll chase the moon all his days. Dick's safe. He's solid and he's safe, and I think you can trust him."

"I know I can. But——"

"I'm not saying that's all of it. We know it isn't, and it lies with you. There's only one thing I'm sure of. You'll have to make your mind up. William was right about that."

"William usually is. But I still don't know——"

"There's one other thing we know."

Jack had intervened suddenly, with a sharpness in his voice to hint that he wished to change the topic; and Mally was willing that he should.

"Whatever you—er—decide for later, Marriott must leave here. That's not a matter for choosing." He turned sharply as he spoke. "You understand it, Jane? There's a warrant out, and Messengers seeking. You've said he lives with his head in the air. But if he tries to stay here with Mally they'll find him and take him from her. And then he'll die with his head in the air."

There was a quick snatch of breath from Mally. Jane sat rigid, her face taut as she spoke.

"I haven't heard you speak like that before."

"Perhaps I haven't needed to." He turned his gaze suddenly. "I'm sorry, Mally. But that's the choice, and you ought to know it."

"Thank you. I——"

"And you will have to tell him of this warrant. For his safety you must. If need be, you must seek him out."

There was not the need to seek him out. He was at the house the next morning, and early. He came riding to the door when breakfast was scarcely done, as if he would take advantage while he could, and be here while the Chandlers were still at Gateshead. He was as fine and splendid as before, still in his golden brown, with the taffeta waistcoat and the Mechlin lace cravat. He was bowing gaily and quickly as Mally stood in the open door.

"I'm early," he said. "Out of season, perhaps. Put it to impatience, and forgive it."

There was sunlight upon him, twinkling on the gold lace and the gilded buttons. His slim and eager face was aglow with pleasure, and there was more than pleasure in his eyes as they met hers. There was a twitch of his eyebrows and a smile that had life and force. He was hard to resist as he stood poised and waiting, his hat now under his arm.

"There's nothing to forgive." She found herself answering as he meant her to. "You are always welcome."

"Thank you." His smile quivered as he spoke. "It's perhaps beyond my deserts, but——"

He was stepping through the door as he spoke, and time seemed to have gone back for Mally. It was all as it had been, and he might have been stepping through another door, as he once had done while she watched from the turn of the stair. Yesterday it had been different, out in the wind, with the horses and the wagonway, and Dick and William present; but now he was alone, and close to her, and in the quiet of the house, and there was a force spreading from him as it had done of old. It set a little tremor down her back, and she had to hold her breathing quiet.

She led him to the lesser parlour, and there was no one

there. Jane was busy in the house, and Jack had somehow effaced himself. She noted it gratefully; yet she knew that she would have no help, and that whatever was coming she must deal with alone.

"You'll know why I come," he said quietly. "I have been parted from you for so long. I had hoped that at last the Fates had turned, and were letting us see each other."

"Are they not?"

"Not as I had hoped. There is Mr. Chandler. I had not known of Mr. Chandler, and what I saw yesterday disturbs me."

His eyes were intent on hers, and she was very still and quiet as she saw the brightness of them, and the eager force behind. She tried to speak lightly.

"Why should it disturb you?" she asked.

"You know very well why it should." His answer came firmly, as if he would put an end to all pretence. "That night in London, at the rout——"

"Yes?"

"There was enough said then to make all plain. You knew then what I hoped, and asked."

He moved, and he was closer to her, with his hands upon her arms. She felt the light touch of them, and a quiver ran through her that she had known before. It was hard now to be at ease; and he spoke again, softly and quickly.

"You were not unkind to me then. You know you were not. And when we met again, up beyond Dilston there, at that inn——"

"Yes."

She murmured it breathlessly, as the memory came; and for a moment he paused, and smiled, as if he too had delight in that.

"That inn, beyond the Wall," he said. "The grey sky, and the river, and the wind there. It——"

"It took my hat. You found it for me. You were all wet, and——"

"I would have done a great deal more than that for you."

He paused again, bright-eyed and eager, watching her. Then suddenly, and before she had even guessed it, she was drawn quickly to him. Her head went back, to look up at his greater height, and she felt his heart beating. Then he had kissed her, very firmly and deliberately, and as one who was sure of himself and her.

"So!" he said quietly. "It was so then, and it is so now. Shall it not be so again?"

"But——"

"I cannot think that Mr. Chandler has your heart and love. He would pretend it so, but he deceives himself."

He said it firmly, but then he waited. His hands were still on her arms, but now he was very still and silent. She looked up to him again, meeting his eyes, and knowing what he waited for.

"It is so, is it not?"

He was insistent, and he had all but conquered. He was very close, very strong and vital; and cherished thoughts and dreams were leaping in her now, throwing care to the wind, and bidding her be sure at least of this. Her lips quivered, and she found herself lying closer against him. Her mind had gone back, to the rout, to the card room, to the bridge by the swirling river, and for the moment she made no answer.

"This Mr. Chandler, he deceives himself?"

That was his mistake. He had spoken again, pressing and urgent, impatient for his answer, and he would have done better to leave alone. One mention of Mr. Chandler brought it all back to her. There was more to this than the charming Captain Marriott, and a longing glance on Lady Chandler's stair. There was Dick Chandler, too, and Colonel Storm. There were Jacobite meetings, galloways in the night, and uncle John who must be kept from harm. There were the King's Messengers with a warrant signed, and there was Black William with a purpose yet unknown. There was more than Tony Marriott, and more than herself. She had a duty here, and she knew that she must do it.

She tried to speak calmly.

"I do not know what Mr. Chandler supposes. So I can't know whether he deceives himself or not."

"Then let us forget him. I've no wish to speak of him. It's you I'm here to speak of. You and me."

"But you must not stay here. It's not safe for you."

"Why not?"

"Because——" She was suddenly exasperated at his blindness to it all. "Because you're Colonel Storm. There's a warrant for you. Didn't you know?"

"Now did I?" He seemed in no way disturbed. "I thought there might be, at some time. Do you say there is?"

"I've just said it, haven't I? Do you think I wish for you taken? You'll have to go from here—now."

"Oh, not so much. Who told you there's a warrant?"

"William. If you don't know who that is, it's Esquire Chandler. No—don't say anything. Just listen."

It came pouring from her, a quick torrent of words, as if she could not now stop, and must rid herself of this. He listened quietly, yet his bearing did not soothe her. He seemed to be listening more from courtesy than from any feeling of alarm, and when she had ended there was almost a smile on his face.

"It's not very bad," was his comment. "Do you know who laid the information?"

"No."

"Willoughby, I'm told. He—er—resents something."

"I'm not surprised." Her memory was suddenly vivid of Mr. Willoughby, drunken in the card room, and then sprawling on the floor. "But what do you mean—you're told? Did you know of this?"

"I knew something of Willoughby's exertions. In those circles in London there was a deal of gossip. Too much, perhaps. So it was not very hard for Willoughby to learn something of me. For the same reason it was not very hard for me to learn something of Willoughby."

"Yes?"

"So a little dust was put before his eyes. I became Mr. Farquhar, and it was put about that that was my true name, and Marriott no more than a name I had used. It's said that Willoughby has sworn an information against Mr. Farquhar, who does not exist."

"Oh!" It was pure exasperation again. "Who do you think will be deceived by that? William Chandler won't be."

"Perhaps we must wait and see."

She was almost speechless as she looked at him, watching

his untroubled face, and knowing that she had made no true impression. It was the same with all of them, she thought; all over-confident, all over-sure, all under-rating the abilities of others. Mr. Peaver was the same, and so was uncle John; and she could almost think that only a man of that sort could be a Jacobite at all.

She tried again, speaking slowly and with a laboured patience.

"There's a warrant, and there are King's Messengers, and they'll be seeking for Colonel Storm. I've told you you must go."

"I didn't come here for the purpose of going."

"I know you didn't. But now that I've told you——"

"Mally, do you wish to be rid of me?" He was suddenly close to her again, and his hands were on her shoulders. "Mally, this it not for young Chandler? You're not saying——"

"Of course I'm not." She felt herself desperate with him now. "It's for your safety."

"Oh, my safety? I think that must wait its turn."

"It can't wait. It——"

"It must and it shall. What do you suppose I am?" The brightness was in his eyes again, and she felt herself drawn closer to him as he spoke. "You know well what I came for, to lay all before you, to seek both hand and heart."

"Yes. But——"

"Do you suppose I'm to forget it, to run for hiding like a rabbit, because some frightening tale is told? Is that what you think of me?"

"You know it isn't. But——"

"Then don't ask me to do it. We'll talk of your tale another day. Meanwhile——"

"There may not be another day."

"Oh yes, there will. There'll be no warrant here this week. Now please, Mally——"

He stopped short, and for a moment he held her fast and watched her, while she felt the force that was in him. Then abruptly his hands moved, pressing her against him so that her head must go back, and he was kissing her as he had never done before. It was utter surprise, done without hint or warning, and for an instant she was in exultation that he should have such wish for her. She lay in his grasp, letting him have his way, sensing all the power that was in him, the fragrance and the magic he had always had for her. Yet it was not as it might have been a day ago. Exasperation was still within her, and fears for him and others; and that quiet corner of her mind stayed clear and cool, sure that her wits were the sharper, and that in his ardour was his weakness. If he wanted this enough, she might yet have her way with him.

He released her, stepping back a little and looking down at her, and for a moment she would not meet his eye. She looked down to the floor, and his voice seemed to come from a far distance.

"You will say the word that I ask ? In the days to come you will stay true to me ?"

"The days to come ?" She roused herself, and there was a ring in her voice as she answered him. "And what will you be doing then ? Thrusting yourself into every danger, as you make your plot ?"

"I shall be loyal to my King. Would you have me less ?"

"I would have you in less danger. I would have you away from here."

"I shall not go from here till you say what I ask." He answered her in the instant, and he spoke with a slow determination. "I am not to be run from here by an idle tale. If it were true, if I knew it to be true, I should still not go."

"But——"

"I would rather face the Messengers, if they were here at the door, than go into the dark with a mind tormented. While I wait for your word, I shall await it here."

"But don't you see——"

"If you would have me go, you must say that word."

"I shall not say it unless you *do* go."

She answered him hotly, and perhaps imprudently. He stayed very calm, considering her carefully, and she had already guessed what he would say.

"If I promise to go, will you first put me at ease ?"

"How ?"

She said it feebly, as dismay came in, and she saw what

faced her. If she did not say what he wished he would stay; and if he were taken she would feel that she had kept him to his death. Her forehead felt wet as she thought of it; and the memory came of all that had passed between them, of all the dream and hope that had been hers from him. She stirred, moving almost towards him, held back only by the thought of his plot, and the madness he would lead her into.

"Will you?" His voice came quietly and insistently. "Will you promise, if I go, that you will have no more to do with Mr. Chandler, nor make any attachment with him?"

Again he had blundered. The mention of Dick Chandler set another train of memory clear before her; the ship in the sunlit river when he came aboard to greet her; the jolting chaise in the dusk, his understanding of her troubles, and then his big form, stiff and lonely by the door as he faced a hostile greeting and stood sturdily for his father; and then she was remembering his farewell in the dark by the waiting chaise, and how it had lingered in her thoughts as she turned to go to Jane. It was a rush of memory, pressing in unsought, but it sufficed; she could not, at this moment, promise no more to do with Dick Chandler.

She lifted her head and spoke unhappily.

"I can't promise that," she said. "Dick Chandler has been good to me, very good, and I can't say to him that I will speak to him no more. I couldn't."

"Very well." His voice was as quiet as hers, but she saw how his face had set. "Then I stay here, come what may."

"But you mustn't. You——"

"I stay. It is not what I hoped for, or indeed what I had thought to have. It had seemed in London——"

"Please!"

"As you wish. But I will not be frightened hence to make room for any other. I serve my King, and always I shall serve *you*."

He moved quietly across the room and took his hat and gloves.

"Now I think I should go. For one morning we have said enough, and it is not making us happy."

"Tony, I——"

No more words would come, and by the door he stopped,

looking gravely at her, as he had done on Lady Chandler's stair. He almost moved towards her; and then, very slowly, he shook his head.

"I think you are still of that mind. Or perhaps you do not know your mind. I shall pray for that, and I shall come to you again. In a matter of hours I shall come again. Truly, your servant always."

He was gone. Her eyes were not clear, and she did not see him go. She heard the latch; she heard a murmur of voices as if Jack Harvey had come to do the courtesies; and then she was alone, staring at a bleak shut door in a room that was sad and quiet; and her memory was of Lady Chandler's stair, and the card room at the rout.

She never knew how long it was before the door was quietly opened and Jane came in. She had an air of purpose, yet in the doorway she stopped short and was staring at Mally.

"Now—now what?" she asked.

"Oh, Jane!"

Words stopped again, and Jane stood waiting. Then the air of purpose came back to her.

"You can tell me later, Mally, when it's easier. Did you hear a horse come here while you talked?"

"I didn't hear anything. I——"

"Well, one came."

There was a note in the short words that cut through the drifting thoughts and brought Mally to the present. Something, as she was sickeningly aware, was wrong, and Jane was trying to tell her.

"What is it?" she said.

"It was a fellow from Henry—from Henry Deane, Mally, in Newcastle—and he sent a letter. You'd better read it."

Without more words she held it grimly out, and for a moment Mally met her eyes. Then she took it.

It began with some greetings, a little cold and perfunctory, and it came quickly to what mattered. Henry had been in earnest, and he was not for wasting words:

I must pass to you some warning for which I hope there is no occasion. My being a Hostman permits me at times to learn of events. Yesterday there came to this town from London

*John Newman and Richard Root, King's Messengers, hav-
ing a general warrant for one Richard Farquhar, alias James
Storm, alias Anthony Marriott, alias etc. One of these names
is that of a man who at your aunt's house in London was showing some concern for Mally; too much concern, as it was
thought. Whether he is the same man I know not; but that
is why I write this letter.*

*He is plainly a meddling and seditious Jacobite, which in
itself is of no great matter. If he is hanged the world will be
lighter for it. But if he should be the same man, and should
perhaps appear at your house for speech with Mally, then will
you please to remember that a general warrant permits search?
I beg pardon if I am too zealous here. But I cannot forget your
uncle's leanings, and the company he keeps; and I do not forget William Chandler on his land. To deal plainly, treasonable
matter found in a house could lead to confiscation of inheritance, with a proportion to the searchers and perhaps a larger
one to Chandler. That is what I fear.*

*I will add that these Messengers do not know where to
search; nor does the Mayor, to whom they have applied for
help. It may well be, therefore, that they will not learn anything to take them to your house. This we may pray for.*

If I can help in any matter, be most ready to call me

Your obedient servant,

Henry Deane.

The paper crackled as Mally's fingers tightened. She looked
up, and found Jane watching her in silence.

"So they've come," said Jane. "When does your Tony
go?"

"He——" Mally stopped short as the full meaning of it
came pressing on her. "Oh Jane, he—he won't go unless——"

The door swung quietly open, and Jack Harvey came in.
He looked as grave as Jane, but he stopped by the door when
he saw that he had interrupted. Jane spoke first, and she was
watching his face.

"What is it, Jack?"

"Haven't I disturbed——"

"Let that wait. What is it?"

"I had a word with Marriott as he went. I asked him about those things in the cellar here."

"Yes?"

"He declares himself not concerned. He says it's Peaver's affair. Peaver sent those things in here, and Peaver will have to shift them."

"Peaver won't," said Mally; and knew that this was true.

CHAPTER XXIX

THE CARRIER'S BOY

MALLY rode out with Jane that afternoon. She thought she must certainly get out of the house for an hour, if only to recover her wits; but the thought of riding out alone, and perhaps being intercepted by Dick Chandler, was more than she could bear. Urgent talk from him would be too much for her just now. It would be too close to this morning's, and she therefore asked if she might for once ride with the others. Jane gave an understanding answer.

A little later, Jane improved on it. She declared that Tony must be warned forthwith of the Messengers in Newcastle; which, she added, was not a work for Mally. It would come better from a man, and would Jack please see to it?

Jack gave the obvious answer, and he went alone as soon as they had dined. Jane and Mally rode a half-hour later, and they did not go to the wagonway. Mally, indeed, was never sure where they did go. She left that to Jane, and Jane plunged into devious lanes while she heard in detail of the morning's talk. It took some time to tell, and then her comments were forthright.

"It won't do," she said. "If you won't marry him, he'll get himself hanged, will he? Romantic booby!"

"Jane, he didn't say that. He——"

"That's what he means. Well, you're not to do it."

"But if he *is* taken——"

"It will be all your fault, won't it? I still say you're not to do it."

"But I couldn't bear it if——"

"Don't get excited. It probably won't happen. He may change his mind when he hears about those Messengers."

"I hope so. But——"

"If he wants to marry anybody, he'll have to behave differently. He's behaving like a fool, and he's taking you for one.

271

And for his own sake and everybody else's you'll have to stand firm."

"I hope you're right."

"I am. Just suppose you gave him his way? What would follow?"

"He said he'd go."

"Go into hiding, I suppose. Then he'd go on with his plot, and if he missed being hanged for that he'd be in hiding for the rest of his life. What a husband!"

"He'd say the plot will succeed."

"With John and Peaver in it?" The lift of Jane's eyebrows showed what she thought of that. "I suppose if he was very lucky he could escape to France, and be an exile there. That's a fine life."

"He was there before——"

"*No*, Mally. If he wants to wed with you or anybody else, he'll have to show some sense. He'll have to give up plotting, and settle down to some proper life."

"He'd say that his honour——"

"Requires him to be hanged. Well, he'd better change his mind. Who the Devil's this?"

They had taken a wide half-circle from the house, and now they were riding a bridle-track on high and open ground. Before them was a slight rise, and down the slope beyond it would be the wagonway. But over the rise a man had come into view, walking towards them as if he had come from the wagonway, and it was sight of him that had brought Jane's question. She looked at him carefully, and then she used the same trenchant tone.

"It's Geordie Wade. I've been wanting a word with Geordie. About those galloways."

Mally was content to leave this to Jane. She had more on her mind just now than galloways; and where those cloaks and drums had come from seemed less important than where they could go to. But she was not disposed to argue, and together they waited for Geordie Wade.

He had undoubtedly seen them, and he was looking almost sheepish as he swept off his battered hat. Jane spoke abruptly.

"You didn't tell me when you left our stable, Geordie?"

"No." He scratched his head awkwardly. "It was Master

Nixon, d'ye see? He come for me to go with him, and I wasn't to tell——''

He stopped, looking down at his boots, and for a moment there was silence. Jane spoke more quietly.

"What weren't you to tell, Geordie?"

There was another pause, while he looked at his boots and looked at the sky, and had one quick look at Jane.

"Geordie!"

Her voice came quietly, and it had the note of one who would remind him of something. Again he looked quickly at her, and Mally began to understand. Geordie had been the stable-boy before he ever joined the carrier, and a habit of respect for Jane had been ingrained in him. He had not forgotten it, and Jane was reminding him of it. She waited, and then she spoke again.

"Do you mean, Geordie, that Nixon said you were to go with him, and not tell me?"

"Aye, that's it." Again he shuffled awkwardly. "It was the galloways, you see, and we had to go quick."

"Where to?"

"York." He was answering by habit now.

"I thought Nixon had gone to the London trade."

"Aye, but the stuff was at York."

"What stuff, Geordie?"

Jane's voice was even quieter, but the tone had hardened. It was not lost on Geordie, and now he was shuffling again.

"I don't rightly know."

"Don't you? But I do."

"Ay?" He was suddenly open-mouthed.

"I know what you've been doing, Geordie. You went to York, and you loaded your galloways with—well, we won't say what—and then you came here. Didn't you?"

Geordie stood speechless, looking at his boots, and he would not meet Jane's eye. For the moment he was the stable-boy again.

"You came by night, Geordie, with the moon—and you had five galloways to unload. You led them to the door, one by one, didn't you?"

"No." He was protesting hurriedly. "That was second lot. First lot we——"

He stopped, his mouth dropping open again, and Mally heard Jane's quick catch of breath. There was silence, while Mally's thoughts went rushing, and she dared not look at Jane. They sat their horses stiffly; and Geordie shuffled, and looked again at the wooden bars that tipped his boots. Jane was very quiet and steady as she spoke again.

"Just so, Geordie. It was the second lot. And where did you take the first?"

"Down yon pit."

Again there was a faint sound, almost of a sigh, from Jane, and again Mally dared not look. In the silence she waited for Jane.

"Which pit, Geordie? Our old one, was it?"

"Aye, that's right. Down at bottom."

"It's water there, Geordie."

"Aye, but in t'shafts."

"What!" For a moment Jane's tone was sharp. "Now who ordered that? Would it be—Mr. Peaver?"

"Aye. He showed us."

The silence came again, as if even Jane must think this out. Geordie stood abashed and waiting, and Mally's thoughts went whirling to a day on her first arrival here. Mr. Peaver was showing her the coal pit, and there was a black and stagnant pool, and water dripping from the rock. Mr. Peaver was pointing to the streak of coal that went slanting down and down, and there were deep dark tunnels cut in it, where men had crawled and toiled. But it was forlorn, finished and deserted; and what better hide could there be than those forgotten shafts?

Mally stirred suddenly as another thought came. She had said to Mr. Peaver that no man would ever use those shafts again; and he had agreed. He had agreed, and had then been suddenly thoughtful; and at that exact moment Geordie Wade had come into view, pushing his head over the rim of the pit. It might have set a thought in Mr. Peaver, especially if he knew already of a need to have skins and prunes in waiting. Certainly he had shown a strange haste. He had gone scrambling from the pit to question Geordie, and when he had heard of Nixon's troubles he had told Geordie to send the man to see him; and within some few days, Nixon had called Geordie from the stable.

There was a quick movement as Jane eased herself from her saddle and slid carefully to the ground. Apparently she meant to come to closer quarters now, and Mally was prompt in dismounting too. Decidedly they must have the truth from Geordie Wade, and the note in Jane's voice showed that she thought the same.

"So Nixon took you away, did he, Geordie? And you went to York? What did you load?"

"The bales. Two to a beast."

"What sort of bales?"

"Long 'uns."

"What does that mean? Did you know what was in them?"

"No. I mean, I—I shouldn't ha' done."

"Meaning what, Geordie?"

He stood unhappily, looking as if he must not tell this. Again his gaze wandered from his boots to the sky, and from the sky to Jane; and what he saw in Jane did not comfort him.

"Mas' Nixon said I wasn't to——"

"Those bales, Geordie?"

It was cold, and utterly inflexible. Geordie met her eyes, and quailed visibly.

"It was a bit o' trouble, like. The second night out."

"From York, you mean? Go on."

Geordie looked at her again, and then he went on. He was past resisting now.

"We'd gone up the straight road, and we were inning, that second night. Piercebridge, that was."

"Yes?"

"You have to cross the river there, d'ye see, to come to the village, and all that timber's rotten."

"A timber bridge, you mean?"

"Aye, and it's rotten. And there was one of the beasts put a foot through. A mare, she was."

"And broke a timber? Go on."

But Geordie was not to be hurried. He seemed to be pulling at his memory, and he spoke in his own slow way.

"The timber just cracked. All rotten, and it brought the mare down. She wasn't hurt, but she came down, on top of the bale, and one of the cords broke. So after we'd stabled the beasts, and seen the mare no worse, Mas' Nixon said we'd best undo that bale. It would need new cord anyhow, and he said we might have spoiled it—broken something. It sounded that way."

"Geordie, what was *in* it?"

"Aye, so we unrolled it. There was a deal of canvas to it, but what we come to in the end was muskets."

"What!"

"Aye." Geordie seemed hardly to have heard Jane speak. "That's what I'd have said, but Mas' Nixon said carbines. He says they're too short for muskets. A musket, he said, is for a man on foot, and these'll be for Horse. Short, d'ye see?"

"Yes, Geordie. I do see."

So did Mally, and there was a candle flickering in the wine cellar, lighting the cloaks and hats that had come in the second load. Those, too, had been for horsemen, and alike they were the furnishings of treason.

"How many of these carbines?"

Jane's voice came again, marvellously steady, and Geordie answered easily.

"Five."

"In a bale? Twenty-four beasts, was it?"

"Aye, but it was half had these things. There was half the bales another shape."

"And did Nixon open one?"

"Aye." Geordie was suddenly grinning. "He said we'd best know what we had. So we uncorded, and it was swords that time. Ready and sharp, too."

"For horsemen again, I suppose. And all put into the pit?"

"That's right."

"Right, do you say?"

It was the first time that Jane had seemed to comment, and Mally heard it with understanding. There was nothing of chance here. It fitted too exactly. Certainly there was a Troop of Horse in sight, and it was to be a Troop furnished for war. Even the drums had been thought of, and a Commission signed for the commander. There was enough here to hang half a neighbourhood, if it should be known; and almost in desperation she heard Tony Marriott's voice again, refusing to go until she had promised him.

"What happened after all this, Geordie?" Jane was flat

and toneless now. "After your second coming, I mean. Where did you go then?"

"Why, it was the house that time. We——"

"Not for *all* the beasts, Geordie. Where did the others go?"

"Oh aye." His face cleared happily as he understood. "Why, across the river we had to go——"

"At Corbridge?"

"Aye, and then up a hill. But I don't know just where. We had to go at night, and I didn't know that road."

"I'll guess it. Have you been back to York for more?"

"No." His face had clouded suddenly. "I thought we was to, but Mas' Nixon's gone away."

"Oh? Are you turned off again?"

"He hasn't said. He's just gone. He didn't take me, or the beasts either. They're still in stable, and I'm waiting."

"Then I shouldn't think you're turned off."

"Aye, maybe." The friendly grin was on him again now. "But I'm sorry I didn't tell——"

"All right, Geordie. I'll forgive you. But when you know whether you're turned off or not, come and tell me at once. I want to know what happens to you."

"Aye."

He was beaming now, perhaps in relief that he had not been blamed for anything, and when Jane turned to her horse, seemingly quite at ease, he ran to hold her stirrup. He did the same for Mally, and then he stood grinning as they moved quietly away. Jane kept composure till they were safely out of earshot.

"Carbines!" was her comment then. "In a coal pit! Peaver must be mad."

"I suppose——" Mally tried hard to make the best of it. "I suppose that's better than in the house?"

"With Black William riding round all day? It's almost William's pit. Of all the addle-witted fools!"

"Peaver? But he didn't know that John would sell the coal. Now I think of it, he did seem disturbed when he knew."

"I wish he'd gone clean mad. Then we could have put him in Bedlam and been rid of him. Could we put 'em all in, do you think?"

"No. I shouldn't think anyone would go down that pit."

"Suppose William gets a hint?"

"You don't think Geordie will talk?"

"Perhaps he won't. But what about Nixon? He knows of it too, and Nixon's a rogue, if I know the face of one."

"I haven't seen him in——"

"Where *is* Nixon?" Jane's face had hardened suddenly, and her voice came with a snap. "Geordie said he'd gone. Where to?"

"Jane! What do you——"

"I don't know. Nixon knows too much."

"Everybody knows too much."

"Need you tell me?"

They had come to the crest of the ground. Before them it fell in a gentle slope, to rise again beyond, and at the foot of the slope, running across their path and rising gently to their left, was the wagonway. This was the lower stretch of it, finished and ready. The picks and spades had gone, and it was deserted except for a wagon of gravel creeping slowly up behind two patient horses. But a half-mile up it, and only a little out of sight, would be the coal pit, old and water-logged, where swords and carbines lay; and Jane reared her head and sniffed at the wind.

"Will the way be up to the pit yet?" she demanded. "That would mean William's men all round the pit. There'll be no chance to make anything safe then."

"Perhaps it hasn't quite got there."

"Let's go and see."

They went gently down the slope to the wagonway, and then turned to ride up it. They had passed the loaded wagon, rumbling slowly up, and then an empty wagon came down, running free and fast, with a man clinging tight to its rim as he worked the brake. It went rattling past, and Mally had a feeble smile.

"That reminds me of Dick," she said. "He once went into the river, doing that."

"Serve him right," said Jane.

They turned a bend in the track, and the scene changed. Here was the old pit, a quarter-mile away, and beyond it was the throng of busy men, the horses and wagons and timbers, all the bustle that went with the making of the new way. The sound of it came clearly on the wind, and at the first glance it was plain that the wagonway was beyond the old pit now. It was a full fifty yards beyond, and the oak rails ran only a few short feet from the pit. Mally looked keenly, and then she turned to Jane.

But Jane was not seeing the wagonway. She was looking a little to the side, to the farther rim of the pit where no workmen were. There was a horseman there, alone on the grass, sitting his mount as if he were waiting for someone. Mally took one look, and then had to steady herself. This was Dick Chandler, and he would certainly see her.

He saw her in the next instant. The brown hat waved; and then he was jogging over the grass to join her.

CHAPTER XXX

SHADOWS DEEPENING

ONCE again she had not quite the measure of a Chandler. If she thought he would be disturbed after yesterday's meeting, she was wrong. He was no more disturbed than his father would have been. He came jingling up with a smile and a wave of his hat. Then he looked cheerfully at Jane.

"Well ?" he said.

"Well what ?" said Jane.

"Shall we start by bickering a little ? We generally do."

"Just as you please."

"I please not to. You're a shade too good at it. I've known hedgehogs smoother." The grin was suddenly on his face. "So I'd sooner be friends."

"You think you're going to be ?"

"I thought we might start."

"Oh, did you ?" Jane spoke truculently, and did not look displeased. "You must have a friendly nature."

"I have, Jane."

"Who said you might call me Jane ?"

"That's the friendly nature." He looked at her solemnly. "I've been trying all day to be friendly with folk."

"And didn't they wish it ?"

"No." There was a slight pause, and still he looked at Jane. "I began by thinking I'd ride to your house—to be friendly with Mally, you see ? I was just thinking of it when Marriott came."

His change in tone was of the slightest, but Mally took it instantly. He was coming to what mattered; and again she marvelled at the way he followed his father. The playfulness that steered the talk, and then the swift easy flick to what he wanted, were just how William would have done it. He even had the same simple look, and she was alert to everything as he went calmly on.

"That was this morning. Marriott was coming back, as if

he'd been to your house, and he didn't look friendly at all."

"Did you speak to him?"

"I offered to show him the wagonway."

"Dick!" Mally suddenly spluttered, and in spite of anxieties. "You didn't? What did he say?"

"Looked all black at me. Very polite, though. Waved his hat. Begged to be excused. Then went off—cantering, too, not trotting. But he *is* polite."

"It's called the polite world, Dick."

"But I wish he didn't look like it."

"Why?"

"It makes folk look at him. Then they ask why he stays with Peaver." For an instant there was sharp shrewd meaning in his eyes. "So I didn't come to see you, Mally."

"Why not?"

"He didn't want me, and I thought you mightn't either— just then."

He had been entirely right, and once again he surprised her with his quick understanding. But he seemed to expect no comment, and the light note was still in his voice as he went on.

"I thought I'd visit you this afternoon. I was just going to do it when Harvey came."

"Oh?" said Jane.

"Yes. He said you'd gone riding."

"So what did you do?"

"I offered to show him the wagonway."

"Dick!" Again Mally found it hard to be serious. "And was he polite?"

"He said he'd like to, but he was busy. So he waved his hat, and off he went—towards Peaver's."

"I see." Mally spoke easily, but she was uncomfortably aware that he had missed nothing. "And then what?"

"I minded my own business. By and by, back came Harvey, and this time *he* looked upset."

"Oh?" Jane spoke quickly, and spared a hasty glance at Mally. "So what then?"

"I offered to show him the——"

"For goodness' sake——"

"But I *did* show him the wagonway. He said he had

nothing else to do now, so we spent an hour looking at it. I like Harvey."

He was looking Jane straight in the eye, and she made no answer. Mally watched, sure that Jane was dismayed by what must be the failure of Jack's mission. He had not persuaded Colonel Storm to go.

"I took him up to the pit yonder," said Dick, and he waved to the new pit up the slope. "And while we were there, we saw Marriott again. He had Peaver with him this time. They were looking at this pit."

"What?"

Mally spoke in alarm, and carefully said no more. Talk of the wine cellar might well have set Mr. Peaver to think of the pit and what was hidden in it, and it would be natural for him to tell Colonel Storm. But to come here in daylight, under everybody's eye——

"Oh yes," said Dick cheerfully. "They were looking at it. They were on their horses, just about where we are now, and they were looking down into it. Of course, I wasn't interested."

"No?" Again it was hard to keep her voice steady. "And then?"

"They rode off—to your house, I think. At least they went that way. And they'd no sooner gone than Harvey said he must go too. Talked about affairs, or something, and then off he went, all in a hurry. So I minded my own business again."

"Yes." She looked at him steadily, and tried to soften her tone. "I'm sorry, Dick, but I'm afraid we shall have to leave you too. It's not that we wish to, but——"

"But it's you like the others, isn't it?"

"I—I don't know what that means?"

"Don't you?" He watched her in silence for a moment. "Shall we just say that of everybody here, I'm the only one who minds his own business? The rest of you are—all concerned for someone else?"

"It's—sometimes hard not to be."

"It might be wise not to be." It came quickly, and then his face eased. "But I do want to talk to you. Shall I come tomorrow, in the afternoon?"

"Yes." She had no notion what tomorrow would bring,

but she could not refuse him this. "I'll try to be free. But now——"

"I won't keep you. Anyway, I'm waiting for my father. He's coming to see the pit. And I expect your affairs are difficult."

"I—I don't——"

"I'm not asking questions. But if I can help, tell me. Good night."

"Good night, Dick."

Jane was wheeling her horse already, and Mally had to move quickly to be with her. She turned to acknowledge Dick's wave, and then she was alongside Jane as the horses stepped delicately over the wagonway and its rails.

"What's it about?" she asked as they began to trot. "What are they all doing?"

"Talking, I should think," said Jane.

"Yes. But what——"

"Jack will have had a word about that wine cellar. You've guessed, I suppose, that he didn't succeed?"

"Yes."

"So I suppose they've decided to have a word with John, and Heaven knows what they'll hatch between 'em. I'll be glad when we're home. How much has Dick guessed?"

"More than he'll tell us. And they won't be silly guesses."

"Not if he's like his father."

"He is."

"I know. He's probably right when he says he's the only one who minds his own business."

"He's right in something else too. He does try to be friendly."

"Yes." Jane sounded terse. "He's also got some sense, and I'm not sure he won't end by being our only hope. Now let's ride."

It was late enough. The November afternoon was shading to a grey dusk when they came at last to the door and gave their horses to the boy. The house stood still and quiet, as if it had known through the years the alarms of men, and had learned to treat them softly. It did not obtrude itself. It was fading into the dusk, and candles would be needed soon, if anyone had the wit to light them.

They went quickly in, and in John's big parlour they found the group they had expected. He was in his own chair, toying with an ale mug, and trying, perhaps, to look more at ease than he was. Opposite, also in an elbow-chair, was Mr. Peaver, still in sober black, his long legs stretched comfortably out, and seemingly no whit disturbed by anything. At the side of the hearth, Jack Harvey stood quietly, as if he disapproved of this, and were watching rather than taking part. It was Tony Marriott who had the centre here. He had the centre of the hearth, leaning his shoulders against it, and he had everybody's attention too.

Certainly he had Mally's. He turned to her at once when she came in with Jane, and whatever he had been speaking of had to wait. The light of welcome was in his eyes, and his smile seemed all for her; and for a moment her mind was a blur between him and Dick Chandler. Then it cleared; and here was the man she had known in that other world.

"Forgive us," he was saying. "It was remiss that we were not at the door. We have affairs, and of some weight, and that's what we must plead."

"Aye." It came in a growl from John in his elbow-chair. "We've affairs, and they're not for women."

There was a note in his voice that brought Mally out of dreams and down to earth on one swift instant. She had heard that growl from him before, on a night when he had quarrelled with Jane, and with one hurried glance she was sure that the same mood had him now. He was ill at ease, not very far from frightened, and it had made him testy now as it had made him then. A care was needed now in dealing with uncle John.

"No?" Jane snapped it suddenly, and then she dealt ruthlessly. "Well, we don't apologize for intruding. We've been talking with Geordie Wade."

"What the Devil's that to do with it?"

The growl had deepened, but Jane was not to be put off. Her forehead was as tight now as her lips, and she was plainly in a mood for any trouble that came. She eyed him truculently and then her glance swept round the circle.

"We've been learning of some galloways. Drums in the wine cellar, and carbines in the coal pit. We ask what's to be done."

She flung her question more at Mr. Peaver than at another, and for once he was disturbed. He was also indignant, and he hastily tried to sit up.

"Now what's this?" he demanded. "What right had Geordie Wade to——"

"Geordie's a simple soul. He told us because he didn't see what it meant."

"But it's most improper. Did you press him to——"

"Where's Nixon?"

Again she cut him short, and this time he sat gaping at her. Tony Marriott leaned forward as if he had sensed that there was something important here; and uncle John came erect with a jerk that slopped ale over his breeches.

"What the Devil!" he growled. "Answer what you're bid, can't you?"

"It's events that do the bidding now. Nixon's gone, and——"

"My God!" He was red-faced and angry now, glaring at her while he dabbed at his wet breeches with a none-too-clean handkerchief. "You're from your manners again, are you? Answer what——"

"By your leave——" Tony Marriott had moved forward, taking the attention of them all. "This is important, and I think we should hear of it. Nixon's a carrier, is he not?"

"Yes." Jane turned swiftly to him as John subsided again, muttering and puffing. "He's the carrier who brought your carbines, and——"

"They were not mine. But you say this Nixon has——"

"He's gone. He's left Geordie with the beasts, and he's gone. I'm asking where."

"Ought I to know?"

"Oughtn't you to guess?" Her retort was instant, and then she faced him squarely. "I've no wish to harrow your feelings, but there's a warrant out."

"So we are told. But——"

"Which ought to mean a reward offered. And Nixon's a rogue. Does it add up?"

"My God!" John interposed suddenly, and there was a twitch of his lips to belie his bold air. "Do you say——"

"*Isn't* he a rogue?"

"How do I know?" He was less noisy now, and some of the high colour had left his face. "I suppose he could be. There's a damned hangdog face to him."

"That's a good word, just now."

For a moment Mally feared there would be an outburst, and certainly Jane need not have said it. He paled, then flushed again and seemed to be near choking, while Mr. Peaver came jumping to his feet in agitation. The white bands were flapping against his black, and he seemed to find no oddity in wearing them while he plotted treason and laid in the furnishings of war. The question slipped through Mally's mind, and then was gone again as Tony intervened once more.

"By your leave," he said again. "We shall better take this calmly, and I do not think we should provoke each other." He was looking steadily at Jane. "Do you think this Nixon will betray for reward?"

"I think it's in his nature." Her answer was quick and quiet. "I suppose he could also tell them that *you* are here. Which is why I think you should go."

"That is for me to judge, and I have said already that I will not be frightened hence."

"I think it's the rest of us who are frightened."

"For whom?"

"You. Ourselves as well."

"For myself, I hold to what I've said." He shot a quick glance at Mally, and then he addressed himself to John. "But I do not like these matters hidden in your house, sir. I think it's indiscreet."

"We did our best." John sounded on the defensive now. "They had to go somewhere."

"No doubt, but it's not a good hide. Nor do I like this laying in a coal pit, with so many having some right to go there."

"Aye." It came testily, and suddenly John turned on Mr. Peaver. "Why the Devil must you put 'em there, and with no word said to me?"

"Really now!" Mr. Peaver sounded both frosty and indignant. "As you've just said, they had to go somewhere. I might as properly ask why you sold a lease to William Chandler, and with no word said to——"

"Hell! Am I to ask leave on my own land, to sell my own——"

"For Heaven's sake!" Jane spoke almost desperately. "It's not a matter of whose fault it is. What are we going to *do*?"

"There is nothing we can do," said Mr. Peaver stiffly. "We must trust in God. We have a righteous cause, and He will not——"

"Aye, aye," said John hurriedly. "But if anything will make it safer, let's do it. What ought we to do?"

He added that blankly, as if he had no notion what to do. He looked almost beseechingly from one to another, plainly asking them to tell him, and Jane wanted no second invitation.

"For pity's sake," she told him, "you must assert yourself here. It's your house and your land, and the word lies with you."

"Aye, aye. Perhaps it does. But what——"

"Let's have those things from the cellar, and let's put 'em in the fire. Let's burn the lot, and——"

"Good God!" said Mr. Peaver, and it was the first time Mally had heard him say it. "That's plain treachery. Wanton destruction of what our King has——"

"King George will take it from you."

"Of what our King has committed to our trust. With money he could most ill spare he purchased these, and gave them to our charge. He trusted us——"

"You mean you don't agree?" said John, and Mr. Peaver gave him a glance that could have withered.

"I do not." He was terse and furious about it. "It's treachery of the blackest."

"Just so." Tony intervened again, and he was still calm and quiet. "We should be prudent certainly, but we must not betray."

"Aye, aye," said John, and he had a bluff heartiness. But he was looking sullen now, as if he were being driven against his will, and Mally took swift note of that. Uncle John, she thought, would walk out of this if he could; but he would not crawl out under the contempt of the others.

"Then what," said Jane acidly, "do you propose? Do you sit here waiting to be taken?"

She was addressing herself to Tony. He drew a long breath, as if he were steadying his temper.

"I don't propose to be taken at all," he told her. "For these things in the cellar, I've a notion of what we may do. It was done once in another house. For the coal pit, that's a little harder, with this Chandler and his men about. I wonder——"

"What the Devil did you put 'em there for?"

It was John, with the growl in his voice again, and Mr. Peaver flushed.

"I put them there, sir, as the best and safest place, and I did not for one moment dream——"

"Please!" Tony's voice was still calm. "We trust each other, if you please, and we do not fall out. I was wondering if we could perhaps remove these things from the pit under cover of night?"

"Where to?" said John.

"There need be no difficulty," said Mr. Peaver. "They may come to my house."

"No." Mally spoke sharply. "With Tony at your house they'll go there at once, and——"

The sound of a horse broke in, a hurrying horse, coming past the trees to the house, and Mally stopped short, with a stabbing fear that here were the King's Messengers at last. She turned, staring through the window at the greying dusk, and it was a single rider who dismounted by the door. He went to it at half a run, and Mally stood numbed, noting the dark-blue coat and yellow breeches, the neat wig and the black hat. This was Henry Deane, and something had brought him in such haste that he had not so much as a servant with him.

The knocker clattered through the house as he plied it fiercely, and in the silent room they looked to each other in question.

"Henry," said Mally, in brief explanation.

"Who?" Jane looked dazedly round the room. "I suppose we'll need candles."

The knocker clattered again, and Mally went at a run.

CHAPTER XXXI

NIGHTFALL

In the hall she found the stable boy, also hurrying to the door. She let him swing it, and Henry almost shouldered him aside.

"Is all well?" he asked.

"Yes." She found herself gaping at him. "So far."

"You say it well. Take me to him."

It was not a moment for manners, and she argued nothing as she led him quickly into the parlour. They were all on their feet awaiting him, and Jane had lit the candles. On the threshold he paused, still booted and spurred, and holding his hat and gloves, and in the circle of them his eyes found John.

"It's of some urgency," he said.

"Aye."

John spoke slowly, as if he did not know what to do. He saw Henry look again round the circle, and that seemed to rouse him. It told him what he could do.

"The—er—Reverend Mr. Peaver. Friend of mine."

"Servant, sir."

"Mr. Harvey. Son of my brother-in——"

"Servant."

"And—er——"

John stopped awkwardly, and Tony came smoothly to his rescue. The polite world knew how to keep its calm.

"I'm a passing traveller, sir, benighted here. My name is Staunton."

"Is it?" Henry spoke with a crackle, and he had a hard and hostile stare. "You've forgotten that I was Lady Chandler's guest last month. Your name was Marriott then, and you were at odds with Mr. Willoughby."

"I beg pardon, sir." He was not in the least disconcerted. "I had failed to remember you. There were so many there that night."

"I don't doubt it." The crackle was still there, and Henry's eyes were as hard as pebbles now. "You're also named

Marriott—joined with some other names—in a warrant that's out. Did you know of it?"

"I'd heard some talk of it."

"You'd best believe it, and quickly. There are two King's Messengers now on their way, with Dragoons. They're fo this house. You've a half-hour, or something less, to be gone.'

"Oh!"

It was from Mally. She was still in the doorway, and her eyes, and all her thoughts, were on the man who was in peril and who yet stood calmly there with the half-smile on his face He seemed quite unmoved, and Mally almost screamed at him. She had never a doubt of the truth of this. Henry had an air now that brought conviction, and she could all but hear the beat of hooves again, the clank of the Dragoons, the rustle of a warrant unrolled for reading. Her thoughts went leaping, wild and fearful, and there was Tony between the Dragoons, and then the judge's trumpets, and a black-robed chaplain praying while a hangman leered. She felt herself white and sick, and she sought wildly for something to shout at him as he stood unmoved before her. No words would come, and she knew that her mouth was open. Then Henry spoke again, and again he snapped his words.

"Thank me that I give you warning. For you, that's all." He turned swiftly to John again. "You'll forgive me that I intrude in this manner, sir. There are some points here that touch our—er—family. I wish to speak of them."

"To be sure——"

Again John sounded vague, and again it was Tony who was smooth and calm. He could have been in Lady Chandler's card room as he spoke.

"If it's family affairs, perhaps we'd best withdraw." He had turned to Jack Harvey, and seemed to be including him in this. "Mr. Lawley will no doubt give us leave."

There was an assurance about it, a calm taking of command. It told Jack that he, too, was not of the family and should withdraw; and that, though he looked puzzled for a moment, he could hardly dispute. He made the best of it.

"By all means," he said quietly. "You'll permit me, sir?"

He hardly waited for John's nod. He was already moving to the door, with Tony at his side, and in a cold silence Henry

stepped aside to give them way. Mally stood stupefied, forgetting that she too was in the doorway; and brusquely Henry
took her by the arm and moved her aside. The two men went
out, and the click of the door seemed to bring life to Mally's
thoughts again. He was going. Suddenly and blindly she was
sure of it. He had taken Henry's warning, taken it with the
quick wit and impassive face of the card room, and now he was
going. He had swept Jack from the room, no doubt to receive
some message, and he was going. For an instant Mally turned,
with a blind instinct to run from the room after him, and
suddenly Jane was at her side, touching her lightly on the
hand. It was needed, and it brought some kind of calm. He
was going, she told herself, but perhaps not far. He would
surely have said some word if this had been his last departure.

She clung to the hope of that as Henry spoke sharply from
the doorway. He addressed himself to John, yet his tone
seemed to take in all of them.

"I accounted it urgent," he said, "or I'd not be here at
this hour of night. Briefly, sir—you'll know that a Hostman
has ways of learning things—I learned yesterday of
Messengers and a warrant for this Marriott. I sent you some
word of that."

His swift glance was at Jane, and then he went hurriedly
on.

"Today I had word of more. The Messengers did not know
where to seek. They had asked the Mayor for help, but he
could not give it. He knew nothing of Marriott. But I heard
today of a rogue come to the Mayor with a tale. He had hope
of——"

"Nixon?"

Jane cut hotly in, and for a moment Henry was silenced.
He showed a flash of surprise, and then he nodded.

"You know of him?"

"Rather too well."

"Oh?" He looked at her coldly, and his face grew harder.
"That could mean that his tale is true. I had hoped it wasn't."

"What *is* his tale?" said John. "You take a deal of words
to come to it."

"Then I'll be briefer. I doubt if it will comfort you. I heard
of this, and I made all speed to the Mansion House. The Mayor

had then heard Nixon and had passed him to the Messengers. I took a look into that room to see him as he talked, and——"

"In God's name, what *is* his tale?"

"As the Mayor told it to me, it is that packages said to hold weapons are in your wine cellar, and others in your coal pit."

"What's that?"

"Nixon says he is a carrier, and——"

"He's a liar, and a damned rogue too."

"I don't doubt the rogue. I wish I were sure of the other."

"Now what——"

"This is not a matter for heat." He cut coldly into John's hot words. "I heard so much, and then I put aside all things as I rode to warn you. I don't ask you to thank me."

"Good!"

"Please to understand. This tale of your cellar sorted with with some more I had heard. It was prudent to suppose it to be true."

"Of all the damned——"

"One moment more. The Messengers believed it. They were calling for horses to ride here, and there'll be a hope of reward to spur them." He paused, looking John in the eye, and he seemed to gather all his forces. "If your cellar has arms, and a scent of treason, you know what will follow? Apart from yourself, the least we can expect is confiscation of all goods and estate."

"Indeed?" A note of contempt had come suddenly to John. "So now we know what brought you. You feared the estate would be lost, and you'd never have your hands on it after all. What anguish!"

"It's fortunate I can keep my temper. Please to note that I left Newcastle perhaps five minutes before these Messengers. I spurred indeed, but what time have you left?"

"Left for what?"

"Need I say it? They'll be here in five minutes. For God's sake, clear that cellar."

John stood staring at him, stubborn and angry, unable perhaps to find an answer; and suddenly Jane turned on him furiously.

"My God!" she said. "If you'd only burned 'em when I told you to!"

There was a sound of horses by the trees, a sound swelling quickly, and not of one horse but of many. Jane almost jumped to the window, and in the same instant Mally was at her side, peering through the glass with her back to the candlelight. It was full dusk now, and hard to see, but there could be no mistake of the dozen riders who came surging past. They were big men, sitting erect, and there was a gleam of steel and shining helmets. She looked, and quivered; knowing that these were the Dragoons who gave force to the Messengers and the Secretary's warrant.

"So!" said Henry behind her. "You've put it off too long. I hope you can lie your way from this."

She turned hurriedly, expecting some hot retort, and it did not come. John was standing stiff and straight, and for the moment his glance was on Mr. Peaver. The old friends were looking each other in the eye, and perhaps something passed between them. They were very still and quiet, and Henry Deane was not in their minds at all.

"It was written on a stone," said Mr. Peaver softly. "Dis Manibus. The Shades watch, and we are not the first."

"No." John was as short and as quiet, and then he turned decisively as the knocker sounded through the house again. "Now we'll deal with these rogues."

Something seemed to have come to him; and Mally, pressing back against the window with her hand touching Jane's, found herself in wondering surprise. The vagueness and foolishness seemed to have left him; and now, with the moment come, he was showing the quality that could meet it. The knocker sounded again, peremptory, with a note of threat and summons in it, and it set Mally's heart pounding in quick alarm. John stopped, and for a moment he had a lifting eyebrow as he glanced at Mr. Peaver.

"They feel important," was all he said; and then he went firmly from the room.

It was dark in the hall, and Jane seized a candle to carry after him. All was still and empty, and there was nothing to be seen of the men who had gone from the room some minutes past. Mally noted it in one swift look, and was thankful. Tony was surely away, and before the Dragoons had come; but she wondered where Jack Harvey was.

There was no hesitation in John. He walked to the door, unbolted it, and flung it open. The others were behind him, and Jane had the candle high and steady. It shone through the doorway, lighting two men who stood in the stone-roofed porch, and flinging a gleam on some others who stood behind, men in dark-blue coats and gilded buttons. They waited stiffly, and it was the men in the porch who had command.

"Mr. Lawley?"

One of the men snapped it shortly, and he stood a little forward, taller than his companion.

"I am John Lawley. Who are——"

"We are the King's Messengers. We've a warrant here."

"Do you say it's for me?"

"It might be." The fellow came forward, pushing himself into the hall, and the shorter man came with him. "It's for one Farquhar, alias Storm, alias Marriott, and he's perhaps here."

"He isn't."

"That's to be seen. This is a warrant of search."

"I'll need to see it."

"All you want of it. Perhaps more."

He was squarely in the hall now, and he looked carefully at each of them. He had a sudden hostile stare for Henry Deane, which was truculently returned. Then he came back to John.

"To make an end of it I'll read this warrant, and you can all hear. It's from milord Townshend, the Secretary of State." He was unrolling it as he spoke. He turned, putting his back to Jane, so that his paper took the light of her candle, and in a rough hard voice he read it quickly out:

Charles Viscount Townshend, one of the Lords of his Majesty's honourable Privy Council, and a Principal Secretary of State: these are in his Majesty's name to authorize and require you, jointly and severally, to make strict and diligent search for Richard Farquhar, alias James Storm, alias Anthony Marriott, and all and every of the places where he may resort or seem to resort; and him, having found, you are to seize and apprehend, and bring, together with all books papers objects persons and matters touching, before me to be examined according to law concerning sundry treasons and seditions

charged against him; in the execution whereof all Mayors
Sheriffs Justices Constables and other his Majesty's officers,
civil and military, and loving subjects whom it may concern,
are to aid and assist you as there shall be occasion; and for
so doing this shall be your warrant.

Townshend.
To John Newman and Richard Root,
  two of his Majesty's Messengers.

The candle flickered as he thrust the paper suddenly at
John.

"Best see it yourself," he said. "You'll know then that
it's signed and sealed."

"And what now?" John handed it steadily back to him.
"There's no such man here."

"No?" The fellow swung abruptly to Henry Deane. "Will
you give a name to yourself?"

"What's that?" There was a gasp of surprise from Henry,
and then a hot flush of anger. "Are you supposing that
I'm——"

"I've asked your name."

"Have you? Then my name is Henry Deane, one of the
Company of Hostmen of Newcastle. You'll learn more of them
if you take that tone with me."

"I'll take what tone I——"

The shorter man leaned forward, plucking urgently at his
sleeve.

"He was in the Mansion House," he whispered. "Behind
the Mayor. I noted him."

"Oh!" The man who was no doubt Newman turned again,
looking keenly at Henry, and then his tone changed.

"We'll take that so, then. All the same, Mr. Deane, I'll
need to ask you if you've seen this man here, by any of his
names."

"No," said Henry.

"He's a treasonable rogue, a damned Jacobite rebel, and
I ask if you've seen him, or any man like him?"

"I've told you I haven't. Mr Lawley is my kinsman, and
this is a loyal and peaceful house. There's no Jacobite here."

Mally held herself stiffly, and dared not look even at Jane.

She had not expected this. Henry was lying staunchly. It might, indeed, be in defence of the estate, but whatever the cause he was firmly at John's side. In that moment she forgave Henry for many things.

Newman looked round him, peering keenly from the one to the other, his face was hard and greedy in the light. Then his eyes came back to John.

"Meaning, I suppose, that the fellow's run. We'll make sure of some more first. We've information laid, and here's warrant of search." His knuckles rapped noisily against the paper. "We'll begin with your wine cellar."

"Do you think to get drunk there?"

"That's enough. I'll need the keys. Sergeant!"

"Sir?" There was a heavy-booted tread in the doorway as a Sergeant of Dragoons stepped through.

"Two or three of your men in here, in case of trouble. Now—the keys?"

"I don't hold keys of cellars. Ask my housekeeper." John had a fine note of disgust in his voice now. "Give him the keys, Jane."

Jane seemed to stiffen, and for a moment the candle shook in her hand. She looked sharply at John, as if she would have confirmation of this, and then she moved slowly to the lesser parlour where she kept her keys. Then surprise came. She was not yet at the door when it was quietly pulled open from within, and Jack Harvey appeared. There was a look of mild surprise on his face, and he blinked as he saw the Dragoons behind.

"Is there some trouble?" he asked. "We were playing backgammon, and we heard voices."

Jane stood speechless, and Mally found it hard even to breathe, as fear joined now with surprise. For there were candles burning in the room, and a backgammon board on the table as Jack had said; and seated at ease by the board, looking for all the world as if his game had just been disturbed, was Tony Marriott, the man the warrant named. And Mally had thought him three good miles away.

"More trouble than some of you will wish," said Newman. "Who do you say you are?"

It was John who answered for him.

"Mr. Harvey is from Stagshaw," he said calmly. "He's my guest, and I vouch for him."

"For what that's worth. And who's this?"

Tony came lazily to his feet. He pushed the backgammon board a little further on the table and came strolling to the door.

"I don't understand," he said slowly. "I'm a traveller, a guest in this house tonight. My name is Staunton."

"You're sure it's not Farquhar? Or Storm? You look plaguey like——"

"Mr. Staunton's name is *not* Farquhar," said John.

"Mr. Staunton is travelling to Carlisle, and has business there," said Henry.

The Reverend Mr. Peaver coughed, and looked more clerical than ever.

"Mr. Staunton," he said, "is well known to me. His uncle is an Archdeacon in the—er—diocese of Gloucester, whose sermons are lately published in fourteen volumes. His parents were my parishioners for many years, and now, being gathered to a greater light, lie together under a canopy of marble, whereon is inscribed a text from Ephesians, the fourteenth verse of the fifth chapter, and a memorial passage setting forth the virtues of ——"

"What the Devil!" said the King's Messenger.

For an instant he stood staring, and looked from one to another. Tony was impassive. Mr. Peaver was bland and benign, and Mally could not resist one darting glance at Jane. She had not suspected Mr. Peaver of such mendacity.

"That'll do!" Newman spoke again, recovered now, and perhaps the harsher for it. "Whoever you are, you'll stay close. We're going to that cellar."

There was nothing for it. A dry cough from the Sergeant of Dragoons was perhaps a warning, and John put a bold face on it. He nodded again to Jane, and slowly she brought him the keys. He held out his own hand for them, and then, with a Messenger at either side, he led down to the cellar. The others followed, Jane close behind him with the candle, and Mally at her side. She looked straight to her front, and dared meet no one's eye. There could hardly be a tale that could explain that cellar.

They passed through the outer cellar that was Jane's, where

her dry stores were for the winter, and it was all as neat and tidy as Jane would have it. Then they were in the ale-store, where the barrels stood on the low stone ramps, the full ones labelled with the date, and the empties with the labels gone. Then they were at the last door, the door of the inner cellar, where Mally had swept and begrimed herself through the length of an afternoon, until Jane had called her to see Dick Chandler.

The key grated in the lock, and in Jane's hand the candle quivered. Mr. Peaver stood rigid. For a moment John paused, as if gathering his forces. Then he lifted the latch and pushed open the door.

The candle slanted violently. The tallow came spilling on Mally's hand, and she heeded it nothing. She was staring at an empty cellar. It lay before them as clear and empty as she had left it herself. There were the flat old wine racks, swept and bare, the naked stone-flagged floor, the blackened walls—and nothing more.

The candle flared as an exultant Jane lifted it high; and with a fierce satisfaction John turned on the Messengers.

"Do you take the floor up now? Or do you think again?"

They glared at him, both of them, sullen and suspicious, and it was the shorter man who answered.

"There's more to this house than the cellar. We'll look further."

"And where?"

"We'll have a walk round. It won't take long to guess where to look."

He turned on his heel and walked angrily out, Newman at his side. John and Mr. Peaver followed, and Henry with them. Tony followed languidly, and the Sergeant, who had found a candle of his own, held it aloft to light them. Jane stayed to lock the cellar, and for a moment Jack Harvey was at Mally's side.

"Jack, what *have* you done?"

She whispered it urgently, and he seemed amused.

"I'll say for Marriott that he has some wits." He held the candle for Jane while she turned the key. "All the same that stuff ought to burn."

"But where *is* it?"

They were in the ale-store now, and for a moment he halted. He reached up and slapped his fingers on one of the tall ale-barrels, an empty one that had no label.

"Jack !"

He heard Jane's quick word, and his smile broadened.

"It was all we had time for, and it was well that I knew where your keys were. Did you like our backgammon ?"

"I thought I was mad—or you were."

He laughed softly.

"We were putting the keys back when these fellows came. That held us in your parlour, so we thought we'd best look——"

He stopped, turning quickly on his heel as the knocker on the outer door broke into sound again. In the cellar it came muffled and confused, but it was the more alarming for that, and they were in a mood now for alarm. They looked at one another, and without a word spoken they went hurrying.

John was already in the hall, the Messengers and the Sergeant at his side. He swung the door open, and the big shape of a man was seen. John moved aside; and Black William, in his boots and his merchant's clothes, stepped purposefully in.

CHAPTER XXXII

THE DISPOSER

HE stood for a moment at gaze, in his brown coat and his neat plain boots, solid and unassuming. Newman looked him over, and then pushed aggressively forward.

"So you're another, are you?" he said. "What's your name?"

"Who the Devil are you?"

It was said quietly and instantly, with no lift of the voice and hardly a turn of the head. Newman recoiled and then his head reared angrily.

"I'll teach you who I am. I'm a King's Messenger, and——"

"Are you from the Secretary?"

"I am. And——"

"If you take that tone with me, you'll go back to the Secretary. My name is William Chandler, and I don't have impudence from catchpolls."

"Catch——"

"Did the Secretary see you?"

"Yes."

"Then you'll have heard my name. Did you?"

For the instant his voice had sharpened, and he turned his head, looking the man in the eye.

"Why—why yes, sir." The truculence had gone suddenly out of Newman. "He—he said——"

"Then mend your manners." He turned abruptly to the other. "Who are you?"

"Richard Root, sir." The man was standing stiffly. "Also a King's——"

"What are you doing here?"

"We're in search, sir. Of one Farquhar, or Storm, or——"

"I've heard of him. Some tale ran that he was lodged with a Mr. Peaver."

"Yes, sir." Newman stepped forward again, and he was more confident now, as if he had found authoritative support in William. "That's Mr. Peaver yonder, but——"

"What of his house?"

"Empty, sir. We went there first."

"And then your rode here, did you? Across my wagon-way?" He nodded. "My son told me he'd seen you."

He paused and looked round him, and for a fleeting instant his eyes met Mally's. They were gone in the same instant, but already her thoughts were leaping. That had been intentional, and she knew it and had read his message. He was here because Dick had told him something; and if Dick were involved, there must surely be some friendly intent in this. It brought a surging of a hope that had all but died. And suddenly she saw that Tony Marriott, whom they were seeking here, was not six feet from William; and William, who had talked with him the other day, did not seem to know him.

There was a moment of silence. William stood brooding, as if sunk in thought. Newman was plainly itching to speak, and was as plainly waiting for William. Mally saw it; and in the same flash of thought she knew that everybody else was waiting too. William had walked quietly into the house, and by his mere presence he had gathered everything to himself. They were standing round him in a circle, and they were all waiting. There was a quality in William.

Newman stirred impatiently, and William looked up.

"We were hoping you could tell us of these men, sir. We've only heard what they say themselves, and——"

"Need we talk here? There'll be a fire, I suppose?"

"To be sure there is." John came suddenly to life, as if he had remembered that he was host. "Come to my parlour, pray."

"As you will." William turned, and his eyes were not friendly as he looked steadily at John. "I'll be sorry if you're taken in a treason, Mr. Lawley. I've no ill will, but you should understand that I serve the government. Let there be no doubt of that."

He stood for a moment as if to let it sink in. Then he turned and walked with slow tread into the parlour. The others followed, and Mally did not look at Jane. As always with

William, there was a little more than she had thought; and she still had not the measure of him.

He put himself against the hearth, comfortably warming his breeches as he once had done before, and she saw how firm and solid he looked. His face was a brooding mask now with tightened lips and a little spreading of the nostrils. There was nothing left at all of the impish William she had sometimes known.

He turned hard eyes on the Messenger.

"What was it that you wished to know?"

"About these men here, sir. Whether they're what they say."

William nodded.

"Mr. Lawley is the owner of the house. Those are his nieces. He's of good standing, and I know nothing against him."

"Yes, sir. And——"

"Mr. Peaver is said to be a Non-juror. That's unfortunate, but it's not a treason."

"Not in itself, sir. But——" Newman was looking dissatisfied, and then he seemed to pass it for the moment. "What of this one, sir? He says he's of Newcastle."

"He is."

William spoke grimly, and his eyes were on Henry Deane, standing stiffly with a cold white anger showing in his face. Mally saw it, and she remembered how these were ancient enemies. This might be William's moment, if he cared to use it.

"He's of the Hostmen's Company at Newcastle." William brought his eyes back suddenly to Newman. "He's of substance there and repute, and I'm sure there's nothing against him. You might be wise not to meddle. He counts for something."

"I—I'm glad to know it, sir. I——"

"I'll thank you for saying it." Henry broke in suddenly, and he was addressing William. "It's true, I hope, but it's perhaps a little more than I'd expected."

"You may at all times expect the truth from me. I serve the government, and that's done by truth. We have that sort of government. Now what more?"

"This one, sir?"

"Mr. Harvey is from the next County, and he's of good name there. I've heard nothing against him, and I don't think there is anything."

Again Newman looked round, and Mally had to steady her breath. There was only Tony Marriott left, and William was insistent that he would tell the truth. So far, she noted, he had done exactly that.

"This one, sir? He says his name's Staunton, and he's a traveller here."

"Then don't ask me to know him. I can't know every man who travels through the County."

Mally hoped she had not moved. There was quickness in William; and it could even be said that he had kept from untruth.

"Yes, sir, I see that." Newman spoke slowly, and there was open suspicion in his voice. "But——"

"You say you seek this man—what was his name?"

"Farquhar, sir. Or Storm, or——"

"Colonel Storm, from what I've heard. But has he been seen here?"

"Not exactly, sir. There was a tale he was lodged with Mr. Peaver."

"You said he wasn't there."

"No, sir. But——" The man hesitated, and then he seemed to make up his mind, as if he were now sure of William's good faith. "There was information laid, sir, of some arms and other furnishings here."

"Nixon's tale?"

William spoke shortly, and Mally had not even a surprise that he should know about it. If this tale had got to Henry it would certainly have got to William too.

"Yes, sir." Newman sounded more surprised than Mally was. "But——"

"Nixon's said to be a rogue. Probably he's a liar too. Did you know that?"

"Oh yes, sir." He had a sly grin now. "The most of those who inform are rogues. There's hardly any other sort that will. But they sometimes drop a little truth with their lies."

"Yes?"

He did not sound encouraging. There was something grim in his tone, and his eyes were turned very straightly on Newman. The man faltered, and then he seemed on the defensive.

"We had to act on it, sir. So when we found Peaver's house empty, we came here. If we could find those things——"

"What things?"

"Soldiers' cloaks, sir, and hats, it was said."

"By Nixon?"

"Yes, sir. In the wine cellar here, he said. So——"

"Have you looked?"

"Yes, sir."

"Well?"

It was as grim as before, and again the man faltered. He hesitated; and Mally, with her every sense at its highest pitch, was watching William. His lips seemed even tighter than before, his eyes harder; and with some deep stir of insight she knew that even in William there was a tension now. He had flung his question; and, perhaps alone among them all, he did not know the answer.

"They weren't there, sir."

"Weren't they?" His answer was immediate, and perhaps only Mally saw the faint easing of his jaw. "I suppose you're ready to account to the Secretary for this?"

"Sir! If you please——"

He was taken aback, frightened, and at a loss to understand. William looked him over coldly, and then took the same quiet tone.

"Did you expect these cloaks to be in a cellar after your goings-on in Newcastle? I'm told you held a small court there? You went to the Mayor, didn't you? And proclaimed a reward?"

"We had to, sir. We——"

"And when this Nixon came, you must needs be at the Mansion House to hear him. You had him in a room next to the Mayor's, didn't you, with half the ears in Newcastle pressed to the keyhole? Is that the way to keep a secret?"

"We—we did our best, sir."

"Then it's a damned poor best."

William said it tersely. He paused, almost as if he were

waiting for something; and then he spoke in a cold deliberate tone.

"You seem to have let half Newcastle know of Nixon and what he told you. I suppose it puffed you out to feel important there. Then you come riding here—you waste your time at Peaver's first—and you expect to find a cellar full of treason."

"But indeed, sir——"

"I don't know whether that tale of Nixon's was true or not. But if it was true, you've left time enough for anything to be moved from any cellar. What do you think to do now?"

He flung it abruptly, and it so disconcerted Newman that he could only stammer. It was Richard Root who had to make answer for him.

"We'll search every inch of this house. There can be secret hides in houses."

"Is this house old enough?"

It was not. Even Mally was sure of that. The house was old enough to be mellow, a century or so, perhaps, but it did not come from the days when men built hides in their homes for secret priests. An ale-barrel was the best it had; and if these men where to search in earnest——

"Who's this? Another of 'em?"

William had heard it first, the sound of a horse on the dark stony drive; and if it brought relief from one tension it brought the alarm of another. It was a single horse, not another troop; but nerves were fraying now, and they were in a mood to find much in little.

It stopped. There was the crunch of a boot, and then again the knocker. William looked to the door, and Mally was the nearest to it. He caught her eye and nodded.

He turned away at once, but she knew she had had her orders, and they were not to be disputed. She opened the parlour door, and as she slipped into the hall she heard his voice again.

"You need not hope for priests' hides——"

She shut the door behind her, and suddenly she was frightened. There was no light now except the candle she carried, and shadows were jumping as the candle swayed. Behind her was William, whose intentions were at the best not plain; and before her, through a bolted door, was—what? She had to grasp herself firmly, pushing down what was almost a wish to run away and hide. Then, with what calmness she could find, she slid the bolt and pulled the door; and it was Dick Chandler who stood alone in the cold dark porch.

He stepped quickly in, and himself pushed the door to and latched it behind him.

"Mally!" he whispered. "I haven't seen you for days."

"You saw me about two hours since."

"With Jane. That doesn't count."

He gave her no warning. His hand closed over hers that held the candle, as if to steady it. His other hand came behind her, and he kissed her quickly. For an instant she was pushing back; and then she found herself pressing against him, clinging to him, holding tight to him. There was something big and friendly here, and all her instinct, for the one swift moment, was to cling tightly to it. He was kind, and to be trusted; and the world was mad.

She saw the smile on his face, the unhurried confidence he seemed always to have; and her eye moved down, noting the splashes of mud on him, the specks of coal-dust on his white cravat. He had come to her straight from his work; and memory took her on its wing again, and he was speaking of the work he sometimes did, and approving because she was dirty from clearing her uncle's cellar.

The thought woke her sharply. She had cleared that cellar for cloaks and drums; and now she was in a cold and ill-lit hall; and through the parlour door was Tony Marriott, and the King's Messengers, and William holding inquisition.

"Dick!" She spoke urgently now. "What is it? What brings you?"

"My father told me to. Is he here?"

"Yes. Come along."

She was all but running now. She pushed the parlour door half open and slipped quickly in, with Dick close behind her. William was speaking, but he stopped abruptly; and Tony, still and quiet at Mr. Peaver's side, turned to look sharply at Mally, and perhaps more sharply at Dick. His eyes came back to Mally, and what she read in them pulled at her. She moved quickly round the back of the room, and then she was at his side; and quietly, unseen by the others, his hand closed over hers.

William was silent, and perhaps he had not seen where Mally was. He was looking at his son, and for a moment they faced each other across the room, with not a word said. Then William turned again to the Messengers.

"That is my son, and you need not suspect him of treason. Dick, if you wish to speak with me, you'll have to wait. I'm busy."

"Aye, aye."

Dick spoke easily, as if whatever he had come about had no great hurry. He propped himself comfortably against the wall, and William seemed to forget him. He spoke again to Newman.

"You'll have to think further. What else did Nixon say? Something about arms, wasn't it?"

"Yes, sir. Carbines, he said, and swords. Hidden in a coal pit."

"Have you looked for them?"

"No, sir. We——"

"Isn't it time you did?"

"We shall, sir, tomorrow."

"You might be too late tomorrow."

Tony's fingers tightened suddenly on Mally's, as if he, too, had caught the grim note of that, and wondered what was coming. William looked the Messengers up and down. Then he spoke with a note of impatience.

"You've found nothing here, and I don't think you will. Nixon is more likely to be a liar than not. But the test of that lies in the coal pit. These people may have had time to clear a cellar, but not a coal pit—yet."

He paused, and Mally tried to press Tony's fingers with an assurance she did not feel. William had put it a little too clearly, and his summing-up had been exactly right.

"Have you tried searching a coal pit?" he asked abruptly.

"No, sir. We——"

"Then it will be something new. You won't enjoy it. How many men have you?"

"Twelve, sir, in all."

"You'll need them. You'll have to work at the bottom and probe the shafts. And mind the water."

"But——" The man looked at him unhappily. "You don't mean tonight, sir?"

"You're not frightened of the dark, are you?"

"No, sir. But——"

"Other folk mightn't be." He looked significantly round the room, and then grimly at Newman. "I doubt if Mr. Secretary would be pleased."

"No, sir." The man spoke hurriedly. "But at night, sir, and in a pit—we'll need lanterns, sir, and——"

"I didn't suppose you were a crew of cats. Ride down that wagonway for a mile or so, and you'll find an encampment where my men are lodged. Borrow lanterns there."

"Yes, sir." Newman spoke resignedly, and he was beyond disputing anything now. "I'd best leave a man or two, sir, to——"

"You'll need all you have. I'll stay here and keep an eye. Whatever you find, let me know at once."

William leaned comfortably against the hearth. The Messengers looked at each other, then at William, and seemed to get no comfort. From the back of the room the Sergeant moved stolidly forward, as if one duty were the same as another to him. There was a general stir as the Messengers trooped out after him; and then, from outside the house, his voice could be heard in gruff terse orders. There was a jingle of harness, another shouted order, and then a crunching of hooves as the cavalcade moved away. The bolt of the door slid noisily; and Jane, who had gone to the hall to see the end of them, came quickly back to the room. She shut the door, and for an instant she looked at Mally.

William had never moved. He was still where he had been, planted before the greying fire, with his feet apart and his face impenetrable; and all of them were waiting for him.

He looked up, and his face was sombre as he spoke.

"You're a fortunate man, Mr. Lawley."

"I—I won't disagree." John spoke slowly, and with his eyes on William. "Perhaps I've to thank you for something."

It was in a tone that Mally had not quite heard from him before, more sober and thoughtful, as if he had perhaps learned something tonight. It had no response from William.

"That's not certain," he said slowly. "I'd not have you deceive yourself. Do not suppose that I'm a Jacobite, or that I've any liking for that cause. I think it's a poison in the land. And in this County, God helping me, I'll stamp it utterly from sight, and by any means I can. Have no doubts of that."

His words fell slowly, fell into a silence that was deathly, and there was no movement, and no answer. There was a faint sigh from someone, and the silence came again. Mally stood as still and hushed as any; and from the depths of her she knew that here, at last, was the real William.

He stirred, bringing his feet together. Then his face eased, and he spoke to his son, briskly and surprisingly.

"It's all clear?"

"Yes." Dick pushed himself away from the wall, and spoke as crisply. "I kept four men back with me, and we got it moving."

"But it's all gone?"

"Yes. There wasn't as much as we'd thought, and it all went in one wagon."

"Heavy for one. What did your driver think?"

"I told him he could lose the brake when he got to the staith."

"Lose it?"

"Aye." There was a sudden grin on Dick. "It'll leave the rails there, and go across into the water."

"As *you* once did, hey? I suppose it might as well. The river's no bad place for carbines."

There was a scrape of feet as Mr. Peaver reared his head at mention of carbines. He looked round him querulously, as though seeking enlightenment on this and John looked as puzzled as he. Mally was staring at Dick, too startled to be discreet.

"Dick!" she said. "You mean you've——"

"Oh aye, we got 'em away. It's all safe." He was grinning cheerfully at her. "But it's a good thing I don't mind dirt."

He was flicking specks of coal-dust from his coat; and suddenly Mr. Peaver flared into indignation. Apparently he had understood.

"Do you mean to say that you have interfered? That you have taken my——"

"Yes, I have." Dick rounded on him bluntly. "I've taken the lot, and——"

"Good God! Do you know that's——"

"It's sense," said William tersely. "And to bring you to your own senses, would you have preferred those Dragoons to take them?"

"It's theft! It's——"

"God pity you!" For a moment William's voice rose in contempt. Then he was himself again. "I told you you were fortunate, Mr. Lawley. So, perhaps, is Colonel Storm."

It came very quietly, but it lost nothing by that. He was utterly still now, steady-eyed and forceful; and at Mally's side Tony Marriott stood a shade more stiffly. For a moment he turned to Mally, and he even had the ghost of a smile.

"You once warned me that these people talked too much. They seemed to have talked of everything, and I did not heed you in time. I'm sorry." The smile flickered again, and then he turned carefully to William. "Now, sir, you seem to know it all. What do you intend?"

"That, perhaps, depends on you. I've already done you some service."

"With the Messengers? I know. I'd thank you for it, if I were not unsure of the end."

"I'm unsure myself. I've said that it depends on you."

The room was very still. William was as steady as rock when he spoke again, slowly and carefully.

"Will you, perhaps, drop this nonsense, settle to some good life, and take the oath of allegiance?"

"To a German usurper? No. You perhaps expect me to thank you, and you no doubt mean it well. But I am not a traitor."

"To King James, you mean?" He nodded. "I'm sorry, though it's the answer I expected. You are of that breed. That's what I'm sorry for."

"How?"

"You are of too good a sort to waste your life. And too young also." For a moment he was the older man, looking

at the younger; and then his face hardened again. "Nevertheless, I serve the government."

"I see." There was a slight intake of breath, just to be
heard in the silence. "So you will call back the Messengers,
and——"

"I shall not." William snapped it suddenly. "A pair of
damned scoundrels, who serve their own pockets. All they hope
for is reward. I serve the government, not them."

"What the Devil do you mean?" Henry Deane spoke
suddenly, bursting into open anger as if he could contain
himself no longer. "I've never known you yet serve anybody
but yourself."

"You've never looked very hard, have you?" William
turned to him quite placidly. "I haven't asked yet what
brought *you* here tonight."

"I don't need——"

Henry stopped, and his mouth shut quickly, as if he had
remembered. William nodded.

"Just so. Perhaps it was to save an estate. But I'll not ask
questions."

"You'd better not."

"No. But what matters is that I serve the government.
And before an hour is gone I think you will be serving it
too."

"What does that mean?"

"Wait and see." William seemed to dismiss him as he
came quietly back to what he wanted. "I said the government,
Colonel, not the Messengers."

"I know. I don't say I understand."

"There was an information sworn—by one Willoughby,
I'm told. If this goes back to the Secretary, you know what
will follow."

"I can guess."

"Exactly. But that's not the true interest. What's needed
is to make an end of treason, and to do it without a noise.
Martyrs and hangings don't help. So I think we'll do this
quietly."

"But how?"

"I'll contrive your escape to France."

"What!"

Mr. Peaver had burst out again, hot and indignant. "I'll not permit this, do you hear?"

"You can't stop it."

"Can I not?"

"No." William turned patiently, as if he knew he must deal with this. "At least, you can't retain him to your service. You can see him go, or you can see him hanged. But that is your choice. You can't retain him."

"No doubt I cannot. But the cause can." He was very tall and erect now, and the light in his eye was hardly of Earth. "Please to understand, sir, that Captain Marriott was in no way concerned with any matters placed in that pit or in the cellar here. That was my work alone, and I hold myself responsible. Proceed against me as you please, but you cannot place it upon the innocent."

"Meaning that you'll hang in his place?" William looked at him almost good-humouredly. "I almost think you would. But it wouldn't save him. You'd merely hang with him. Be pleased to understand that your plot is at an end."

"It is *not* at an end. You may set it back a little, but that is all. In some few months——"

"You would bring death to some and ruin to many. That is all."

"We shall bring a Crown to a King, and——"

"For God's sake, man——" John burst in, suddenly and angrily. "You can see it's at an end, and perhaps as well. Do you learn nothing?"

"Learn?" Mr. Peaver swung to him, hard-faced and fanatical. "So you leave us, do you? Then I learn so much, the true from the false."

"Could this not wait?" said William. He pushed between them; and then, as Mr. Peaver subsided into mutters, he turned again to Tony. "I mean your plot to end, or God knows what bloodshed there'll be. So you go or you hang, and of the two I'd prefer you to go."

"Go?"

It came very quietly; and suddenly he turned aside, and in that instant he looked at Mally.

"Tonight," said William.

"What!"

"I said tonight." For the instant William had looked at Mally too. "I'd not be hard, but it's needful for your safety. Those Messengers will come back."

Henry Deane snapped his fingers irritably, as they had once drummed on Lady Chandler's table.

"How is he to go tonight?" he demanded. "How is he to go at all, with a warrant out and half Newcastle warned?"

"Well thought of," said William calmly. "Fortunately I thought of it first."

"What does that mean?"

"It means that you'll help, as I said you would. He rides to Newcastle tonight—with you."

"Me?"

"You wish to preserve this estate, I think? So you'll ride with him, and at any need you'll vouch for him. That should make it safe."

"Of all the damned——"

"It's very convenient. At Newcastle you take him to the quay and put him aboard the *Derwent Rose*. The Master has orders."

"He would have! Your ship, I suppose?"

"Not quite. But in the London river he'll not go ashore. He'll board the *Harvest Moon*, and that's my brother's ship. It brings him prunes from France, and wine. So it can take a cargo back. It's all arranged."

William nodded placidly, and then he was very grave and quiet again.

"Now, Colonel, it rests with you. But I'm afraid it's the one or the other. Unless——"

"Unless what?"

William watched him steadily, and then he was even quieter.

"Unless you will change your ways and end your plottings. We could make it easy for you, and you could live here then."

"As a turncoat."

"As a man of sense. You could even——" For a moment William paused, and his glance was at Mally. "You could even lay suit to a lady."

"Mally!"

He had turned to her, and she saw his lips tight, and his

face strained and hard. His hand was upon her arm, and from behind her she saw Dick Chandler move quickly forward, as though he had a word to say on this. And, very quietly, William spoke again.

"You may choose, if you wish, to be an exile. It is no good life, but you may choose it if you wish. But can you, properly, press or persuade another to it?"

There was no answer. There was nothing but a twitch of the lip and a slow intake of breath. His hand quivered on her arm, and she saw that his face was white. And William spoke with slow finality.

"A lady who shared your loyalties—perhaps. Another—no. There are men who might press that, but they are lesser men. I do not think you will."

"No." It came from him stiffly, and very slowly. "I cannot ask that. Unless——"

He turned suddenly to her, holding her now with both his hands, and she saw the appeal in his eyes, desperate, and for what he would not say. It was the appeal to say it for him, of her own accord, and to take a frightening fearful life. She saw Jane move forward, fierce and determined, and even uncle John, as if they would hinder her at need; and close at her other side she felt Dick Chandler's presence. They blurred into nothing; and through the whirl and chaos of her thoughts she felt a force upon her, clear and exact, coming from beyond her, making her turn her head. She had to do it; and she was looking into William's eyes.

Then he looked from one to another, and seemed to address them all.

"I think we are decided," he said.

CHAPTER XXXIII

WIND FROM THE NORTH

I<small>T</small> was dark outside the house. Cloud had screened the stars, and from the north a wind was blowing. It was rising and freshening in little gusts that set the tree-tops swaying, and it brought spatters of cold thin rain to hint at more to come. There was a sighing in the trees, and at times a rustle as a dry old leaf went whirling; and then the rain would come again, a few cold drops in the blackness, passing and forgotten.

Mally stood alone by the door, cold and unhappy, with a cloak pulled loosely round her. She waited in the blackness, seeing only the cloud and the swaying trees, and her thoughts were as dark as the cloud. He had asked this of her, and she could do no less.

Faintly, beyond the end of the house, a horse clopped, and a boot struck on a stone. A gleam of light appeared, quavering in the dark, and then a lantern came in sight, and another; and she knew it was Jane, who had gone with Jack to give help with the horses. The riders came after them, faint blurs, hardly to be seen; and one was Henry Deane. They came towards her, led by the swaying lanterns, and she went out in the dark to meet them. They saw her, and Henry stopped. The other came towards her.

He dismounted, and he was close against her. Dimly, and with half her thought, she saw the lanterns one each side of Henry, and vaguely she heard voices; they were holding him in talk, and carefully leading him away. Then Tony spoke.

"I'm more unhappy than I've ever known."

"I know."

She answered him softly, and she felt his arm round her, gently pressing.

"I've to go to the King, and report defeat, and failure. But it's *you*——"

"Don't say it."

"I must." She felt his arm quiver. "If only——"

3<small>1</small>5

"Must you go?"

"Yes. I could not change coat, and be a traitor."

"But——"

"No, my dearest. I could not. And if I did, I should not be what you have known."

"No."

"I am the King's man. I serve him, as my father served his father, and I must not betray."

"Would it be——"

"You know it would. So I must go."

The wind came as a gust, buffeting them, and setting her cloak flapping. She clutched at it; and in the dark he bent down and tied it for her.

"So!" She heard the catch in his voice as he said it bravely. "I've done it for you, and perhaps it's the last I shall ever do for you. I'd have done so much."

"Tony!"

She was clinging to him, pressing herself against him, and she felt her face wet. She looked up, wet-eyed and wretched, and his lips came against hers, pressing, pressing, giving to her and taking from her, and she knew the force that stirred and rent him. Her eyes had shut, and even the black line of the trees had gone; and there was no time or meaning.

"It's done, my dear." He had parted from her and was whispering softly. "We tried, both of us, and it might have been. But the Fates had the dice, and to linger makes it worse. The man spoke truth."

"What?"

"You could not come with me. It would be greed, not love, that took you. Even at heartbreak I'll not do that. Good-bye!"

"Oh, Tony! I——"

"Good-bye, my dearest. God bless and keep you. Now let me go. Words hurt, but memories will stay."

Once again he held her to him, and all sense of time and present went. She lay limp and yielding, giving whatever was hers, feeling for him and longing for him. Then he put her from him and steadied her on her feet.

"Goodbye, my dearest—memory."

He whispered it; and the cold rain spattered suddenly as he turned and took his horse. He mounted, and somewhere in the dark an impatient Henry moved to join him. Two lanterns lifted, and a hand waved in farewell. He was a black shape against the sky as he wheeled his horse, and went. His shape faded; the hoofbeats passed into the trees; they were muffled, and were gone.

There was a slow footfall, and a lantern swayed as Jack turned towards her. She saw him dimly and without understanding; and she saw Jane move more swiftly, to go to his side and turn him away. They left her, going slowly to lock the stable door; and Mally was alone.

She turned her face to the wind, and it came to her cold and strong. It came from the north, came from the high clean lands where a Wall ran, and a river flowed, and a stone was let into a tower with letters deeply cut; and another had kept faith tonight with his Gods and his Dead. It was blowing from the north, and it would be a fair wind from the Tyne. Soon he would be boarding the ship at the quay, with the wind to take him from her; and memory turned crazily, and she was herself in a ship on a sunlit day, and there was a launch alongside, and Dick had come to meet her.

A bar of light leapt into being, swinging across the ground, and she knew that the door had opened. She guessed on the instant who it was; and she was wrong. It was William who stood in the lighted door.

He came slowly to her, and she knew he had a purpose. He came close, and stopped, and in the light from the door he watched her face. The door swung to as the wind caught it; and the light had gone.

"It's hard?"

His voice came out of the dark, and she heard the question in it.

"Perhaps too hard. He—he called it heartbreak."

"Yes." His voice came quietly. "But he was not the man for you. Perhaps not for any."

He was a black shape in the dark, and she could not see his face. He seemed to want no answer; and slowly he spoke again.

"He would not have given you his best. He has vowed it to his King, and that comes first. The best to the King, and you'd have had what's left. That, and no more."

She stood silent, knowing no answer, and her memory was of Lady Chandler's stair, and of the beat of her heart as he turned and saw her there. But even then he had been seeing a lady to her chair, doing his duty to his King.

William spoke again, softly and almost to himself.

"He serves a Stuart King. I wonder why a Stuart should have such men. Do you know what the Stuarts have given their servants, always?"

"No?"

"What you found tonight. Charm and heartbreak. And for it they have men's lives and hearts. And women too."

"Yes."

She said it hopelessly, neither knowing nor caring, and again he waited. The wind came as another gust, tugging at the cloak that wrapped her; and it did not break open. It had been truly tied, and faithfully.

"Now I'll tell you something."

He spoke again, and there was a clearer note in him now. She turned to listen.

"I'll tell you because I know. I have the years behind me. You will not forget him. It's only those who don't know who talk of forgetting. It hasn't come to them."

"No."

"You will remember. But as the years go by you will remember differently. What was unhappy will go dark and dull. What was happy will be clean and bright, because it's a memory you'll live with, going over and over it. You'll treasure it, and be happy with it. Now don't stay out here too long."

He turned on his heel and walked away. She saw the door swing open, and shut again; and she was alone, in the wind and the dark.

The rain spattered again, wetting her face and her hair, and she cared nothing for it. She walked slowly forward, making to the bend in the drive and the trees; and it was where he had ridden as he left her. Her fingers were on the ties of her cloak, feeling the knot he had made, and she could feel his hands again, as he did it for her. He would be aboard the ship soon; and there was a longing in her to be with him there, to untie his cloak, and help him with his boots.

She turned wretchedly, putting her face to the wind, and letting it drown a sob that took her. It was a firm wind now, and a fair wind for the ship. It was blowing from the north, blowing past a pele where a stone was set; and that was the Harvey's home. Jack would be there soon, and he would have Jane with him, and they would be safe, because the plot was done and ended. Uncle John would be safe too, and not all of this had been in vain. There was fair wind for the ship; but it carried Colonel Storm.

His face was before her again, and it mattered nothing what name he had. She saw him on the stair, in the card room, on a wind-swept bridge, and laughing by the river bank with a wet hat in his hand; and again she had to turn her face to the wind, and set her teeth tight. She heard nothing of the boots that were crunching the stony drive, and he was at her side before she knew.

"Dick !"

She turned, startled, as he came surging from the dark, and there was no mistaking the shape of him.

"I wondered where you were. You weren't by the door, and it's raining."

"I know."

He stepped suddenly past her, putting himself between her and the rain, sheltering her and keeping it off her.

"It's time you came in."

"I know. But——"

"You'll be better when you've had some supper. We all shall. Jane's seeing to it."

"Oh !"

She had to think what he meant. She was still thinking when he took her by the shoulders, firmly turned her, and began to walk her in. She went with him quietly, and something was calming her. It was a relief to be told what to do.

"Why did you come for me?"

She said it suddenly, hardly knowing why, except that she wished to hear his voice. For a moment he stopped in his walk.

"I wanted you to know I'm still here. I shall be here for a long time."

"Yes."

She answered him quietly. The calm was spreading through her, almost against her wish, and she knew that it was coming from him. It had done so before, and it would do so again.

His hand touched her shoulder, urging her along the path, and she went quietly with him. She had fallen into step beside him; and that, too, seemed the way of things. She could always match her step to his.

By the door he stopped, and spoke.

"You know what I meant?"

"Yes."

He was close against her in the dark, and she felt his hands lightly on her. She turned quickly to face him.

"Dick, I know what you mean. But I couldn't—yet."

THE END

DATE DUE

ROANOKE BIBLE
COLLEGE LIBRARY

Acc. 1 _____22,059_____

Call No. ___F_____

_____N413_____